Glittering Skies

By Jenna Avery

Glittering Skies

Website: Jenna-Avery.com

For licensing, copyright, and other questions, email jenna.averys.email@gmail.com

Cover art by Ann Bugarin

First Edition

Contents

Suffer the first vision that set fire to the stars.
~ Dylan Thomas

The Universe told me you needed this.

Also Written By Jenna

Contemporary

My Ashes: Memoirs of a Misbehaving Woman
Come Back To Me: A Dark Romance Thriller

The Singularity Series

Through The Folded Stars

Skies of Avalon

Glittering Skies
First Time Friends
Heimlock

Content Warning

If you consider content warnings to be spoilers, do not continue reading.

Seriously. It could/will ruin a revelation that creates tension throughout the whole book.

I'm 100% serious. There are NO graphic assaults, pregnancy, third act breakup, dead animals, or children at risk. There *is* miscommunication. If that's all you need to know, STOP HERE.

While this book is intended to be fun, there are some deeper themes at play. This book contains creepy men, implied SA, parental illness and death, genetic diseases, a controlling father, a submissive mother, and miscommunication that makes sense in the end, I promise.

1

Reverie

Love stories belong to other people; people who aren't like me.

It's for those with empty blood and normal vocal cords. They don't weep with sparkles smearing their cheeks, and doctors certainly don't brand them as infants.

From birth, it's been my destiny to be alone. Perhaps it's why I've dedicated my life to photography. Romance might not be in the cards, but a small part of me hopes it'll transfer through osmosis. As if being around delightful examples of love will force it to ooze into my existence.

No luck in the oozing love department so far. I'm twenty-eight, single, and sitting at a bar, drinking alone.

Well, not entirely alone.

Prestley watches me with a wry smirk, polishing a crystal glass with a slice of mist. As the Whisp proprietor of my favorite puff bar, he's seen me in all moods. Today's dour attitude is more commonplace than I'd like to admit.

"Bad day?" he asks, placing the sparkling glass on a shelf.

I scoff, sitting back on the stool, and crossing my arms. "Actually, no." I sigh dramatically. "They were *so* in love, Prest. You should've seen the first kiss. Steamy as all Hells." I pause, tapping my chin. "Could be because she's a Dragon, and he's a Water Sprite, though."

His thundercloud eyebrows raise. "Some get all the luck."

"And take it from the rest of us," I mutter, my tone sour. My clients never see this level of dourness during their special day; I save it all for my favorite Whisp. Every evening after photographing a wedding, he has a goblet of femire ready when the cloudavator brings me up to his bar.

Reaching for another glass that's already spotless, Prestley wipes it down as he asks, "The one thing you wish you could forget?"

"You're *so* hilarious," I mutter with a scowl. He loves this question because he knows my photographic memory will never let me forget a single moment. "Maybe the groom scratching his crotch mid-vows? He really dug in there like two hundred guests and a videographer weren't watching."

"That's not too bad. Better than the bridesmaid who forgot to put underwear on before dancing."

I shudder. "That isn't just a memory — there's actual photographic proof of her choice."

Thanks to the curse of a photographic memory, I remember every single detail. Not just from today's event, but *all of them*. The flicker of doubt in a groom's eye. The nervous nail-picking of a bride. The dung-colored napkin at table eight from the Culmer wedding two years, six months, two weeks, and three days ago.

The look on my ex's face when he ...

Nope. We aren't going there. Suffice to say, it's a burden more often than not. Not as much as my glitter and song, but damn near close.

Tilting the drink back, I pour the remaining dregs into my mouth and slam the goblet onto the cloud counter.

Prestley narrows his eyes. "I just polished that counter, Reverie."

I lean on an elbow, giving him an inebriated grin. "Come on, Prestley, use a little dew and it'll be good as new." With a chortle, I declare, "Hey, that rhymed."

His pupils crackle with slivers of lightning as he rolls his eyes. "Want another?"

"Keep 'em coming."

"Coming right up." He floats over to the wooden barrel full of femire.

Swiveling to gaze at the scene behind me, I allow myself a moment of appreciation. The sun's setting, its rich hues creating Heavens on earth as the clouds offer a spectacle of colors. Out of dozens in the surrounding area, Prestley's puff bar is the highest. Thousands of feet in the air, I'm graced with the most stunning view of Gondora, the City of Clouds.

Only a handful of times each year do the clouds clear. Otherwise, the floating city nests inside fluffy clouds, with mist rolling between the glass domed roofs and under the golden bridges connecting clusters. Air traffic zips through; a colorful array of Dragons, and other flying species. At this time of day, all the glass and gold remind me of an elegant engagement ring caught in rainbow light.

Glancing at my glittered veins, I raise my slender hand, allowing the light to catch the multi-faceted lines covering my body. They're all colors of the rainbow, their pastel shades matching my iridescent hair, reflecting the light like a crystal suncatcher.

The soft purring of the cloudavator draws my attention. A lavender male Gargoyle, featuring wings with membranes the color of eggplants, rises through the cloud line, his long silver hair glowing in the sunset. He's already watching me with an expression I don't understand. My heart does a little pitter patter, forcing me to look away. I'm here to get drunk — nothing else.

Prestley drifts over with my newest drink in his fluffy palm. Unfortunately, he catches my observation *and* avoidance of the Gargoyle. With a knowing smile, he places the goblet in front of me. "A little fun wouldn't kill you, Ree."

I shoot him a dirty look. "I can be fun."

He makes a show of judging my black sweater and pants. "Do you own any other colors?"

"Yes," I shoot back defensively. "I also love the color purple." I lean down to grab a shoe, lifting it like it's proof of my diverse wardrobe. "And my shoes are pink!"

He chuckles. "Didn't you buy those shoes because they were twenty percent cheaper and at the time, you needed a pair immediately?"

I rolled my eyes so hard, it actually hurt. Placing the slip-on shoe back onto my tired foot, I snap back, "Just because I'm prudent with my money and prefer comfort over style, doesn't mean I'm not capable of having a good time."

Prestley smirks, his eyes flicking over my shoulder. Before I can see what has his attention, I hear a deep voice of velvet. "Is this seat taken?"

My shoulders tense as I white knuckle my drink. Prestley raises his eyebrow, mocking me before giving the source of the voice a genial smile.

"Well, hello Luca. No, I believe that seat is currently empty."

Damn Prestley. Damn him to all twelve Hells. Instincts have me adjusting my sweater and hair to cover my siren brand. The less this stranger knows about me, the better.

Hunching over my drink, I try to ignore the enormous form sliding onto the stool next to me, holding my breath when shadow blocks the sunshine. It doesn't bother me to lose the warmth, but the assumption irks.

I turn, ready to snap at the stranger for his lack of consideration — *because it's about the principle of the thing* — and the words die on my tongue.

My gaze trails up to silver eyes caressing my face with uninhibited fascination. A wide, dimpled smile splits across a chiseled jaw. A sloped nose juts out from beneath a broad forehead, with thick black eyebrows raised as the man observes me in return.

He must notice my ire, though, because he asks, "Are my wings bothering you?"

To my surprise, he tucks them in tight, allowing the sunshine to beat down on my shoulders. The returned warmth of the sun is suddenly too much with the new heat coursing through my body.

I shake my head. "No, it's fine. Don't tire yourself out on my account."

Tearing my eyes away from his suede-soft pale purple skin, I take a sip of my drink, trying desperately to focus on the fruity burn.

It's not that I hate men or want to be alone. It's because when men find out I'm part siren, they think I'm potentially tricking them, because there's no way they could possibly be attracted to a siren without being manipulated. After twenty-eight years of begging them to believe that I didn't manipulate them into fucking me or feeling affection, I'm ... dedicated to embracing loneliness.

A thick finger taps the bar top in front of me. "What're you drinking?"

After taking a long, pointed sip, I mumble, "Blackberry femire."

"Sounds delicious." A pause, then, "Prestley, be a doll and get me a goblet of the same?"

My head shoots up, finally giving the man a proper examination. If I didn't know any better, I'd say he's yet to look away from me since sitting. Two matching dimples in his broad grin send an unfamiliar zing of desire to my core. That beautiful, beatific smile reveals elongated pearly white fangs.

I smash the tiny part of my brain wondering how they feel on skin.

Giving him an exasperated groan, I say, "I'm not going to sleep with you because we drank the same drink. So, don't bother."

His head jerks back, the smile twisting into a disgusted frown. "Excuse me?"

I motion to him — every muscular, meaty inch — and say, "You're sitting here because you saw a Glyridite sitting alone and thought, 'Huh, she's pretty. Maybe my Saturday night could be better with some glitter on my cock and rainbows in my mouth,' right?"

All amusement washes away from his expression. For a split second, my anxiety spikes at the darkness spreading in his eyes. "I assure you, Miss...?"

"Nonya."

He smirks. "I assure you, Miss *Nonya—*" I swear he tries to swallow a laugh as he says my fake name. "—that if I wanted to fuck you, it wouldn't be by spending fifty corals on a drink." His eyes flick to Prestley. "No offense, Prest."

"None taken," my betrayer of a bartender quips as he places a goblet in front of the man. "Her name is Reverie, by the way."

"Prestley," I say sharply, glaring. "*Boundaries.* I'm going to glitter this entire goddess damned bar if you say another word."

His mirth fades. "Don't you dare. I'd hate to ban you for life."

"I'd clean it up," I mutter. Glitter's greeted with nothing but disgust in most of Gondora. Just my lot in life, I suppose.

His puffy lips purse. After shooting another withering look, he levitates away, leaving me with my conversational captor.

"For someone who's supposed to be the embodiment of puppy kisses and rainbows, you sure are a sour black cat."

Whipping my head to glare at the offensive man, I stab a finger toward his face. "That's a stereotype. Plus, puppy kisses are too wet to be a symbol of happiness. That's asinine."

He raises a dark eyebrow. "Wetness doesn't equal happiness for you? What man convinced you of this?"

My cheeks heat; from rage or humiliation, I can't decide. "You're so crude. That was incredibly inappropriate." I grind my teeth. Motioning to the half-empty puff bar, I ask, "Why did you sit here and not in any of the other dozen empty chairs?"

"Maybe I wanted to be the pot of gold at the end of the rainbow."

Stunned, words fail and my jaw drops, then snaps shut with a loud crack as my teeth gnash. "Is that another sex joke?"

He shrugs a broad shoulder. "You clearly have such a filthy mind, Miss Nonya. Are you the type of woman who blames her own dirty thoughts on a stranger?"

With a growl of frustration, I turn away, determined to finish my drink and leave. I do *not* care about his consuming presence, or those fangs, or that smile, or those muscles.

I *really* don't.

Scanning the bar, I search for a familiar face to finagle a rescue from, but the only one is Prestley, who is watching this interaction with self-satisfied amusement.

Dunghole.

I sense the Gargoyle's gaze on the back of my head, but I steadfastly refuse to give him what he's clearly looking for. He's an attention-seeking jerk, only offering maddening quips and dirty jokes. Like every other man on this continent.

"The name is Lucasta, by the way. But friends, and my lovely mother, call me Luca."

My molars grind to dust as I refuse to respond, keeping my back to him. I take a deep gulp of my drink, wishing the fizzy burn didn't prevent me from guzzling it. The last thing needed in this moment is making a fool of myself *and* sending puke onto an unsuspecting pedestrian on the bridges below.

The cool shadow, blocking the last lingering bits of light, shifts. "I personally don't actually like being licked by puppies or hounds. I'm a chimeragon lover, actually. I have one waiting for me at home. His name is Reginald Destau. Reggie for short — his full government name is reserved for when he eats my slippers or that one time he turned my Aunt Libby into stone."

I nearly choked on the liquid in my mouth. Sputtering, I break my vow of silence to peer over my shoulder. "Is she still stone?"

He chuckles, a warm, enveloping sound. "Lucky for her, she's also a Gargoyle. It was a temporary setback for her day, but she's refused to visit since." He actually sounds annoyed by her choice.

"Can you blame her?" I say incredulously.

"Yes," he says defensively. "It lasted for three minutes. He's mostly a chimera; only one-fifth of a Gorgon. It's never permanent, and he did it because she refused to give him a bite of her muffin."

Against my better judgment, I ask, "What kind of muffin?"

He frowns. "Why does that matter?"

"Because if it were lemon poppyseed, that means Reggie is unreasonable, because who would get that upset about lemon poppyseed?" A smile begrudgingly lifts at the corners of my mouth. "But if it was for an apple streusel muffin, then I'd say three minutes wasn't enough."

The smile spreading across his face is so charming that a teeny tiny piece of my hardened heart thaws. "Ah, so you *can* be reasonable."

"About muffins," I clarify. "But very little else."

"I'll keep that in mind," he says in a conspiratorial tone.

I allow myself to get immersed in the swirling mercury of his eyes; just for a second — to prove I'm not actually unreasonable. The longer I look, the faster my heart thumps. Twilight twinkles behind him, the rising sister moons casting an ethereal glow against the silver strands pouring over his shoulders like liquid starlight.

The growing warmth in my belly is uncomfortable. Again, ignoring my better judgment, I spin on my barstool to face him fully. My long legs bump into one of his thick thighs, but he doesn't react. He just ... watches me.

Who is this man? Why is he so enamored? I'm a Glyridite. He doesn't even know I'm part siren. It's a misplaced fascination.

"So if you don't want to fuck me," I say quietly. "Then why did you bother sitting next to me?"

"The sunset."

Dumbfounded, I jerk my head back in surprise. "The sunset?"

He nods. "You watched the sunset like it was a work of art worth memorizing."

Now is probably not the best time to mention my photographic memory. "Well, I appreciate beautiful things."

"Me too," he murmurs, the intensity of his stare making me squirm.

Trying to diffuse the confusion making my insides feel funny, I say, "I'm not going to sleep with you."

"But perhaps have a drink with me?"

"A single drink," I agree. "Nothing more."

"Nothing more."

We both take a sip of our beverages, never breaking eye contact. Maybe Prestley is onto something; it's been years since I've trusted anyone with my heart. Would it hurt to try once more?

Besides, what kind of wedding photographer would I be if I didn't give Fate a chance?

2

Reverie

One Year Later

After this date, I'm giving celibacy strong consideration. It's a testament to my die-hard romantic heart that it hasn't happened already — but this shamrock-green male Orc might be the final reason.

Especially since the next thing out of his mouth is, "How many men have you slept with?"

Eww.

We're at a bar called No Name, the type of place that offers deep shadows for privacy, comfortable booths, and a simple menu. Before I arrived, he'd chosen a booth in the furthest corner, with the darkest lighting.

Red flag number one.

Unfortunately, red flag number two is the fact that he can't seem to stop talking about sex. I mentioned photographing weddings, prompting him to ask what species have sex at their ceremonies. When I mentioned loving puff bars, he asked me if the cloud edges are stable enough for fucking.

So, this asinine question shouldn't surprise me, but it does. Because who in the Hells asks these kinds of questions on a first date?

This man, apparently.

Inhaling a steadying breath, it's a struggle to not snarl when I say, "I'm not sure why that's any of your business, Maureo." I cock my head. "Why? How many partners have *you* had?"

After eyeing my cleavage, Maureo scoffs, waving a large hand flippantly. "It doesn't matter how many women a man has been with. It only improves his worth."

Staring at my almost-finished glass of femire, I see-saw my jaw. *This fucking guy.* When I refocus on his mediocre features, I bat my eyelashes. "One hundred."

It's not a hundred. More like less than half of that, but I'm aiming for shock value here.

As expected, Maureo sputters. "One *hundred?* I knew sirens were loose, but that's outrageous, honey."

Maureo leans back on his side of the booth, appraising me with new eyes. His lewd gaze cramps my stomach with dread.

Since this is a blind date, I dressed for the likelihood of creepiness. I'm wearing a black shirt that shows enough cleavage to entice — I'd hoped he'd be nicer, okay? — but carefully hides my brand. My pants cover everything below the waist. Yet, I still feel naked under his hungry gaze.

A sinking lump of dread settles low in my belly.

One ... two ... three ...

He pats the ocean of space between us. "Come closer, honey. You're so far away. I don't bite ..."

Dating in Gondora is exhausting. Sighing, I toss back the rest of my femire, then say, "Why in the twelve Hells did you ask me out on a date? This isn't a date — it's a sex interview, one I did *not* agree to."

Maureo's expression darkens. "Yureka said you enjoyed having fun."

Yureka and I are about to have an in-depth conversation about how to vet potential dates. Grabbing my purse, I shift out of the booth. "Yes, dunghole, *fun.* As in getting drinks and discussing how we were bullied a lot as children because we were ugly."

I flick my gaze over his less-than-impressive features. "Something you apparently never grew out of."

Slapping enough corals on the table to avoid him chasing me down to pay my share, I snap, "Don't worry, Maureo, I'll pick up the mantle of being your adult bully. Learn how to brush your hair. Find a new cologne. You smell like the underside of a hydra's tail."

None of this is true either, but I hope my words haunt him.

The Orc sputters, clenching his fists. Before he can collect himself and possibly start a physical confrontation, I hurry out of the bar.

After summoning a Dragxi, I text Yureka, who is both my wedding assistant and a friend.

Reverie: I'm on the way, but whatever cesspool you dragged that one from needs to be quarantined. He asked how many people I've slept with.

Within a minute, a blue Dragxi appears, wearing a wooden seating saddle. The Dragon looks at me with one blue eye.

Where to?

"Brawling Battle Gym, please."

Got it.

The Dragon takes off into the puffy clouds settled low in the city today. Thanks to the Dragon's magyck, the wind's kept off my body, allowing a peaceful journey. I'm not in the mood to step into a crowd, but Yureka's been begging me to go out with her to some fight night at a local battle gym.

Personally, I think it's barbaric. Fighting for sport? Training to kill after going to work in an office, wearing a suit? I swear, only men invent these kinds of things. I suppose it's better than the times of old, where all species battled it out for power. We're *civilized* now, apparently.

So civilized I'm paying seventy-five corals for the possibility of having blood spattered on my clothes. I examine my all-black outfit. The blood wouldn't show up, but I'd know it was there.

When my phone vibrates, I check Yureka's text.

Yureka: He did not! Oh my goddess, that's absurd. My mother knows his mother from a local social club for forest dwellers.

Reverie: Well, let her know that he's sex obsessed and said sirens are normally loose.

Yureka: I'm buying your drinks tonight.

Reverie: Hells yes you are.

Putting the phone back into my bag, I stare blankly at the buildings passing by. The sun is almost set, so most of the buildings are lit, with the glass domes illuminating the sky.

It's difficult to not be depressed about another failed date. I'm a wedding photographer who can't find a relationship to last more than a few months. Every week, I'm capturing so much love with my camera — but as part siren, society decided my worth the moment I exited the womb.

After spending years being objectified, used, and rejected, I want someone of my own. To walk down the aisle with a partner smiling proudly; to spend the night celebrating with loved ones. Yet, after all these years of trying to date, it always ended in rejection.

A year ago, I thought maybe, just maybe, things could be different.

But since that night at Prestley's, since Lucasta ghosted me, that hope has dwindled each day.

My phone rings. It's Kahlo, my second photographer. Frowning, I answer.

"Hello?"

His words slur as he says, "Ree, I've made a mistake."

Dread creeps into my veins like smoke. "Elaborate."

"I was slimed by a Slogoth."

Immediate rage has me snapping, "How in the Hells do you miss a Slogoth, Kahlo?"

A fucking Slogoth, of all things. A towering soft-bodied creature of slime, hired to clean the streets of debris. Its slime isn't actually poisonous, but it instantly removes any toxins or dirt. Considering Kahlo loves to imbibe gibbonroot every day — to *relax*, or so he claims — it's no wonder it wiped him out so entirely.

"It doesn't matter how," he says dismissively. Which means he probably tried to impress a woman. "But the doctor said I'm out for the count until next month. Can't use my arms or legs or ... anything. As is, I have a nurse holding up—"

"What!" I shriek, panic thrumming my heart to a painful pace. He's supposed to be working at the wedding *tomorrow.* "Kahlo! This is the busiest month of the season!"

"I know, I know." He sounds embarrassed, but not nearly enough for the severe headache this will cause. "Look, I asked my cousin. He confirmed he can join this month."

Instantly suspicious, I ask, "Is your cousin even a photographer?"

"He is. Really good, too."

"If he's so good, why is he available?" There's silence, which amps up my anxiety. "Hello?"

Kahlo sounds cautious as he explains, "He recently had to scale back on shooting his own weddings; does mostly second shooting now. Less pressure."

A plausible reason. Barely. "And he'll be there tomorrow?"

"Yes, he already confirmed. I sent him the timeline and shot list."

I pinch the bridge of my nose. "This is a disaster, Kahlo. The Orc wedding at the end of the month needs someone who can travel with me. They're Orc royalty — I can't fuck this up. Did you confirm that one as well?"

"All of them are confirmed," he assures me.

My trepidation eases. That makes this less of a disaster, but still stress inducing. Working with a whole new person, a man no less, is not my favorite thing. "He better be a quick learner."

"He is," Kahlo says quickly, albeit slurred. There's murmuring on his side of the line, then he says, "I have to go. Turns out there's a dozen shots required after being slimed."

"They better miscount and give you thirteen," I snarl. "You owe me big time."

"Love you too, Ree." He sounds genuine, but he can fuck off right now. A Slogoth? There *has* to be a woman involved, because he may not be the brightest bulb, but that's a level of stupidity even *he* normally doesn't exhibit.

"I hope it's fourteen." I hang up.

Unbelievable. My upcoming weddings are extravagant and hard won. This past year, it's been difficult running a photography company as a solo artist. There's a particular company, Stone and Skies Visuals, that keeps underbidding me. Potential clients continue sending emails to let me know this company gave them a better deal.

It's been frustrating, to say the least.

In a cut-throat industry, the solution usually is to increase marketing and maybe lower prices. But having no roommate — because who in the Hells wants one of those? — means my apartment is more expensive. Do I want to save money, live with a stranger, and charge less? Or keep prices the same, hope more clients choose me, and pray the rent doesn't rise?

Quite the conundrum.

When the Dragxi lands, I pay and hop off, immediately spotting Yureka. Her bright green skin and hair stick out against the blue Elves behind her. She's standing in a long line that snakes around a black brick building. When the metal door opens, presumably the entrance, I hear pounding music and gleeful hollering. I should've brought my earplugs that I wear at wedding receptions.

Sighing, I walk over to Yureka, giving her a hug. Taking stock of the people waiting in line, I'm surprised to find a wide variety of species. Elves, Witches, goblins, various flyer species, and even a cluster of pixies hover in the air next to some Cyclops.

The moment I'm close enough, I exclaim, "You will never believe what happened."

Yureka grimaces. "Er, I set you up with a dunghole Orc?"

I wave away the words, already over it. A bad date is normal at this point. "Yes, but besides that, Kahlo got slimed head to claw by a Slogoth."

She arches a forest-green eyebrow. "How in the Hells did he pull that off? Aren't those things like twelve feet tall?"

I throw my hands up. "Fuck if I know! He claims to have a cousin ready to step in tomorrow." I let out a sound of frustration. "*Ugh!* This is terrible timing."

Yureka, ever the peacekeeper, puts a hand on my arm to give it a soft squeeze. "It'll be okay. Kahlo is a bit of an idiot, but he also wouldn't send an amateur."

I sigh, scanning the line again. It's doubled since I arrived. "You're right. But I swear, I should fire him over this."

"Maybe." A crease deepens between her brows before she throws her arms around me. "We'll figure it out, okay?"

"Thank you," I say, the words muffled in her hair.

"But that's a Future Us problem," she says, smiling. "Let's enjoy tonight, okay?"

I exhale sharply. "Fine, you're right." Craning my head to see how many more people are in front of us, I ask, "Is this actually that popular?"

Excited about the topic change, Yureka practically hops in place. "Oh yeah. I was lucky to snag tonight's tickets. The headliner features a Regenerator, which means 'death' is allowed." She uses fingers to air quote the word 'death.'

I frown, not understanding. "So, people die here?"

She shoves my shoulder playfully. "No, silly. It's a Regenerator, so it can only die by fire or drowning. Neither is allowed in the arena without special permits."

Still not quite sure what to expect, I nod along, pretending to understand. We discuss the different fight rules, half of which I don't understand. Before long, we're handing in the tickets and entering the building.

I hadn't paid attention to the size of the building, but the inside is ginormous. Brightly lit, like the sun itself is right overhead, it's also packed. There are more species in here, including a group of Satyrs — they love a good gambling situation — Orcs, Angels, ghouls, phantoms, and even some Gargoyles.

I study them, not intending to compare them to Luca, but I do. The species has skin that is different shades of purple and blue, but otherwise, their features can vary. Some have red hair with twisting horns. Others have black hair with yellow eyes. None have white hair like Luca, though. None are as muscular, either.

Stop it.

I don't need to think about him whatsoever. The fact that a year later, he still plagues my thoughts, pisses me off.

I squeeze through a pair of Sprites, careful of their delicate wings. One of them, the taller man, leers at me. I ignore him, keeping close to Yureka as she guides us through the crowd.

Finally, she finds our seats on the lower level. The arena itself has staggered stadium seating, each level offering enough space for wings and large hindends. Smaller species like us are relegated to the front so we're safe from trampling. It also means we naturally have better seats. Small creature privileges, I guess.

As we sit, I watch the fight already underway. It's between an Ogre and a Cyclops with no weapons. Just using their strength and smarts. Well, smart is a generous term because neither species are known for their intelligence.

“Would you like something to drink, miss?” An orange pixie flits out in front of us, holding a small pad of paper. We both order beers, and focus on the fight.

Normally, I’d prefer to be curled up in bed to watch a movie or read a book. However, I have to begrudgingly admit it’s thrilling to feel the energy in the air and hear the roar of the crowd.

When the Ogre passes out from a pretty vicious punch, the referee declares the Cyclops the winner, and the crowd screams in approval. A pair of Orcs drags the Ogre out of the arena, trailing blood across the sand.

The roaring cheers die down as the attendees chatter about upcoming bets. Apparently, the next fight is a Regenerator and some Gargoyle who never loses.

“Two beers,” the pixie says, using wind magyck to levitate our mugs of golden alcohol. I thank him as Yureka pays. He grins and flies off.

Taking a sip, I grimace. “This is disgusting.”

Yureka chuckles. “Well, if you want good booze, go to Prestley’s. This is part of the *experience*, Ree. Stop finding reasons to not be here and enjoy yourself.”

Frowning at her call out, I sip my beer again, pretending it’s delicious. "Mmm, *so* good."

Yureka pats me on the thigh. “There you go. The more you drink, the better it gets.”

“Doubt that,” I mutter, watching the bloodied sand get covered by some Elf attendants.

After a few more sips, I'm relieved when the horn is called, announcing the next fight. In the center of the arena, a presenter suddenly appears. A male phantom grins at the crowd, lifting his translucent hands.

“Wings and fangs! Have I got a treat for you! A highly anticipated battle between Richor the Regenerator and Lucasta the Lucky, the undefeated champion of over fifty battles!”

Beer spews from between my lips.

3

Reverie

Sputtering, I wipe my mouth dry, looking around frantically. Surely, the phantom misspoke. Luca is *not* here, doing a battle with a Regenerator.

Except there he is, stepping into the arena, his powerful legs bare. All he's wearing is a fucking loincloth cinched around his crotch. I steadfastly ignore the bulge between his legs. His chest is bare, revealing delicious pectoral muscles.

Somehow, I'd forgotten.

It must have slipped my mind how handsome he was. The crowd roars, and he grins. *Fuck, those dimples.* His fangs flash, and my mind betrays me, remembering too much. Unfortunately, after that incredible kiss on the cloudavator, I know *exactly* how they feel.

I'd waited an embarrassing amount of time for him to text. My pride wouldn't let me send one first, but the more time that passed, the more angry and embarrassed I became. The official date I'd been so sure would happen never appeared.

For too many nights, I thought of the way he'd kissed me. The way his tail—

No.

My thighs clench. I smack them, cursing their betrayal. He ghosted me and is undeserving of neither my admiration nor imagination. He is not sexy.

No.

No, he is not!

The crowd surges, including Yureka. She looks at me still sitting, twisting her brow in confusion. "What's wrong?"

"Nothing," I mutter, holding my beer in front of my mouth, propping my elbow up with my forearm.

Luca laps up the praise, throwing his muscular arms in the air. The crowd chants *his name*; it's my own personal Hell. A mocking chorus of heartbreak. I'm tempted to tell Yureka I have to go, but I know her; she'll refuse to let me leave. I'm stuck.

Richor the Regenerator steps into the arena to another wild chorus of cheers. He's a bi-pedal creature with black skin and white eyes. A menacing smile reveals a mouth full of jagged white teeth. Twelve-inch claws slide out from his fingers. Black shadows unfurl from his back, becoming solid, turning into leathery wings.

He's genuinely terrifying.

Richor and Luca meet in the center near the presenter, laughing while shaking hands. Luca's smile is so stunning, I'm forced to look away. Dunghole.

The presenter explains it's a friendly fight; Richor is permitted to be dismembered, but not Luca.

No, that doesn't give me relief. Why do you ask?

The presenter rushes out of the arena. Another bell sounds. The crowd screams so loud, I almost drop my beer. Placing it on the ground by my feet, I cross my arms, rooting for the Regenerator.

Richor and Luca circle one another, exchanging jokes too quiet to hear. Luca's skin glistens with sweat, like he warmed up before this. *That's not sexy.*

Richor is the first to strike out with a claw. Luca easily dodges it by jumping backward, laughing. Feinting right, he punches left, slamming a fist into Richor's face. The Regenerator's head snaps back, and blue blood trickles out his nose. *No, that does not make me proud.*

Raising a finger to his nose, Richor inspects it, then gives Luca a feral smile. They both lunge, delivering a series of punches. I gasp when Luca's cheek splits from a well-placed claw. He doesn't notice, ducking from the next hit easily.

When Richor tries to punch again, Luca's skin turns a metallic periwinkle as he shifts into his scora form, where his skin becomes impenetrable. At the same time, he flares his wings — no, his wingspan is *not* impressive; stop wondering — and pivots, bringing a wing toward Richor's head. The Regenerator has no time to react as his head is promptly lopped off.

I shriek, completely taken aback at the spray of blue blood pumping into the air like a geyser. I've never seen so much blood in my life.

Luca's head snaps in my direction. We lock eyes. His jaw drops, looking as shocked as I'd been when he reappeared. Maybe he'll ignore me. After ghosting for an entire year, there's no reason for him to engage with me.

A slow, feral smile spreads across his handsome face. My heart convulses as violently as Richor's decapitated body does. Luca steps over the corpse, stalking toward us. He won't hop the wall, right?

At the mere idea of him doing that, my eyes dart around, hoping to find an escape.

Shifting back to his normal form, Luca rests both arms on the edge of the wall, like he's talking with a friend at a park.

"Hey there, Reverie. Fancy seeing you here." He dips his chin to Yureka. "Hello there, Reverie's friend."

Yureka titters like an adolescent girl. I'm tempted to throw her at him so he'll stop talking to me. The two rows of onlookers turn their eyes appraising the visible veins of glitter. I give Luca a flat look, refusing to say anything. He's embarrassing me on purpose.

When I don't answer, he says, "Sphinx got your tongue?"

He thinks he deserves *anything* to do with my tongue? "Why don't you go fuck yourself, Louie the Lamentation or whatever your name is. Go focus on being a barbaric fighter in a loincloth."

He pretends to be hurt, placing a clawed hand over his heart. "Still mean, I see."

A Sky Sprite in the front row looks at me with completely blue eyes. She actually looks furious. "Are you being mean to Lucasta the Lucky?"

"What? No!" I snap, pointing at my chest. "He was mean to *me.*"

Luca gives a low chuckle. The sound raises my blood pressure. "I understand why you're sad. Why don't you let me explain?"

"There's nothing to explain," I snarl. "You ghosted me for over a year. And I'm not *sad.* I don't even think of you. What's your name again?"

Lies, lies, lies.

Luca lets out a full, deep laugh, not buying the lies for a second. This bastard ... What did I ever see in him? Aside from the muscles, dimples, wings, tail, and that smile, of course.

The Sky Sprite looks at Luca, appalled. "Did you do that?"

How in the Hells did this become a crowd participation conversation?

Luca shrugs. "I have my reasons, Rebrecka."

Rebrecka the Busybody turns to me. "He has his reasons."

"Thank you, Rebrecka," I mutter. That's when I notice Richor's head is halfway reformed. I point at the reviving corpse, gratified for a distraction from this tortuous conversation. "Looks like you have something else to focus on."

Luca doesn't react; he just keeps smiling. With an exaggerated pout, he says, "I don't think I can continue. Not without you promising to hear me out."

I cross my arms, scowling. "No."

He mocks me by crossing *his* arms and popping out his hip. "Yes."

Maybe if I transform his eyes into glitter, this Gargoyle will get it through his big, fat, handsome skull that I'm not interested. Richor's head is fully reformed, and he shakes it, as if clearing away cobwebs. Smugly, I point over his shoulder. "Your opponent is going to kill you."

Luca shrugs. "Maybe I'd rather die than never have you hear me out. Say yes."

Rebrecka huffs with irritation. "Just say yes. I mean, *look at him.* Are you really turning *that* down?"

"Yeah," Luca laughs, motioning to his *very not impressive* form. "Are you going to turn this down?"

Richor stalks toward Luca; a little wobbly, but the intent is clear as he makes his claws longer. Since I just saw Richor get decapitated, I'm not interested in seeing a Gargoyle bleed out. Even if it's *this* Gargoyle in particular.

"Luca!" I shriek. "Behind you! Stop talking to me!"

Luca sighs, shaking his head dramatically. "I can't see anything else except for a Glyridite who won't hear me out."

When Richor is five feet away, close enough to stab Luca in the lungs, I scream, "Fine! Text me, you *fucking idiot!*"

Luca shifts into his scora form to avoid being stabbed, Richor's claws bouncing off the impenetrable periwinkle skin. Ignoring the blow, the maddening Gargoyle flashes long fangs as he laughs. It's full bodied delight.

With a wink, he declares, "Text you tomorrow, Reverie."

"I hope you lost my number, dunghole!" I call out with cupped hands so he can definitely hear me. But since he didn't ask for it again, that means he does. Which makes it less acceptable to ghost me.

He's going to regret this. I'll make sure of it.

Whirling around, Luca flares his wings. It's stunning to see them splayed out, the dark membrane resembling thin silk. With one swift pump, he's airborne. Richor follows on wings of midnight. They continue to punch and claw one another. Yureka bumps my shoulder with hers.

"You have to admit, that was kind of hot. He was willing to be stabbed for you, just so you'd hear him out. Who is he?"

"Pure fucking manipulation," I seethe. "He's just some guy. I doubt he'll text. That was absolutely uncalled for."

The rest of the fight is equally impressive, with Richor losing after Luca severed both legs from his body. When he does his victory lap, he pauses in front of me again. He holds up his thumb and pinky finger to his ear in the shape of a phone, then winks.

I glance at his groin, then back at his face. Raising my pointer finger and thumb, I separate them by an inch with a scowl, implying that *something* is small.

The goddess damned man puts a hand to his heart, miming the implication of being shot with an arrow. I sit, focusing on my beer. When I look back, he's moved on.

I hope to never see him again.

4

Luca

Watching your only parent waste away is its own special kind of hell, filled with hushed tones, sad eyes, and muttered apologies while feet shuffle away.

Through it all, my mother has kept her chin held high, always ready with a good attitude. Like today, for example. Despite this being day four in this brightly lit hospital room, she watches me with amusement while my tail twitches with frustration.

I'm sitting in a chair by her bed, like an acolyte praying for a mother's love. It's been almost two hours since I arrived, and so far, I've helped brush her silvery hair, played card games, and told her wedding horror stories. The clock is ticking, marching toward the inevitable.

Two minutes. I need to leave in two minutes. My tail thrashes.

"You're going to break the tip again," she teases, voice like worn leather.

The words make my tail thrash harder. Lifting her hand away from the blue blanket, I say quietly, "I hate that you're here."

My mother smiles faintly, rubbing the delicate pad of her thumb over my knuckles. "Luca, my light; do not fret over what cannot be changed. The Fates will deliver regardless of a sour rejection."

Flowery words for rotten moments. I'm losing my mother, and she wants me to not worry? Ridiculous. It's all I've done for the past year. Longer, honestly. Since Dad died five years ago, I've worried. I'm thirty-three years old and I'm about to be an orphan.

Instead of saying that, though, I deliver a strained smile. It's growing difficult to present a mask of enthusiasm nowadays. "I'm heading out to photograph a wedding. Do you need anything? I'll be here bright and early to bring you home."

She gives my hand a squeeze with stiff fingers, then pats it. "You can come around lunchtime. Make sure you rest. I can wait."

"Alright." *Not alright*; I'll be here at eight in the morning so she can maximize her day at home. She loves to watch the waterfalls and admire the rainbows. "Text me if you need anything."

"Okay," she says, smiling with an impatient tone. "You know, I took care of myself just fine for sixty years."

Raising an eyebrow, I give the IV in her hand a pointed look. "Our definitions of 'fine' appear to be different."

My mother, in all of her sweetness, says, "You never were good in your language classes."

"Good*bye*," I say with a genuine grin. Kissing the pale purple skin of her forehead, I inhale her scent of lavender. Not loud enough for her to hear, but deep enough to remember when needed. The distant thought isn't buried well enough to prevent an excruciating tug of grief in my heart.

Alone.

I'll be all alone. Soon.

"Find a pretty bridesmaid," she calls as I close the door behind me. I leave a derisive snort in my wake. Her optimism is borderline delusional. My smile drops the moment she's out of sight. I can't *breathe* in here.

Shaking my head, I make my way through the maze of hallways and out into the bright, warm sunshine. It eases the tension soaking my body.

The fresh air shifts my reality, leaving Mom in one compartment of my mind to settle into the reality of being a photographer today. This reality is the one where I step into borrowed moments.

It'll be nice to have something to do today. Get my mind off things for a little bit. *Almost* like a blessing.

The fact that Kahlo was somehow slimed is ridiculous. What makes it more absurd is that he thinks covering a month of weddings is equal to helping me move boxes for one afternoon.

Logic isn't his strong suit. Kahlo is fun, but a little short on brainpower. Trying to call out the nonsensical logic was fruitless. He pointed out that I needed the money, and that shut me up. My marketing fell to the wayside last year, when weddings this season would've been booked. With no weddings of my own, I'm forced to second shoot when possible and pray business appears out of the sky.

These hospital bills aren't cheap.

However, the excitement of shooting a wedding again puts a pep in my step. For the first time in a year, I have something to look forward to. Aside from texting Reverie, which I'll do a bit later. Seeing her last night was a thrilling shock, but I won't let her get away this time. Too many nights have been spent thinking of her.

The pre-wedding anticipation reaches a head as I arrive at the address provided by Kahlo. It's a stunning hotel, built specifically for all types of species to relax and, in today's case, get married. It's designed to resemble the outdoors, with mossy flooring, and waterfalls pouring between panes of glass. It offers a mix of real and artificial light that changes to reflect the light outside. At night, they have small gem lights installed in the ceiling to resemble the night sky. It's one of my favorite places in the city.

Pulling my rolling box of gear behind me, I stride through the entrance, enjoying the cool air caressing my skin. I'm wearing my normal wedding attire: a black suit and white-collared shirt. Since the world of fashion has yet to invent claw-safe shoes, I'm also barefoot.

My moonstone-colored hair's pulled back with a black braid of leather. I look pretty damn snazzy if I do say so myself.

Full of confidence, I walk up to the front desk. The pale Witch with brilliant orange hair greets me with a toothy smile.

"Hello, sir. How may I help you?"

I tap the counter with a pointed claw, offering my most dazzling grin. "I'm here for the Fularoy wedding. Do you by chance know where it's located?"

She sweeps a hand toward a dusky hallway. "Through the Hallway of Twilight, on the left. The reception is in the Pillared Ballroom, but I believe the couple is preparing on floor one hundred seventy-two. Would you like me to confirm that you're expected, and print a key?"

Leaning on my forearm, I beam, delighting in the pinking of her cheeks. "That would be wonderful ..." My eyes flick to her name tag. "Rylaya."

"O-of course, sir." She's visibly flustered as she lifts a phone. "Please give me one moment."

While she does that, I glance past my wings to observe meandering guests. I love watching people walk through the double doors and gasp with delight at the decor. This hotel deserves to be appreciated, especially the large pond in the center of the entrance hall, containing no less than a hundred koi with a dozen water pixies living in the lilies.

"Sir, here is the key. They said you can go right on up."

Returning my focus back to Rylaya, I grab the key card, saying, "Thank you so much, Rylaya. I hope you have a wonderful day."

She titters, batting her orange eyelashes. Shoving off the counter, I tug my gearbox behind me as I walk toward the elevators. Stepping in, I press the floor button, peering through the clear walls as it shoots into the sky. The hotel itself has two hundred floors, with the top fifty being penthouses.

Taking a deep breath, I exhale, cupping my mouth to check my breath. Minty fresh. Adjusting my light purple tie — Kahlo told me the company colors are purple and black — I mentally prepare for whatever chaos arrives when the doors open.

After ten years as a photographer, I've learned there's no such thing as "seen it all." There's always, *always*, something new to discover. It's one of my favorite things about weddings.

The elevator dings and the doors separate.

Revealing utter chaos.

Invigorated, I step out, then step back as a female Satyr bounds by, screaming something about wrinkles in her dress. Wrapping my tail around my thigh to keep from tripping anyone, I gingerly step to the side as another Satyr follows, screeching after the first one, holding a steamer.

Grinning, I search the room. Kahlo told me to find a female Forest Sprite named Yureka, who would have the schedule of the day ready. All I see are woodland creatures in various states of undress. It's the living room of the penthouse, but that doesn't prevent woodland creatures from getting half-naked. Their sense of propriety is more ... flexible.

Still, I'm cognizant as I scope out the scene, making sure my gaze lingers nowhere but faces. Finally, I spot a woman who could—

Sluggish tar coats my insides when I see who must be Yureka. She's wearing a black pantsuit, holding a clipboard, with green skin and dark green hair pulled into a high ponytail. Her large eyes watch the female Satyr in front of her, nodding in agreement.

Yureka is the woman next to Reverie last night.

She catches my eye, noticing the gearbox. Her eyes widen. With a nervous expression, she waves me over. Trying to steady my weak knees, I dodge scurrying wedding guests as I cross the room, flashing smiles at anyone willing to make eye contact. My first job of the day isn't taking pictures — it's establishing trust as fast as possible. I find the smile I inherited from my mother the best weapon in this goal.

Yureka pulls away from the Satyr in front of her, promising to call someone, then turns her focus to me. Holding out a slender hand, she clears her throat. "Hello, I'm Yureka. Do you prefer Lucasta or Lucasta the Lucky?"

I chuckle. That damn nickname Kahlo insists on. All because I won a contest when we were six years old. It was a damn fruit basket, but he's insisted on the nickname since. It's why Richor chose it for me all those years ago before my first battle. "Actually, it's Lucasta, but you can call me Luca."

Yureka's phone chirps; whatever message she receives pales her face. Flustered, she pulls two sheets of paper from the clipboard. "Okay, L-Luca, here's the schedule for the day. You'll be with the groomsmen, of course, until the First Look at three."

With high, delusional hopes, I ask, "Who is the other photographer? Kahlo didn't tell me their name. He's not the best with details."

Yureka smooths a loose strand of hair behind her ear. "Yes, it's a good thing he isn't a planner." She nibbles her lip. Behind us, the elevator dings again, catching her attention. Her mouth shuts as her eyes widen further. "Um, well, she's here now."

I follow her gaze, ready to smile at whoever I'm helping today, but my mouth dries as the woman steps out. Her aquamarine eyes scan the room, quickly homing in on the biggest creature in the room. Me.

There's too much noise in the room to hear the word, but I see Reverie's plump lips open as she mouths — with vicious ferocity, might I add —"*You.*"

Fuck.

5

Reverie

This damn purple dunghole.

The tormenting subject of my dreams. Every night, he's floating with me in the sky as he presses those curved lips against mine, promising to call the next day. All over again, I feel the excitement dying, as each day passed without a text or call. It shifted into anxiety, then insecurity, and finally, anger.

After last night, the embers of said anger are fresh, sparking glitter at my fingertips. Curling my hands into fists, I flash a stony look at Yureka, as if this is her fault. She appears just as blindsided, which means she most likely just found out herself.

I'm going to *kill* Kahlo.

Shoving down the visceral emotions punching against my ribs, I put on my mask reserved for weddings, allowing a wide, welcoming smile to light up the room. Raising my hands to the twenty-foot-tall white ceiling, I don't announce myself — I let the rainbows do that for me.

The room fills with a shimmering collage of color. The Satyrs giggle with excitement. All around is happy commentary, pointing at me as I plaster a smile onto my tight face.

Louelle, the bride, hops over to me, her blonde hair streaming behind her. A crown of daisies sits right above her pointed ears, with flecks of glitter lighting her large, brown eyes.

"Reverie!" she squeals, flinging her arms around my waist. "I'm so glad you're here. I knew your entrance would be epic, but that was incredible."

I lean down to hug her back. "I'm so glad you loved it! Where's Olor getting ready? My second shooter will be with him until the First Look."

Ignore him, ignore him.

Louelle beckons over her maid of honor, Strella. "El will bring your second shooter to him. He's getting ready in the attached suite at the end of the hallway. We're getting ready in here for now, then I'll get dressed in the bedroom."

I direct Strella to *him*, and wave over Yureka. She gives *him* one last glance, then bustles over. As Louelle skips to the buffet of vegetation, Yureka sidles up to me against the wall.

While I busy myself with pulling out photography gear, she hisses, "I had no idea, Ree. I found out five seconds before you did. Do you want me to make him leave? Because I'll kick his plump ass out the door if you want me to."

Ignoring her comment about his rear-end — even if I agree — I shake my head. "No. As much as I loathe to admit, we need him. There was no one else." Attaching my cameras to my harness, I say, "We can be professionals. Kahlo said he's an expert, so I have to trust that we can both be adults here."

"But—"

She falls silent when I cut her off with a look. "No. We don't discuss it. You don't discuss it. We are professionals, right?"

She hesitates. "Yes ..."

"Save it for the bar tonight, then."

It's amusing how relief drops her shoulders. Yureka is a good friend; she knows all about my experience with Luca, even if she didn't know who he was until I explained last night after the fight. But her wanting me to be okay won't actually make me okay.

After spending over a year being furious with myself about giving him a chance at all before being ghosted ... I've spent this time feeling stupid. His reappearance, acting like it's easily explained away, is infuriating. And now, a *whole month* with him?

I can't do it.

Ensured all of my immediate gear's attached to my body, I ask, "Is he still behind me?"

Her mouth twists in uncertainty. "Yes?"

"Damnit," I mutter. Closing my eyes, I count to five. As they open, Yureka watches me transform my frustrated expression into one of joy. Always joy on wedding days. Wedding photographers don't have the luxury of any other emotion.

Turning on the ball of my foot, I find Luca still waiting in the same spot, staring. Not doing his job. Irritated, I make my way through the crowd, stopping to offer compliments to help build rapport. It's only ten hours today, but in those ten hours, I need everyone comfortable around me to get the best photos.

Those storm cloud eyes watch me approach, revealing no emotion. His body language is lax, but the way his knuckles blanch around the handle of his gear case, I know he's just as good at hiding his emotions as I am.

Like all those nights ago, I revel in his height. Being a taller woman myself, it's a pleasant experience. *Don't think about it.*

We have a job to do; that's it.

With a saccharine smile, I say, "What was your name again?"

Amusement crinkles the corners of his eyes. "You can call me either Mr. Nonya or Luca."

Oh, fuck this guy. Swallowing hard, I say, "Good to know." Scanning the room, making sure no one is watching too closely, I say under my breath, "Are you sure you're comfortable working with someone you don't like?"

His eyebrows jump, then scrunch together in confusion. "Who don't I like?"

It's my turn to look confused, but I wipe it away immediately, returning to my pleasant mask. "It doesn't matter. We're professionals, and there's no need to discuss anything outside of doing our jobs. Got it?"

"Reverie, I—"

"Got. It?" I grit.

"Got it."

His face falls for a split second before smoothing into neutral. I glance at the pieces of paper in his hand. "You have the schedule?"

"Yes."

"Good." I point at Strella, who catches the gesture and walks over. "She'll show you where the groom is getting ready. His name is Olor. The bride is Luelle. They're having the typical Satyr ceremony, with a lot of frolicking while drinking wine. Louelle will serenade Olor with her flute before the 'I dos.'"

"Understood." He neatly folds the schedule before shoving it into a pocket. He's handsome in his tailored suit. I can almost feel the heat of those rough palms on my cheek.

Catching myself staring, I focus on greeting Strella. We shake hands, and I introduce her to Luca. His demeanor is welcoming. She takes to him right away, leading him to the room where Olor waits.

I close my eyes and count to five again, trying to dull the anxiety thrumming in my blood. I can do this.

I'm a professional.

I'm a professional.

I'm a professional.

Maybe if I repeat it enough times, it'll wash away the renewed heartbreak.

***

To my surprise, Luca is not only a professional — he's *really* good at what he does. When I'm not focused on taking pictures, I observe him from afar. He's inventive with the angles, always ready to offer a guest assistance, and takes direction without question.

It adds to my resentment.

We're almost at the ceremony, and he still hasn't tried to discuss why he ghosted me. Which makes me angry in a very unreasonable way. Mainly because I told him not to, and he's respecting my boundary, like a *dunghole.*

I need to get a hold on this anger.

Is there anything he could say to fix what he's done? It's been over a year, so it's not like he hasn't had time. No one is *that* busy.

Even as the three of us, Yureka included, walk toward the ceremony site on the first floor, none of us says a word. The way Yureka casts him furtive glances means her curiosity is burning. It's only a matter of time before the self-control snaps, so I need to separate them.

"Yureka," I say, pausing mid-stride. The two of them stop, surprised. Pulling out the timeline, I point at the shot list inserted in the middle. "Can you go ask the planner who is going to be gathering these people? I want to make sure we use the time wisely after the ceremony since they only gave us twenty minutes."

For the millionth time today, she hesitates. My eyes flash a warning. She straightens, nodding curtly. "Yes, of course."

Rushing down the cobbled pathway and almost running into the abundance of greenery, she lends me one last backward glance before disappearing around a corner.

Refusing to give Luca attention, I continue walking, his large presence more than a nuisance. Instead, I focus on running through the shots I'll need covered during the ceremony. Pulling out the image request list, I skim the bullet points. It's already memorized thanks to my skill, but I need something to do with my hands.

Grinding my molars, I note the personal request for an aerial shot.

I point at it, still refusing to look at him. "Will you be able to get the aerial shots during the procession and wine exchanges?"

"Of course."

"Make sure you don't miss the flower necklace exchange."

"I won't."

His short answers are infuriating, especially since I know he's trying to respect my boundaries. Why does he respect me *now?*

The deliciously low voice haunting my dreams says quietly, "Reverie. I'm really sorry I never called."

So much for respecting the boundary. I'm both thrilled and even more furious.

The shot list crinkles in my tightening fist. A lump burns in my throat, and it's an effort to swallow the emotions. "*I said* we won't *talk* about it."

"I'm sorry, regardless." The regret in his voice has to be a ruse. Because why be sorry, but never fix it?

Halting in my steps, I check the empty path, then direct my steaming rage at his handsome face. It's tempting to jab a finger into his broad chest, but I'm not about to assault a co-worker. Instead, I snarl, "Your apology isn't needed. You didn't have to lead me on, you know. You could've let me down gently. I'm a grown adult who can handle rejection."

Unidentifiable emotions flicker across his face, deepening his frown. "Reverie, I didn't reject you."

I scoff, continuing to walk. "Could've fooled me these last three-hundred-eight-two days."

Luca inhales sharply, keeping pace next to me. With a tone filled with curiosity, he asks, "You're ... counting?"

Shit. It's not like I was marking a calendar or something like a lovesick child; my photographic memory also has an uncanny ability to mark the passing of time.

Trying to blow it off, I say, "No, of course not. I just happened to buy a subscription to FloRyte the day we met, and I just renewed it."

Why did I say FloRyte? I want to smack my forehead and knock out some of this brain-smothering fury.

"Right. Because your laxative prescription is due? And not because you think about that night?" His tone says he doesn't believe me at all, but I don't care. He doesn't need to know about my skill. Luca doesn't deserve to know that part of me.

"Don't flatter yourself," I mutter. Finally gracing him with a scathing glare, I demand, "Now, enough of this. You apologized to feel better. Goody for you. Can we go back to being professionals?"

I ignore the way my heart pangs at the hurt on his face. No, there's no reason to care that my barbed responses hit their mark. He deserves it.

We reach the ceremony site, and I'm temporarily stunned. This is one of my favorite hotels in the city, and the view before us is exactly why.

Large gumdrop trees reach for one another, offering a dappled shade, their colorful fruit ready to plop onto the mossy ground with explosions of color and scents. Logs hand-carved into elaborate benches lay in a circle, surrounding an arbor made of ivy vines covered in spring flowers.

Off to the right is a small quartet of Elves, their nimble fingers warming up string instruments. Guests mill about, offering laughter and hugs to one another. The heady scent of eucalyptus comes from the arrangements placed between the logs. For a split second, I forget my anger, enthralled with the moment.

"I love this ceremony site," Luca murmurs, pausing next to me.

Unsure if someone is watching us, I spear him with a look, wishing I could shoot glitter from my eyeballs into his. But since I need those silver eyes, and I can't actually shoot glitter from mine, I let myself enjoy the imaginative visual.

"Kahlo says you're good at your job."

He nods. "I am."

Tilting my head, I ask, "What's your company?"

"Stone and Skies Visuals."

My blood pressure skyrockets. I imagine bludgeoning his head in with both of my cameras. The effort required to keep my expression neutral might put me in an early grave. "Did you say Stone and Skies?"

He cocks his head, confused. "Yes?"

"Are you aware of my company name?"

His broad brow pulls together with uncertainty. "Actually, no. Kahlo and I rarely discuss work."

"It's Edges of Glitter."

Understanding dawns. He knows *exactly* what he's done. "Reverie, I—"

"Are you really so dimwitted that you had no idea who you were working with?"

"Reverie—"

I hold up a hand. "Do your job. I don't want to listen to your excuses, which are most likely Pegishit."

Luca flinches, and his shoulders drop. I spin, refusing to hear anything else he has to say.

Lucasta Destau is responsible for almost every potential client I've lost in the last year by undercutting every single bid. He's a direct competitor, something Kahlo definitely should've known. I'm going to strangle that man with fists full of glitter until they leak out his nose.

"Reverie." Luca calls after me, sounding too desperate.

Shoving my arm behind me, I lift three fingers, bending the middle one, a sign of disrespect. I need to find a new second shooter by next weekend if it's the last thing I do.

6

Luca

My mother tells me any chance possible that I was born full of light and happiness. My name means light, so maybe she was correct.

Right now, though, I feel dark.

Watching Reverie retreat, giving me the middle finger, makes me want to make a fool of myself and beg for forgiveness. *Three hundred eighty-two nights.* Her admission stuns me. She doesn't appear to be the type to keep a tally, but the exactness is disturbing. I'm certain it's not because she's constipated, although the expression she keeps giving me might convince me otherwise.

Regardless, she knows how many days and it hurts. Because that means I had three hundred eighty-two missed opportunities.

Shame fills me as I follow her, staking out a spot for my gear. Finding a tiny alcove on the outskirts of the ceremony site, I switch out lenses, self-flagellating myself the entire time. Reverie is angry, which means she's actually hurt. I've *hurt* her. It was never my intention, but the way she's behaving, she'll never give me a chance to explain.

Even if the reason is logical.

But is it? Have I really never had a single moment to myself in the last year to contact her? Of course I have. In fact, six months ago I did just that, typing out a whole message. My thumb hovered over the Send button. Thirty seconds into meeting, she thought I wanted to fuck her; what would a random text after six months do?

She didn't text me either, so I assumed she didn't want me.

It'd hurt to delete that unsent message, but I thought I was being an honorable, sensible man.

I was very, *very* wrong.

There's the matter of being business rivals. Well, at least in her eyes, we are rivals. I always considered Edges of Glitter to be a competitor in the way that we're in the same industry, but also serving two different markets. All of the clients who chose my company prefer high amounts of discretion and curated productions. Edges of Glitter is known for ... glitter and rainbows. That's not a bad thing — we're simply different creatives. My work is more reserved, while hers is radiant. There's no other word for it. I've admired her work for years. If I had known she was the owner of Edges of Glitter ...

I'm so fucking stupid. We hadn't talked about our careers that night at Prestley's, but I should've asked.

Now is not the time.

Checking that all of my gear's secured, I turn toward the crowd. Pastel rainbow hair bobs past guests, Reverie's long legs keeping her above the sea of horned heads of hair. The night we met, it had been a pleasant surprise to discover those long, muscular legs brought our faces closer than I'm used to. Being almost seven-feet-tall makes it difficult to find partners who don't cause back pain when I kiss them.

She'd been perfect in my arms, all passionate softness. The way she'd look at me with those clear blue eyes, a small hopeful smile on her full mouth ...

A pang of mournful regret threatens to consume me.

Focus.

Battering down the memories with a mental sledgehammer, I focus on doing my job. Nothing else. When the ceremony begins, I fly high into the trees, carefully avoiding the juicy fruit to prevent an over-ripened catastrophe falling onto the guests below. While I can usually separate work from my personal life, my eyes still trail the woman full of vibrant smiles.

I want those smiles.

When she uses glitter to encapsulate her lens to add drama to her images, I think of her barbed joke about glittering my cock. It throbs at the memory. I stab a fang into the inside of my lip, desperate to stay professional.

I never in my life thought I'd crave glitter on my cock, but for her, I'd happily resemble an art project every single damn day.

But the only way I'd get the opportunity is if I can convince her I'm not a total dunghole.

By the time the ceremony's complete, and my memory card is full of frolicking Satyrs guzzling wine with cheery red cheeks, I'm determined to explain things to her. Beg for another chance.

Except I don't get the opportunity. Any time I approach, she walks away. During dinner, when I try to sit with my vendor meal, she leaves the room. Yureka delivers every single one of her requests. When it's over, the assistant pays me with a polite, but decidedly cool, thank you. When I hand over my memory card, Yureka reminds me to check my email for details about the next wedding.

This is going to be the longest month of my life.

***

After showering in my oversized bathtub and making a quick sandwich in my luxuriously appointed kitchen, I call the source of my havoc.

"You could've told me your boss is named Reverie Songlight," I seethe, clutching the phone to my burning ears. On the other side is a very confused Kahlo.

"Why does that matter?"

Growling, I pace my apartment, careful to keep my tail close so I don't knock over another lamp. My lamp budget is maxed out due to my overly twitchy tail when I'm agitated or nervous. "Kahlo, I know we agreed to keep our wedding shit separate, but you could've told me it was Edges of Glitter."

"So?"

This man *deserved* to be run over by a Slogoth. "*So.* Do you know my company name, Kahlo?"

I can almost hear his nonchalant shrug. "No."

"Stone and Skies Visuals." Silence. Yeah, this dunghole knows he fucked up. "Exactly. And you remember that woman I met at Prestley's over a year ago?"

"No." He breathes the word as if the shock is truly, fully hitting him. "Why in the Hells didn't you *tell* me she was a Glyridite?"

"Tell you?" I whip around so fast that the control over my tail snaps, and there's a crash. Closing my eyes, I take in a deep breath, mentally setting aside a hundred corals for another lamp. Willing patience into my heated veins, I say slowly, "Kahlo. When have we ever had a full conversation about our love lives? The last woman you dated, you told me she had dark hair, nice eyes, and an ass rounder than a beach ball. That's it."

"It was a nice ass," he agrees.

Snatching a pillow from my white overstuffed couch, I shove it against my face for a long, satisfying scream. Even held at my hip, I can hear Kahlo's tinny voice babbling about the woman he dated. Entirely missing the point.

When the rage inside me is curbed, I lift the phone back to my ear and interrupt his story about the woman he screwed in a bar's bathroom.

"Kahlo!" I bark. He smartly shuts up. "I can't do this for the next month. She hates me. She won't listen to me."

"Just tell her, Lucky. She's not unreasonable."

"You must not know her well," I mutter.

"What?"

"Nothing. She won't talk to me."

He sighs like I'm a petulant child interrupting his laying in bed, regaining use of his fingers. "Luck, I don't know what to say. I told you lifting those boxes with my back problems would have a cost."

"You had a bruise on your back from *fucking an Orc on rocks.*"

My cousin, in all of his brainless glory, has the gumption to say, rather gleefully if I might add, "Oh yeah! Worth it, if you ask me."

"Next time I see you, I'm stoning your face in."

He clicks his tongue in admonishment. "Lucky, you're being dramatic. It's three more weddings, not a prison sentence. Are you so unprofessional that you'd cancel because a woman is being mean to you?"

Yes. "No."

"Then it's settled." He sounds so damn smug, I'm tempted to rip this pillow in half. But I already have to replace another lamp; I don't need to add a pillow to the tally.

Grinding my fangs, I grit out, "You're going to owe me big time."

"Maybe," he admits. "But take pity on me. I'm an invalid."

"I'm going to make you a lifetime invalid if you ever pull this shit ever again."

"Maybe I'd fall in love with a healer, and we'd have six babies that look like me. I'll name the oldest son Lucasta."

I hang up.

7

Reverie

Cover your arms, Reverie.

My dad's voice chides inside my mind while I examine my reflection. Wearing black pants and a tank top, I'm pretty cute. Even my hair, normally a little unruly in its waviness, is behaving.

In my hand is a green sweater. Soft armor. I'm due at the entrance of the farmer's market in thirty minutes, and I cannot decide whether or not to show skin. On one side of the coin, my father will have a few things to say. Eventually, he'll force me to wear it. The other side ... I could be comfortable in the spring air.

Grabbing the sweater, I stuff it into my oversized purse. A temporary compromise. Boundaries with my parents are hard.

I'm dismounting the Dragxi with five minutes to spare, but they're already waiting. Mom's ashy blonde hair is pulled back in a neat ponytail, her eyes shining when she spots me. The only physical traits I inherited from her are my height, curvy figure, and her smile.

Dad's arm wraps around her waist when they both wave. His dark blue hair, with streaks of rainbow scattered throughout, is perfectly styled.

They're both covered from head to toe. My father's wearing a turtleneck to hide the veins on his neck. The ones you *can* see are thick and darker colored.

"Hello, Popsicle." Mom's the first to hug me, using the childhood nickname chosen from the summer where I exclusively ate popsicles.

"Hey, Mom."

Then it's Dad's turn. Half a foot taller, he presses me into his chest with an enthusiastic hug. His voice rumbles in my ear as he says, "You're beautiful, but please tell me you brought a sweater."

And there he goes. I step back, frowning. "It's pretty warm today. I thought it would be nice—"

"Now, Reverie," he says, giving me a stern look with cobalt eyes. "You know it's more about making sure others are comfortable."

"Spark." Mom places a tempering hand on his elbow. "Maybe it's okay if—"

"It'll make *me* more comfortable." He eyes my bag with raised eyebrows, because this isn't our first or last discussion on the subject. My dad knows there's a sweater in the bag.

Shame burns my cheeks as I pull out the sweater, sliding it on without another word. When my body is fully covered, Dad nods, motioning for us to go into the farmer's market.

My parents are good ones, but my dad was apparently bullied a lot as a kid for being a Glyridite. Naturally, Mom was too, for being part siren. They're protective and want me to be happy. Not for the first time, I wonder why they never left Gondora. Travel has never been a focus for me, so maybe the whole of Avalon is like this.

"Come," Dad says, ushering us forward. "I heard there is a new bread baker we should try."

We make our way through the slow-moving aisles, pausing to taste samples. As per the routine, when we pass the small coffee stand, we all buy hazelnut lattes. Mom and I love a little cinnamon sprinkled over the milky foam.

My stomach churns when we stop at Dante's stall. He's a Glyridite specializing in potions, tinctures, and spells. Mostly patronized by

Witches, Dante also sells glittering wares like plates, utensils, and shirts to bring in other customers.

Glyridites aren't common in Gondora. Glitter itself may not be toxic in any form, but people treat it like an incurable disease because some bits can be left behind when someone uses the power. Unlike me, Dante doesn't incorporate glitter into his business, which Dad appreciates.

Unfortunately, Dante also has a crush on me ... even though he's fifteen years older. When he spots us, his shoulders square, and he rubs the outside of his mouth. Coming around the table, he holds out toned arms I'm supposed to step into.

Instead, I stand there, receiving the hug with a stiff spine. Fingers briefly drag across the top of my pants, almost indecent but not enough to make a fuss over it. His voice grates on my nerves as he says, "Ree, it's good to see you."

Why does he have to be Glyridite? With any other species, my parents would've avoided him the moment I said I was uncomfortable — which I have, *multiple* times. But thanks to the glitter in Dante's veins, Dad insists on stopping to support a fellow glittering freak. Except Dante can show off his arms. Me? I resemble a maiden priestess.

Okay, that's a little dramatic, but still.

Mom smiles faintly over his shoulder, knowing how I feel about Dante. Dad, however, is blind to it all; either on purpose or by accident, it's hard to say.

He claps Dante on the shoulder with a wide grin. "Dante, it's good to see you."

"You too, Mr. Songlight." Dante won't take his light blue eyes off of me, his teal and rainbow hair a little messy. Laugh lines crease the corners of his eyes, as well as a deep groove of past emotions cutting across his forehead.

After hugging my mom, he says, "Haven't seen you here in a little bit, Ree."

"Uh, yeah." I shift away, rubbing my arm. "Been busy."

"Busy! Too busy for a lovely morning with your parents?" he teases.

It's impossible not to lift my lip in disgust. Every time we speak, it's like he's trying to prove to my parents that he can be my new parental figure. The familiar, festering fury of how men treat me rears its ugly head. *Who the hell does this guy think he is?*

"Are you chastising me?"

"Ree," Mom admonishes, shifting to place a hand on my shoulder. "Be nice."

Be nice, Reverie. Cover up, Reverie. The broken soundtrack to my life. Exhaling slowly, I give Dante a saccharine smile. With a soft, disingenuous feminine voice, I say, "Sorry, what I meant to say was, 'Are you *fucking* chastising me?'"

"Reverie Vayla." My name is sharp against Dad's tongue. The three of them gape at me like I've grown eight hydra heads, instead of maybe, I don't know, trying to set boundaries?

I wince. This will result in a lecture about ruining my future with a sour attitude. Might as well really fuck myself over. "I'm going to take my latte over there—" I point at an empty bench. "—and you both can join me when you're done chatting with this ..." I examine Dante with a wrinkled nose. "... this man, who is closer to my father's age than he is to mine."

My mother gasps, giving Dad a nervous look; my patriarch is incandescent with anger. Dante's brows dip in disappointment, like he's ready to lecture anyone willing to suffer through it.

No, thanks.

Spinning on the toe of my boot, I stalk over to the bench, sitting with a huff. Now comes the theatrics of how I'm not getting any younger, and *something something* dying alone *something something*. They act like being twenty-eight and single is a curse. But have they met the available men in Gondora? Few would win an award.

Except for Luca, but that does *not* matter right now

"That was incredibly rude, Popsicle," Mom says, voice soft as she sits next to me.

Staring at my coffee cup, stewing in my anger, I hiss, "I'm not stopping at that tent anymore. He's creepy, almost grabbing my ass each time, Mom."

"I don't think that's—"

"It is," I insist. "Why can't you—"

"Reverie Songlight," Dad barks, barely in his seat before the patriarchal lecture begins. "That was *uncalled for.* What has gotten into you? We're trying to have a nice morning, and you have to use foul language like that in front of a small business owner?"

Unpeeling my tongue from the roof of my mouth, I stop grinding my teeth long enough to say, "He isn't a random business owner, Dad. We all know he wants to go on a date with me."

He gives me an incredulous look. "So? You could stand to go on a date, Reverie. You aren't getting any younger."

I've heard that phrase so many times since I turned twenty, it's immediately exhausting. I've heard it so much, it's only offered encouragement for me to stay in unhealthy relationships.

It's never enough. It'll never *be* enough.

The fighting spirit raising my heart rate poofs out of existence. My shoulders sagging, I study the grain in the wooden tabletop. "Sorry. You're right."

He dives forward as if I haven't spoken. "I mean, really, Reverie. Showing up without a sweater on, to distract everyone else? Being rude to a family friend? What is *wrong* with you?"

Mom frowns, a line deepening between her brows.

At least they worry — not everyone has parents who worry. Arguing with them because they worry would be dumb.

My cheeks burn for a different reason now. "Okay. I'm sorry. Won't happen again."

It will *totally* happen again, but this is the quickest way for both of us to move on. Doesn't make the words sting less, though.

"I would hope not," Dad grumbles, mollified. He glances around. "Oh! They have fried hippogriff." To Mom, he says, "You've been wanting to try that, right?"

Her face lights up. "Yes!"

Dad stands, smiling at me with a soft expression. "Would you like some? Looks like they're kebabs."

Relieved at the brevity of the lecture, I nod. "Sure."

After pressing a kiss to Mom's forehead, he winks at me and heads to the back of the line.

"Thanks for the back-up," I grumble, staring at my lap so Dad can't read my lips.

"Now, Reverie, that's not fair," she says in a stern tone. "Your father is right; we worry about you. I know Dante isn't ideal, but you'll be so much happier in a family."

Glancing up sharply, I say, "Women don't need families to be happy. I'm fine right now."

It stings more because I'm just that — fine. Not great or good. Just fine. But the solution to happiness isn't finding a man ready to create a family. No matter what my parents insist on, it just isn't. They seem happy enough, but it's probably because Mom submits to him more than anything. I've never heard them fight.

And even though I want to be married, to have someone of my own, I don't want it to be at the expense of my freedom. What they're asking for is for me to accept a specific identity — a mother and wife — for the *possibility* of being happy.

I refuse.

She places a hand on my thigh. "Hey."

When my tear-filled eyes meet hers, she softens her voice. "I want you happy, Popsicle. We're concerned. Can you blame us for wanting our daughter, our *only child*, to be happy?"

Call me a coat rack for all the hopes and dreams flung onto my limbs. "Let me figure it out without the pressure. Please?"

"Of course," she presses a kiss between my eyebrows. "How's work? Any interesting stories so far?"

And just like that, the topic changes. Crisis averted with supplication. Shifting my mask to one of happiness, I smile. "Let me tell you about the Satyrs this past weekend."

While I prattle on about the wedding, a tiny space in my mind wonders what Luca would've done in my shoes — if he could wear them, of course. Something tells me he wouldn't have apologized.

Why do I keep apologizing?

8

Luca

A fist collides with my cheek, knocking my head back. I barely feel it. Snarling, I swing with my elbow, missing Richor's mouth. He laughs, not realizing it was a distraction. Shifting faster than he can process, I duck, flaring my wings mid-spin.

My opponent isn't fast enough — as he jumps back, his right arm is too far forward, until it's not. My wing hits its mark with a quiet squelch.

Half of Richor's pitch-black arm lands on the sand.

Wiping sweat from my forehead, I flash him fangs with a too-wide grin. "Whoops."

Richor gives me a nasty glare as he picks up his arm. His blue blood gushes from the stump below his shoulder until the flesh begins to stitch itself back together. Growling, he shakes the displaced limb at me. "Come on, Luca. I can't lose all of my body parts before the actual battle. I'll pass out before there's a chance to stab you."

Snapping my wings in, I grab my water bottle. "You're just bitter that you didn't see that coming."

Richor scoffs, tossing the arm next to the leg and hand I'd lopped off earlier. "Without me, you'd never get to actually show off. You should be thanking me."

Spitting out blood with some water, I laugh. "Sore loser."

Richor's milky white eyes narrow. "Being a Regenerator can be lucrative, but for once, I'd like to cut off someone's arm."

"Here, take mine," I offer one of my arms.

He snorts. "How would you jerk yourself off?"

Shrugging, I put the water bottle back on the bench. "I have another hand."

He rolls his eyes, rubbing a towel over his sweaty face, one of his claws accidentally ripping through the fabric. "If you're only using one hand to jerk off, you're not using your imagination enough."

I pause, giving him a wolfish grin. "I do have a tail."

Even without pupils, I sense his gaze flicking to my dexterous tail with its blunt end. I raise it and wave the tip at him. He jerks back with a sneer of disgust. "I don't want to know," he mutters, tossing the ripped towel on the ground. "Come on, one more round. Then we'll rest."

Cracking my neck, I shake my arms to loosen the muscles. "We have to put on a good show tonight."

Richor and I have been battle buddies for over a decade. As a Regenerator, his battles are more for entertainment than earnest efforts. Losing body parts doesn't hurt him, making him an excellent way for a warrior to show off their abilities without doing actual harm to someone. He gets paid *a lot* of money for the service.

He flares his wings as he rubs a bicep absentmindedly. "I need to have Sethe come visit. We haven't had a duel between two Regenerators in almost a year."

Inhaling a steadying breath, I hone in on his micro movements, anticipating his attack. He's trying to distract me with conversation — it won't work. In the arena, I'm in my element; my body sings with the violence I keep tempered; at least, most of the time.

"Speaking of a year," I say as we circle one another. I catch the way he drops his shoulder, but I know it's a distraction. "Remember that Glyridite I mentioned meeting a little over a year ago?"

There. Richor flares his wings to draw attention, but his thighs bunch. As he leaps in the air, I catch his foot and twist. It flips him over, forcing him to land on all fours. Taking me by surprise, he leans forward on his hands and bucks, kicking me straight in the chest.

Air escapes my lungs as I stumble back. *Fucker.* While I find my footing, Richor somersaults in the dirt and propels himself to standing. I'm already charging as he spins. His eyes widen with shock as I lower my head, slamming my forehead into his chest.

He flies six feet backward before landing on his ass. I bark out a laugh at his bewildered expression. Flipping his body to standing, he snarls, "You mean that woman you moped about for months?"

I throw a punch, landing my fist on his temple. "I didn't mope."

In a whiney voice that *does not* sound like me, he drawls, "'*I should text her. She was so beautiful. It's too late, though. Wah wah.*'"

Snarling, I slam an uppercut to his chin, snapping his sharp teeth together. "I did *not* cry."

Richor gives me a dry look, then open-palm slaps me in the face. "You definitely cried. Lubed up your dick while jerking off with your tail, you sick fuck."

The sting on my cheek emphasizes my frustration. "I didn't realize I'd had an audience, you little freak."

I return the smack. We hold eye contact for a second; then we both lunge, tumbling to the sand in a sweaty, bickering mess.

"I like to watch you jerk it to Pegasus porn," he hisses, elbowing me in the ear. I shake my head, trying to get rid of the stars sparkling in my vision.

I grab his hair to dig his face into the sand, then let go. Standing, I shoot back, "It's only because it reminds me of your sister and her voluptuous ass."

Spitting out the sand, Richor snarls, "Don't you look at my sister's ass."

"So you *know* it's voluptuous?" I shake my head in mock disbelief. "Why are you staring at your sister's ass, Richor?"

With a war cry, he leaps onto me with the rabid energy of a deranged harpy. We trade punches until we're both heaving for air, bent over, trying not to pass out.

Catching his eye, I grin, wiping away blood. "Seriously, why are you looking at her ass?"

"Shut the fuck up," he grumbles, swaggering over to his water bottle. After taking deep gulps, he asks, "So. The Glyridite. Did you finally grow a pair and call her?"

I sit heavily on the bench, wincing at the soreness of my legs. "Worse. She was at the wedding. Kahlo apparently works for her."

Richor swears, then chuckles. "And how did she take it?"

I think of the fury rolling off the colorful woman who hates my guts. "Wonderfully. So great. Hugged me, even."

Richor's face contorts in confusion. "Really?"

"Fuck no." I laugh. "She all but told me to jump off a cliff with clipped wings."

"I like her already," he deadpans. "Did you tell her why you disappeared?"

My happy mood shifts into something darker. "No."

He appraises me for a long, painful moment before finally saying, "Do you like her?"

I think of Reverie's smile. Rainbow hair. The beauty she sees in the world. "Definitely. She's something special."

"You should tell her."

I look away from my long-time friend, refusing to entertain his advice. Leaning forward on my knees, I stare at the sand. "We're just working together. She doesn't need to know anything about me."

"And if it gets more serious?" Richor sits next to me, all of the vicious energy from before gone. Concern rolls off him in waves. It makes me want to leave this conversation behind. I regret bringing up Reverie; it could turn into absolutely nothing. Maybe that entire evening at the bar was a fever dream. I've over-romanticized it all.

"I'll tell her. But she hates me, so it most likely won't come to that."

Richor is silent. When he doesn't speak for a couple of minutes, I glance at him. The pity on his face pisses me off. "Stop staring at me like that."

To my dismay, one of the greatest fighters in Gondora puts his clawed black hand on my shoulder. In a quiet, serious tone, he says, "Lucasta, you deserve to be happy. You deserve to be loved, even if you don't think you do."

I shake his hand off and stand. Painful emotions choke my throat, and I have to clear it before I can speak. "Your version of foreplay leaves much to be desired."

Something indecipherable flickers across Richor's face before it disappears. A smile spreads across his face, revealing pointed teeth sharp enough to bite through bone. "I could give a blowjob."

I shake my head and cross my arms, relieved to move on from the seriousness. Richor is a good friend; I just don't have the capacity for this conversation right now. "The only Regenerator I want a blow job from is your sister."

He's lunging before the sentence finishes.

9

Reverie

Kahlo is ignoring my texts, which means one of two things: he's died of Slogoth slime poisoning or he's spoken to Luca and understands how badly he fucked up.

I hope it's both.

Checking the time on my phone, I glance around the restaurant, hoping my best friend Malona shows up soon. She's chronically late, and I'm obsessively early, which means I've been sitting here for thirty minutes.

This is our favorite restaurant, Manna From Heaven. It's owned by a family of Seraphim, using their Heavens-given talent to offer the most inventive meals in the city. My favorite is simple: angel hair pasta covered in butter, garlic, and topped with slivers of dove.

Sipping my cup of green tea, I watch fliers pass by the window, hurrying to places unknown. Manna From Heaven is situated six stories above the street below, so we aren't high enough to see the horizon, but the wing traffic is interesting. Perfect for keeping my mind busy.

Luca reappearing throws a wrench into not only my month of weddings but also the thick wall of solitude I've hidden behind for years, fortified by his disappearance. Maybe to him, it was a simple conversation with a random woman. For me, I allowed myself to hope, just for a second. I gave into that smothered desperation to be *seen* beyond my bloodline.

"What's your favorite color?" I asked, mesmerized by his silver eyes lit by moonlight. They were warm, cradling my essence as if I were the only thing in existence. No one had ever made me feel like that, especially none of the dozens of men who'd tried to pick me up here in this very bar.

Those eyes searched mine before he said, "Turquoise."

The color of my eyes. My face flushed, and I averted my gaze, my hands trembling. "You're just saying that."

"You don't think I love the color of tropical oceans and the happiest of skies?"

I gave him a sharp look. "Gargoyles hate oceans."

"It would be a beautiful color to drown in."

The memory heats my body and grinds my teeth. I was so foolish to have believed any of it was real. He probably went home and crawled into bed with a girlfriend. Never thought of me once. He's probably like the rest of them. I can't fall for anything he says.

"Hi, hi, hi!" Malona breezes over to my table, her light pink feathered wings trailing behind her. Grateful for the respite from my cruel thoughts, I stand, holding my arms out for my best friend. She's an artist working at one of the top galleries in Gondora.

Her tightly coiled black hair springs from her head in an oversized dome, wider than her shoulders. Streaks of light pink stripe the curls, matching her wings. A smudge of blue paint sits at the top of her dark cheek. Her clothes, baggy and comfortable, have specks of paint colors.

We exchange hugs, then sit. Her energy is frenetic as she looks around the room while simultaneously grabbing the menu, despite knowing exactly what she'll order.

"You're late," I say.

"The world is too fast," she responds in a lyrical voice. It's the typical response when, in reality, it's her own mind moving too fast for her to catch up. Ignoring my unimpressed glare, she waves our waiter over.

The Seraphim pauses at our table, his eyes lingering on my glitter veins a little too long for comfort. I pull my hands into my lap, wishing I'd worn something long-sleeved.

As she asks questions about the specials, I watch my best friend enthrall the Seraphim. She's a Cherub, appearing sweet with her wide, honey-colored eyes and dazzling smile that can thaw even the surliest goblin. She's used this to her advantage more times than I can count.

We've been friends for almost our whole lives, and I'd do anything for her, but sometimes, she's too ... too *on,* if you know what I mean.

When the Seraphim's done taking our order, Malona turns her light onto me. For the first time since I stepped out of the elevator at yesterday's wedding, the tension melts away. The charm of Cherubs; a welcome one at that.

"Hi," she says softly.

"Hi," I respond, relieved. "You wouldn't believe what happened."

Her face lights up at the promise of gossip. "Tell me *everything.*"

When I'm done regaling her with my personal nightmare, she's staring in shock. "*The* Gargoyle was there? I can't believe it. How do you feel about it?"

"Angry," I admit. "The dunghole had the audacity to be sad when I confronted him. *Sad!* Can you believe it?" Balling my napkin in disgust, I throw it on the table. "He's no different from the others."

Malona gives a little shrug, bristling my wariness. "Maybe he has a good enough reason."

My eyes slit in irritation. She knows exactly how men treat me. "Don't you dare side with him."

She sighs, stirring her soda with a straw, studying the bubbles fizzing against the ice cubes. "I'm not on his side. I'm always on your side, Ree. I think it's disgusting how men treat you."

"But?"

"But," she continues, tension pinching her features. "You didn't give him a chance to explain. Maybe there's a superb reason. What if he was kidnapped by a pack of Druids and kept captive until two days ago?"

"And appeared to photograph a wedding?" I respond dryly. Her reasoning makes no sense. If he *really* wanted to, he could've left a note at Prestley's.

She shrugs again. "I'm just saying, life is crazy. There are actually numerous reasons that held him from contacting you. If he seems sad, maybe he is."

"You're supposed to tell me I'm right," I shoot back, frustrated with her words, knowing she's probably right. He *had* appeared sad. Yesterday wasn't the time or place to discuss it, but maybe ... maybe I could invite him out for coffee. Bury the hatchet so the weddings aren't so complicated.

Regardless, I'm not giving him another chance to break my heart. He's a competitor. He *stole* business from me. Six months ago, I almost landed one of the biggest gigs possible. It would've placed my work on the front page in the biggest magazine in town. After meeting with them, the couple declined to hire me, stating in their rejection letter that they'd found a photographer that promised them more for less.

Knowing it was Luca is infuriating.

"I'm just saying," Malona says, dipping her chin and pursing her lips. "You're more prickly than a harpy filled with spears."

It's irritating that she's right. "I'll take your words into consideration," I say, watching the approaching waiter with our food. Digging into my pasta, I ask, "So how are things with you and that ghoul?"

Her pink eyebrows furrow. "Who?"

I raise an eyebrow. "The ghoul? The one you said was possibly The One?"

After a pause, she lights up. "Oh! Ricky! Yeah, no. He liked to collect toothpaste caps and keep them in a drawer. There were hundreds. It was too much of a red flag."

Giving her a smug grin, I say, "Maybe he has a good enough reason? Have you tried talking to him?"

Her expression sours at my mocking of her previous words. "I was okay with it until my toothpaste caps disappeared."

"So?"

"It was a fresh tube," she declares, shaking her head in disbelief. "The toothpaste oozed all over my marble counter, staining it. He didn't even apologize."

"That's red flag behavior," I agree.

She thrusts her hands into the air in vindication. "*Thank you.* That's what I said."

As we catch up with the other mundane things happening in our lives, I can't help but stew over her advice. It couldn't hurt to at least try being civil with Luca. It's near impossible working alongside wedding photographers you can't stand. If anything, I'm doing what's best for my clients by making peace with him, even if his actions still hurt.

And I'm absolutely dedicated to my clients. No matter what.

10

Luca

It's the first of the week, which means it's rock climbing day. Almost everyone I know thinks it's bizarre for a Gargoyle to climb rocks, but it's great exercise. The amount of mindfulness required helps empty my brain.

Plus, if I fall, I can fly to the ground.

As I'm double checking all the gear, my phone rings. It's a shock to see Reverie's name on the screen. After all this time, I never deleted her contact information. I'm glad of it. I'd planned to text her after climbing, so this is a treat.

Grinning, I answer. "Hello Miss Nonya, how can I help you on this beautiful day?"

My words are met with silence while she most likely works through the reference. We can't act like our semi-date didn't happen; I refuse.

As expected, she brushes it off. "You never texted me. You said that night you'd text me." She pauses, then says angrily, "Actually, *both* nights you said you'd text."

I withhold a frustrated sigh. Her anger is understandable on both accounts. I've thought of her every day this past year. Not that she'd care if I admitted this.

When I heard a woman scream during the battle, every instinct homed in on the sound, as if my heart knew its match was nearby. My stomach nearly fell out of my ass when I saw the bluish green eyes that have haunted me for months.

Taunting Reverie, seeing her face pinkening with anger, was also an unexpected delight.

And yet, I didn't text either time, for good reasons. The most recent being her boundary and vicious words.

Keeping my tone even, I say, "I didn't think you'd want to talk about anything not business related."

She sighs, sounding more burdened than a hydra with fifty heads. "I was talking to my best friend. She thinks I should hear you out."

Color me stunned because that's entirely unexpected. A flutter of hope rises, sending my heart galloping. "Hear me out?"

"Yes," she says impatiently, "About why you rejected me."

Again with that word; *rejection*. "Reverie, I didn't reject you. Life simply got in the way."

"For over a year?" she says with disbelief.

For *more* than a year. Life has never stopped with its punches. Unwilling to scare her away, I say, "Do you want to talk about it in person? I'd hate for you to hang up if you don't like what I have to say."

"Fine. Does two days from now work?"

I can't wait that long. Knowing that she's willing to hear me out is too exciting to wait on. Glancing at my gear bag, an idea forms. I chirp, "Nope. I fear I'm positively swamped every single day forever except for right now. I'm about to go rock climbing. Come join me."

"Rock climbing," she repeats. "You're a Gargoyle."

"So I'm reminded every time my wings knock into someone," I say dryly. "Join me; it'll be fun."

"I don't know ..."

Now that I know she's on the hook, I desperately want to reel her in. "Kahlo told me he thinks you'd be awful at rock climbing. He's probably right." Untrue, but she doesn't know that. "We can go get coffee if sitting is more your speed. I'd hate to break you."

I pause. When she doesn't respond, I click my tongue. "You know what? Let's go get coffee. You do seem pretty fragile."

I hear a tiny growl of frustration, along with the muttering of my cousin's name. "Fine. Send me the address."

"Happily. See you in two hours."

Shooting off the address, I glance at Reggie, who's watching me with a baleful expression. He loves to go rock climbing with me, except he's absolutely awful at it and will fly alongside me. Which wouldn't be too bad if he also didn't land on my shoulder and force me to let go every two minutes.

Scruffing his dark mane, I say, "Sorry, buddy, not today. I have a pretty lady to impress."

He snorts, closing his eyes for an afternoon nap.

***

Reverie arrives on a red Dragxi, hopping off gracefully and paying a handful of corals. She pats the Dragon on the shoulder.

"Thanks, Fynn."

The Dragxi chuffs in appreciation, then flies away.

For a moment, I forget how to breathe. As usual, she's wearing black, offering a beautiful contrast to all the colors that make her ... *her.* Hair pulled into a messy bun; her crystal blue eyes find mine. They're a shade of vivid skies and make my heart soar.

Hot pink sneakers offer the only color in the outfit of black leggings and a long-sleeve top. Why in the Hells did she wear long sleeves? She's going to be sweltering in that.

Gingerly stepping onto the pathway of rocks leading to the cliff-face, she averts her eyes as she examines the surroundings. It's a spot with two options for difficulty.

Grinning, I sweep my arms wide. "Welcome to Devil's Cheek."

She mutters under her breath, and I'm so unbelievably charmed by her surly attitude, I should have my brain examined. Especially since I can't resist needling her.

"What's that? I didn't hear you."

She jerks her head up, her blue eyes stormy. "*I said,* of *course* it would be named that." There's a flicker of fear as she examines the rock face. "People actually climb that? I've never done this before."

"Yes, but there's a beginner's side over here." I motion to a much shorter section of the cliff face, about fifty feet high.

Relief softens the tension in her expression. Exhaling sharply, she eyes the bag of gear before glancing around. "No one else is here?"

I shrug. "Not right now." A look of unease pauses her steps, and I want nothing more than to make her comfortable. "Please don't worry. We're going to climb today — nothing more."

Reverie eyes me with suspicion. "Nothing more?"

The echo of our first conversation stabs painfully. I nod firmly and motion for her to join me at the bottom of the facing. Her hips sway as she approaches, the breeze playing with strands of her hair. The scent of raspberries waters my mouth.

Her eyes crane up the cliff, jaw opening. Again, fear flickers across her face. I'd never let her fall, ever, but maybe this could be a good challenge for her.

"So ..." She nibbles on that plump lip. "What do I do?"

I point at her ridiculous shoes. "First, take those off. I have an extra pair that should fit you."

Reverie grimaces with disbelief, but goes to the boulder to sit. I dig into my bag and pull out the small pair I stopped at the store to buy thirty minutes ago, taking a rough guess on the size of her foot. Since I've never owned a pair of shoes, the sales associate had to help me decipher the right size based on her height.

It's a relief when they fit perfectly. She winces, tugging at the back of one. "They're so tight."

"You want them tight," I affirm, repeating the words of the sales associate. "It helps you grip the rock better."

"If you say so," she mutters, still unconvinced.

Chuckling, I turn toward the rock face. "Let me go set the anchors and rope. Then we'll get started."

Spreading my wings wide, I shift my body into scora stone. It's not like normal stone; it's impenetrable, but also makes me lighter by at least a hundred pounds. My purple skin shifts to a more iridescent periwinkle, catching the light of the sun. Behind me, Reverie gasps, and a smug, masculine part of me thrills at her reaction.

I make quick work of checking established anchor points and adding a couple new ones, digging my retractable claws into the rock as I shove the anchors into crevices. Sliding the rope into the necessary spots, I glide down to the ground, then wave her over.

Tentatively, she walks to my side. I hold out a harness, kneeling to help her step into it. Even though she could do it herself, I much prefer to help slide it over her thick thighs. What she doesn't know won't hurt her; in this regard, at least.

Once it's comfortable, yet tight enough, I lead her to the wall and snap the first carabiner onto her harness. Then hand her a helmet. Giving the rope a firm tug, I give instructions. She stares at me, listening intently, like she'll remember every word.

When she confirms she's ready, I wait patiently as she begins the climb. She's a natural, finding the best crevices and crags. She listens to my advice without attitude, which is a surprise. Maybe we'll be a better team than anticipated.

At the ten-foot mark, there's a tiny ledge for people to rest at. It's also at the point where her rope needs to be attached at the next anchor. I fly the four additional feet easily. She watches me silently as I unlatch and reattach equipment. She's quieter and more observant than expected.

"You ready to keep going?" I ask, staying level with her, keeping the gusts from my wings as gentle as possible.

That's when I see it: the quiver on her lip. It's so small that if I weren't already obsessed with seeing every little expression, it'd be easily missed. Will she go home if I ask her what's wrong? We're existing in comfortable silence, and I don't want to ruin it by being overbearing.

Reverie says nothing, though. She nods and stands, her knees wobbling. I shoot forward, hands ready to grab her. Resting against the cliff, she holds up a hand.

"Don't." The word comes out harshly. Swallowing hard, she studies the ground. "Sorry. I'm more scared than I thought."

"You're hiding it well," I murmur.

She gives me an unreadable expression. "I hide a lot of things well."

Trying to distract her, I ask, "How long have you lived in Gondora?"

Her head jerks back in surprise. "What?"

"Just trying to keep your mind off things." *And trying to know you better.*

"My whole life. My parents moved here before I was born."

"Are they still alive?"

I can tell some of her fear has dissipated by the way her shoulders loosen. "Yeah. Are yours?"

With a sad smile, I say, "My mother is, but not my father."

"I'm sorry to hear that," she says quietly. "Any siblings?"

"None. You?"

"Same."

"Do you like living in Gondora?"

Reverie's expression sours. "Why do you want to know?"

I knew the simple answers were too good to be true. It's not currently worth pushing, since I don't want to upset her right now. To keep the mood lighter, I tease her with, "Does this mean it's a good time to discuss how we're going to work together these next few weeks?"

Narrowing her eyes, she curls a lip in disgust. "No. It is not."

Holding up both hands in surrender, I grin. "Well then, Miss Nonya, get going. I'm ready for lunch."

She's trying to hide it, but I see her hands shake as she finds the first crag. The sudden sharp metallic scent of fear hits the breeze, breaking my skin out in goosebumps. Frowning at the rebellion of flesh, I ignore the anxiety lighting my nerves. She'll tell me when it's too much. I have to trust that. Reverie has made it clear she does not appreciate overbearing men.

Sweat beads on her forehead as she searches for the next handhold. Silently, I curse, realizing I forgot chalk. Where I have long claws that easily dig into most types of rock, she has blunt fingers.

Just as I'm about to recommend we stop, she cries out. Her left hand loses its grasp. She panics, scrambling to find a new grip, but the rocks crumble under her frantic movement. A foot slips. I swoop in, arms at the ready. Reverie screams with terror as her body gives out, falling backward.

Right into my arms. Exactly where I want her to be.

Cradling her, I flap my wings as I peer at her with pride. Despite falling, she tried. Fear coats her scent, and her face flushes with exertion. Panting, she appears to forget how angry she is at me for a moment. With wide eyes, she says, "You caught me."

She sounds so surprised, my gut squeezes with regret. She genuinely believed I would let her fall to the ground? "Reverie, I will always catch you."

Her jaw ticks, and the vulnerability disappears. Expression shuttering, she refuses to meet my gaze. I'm unsure what about my words set her off, but I'm already recognizing when she's hit her limit.

Within a second, my claws are on the ground, and I'm helping her stand on shaky legs. I loathe letting her go, already craving her in my arms again.

Her fingers tremble as she tries to undo the harness, but they're still slick with sweat. Cursing, she gives me a plaintive expression, and I smile, kneeling at her feet.

Exactly where I want to be.

"You did well," I murmur, keeping my touch gentle as I loosen the attachments.

"I don't know if rock climbing is for me," she admits.

I huff out a laugh. "It's good to try new things. You made it pretty far for the first time."

"Why do you like to climb, since you're a Gargoyle?"

I stay focused on the piece of equipment, afraid that if I make eye contact, she'll bolt like a terrified lamb. Instead, I revel in the slice of pale skin revealed when her shirt shifts. At the glittering veins decorating her body.

"Gives me something to do. Keeps my mind and body strong, with a challenge. Beats lifting weights every day."

When the harness gets stuck on her belt, it jerks her forward. Fingers dig into my shoulder, and breasts rub across my forehead. My breath hitches as a painful roll of need shoots straight to my groin.

"Sorry," she says quickly. Her cheeks flush bright red.

Swallowing hard, I refocus on the harness. "My fault."

The harness slips over her hips, and she steps out of it, almost stumbling when she backs away from me. Pupils dilated with adrenaline, Reverie watches me with a mix of heartbreak, anger, and ... is that desire? Surely not.

Without another word, I collect the gear into my pack. When it's all situated, I face her. She's sitting on the same boulder, grabbing her pink shoes. Long rainbow strands fall forward as she focuses on switching the footwear. Her fingers shake as she ties the shoelaces, but otherwise, she's doing an excellent job hiding her emotions.

This has been my first one-on-one time with her since that night all those months ago. It's an opportunity to be honest. But transparency has a cost — one I'm not quite willing to pay yet.

There's a tenuous truce right now, but we came here with a purpose.

Setting aside the climbing shoes, she raises her eyebrows expectantly. "Okay. I did the climbing. Now, will you explain things to me?"

Anxiety crackles in my chest as I consider exactly what to say. With more weddings ahead of us, it's important to not burn this bridge, even if it's only professionally. She might be my direct competitor, but I'm not going to sabotage her upcoming weddings purposefully.

Which means some things must stay hidden; for now.

Swallowing hard, I nod. “Alright, but first, let’s get you a snack.”

11

Reverie

My whole body's weak; I'm afraid that if I stand, I'll fall over. Luca watches me like he's trying to memorize my every movement. Sweat drips down my spine, plastering hair to my neck.

I wish it'd been feasible to wear a sleeveless shirt in this heat, but he'd see my siren brand. I can't bear the thought of him viewing me differently, even if it led to my losing grasp on the rocks, forcing him to catch me.

He caught me.

Like some hero in a fairytale, Luca caught me in the air like it was nothing. It was the sexiest thing I've ever experienced. The way he looked at me ... with pride? I don't know what to make of that. He barely knows me. Why does he care so much after ignoring me for a year?

This exact question is why I'm eager for him to explain. Instead of giving a straight answer, Luca pulls out a water bottle and a bag of nuts from his pack.

Handing them over, he commands, "Eat."

"No, thank you." I go to push them away, but he places the items in my lap and steps back, forcing me to take them.

Sighing, I take a sip of the water and chew on a handful of nuts. Almost instantly, my body calms, the adrenaline dissipating.

"Did that help?" he asks, crossing his arms. He's wearing a light blue sleeveless shirt, and it's impossible to not notice how muscular he is. Gargoyles are strong, but he's so ... *extra*. Everything about him is extra. Instead of a flat belly, it's a little round, but it's more of his body type than a sign of overindulgence.

He's probably extra elsewhere, too.

No, I'm not going there. Shoving the rogue thought away, I ask, "Are you going to explain yourself? Or do you think these nuts will distract me?"

The second it comes out of my mouth, I know it's a mistake. His entire face lights up with a devilish grin.

"*Don't*," I seethe. His grin stretches. I point a finger. "Do. Not."

"What?" He feigns innocence. "I'm merely wondering if you're easily distracted by nuts?"

Grinding my teeth, I toss the bag at him. He catches it, still grinning from ear to ear. "Knock it off and get on with it. Or I'm summoning a Dragxi."

This sobers him. For whatever reason, he wants me to stay. "Fine. Can I apologize again for not calling?"

"Yes, but you've already done that. Now explain yourself."

"Right," he says more to himself. To my surprise, he begins pacing, his thick tail whipping against blades of grass. "I hadn't expected to meet someone, especially someone like you—"

"Like me?" I interrupt.

He cuts a look, silencing me. "Yes. Like you. I was having an awful day, so when I saw this beautiful woman sitting at the bar all alone, I thought, 'What's the harm in saying hello?'"

I want so badly to ask him why me, but I bite my lips close. His own lips twitch like he wants to smile. Instead, he continues, "I never rejected you, Reverie. Nothing I did or said was a lie. I thought of you every single one of those three hundred eighty-two nights. Life got in the way. You understand?"

He swallows hard, studying the ground. "Things happened. I knew I couldn't give you the one hundred percent you deserved. By the time I realized it was a mistake, I was afraid of it being too late. Someone like you would be snatched up quickly, and I didn't want to reach out to confirm I'd lost the opportunity. I'm ashamed of my cowardice."

I nearly laughed in his face. Someone like *me?* He wouldn't say that if he knew I was part siren. "You thought I would be snatched up? I'm a Glyridite."

He pauses in his pacing, giving me the most absurd look of confusion, like he cannot fathom a reality where that means something foul. "What does your bloodline have anything to do with it?"

"People hate my powers." How does he not *know* this? "You know, I was eleven the first time a man asked me if there was glitter in my underpants?"

Luca blanches, and I barrel ahead. "Yeah. When I was seventeen, I lost my virginity to a guy who bragged about 'how much glitter oozed out'"

I didn't sleep with anyone for a year after that. The shame ensured that the second someone showed me any level of interest, I'd break their desire to acknowledge me within the first sentence or two.

Luca's wings flare out violently. "That's fucking disgusting," He resumes pacing. "I don't care about your bloodline, Reverie." His gaze sharpens in response to my dubious stare. "I *really* don't. That's not remotely close to being the reason for my choices."

My jaw clenches painfully as I suck in a steadying breath. "Then what was it, Luca?"

He pauses again, spinning to face me. A flicker of something — insecurity, maybe? — passes over his expression before disappearing. After a beat of silence, he asks quietly, "Would you accept the answer that things became complicated?"

"Overnight?" I say, incredulous.

"Yes," he says firmly. "Overnight. Sometimes that happens, you know."

His tone isn't condescending, but it feels like it is. His half answers are as annoying as they are lame.

I stand, grateful for the steadiness of my knees. "I'm tired of men using me for entertainment."

Luca's face twists with anger. "Reverie, that is *not—*"

I hold a hand up, cutting him off. "If this is the best you can do, explanation-wise, then thank you for the vague reasoning. Really clears things up."

It's difficult to admit, but I'm still hurt by his disappearing act. And this poorly executed attempt at explaining exacerbates it. It's almost like he's patting me on the head, and telling me to accept his excuse like a good girl.

If Luca truly wanted me to understand, there wouldn't be so much obfuscation involved. 'Life happened' isn't a good enough reason for me, nor is acting like somehow a Glyridite siren being snatched up for being *such* a catch. I almost scoff at the thought.

Pulling out my phone, I summon a Dragxi, then tuck the phone back into my pocket. Pettiness has me taking a step closer to Luca. Releasing translucent glitter into a whirling vortex into the air, I turn it lilac, slightly lighter than the exact color of his skin.

Focusing wrathful eyes on him, I beckon him with my other hand. "Come here."

Still confused, he approaches like I'm an unpredictable animal, while also keeping an eye on the glitter. Instead of the disgust I'm used to, he's mesmerized. I don't know if that means he thinks I'll be a unique fuck or if he ... likes it.

Well, we'll see how he feels in a few days.

When he's close enough, I snatch his wrist to yank him closer. Well, I attempt to yank — the man weighs over four hundred pounds. He *allows* me to pull him closer.

Before he understands what I'm about to do, I twirl the glitter around my pointer finger. Locking eyes with him, I draw.

Luca doesn't watch what I'm doing; he's entirely homed in on my face. This close, I'm forced to inhale his scent of petrichor, layered with a deeper scent that is completely him. It does nothing to quell my growing anger.

"You think no one should care about my glitter? It's useless. It offers no defense; no benefit other than aesthetic. It's not a useful power — people view it as a nuisance. More than a nuisance. If I forget even a spec, people berate me for destruction."

My voice cracks. I clear my throat. "People love it as a party trick, but no one wants to shake my hand. Few will hug me. They're afraid it leaks from my pores like a contagion."

Luca's free hand raises, as if he wants to comfort me, but then falls back to his side. For some reason, that makes me angrier. Is he afraid of touching me? He wouldn't be the first to be afraid.

Sometimes, it's like a sickness under my flesh. Too many showers spent sobbing trying to scrape away these veins that tell the world what I am. No matter how much I scrub, it'll always lead to people treating me like I'm a walking illness.

My parents instilled the need to hide my powers. Make them as small as possible. It's the only way I'll be accepted into this world. I'd wear the layers of clothes and make apologies for my existence, until shame became so consuming, I needed to take control.

Appalled isn't a strong enough word for their reaction when they discovered my intent to focus Edges of Glitter on my powers. But I needed to make peace with this part of myself, even if it's all party tricks. It was pure survival at the time, and I'm very fortunate the gamble paid off.

With each word, the confusion leaks from Luca's expression, until there's only pity. I hate that even more.

Releasing his arm, I suck the remaining glitter back into myself.

Breaking eye contact, unable to tolerate the vulnerability anymore, I stand. "Luca, you think you want to know me. You don't. You think I'm a pretty art piece with some intriguing attributes that might make for a good sex story."

Turning away from him as he examines my art, I check on my incoming Dragxi, relieved to know it'll be here in less than a minute.

"Reverie ..." He whispers my name, but I won't make eye contact. I don't want to see any lies or pity or whatever he thinks is the right thing to say.

"Don't bother, Luca." A sharp emotion slices through my throat. Swallowing it down, I force out, "I'll see you at the wedding. Yureka will text you the details."

"Reverie, *look* at me." His voice is more forceful than it's ever been.

My eyes meet his silver irises like a magnet, unable to break away as he takes a step closer. In my peripherals, I see his tail twitch with agitation.

Running fingers through his hair, Luca says, "You are *not* a pretty art piece to me. You can run; you can be mean to me. It's fine — I can take it. But *do not* leave today thinking that about me."

This time, when he takes a step closer, I take a step back. Luca's mouth flattens at the movement, but he doesn't close the distance between us. My pulse beats wildly in my veins, and I want to cover my ears. I can't let him break through my defenses. I just can't. Digging my nails into my arms, I let the sting keep me focused.

My voice shakes as I say, "I think we need to keep things professional. We don't need to do things like this—" I motion to the cliff. "—to work together for the rest of the month. I promise to not make things awkward if you can do the same."

Voice soft, Luca says, "We can be professional, that's what you want."

"I do," I say, the tone not betraying the heartbreak already festering. This is for the best, to protect myself, but the way he watches me makes it also feel like a mistake.

The silver Dragxi lands and I turn away from the silent Gargoyle, loading into the seating saddle.

As the Dragon rises into the sky, I chance a glance at Luca.

He's staring at me, expression imploring, but he doesn't call out.

Because he doesn't want me. Not really.

They never do.

12

Luca

A penis. She drew a goddess damned *penis* on my forearm. Which after *four days* hasn't disappeared.

Watching her leave hurt every fiber of my being, but my understanding of what it means to fear rejection kept me from reaching across the invisible divide.

I should've forced her to understand that I don't care about the glitter. I've never understood why others scorn something so beautiful. Sure, glitter gets into *everything*, but that is something I actually appreciate about it.

It proves nothing is immune to beauty.

I'm still thinking that as I shower, trying to scrub the penis away, grinning like a deranged man, happy for a damn dick on my arm. However, it's been there for four days, and I have a wedding to be at in two hours.

With a damn dick on my arm.

I'm positive she made it stick. Short of fileting my skin off, this won't budge. Oh well. Perhaps she'll grant some mercy and remove it today, seeing as I doubt her clients would appreciate a second shooter decorated with a glittering phallus.

Whistling a happy tune, I step out of the shower and wrap a towel around my waist. Reggie rests on the bath mat, licking his dark leathery wings. His golden serpentine eyes focus on me as I walk to the mirror, pulling out shaving supplies.

In the mirror, I grin at him in the reflection. "I get to see her again, Reg."

His round leonine ears flick like he's trying to process my words. "Don't seem so excited, bud." Smearing shaving cream on my jaw, I shave away the stubble. "I'm betting she's going to be extra mean today. What do you think?"

Reggie yawns, resting his snout on his black paws. I nod, more to myself than to him. "Yes, I think so, too. Perhaps I can bring her something to soften the blow."

The thought of giving her a gift, even something small, thumps at my heart. One day, I'm going to earn a real smile; not one of those guarded ones she pretends are genuine.

"She thinks I don't like her because of the glitter," I say conversationally, washing out the razor in the sink. "But I can't wait to see her face when I show her the penis." Pausing, I wonder out loud, "Should I name the penis?"

Reggie sighs heavily, followed by a whine. "You're right. That's probably going a little too far."

Putting everything away and wiping the sink, I head to my closet to don my normal attire. All of my gear's ready to go. The familiar nervous anticipation arrives as I head to the front door. Pulling out my phone, I text Yureka that I'm on my way and ask another question. Once she responds, I sling the gearbox over my wings and connect the straps across my chest. Walking over to my balcony, I yell out to Reggie, "Patina will be here in a few hours to walk you. Be nice!"

He chirps in response, but I know he's curled up in his bed in the corner of my room. He doesn't mind being alone for long periods of time, making him the perfect pet.

Ready to start today's adventure, I leap into the sky.

***

Today's wedding is for a throuple of Centaurs at a nearby national park. It's set in a mossy forest of giant trees with long, willowy branches. It's home to large birds of every color under the sun.

Yureka is already waiting at the park's entrance, setting up detail shots. Holding a pair of horseshoes, she looks up as I land. Eyeing the two cups of coffee in my hands, she sniffs the air suspiciously.

"Who's the other one for?"

Bending, I hand her one of the cups. "For you, of course."

Her expression twists from surprise to pleased. "Well, thank you." She takes a sip, then groans. "Oh, I love hazelnuts." She stands, leaving the details on the ground. "Do you have a copy of the schedule?"

I pat my pocket. "Right here. Where's Reverie?"

Yureka motions her long fingers over her shoulder. "Somewhere near the jousting corral." She grins, revealing sharp teeth. "I've never done a centaur wedding before — have you?"

"Once or twice." I wink. "You're in for a treat."

Leaving her to the details, I go search for the one person I want to see today. She's difficult to spot, seeing as some Centaurs are tall enough to make most creatures crane their neck, me included. Reverie is tall, but not *that* tall.

I find her in the jousting corral, photographing the groomstuds as they rear, holding jousting sticks. I pause, enjoying the energy she exudes. In private, around me, she's wound tighter than a jumping Basilisk. Here, she's all laughter. Today, it could be real; it could be a mask. Only one way to find out.

As the groomstuds pounds the soft earth, she shouts for them to gallop around the arena, assuring them it'd look amazing. They obey, proud creatures that they are. As they should be, with the way their long legs eat up the earth, plumes of dust in their wake. As Reverie laughs, catching their movements with her camera, I take out mine to take a photo of her. Inspecting the image on my screen, I smile to myself.

She resembles an enthralling creature, wild and free, with her hair in loose strands teased by the wind. Her glittering veins shine brighter as she exudes something special, something I'm desperate to hold in my palms.

She's wearing a long-sleeved shirt with a wide scoop neck. It hugs her generous curves while maintaining modesty. That's when I notice the brand.

A siren's brand. Given to every infant within thirty days of birth. Barbaric and cruel.

I look up, blood draining from my face at the exact moment her camera lands on me. I see the shutter click, which means she's captured the moment I realize she's a siren.

Her camera lowers, her own face showing a matching expression, as if she knows exactly what I've realized. Last wedding, she wore her hair down and refused to be around me, so I can't remember if she hid it or not.

Now, the distinctive brand, the dainty, but cruel mark given to infants, is on full display.

Her joy seeps away, like my dismay sucked it out of her. It's devastating. I've no doubt, knowing how she views the world and how she thinks it perceives her, she assumes I'm judging her.

This explains why she wears so many layers. Especially for rock climbing. She's afraid of how people will view her lineage.

I've never understood the pre-assigned pecking order of Avalon, and more so in Gondora. Why sirens or phantoms are less respected than an Elf or Gargoyle has never made sense. To me, a person is a person; that's all that matters.

Desperate to return that joy to her, I drop my camera, letting it swing on the harness at my hip, and raise her cup of coffee. Her expression becomes guarded as her eyes narrow, already inspecting the cup for trickery.

While the groomstuds are on the opposite side of the arena, I easily leap over the fence, landing gracefully, not spilling a drop of her coffee.

Wary, she takes the offered cup. "Thank you?"

"I asked Yureka what your favorite drink was. She said that you preferred a hazelnut latte."

Her eyes flash with surprise as she takes a sip. There it is — a spark of happiness returning. The smile is small, but it's there. "Thank you."

"I don't care, by the way," I say conversationally, watching the groomstuds as if they're somehow more interesting.

There's a beat of silence before she says, "Everyone says that. But they don't mean it."

My focus homes in on her. "I'm not in the habit of spitting out words that I don't mean."

"Then you don't know enough about sirens."

Doubtful, but I'm not about to argue about her insecurities. Instead, I ask, "How's it going here so far?"

The tension creasing her brow relaxes. "It's already been a long day."

"When did you start?"

She checks her phone. "Four hours ago."

I give a low whistle. "Why didn't you have me come earlier?"

She shrugs and takes another sip of her drink, eyes tracking the groomstuds. "They paid for a certain amount of time."

"Reverie, if you need me to come earlier next time, I'm willing to."

She scrunches her nose. "I can't afford to pay you extra."

"Nothing extra. Just to help."

Really, I'm desperate to spend more time with her. The scent of raspberries zings straight to my cock again. Of course she would smell like my favorite fruit.

My eyes flick to the brand, and she notices. Frowning, she sweeps her long hair in front of it. Tone even, yet deadly, she asks, "Do you have a question to ask?"

"Yes." My grin's slow and feral. Unable to resist a little immaturity, I ask as seriously as possible, "Is it true that if you don't use it, you lose it?"

To my delight, she appears unperturbed. She knocks me down a peg as she says cooly, “I’m sure someone like you has no way of finding out. Everyone knows Gargoyles are promiscuous.”

Definitely mean. I make a mental note to inform Reggie. Unwilling to tolerate the unnecessary rudeness, I lean over to whisper in her ear. “That means we know *exactly* what we’re doing.”

Straightening, I take delight in her response as her cheeks flush a shade of pink that is officially my new favorite color. Now we’re even.

Holding out my arm, I lift the sleeve. “Actually, I do have a question if you don’t mind.” Her glare is icy as she presses her lips together. I twist my arm, revealing the purple penis. “I’m loving this glitter tattoo. It doesn’t seem to want to come off, though. I’m assuming its strength is directly tied to the obsession and desire of the deliverer?”

“Oh, do shut up,” she mutters, flicking her hand above the shiny phallus, sucking up the glitter into her palm, not leaving a single speck.

Sensing the groomstuds approaching, I pull out my schedule, turning on the business facade. “So where would you like me ... boss?”

The question’s met with a clenched jaw and fake smile. She’s so adorable when she’s frustrated.

13

Reverie

Even though I spent days trying to find a second shooter replacement, everyone worth hiring is already booked. Forcing me to work alongside this maddening man once again. Sending him off to continue photographing the groomstuds, I sulk as I walk to the bridal suite, absentmindedly rubbing my brand.

His reaction to the brand was ... unexpected. He'd been shocked, but everyone always is. The brand is taboo enough to draw a small reaction from the most stoic. He recovered quickly and didn't drag out the conversation.

It softens me a little more in my perspective of Luca. That maybe, just maybe, he's not a complete dunghole.

It's a bit of a walk to the getting ready barn, offering plenty of time to seethe over how annoyingly nice that Gargoyle is.

If there were a mean bone in that purple body, it'd be easier to hate him. Rock climbing with him only stoked my ire. He didn't call. He didn't text. Why in the Hells was it so surprising? It's what he does; he disappears.

I exposed myself to him, albeit with lots of anger and a semi-permanent tattoo of a dick. Okay, maybe the dick was a little too far, but he clearly *enjoyed* it, regardless. Any other guy would've been furious. Unless ... unless he likes dick.

Is he gay?

That has to be it. Maybe that's why he's blown me off repeatedly: the life "getting in the way" was him actually impeding someone else's dick.

He's an insatiable flirt, but so are most Gargoyles. Maybe he kissed me that one time to experiment. Luca seems a little old to be experimenting, but late-in-life exploration is normal and valid.

Not caring about the dick ... not calling me ... maybe I'm a terrible kisser? Maybe he doesn't like kissing women? The more I think about it, it could be a feasible reason.

Positive that's exactly what it is, I smile to myself and sip the delicious coffee. I don't have many gay friends — I don't have very many friends to begin with — but maybe he can become my gay best friend.

Stepping into the getting ready barn, I'm greeted with lots of laughter and merry singing. Centaurs are known for boisterous celebrations. By the end of the night, I'll be absolutely wiped.

Inside are six bridesmares, and the bride, Sorrel. She has long red hair falling to her withers, freckled skin and pert breasts. Centaurs aren't fans of shirts. Her hooves clack on the stone floor as she shifts nervously in place. As soon as she sees me, she squeals, motioning me forward.

"Ree! I'm glad you're here! You said gold's best with my coloring?"

Sorrel is a blood chestnut mare with a rich red coat. When we first had our consultation, she raved about my glitter, declaring that instead of the typical topless centaur style, she wanted glitter to cover her torso.

It feels fantastic to help her look ravishing on her wedding day, *and* to have my skill set embraced.

Standing on a step-stool, I hover my palms in line with her nipples. "I think it'll be splendid."

Taking a calming, steady breath, I conjure my glitter. It slowly spins out of my hand like a glistening gold tornado. I direct it to swirl around her flesh. It solidifies on her skin in beautiful filigreed swirls that encircle her breasts and spread along her breastbone, clavicles, and down her arms.

When it's done, she inspects her reflection. "Oh, Ree, this is stunning." She claps her hands, tossing back her thick mane of curls. "Better than I imagined."

Giving her a satisfied smile, pleased to have my power welcomed, I dip my head in acknowledgment. "My pleasure."

"Can you do me, too?" a bridesmare asks, clopping forward nervously. She's a dapple gray with long, straight strands of white hair. Grinning, I nod, motioning for her to stand in front of the stepstool, allowing sterling glitter to do the same to her dark brown skin.

One by one, I decorate each mare, giving them unique designs and adding it to their faces. It's a rare treat to share this beauty with so many people excited to experience it.

When I'm done, I begin taking photos again, laughing with them as the bridesmares apply finishing touches to Sorrel's maroon tail, weaving in flowers after braiding it.

"What is on your chest, Sorrel?" an older mare shrieks, stomping into the room. She's a palomino with a white mane and tail. Her heavy breasts lay flat against her flabby belly. I grimace at the glare on her face, aware of where this is going.

"Mother, I wanted glitter," Sorrel says nervously. "I told you that."

"And *I* told you it's unbecoming for a Centaur to wear anything unnatural on their wedding day," the mother snipes. "And where is the woven weed veil I gave you? The one every mare has worn on their wedding day since your great-great-great-grandmare?"

Sorrel gives me a pained expression. "I really want to wear this, Mother. And that veil is hideous."

The mother gives me a nasty look. "Take your unnatural ..." Her nose wrinkles with disgust, clearly holding back the words she'd prefer to say. "... *glitter*, off my daughter. And everyone else."

For a moment, I pause, waiting to see if anyone speaks up. Defends me.

No one does. As usual.

Studying my shoes, I lift a hand to absorb every bit of glitter off all seven mares. It takes deep focus to remove every spec. My skin burns as I re-accept the glitter; I'll have to expel it later. Hiding the heavy defeat in my chest, I smile at the drawn, sad faces of pity.

"So, are we taking veil photos?"

***

By the time we sit for our vendor meals, my feet ache and my knees beg for ice. All the vendors are sequestered in a side room, away from the glamour of the wedding reception. Stacked chairs fill one corner of the room, next to an overflowing trash can, and a tattered couch that's seen better decades.

In the center is a large round table. After taking the vendor meal from the wedding planner, I find a seat. Next to me, Yureka sits, tapping nails furiously against her phone screen. Across from me are the DJ, his assistant, and the wedding planner's assistant.

It's been a long day, especially since Sorrel's mother was nit-picky about everything, going as far as interrupting the ceremony to make sure the veil — the hideous, half-rotted veil made of grass — was situated properly.

When the jumping course began and one of the grooms started an unplanned jousting fight with his brother — which ended in bucking, resulting in a horse-shoe sized bruise on the groom's chest — Yureka gave me the most comical look of bewilderment. I don't think Centaur weddings will be for her.

Just as I'm about to take my first bite of overcooked chicken, my fork pauses mid-flight as Luca steps into the room. He's so big, the room shrinks. He gives a lazy grin as he aims for the empty chair next to me.

Damn. I'd been successful in avoiding him today due to all of the different activities. I'm too tired to muster irritation, real or fake, so I chew on my rubbery chicken and ignore him as he sits.

The other vendors chatter among themselves, gossiping about other vendors in the industry. I keep my mouth shut and thoughts to myself — I'm not about to get wrapped in needless discourse.

Luca appears to be the same way, his focus entirely on eating his food. Against my arm is the heat of his skin. My muscles ache so much, I'm tempted to lean closer to soak some of that warmth up. He smells of rain and earth, a soothing scent. Once again, we're in a pleasant silence, despite the conversation going on around us.

I'm still angry with him, especially since he *still* hasn't reached out, which increases my frustration. There's something good here between us, but neither of us appears willing to be the first to explore it in earnest. He won't text, so I won't, either.

But what would it be like to be the first to bridge that gap? Can my pride even allow it?

Suddenly, Luca tenses. My focus shifts to the frustrated twitching of his tail against my ankle. I frown, looking at the floor where his lilac tail thrashes.

"What do you think, Reverie?"

I jerk my head up. I've been so distracted, I've zoned out the entire conversation. The DJ and his assistant are staring with open curiosity. The wedding planner's assistant shifts in her chair, clearly uncomfortable. Yureka places her phone on the table, casting me a nervous look.

I've missed something important. "Huh?"

The DJ, whose name is Tireen or Tollop or whatever, gazes at me with a smile I don't think I like. It's condescending, immediately raising my hackles. He's a Wood Sprite, like Yureka, except he has dark green skin and black hair.

"I was asking Runan here if it's ethical for sirens to sing at weddings."

The blood in my veins freezes. A loud buzzing fills my ears, blocking everything out. Reality narrows to his ugly face, erasing everything else. I'm too busy visualizing drowning him in thick ribbons of rainbows to think of anything coherent.

Appearing pleased with my reaction, the dunghole leans back in his chair and crosses his arms. "See, I was saying it isn't, because then how does anyone know if what they're experiencing is real? Plus, what if the wedding becomes an orgy?"

Runan chuckles. "Could you imagine? I agree; it would be unethical."

Next to me, Yureka's also frozen in place. She's probably never seen siren-related bigotry up close; this is unfortunately not my first time someone tries to use me as a monolith, speaking for all sirens.

The unfortunate fact of this whole situation is that I'm not willing to lash out at a wedding and jeopardize my client's big day. So, leaping across this table is out of the question.

"I'm *part* siren," I mumble, hoping he'll drop it.

The DJ smirks. "Of course, you're also a Glyridite. You use it as part of your branding. I think that's so smart, using your ..." He motions to my body. "Uniqueness to your benefit."

"That's enough."

The words are so soft, I barely hear them over the roaring in my ears. But in the corner of my eye, I see Luca lean forward, placing closed fists on the table. The DJ ignores the warning signs.

"Have you ever sung romance to a couple? Is that even legal? I don't think it is. Have you done it? Could you—"

"Enough." Luca pounds the table, making everyone jump. Forks clatter to the floor, and the wedding assistant's drink spills over. I shrink into my chair, hating the shame appearing from the DJ's words. They aren't new questions, and they'll never stop coming. This is why I stick to myself most of the time.

The DJ's eyes widen, and he holds his hands up. "Sorry, I was asking out of curiosity. I mean, look at her. She's a mixed breed—"

Luca shoots up, fury radiating off him in hot waves. His skin shifts to scora stone as his wings flare out. After seeing his display at the battle arena, I know exactly what he's capable of. He could kill all of us without breaking a sweat.

Strangely enough, as I peer up from my chair to watch the display, I feel nothing but pleasure. He's doing this on my behalf. I chance a look at Yureka — she's watching him with awe.

You and me both, friend.

Menacing black claws grow as Luca curls his fingers in threat. "You're a DJ, yes?"

The DJ mumbles something. Luca makes a show of cupping his ear. "What's that? Speak up. You didn't have a problem opening your fucking face hole when it comes to denigrating a woman. Why don't you use your big boy voice with someone your own size?"

No one in this room is close to Luca's size, but I love it anyway. This confrontation is one of the most satisfying things I've ever seen. It's a relief to have *someone* defend me.

No one speaks. The wedding planner's assistant slips out of the room. Luca ignores her, still focused on the DJ. I swear his fangs lengthen as he growls, "I asked you a question."

"Y-yes. I'm a DJ."

Luca leans over, bracing against the table. It groans under the additional weight. Yureka and I scoot back, not wanting to be underneath it if it collapses. The DJ's assistant has become a pale shade of gray, which is impressive, since he's a ghoul. They're already incredibly pale to begin with.

"My name is Lucasta Destau. My company is Stone and Skies Visuals."

The DJ's face contorts with confusion, flicking his eyes at me, as if I'm about to help him.

"Don't you *dare* look at her," Luca barks. "Repeat my name and business."

"Lu-Lucasta D-Destau. Stones and Skies V-Visuals."

"Good. You aren't a total fucking idiot. I'm one of the top wedding photographers in this city, second to this one." He jabs a thumb at me, and I want to kick my feet like a lunatic. Having a gay best friend is *amazing.* "If you ever see my name or her name on the vendor list, you're going to either refuse the job or resign immediately. Do I make myself clear?"

The DJ's green face actually turns a shade of ripe cucumber in his fury. "But you can't—"

"It's either that, or I blacklist you by midnight. Your choice."

"You don't have the power to do that," the DJ seethes.

Luca cocks his head like a predator. "I don't? Are you willing to find out?" When the DJ refuses to answer, Luca tucks his wings in and shifts back to normal form. "Now go do your damn job and don't let me catch you speaking to Reverie ever again."

Both the DJ and his assistant scramble out of their chairs, bolting from the room. My entire body flushes with endorphins and desire. Of their own accord, my thighs squeeze together as I watch Luca go from brutal hellion to a man trying to eat his dinner. Pulling up his chair to sit again, Yureka and I watch in quiet shock as he digs back into his overcooked chicken.

Like nothing happened.

As if my entire world hadn't just upended itself.

14

Luca

Blood thumps in my ears as I settle back in my chair, shame shaking my hands as I reach for the fork. I'm afraid to look at Yureka and Reverie. What if they're scared?

There was no way I could let that man speak to anyone like that, but especially not Reverie. The woman who hates her powers and herself. I'm going to have to report the DJ to my colleagues. He'll be blacklisted, regardless. Men like that don't deserve second chances. He took too much glee in Reverie's discomfort.

Unfortunately, I let my baser instincts take over.

I grimace as I bite into the chicken. It's disgusting. Not all vendor meals are awful, but this one was definitely the product of being left under a heat lamp for too long.

"Luca."

Reverie's sweet voice is a caress to my simmering anger. Keeping my expression as neutral as possible, I drag my eyes to her face. Where I'm expecting anger or fear, I'm shocked to find her smiling. It's not small, but it's not a large one either; not yet. But it's one I haven't seen before, making it all worth it.

"I'm sorry," I murmur, resting my fork on the plate. Neither of them appears to be afraid. Why?

Electricity lights my entire body, from claws to wing tips, when Reverie places a soft hand on my forearm. I nearly groan from the sensation.

She rubs my arm as if trying to soothe me. It feels as if the Heavens themselves are embracing me. She needs to stop because if she continues, it genuinely might be enough to make me cum in my trousers. I don't think I could survive that kind of humiliation.

Frustrated that it needs to be done, I lift her hand from my arm and place it carefully in her lap. She watches her hand as if it isn't a part of her, then stares at me with confusion.

"Why are you apologizing?"

She genuinely doesn't understand. A Gargoyle's pride lies in his self-control. In all things, but especially anger. What I displayed lacked any modicum of self-control. If she were a female Gargoyle, it would be an automatic rejection as a prospective partner.

The door to the room swings open abruptly, revealing an angry wedding planner. I can't remember her name, but she's a bossy Seraphim whose wings ruffle with fury. "What's this I hear of an argument?"

That dunghole DJ went and whined to an adult. Well, two can play that game. I widen my eyes, confused. I glance at Reverie and Yureka. "I don't know anything about an argument. Do you?"

They both shake their heads, eyebrows raised in alarm. Reverie tilts her head, widening her eyes and slightly parting her thick lips as if in shock. "Why? Is everything okay?"

It takes digging a fang directly into my tongue to prevent a bark of laughter desperate to escape.

My girl is beautiful when she's duplicitous.

***

It's a long night, and the DJ plays it smart by not coming near our team whatsoever. Good. I wasn't interested in getting splinters as I crushed his face with my fist. The planner lost interest immediately, fed up with everyone's antics. I don't know what she thought she could do, considering she isn't our keeper.

Reverie is significantly less prickly with me, even offering a small laugh at one of my lame jokes. Each sign of happiness is a balm to the shame residing in my chest. Has anyone ever stood up for her before?

When it's time to go home, we're all so exhausted that packing our gear and supplies is a silent task. Yureka and Reverie keep exchanging glances, as if I don't notice Reverie's every move.

As much as I miss Reggie, I don't want to go home. I want to go with Reverie to Prestley's. When I've attached my gearbox to my back, I walk over to them. Reverie's zipping her gearbox and looks up when she hears my claws. I feel satisfaction as her expression brightens.

"Hey, we're headed over to Prestley's. Want to come?"

"Do Pegasi fly?"

This elicits a giggle; I want to fall on my knees and worship the sound. Yureka's mouth drops, bewildered, watching Reverie like she's a Hydra reproducing heads.

"Want me to carry your gear?" I hold a hand out to Reverie and, to my extreme pleasure, she gives me a shy smile.

"Yes, please. I'm exhausted."

With no small amount of satisfaction, I grab her gearbox and head out of the wedding venue.

***

Sitting at Prestley's puff bar is like coming home. The air is crisp on my tongue, the dew settling over my wings like a blanket. I haven't been this high in the clouds since that night I met Reverie. If I'm not working, I'm sleeping or spending time with Mom.

It's difficult to admit, but I also avoided visiting in case Reverie appeared. Something else to regret, I suppose.

Prestley has three stools set aside, as if he knew somehow I'd be here. We lock eyes, and he grins as only a Whisp can, which is so wide, it's disturbing since he has no teeth.

"Luca!" he booms. "I thought you'd splattered yourself somewhere!"

I roll my eyes, sitting next to Reverie, with Yureka on her other side. "You know damn well I'm too good of a flyer for that to happen."

"That's what Ickanus said." With a serious expression, he fake whispers, "And look what happened to him."

"Prest, Ickanus made his wings out of tar. They weren't real," Reverie chided. I smile at her knowledge.

While Prestley prepares our drinks, I take a moment to appreciate the beauty of the surrounding view. This puff bar is higher than most, due to Prestley being a founding member of the concept. The cloudavator ride takes about five minutes to the launch pad hundreds of feet below. I can fly that, but I've always loved standing on a cloud magycked to be solid.

The sun's slipping behind the horizon, plunging the sky into dark hues of purple, pink, and orange. One of the best times of day. Glancing at Reverie, I see she's taking a moment to appreciate it as well. Like the first time I saw her, sitting in this exact chair.

Back then, the sun was stronger that evening, casting all of her beautiful colors into shimmering flecks of light. She'd appeared ethereal, the corners of her mouth curling. As she stared into the clouds, her aquamarine irises were the most vibrant blue imaginable.

When those eyes set on me, the whole world fell away. In that exact moment, I knew there was no way I could continue on with my life without hearing her voice. It wasn't her high cheekbones or generous curves that propelled me to sit next to her — although they are certainly enticing.

It was the way she watched me, then averted her eyes, like she felt the pull, too.

Now, when those eyes slide to me, I can tell she's thinking of that same moment because she frowns and focuses on the goblet arriving on the bar top.

That's fine; I'll remember enough for the both of us.

Apparently, Reverie and Yureka enjoy thunderstorm foot massages. Tucking our feet under the space inside the bar, I'm delighted with the raindrops pummeling my feet from all directions, as if Prestley commanded a hurricane to assault our toes.

Reverie giggles with Yureka, sharing one of those rare big smiles with her friend. Still not the one I'm seeking, but I gobble it up, regardless.

After a couple of drinks and the foot massages, Yureka bids us good-night. Before she walks to the cloudavator platform, she pauses, placing tentative fingers on my elbow.

Lifting her mouth to my ear, she murmurs, "If you hurt her again, I'll tie you down with vines and encourage an entire colony of wasps to make a home in your gut."

Forest Sprites are vicious creatures. I smirk, knowing that turning to scora stone would prohibit her from hurting me, but I let her sit comfortably in her threat. "Understood."

As she walks away, Reverie frowns at her friend. "What did she say to you?"

I shrug. "Oh, you know, yadda yadda if you hurt her, you're carrion. Normal friend-to-supposed-dunghole things."

Her pinched mouth quirks to the side as she tries to stamp down a grin. "She's a good one."

"Yes, she's good at her job as well."

Reverie nods. "I'm fortunate to have found her. I don't know about you, but the industry has been difficult recently. I was floundering a bit until she showed up, ready to keep up with my marketing and keep me sane on wedding days."

"I understand," I murmur, regret slithering in my belly.

Her eyes shift into slits of suspicion. "You do? Because I've been hearing from potential clients that you're going around, underbidding competitors."

There's no way to explain why without scaring her off, so I shrug. "It's a cutthroat industry."

Even in the paling light, I can see her cheeks flush and that cute muscle in her jaw tick. "That's it?"

Taking a sip of my wine, I watch her anger build. She's so fiery, practically crackling with anger. Like a bolt of unshed lightning. I should apologize, but it would imply that I'd do things differently, and that would be untrue.

Instead, I say, "I won't do it again if I know you're in direct competition."

This doesn't mollify her as I'd hoped. The way her ocean-blue eyes morph into raging typhoons should scare me, but all I can do is watch, enthralled.

When I see flecks of glitter shoot from her fingertips, I say, "So what got you into wedding photography?"

Reverie's face twists with anger, like she's ready to scream at me, until the question registers. It's a pleasure to see the anger wiped from her face, replaced by a stunned expression. When she isn't scrunching her nose with disgust or glaring at me like I'm the dung under her shoe, she's incredibly stunning. In the moonslight, her skin glistens faintly, like the fibers that make her are glitter, too.

"What?"

I motion to her with my glass. "You've been doing this for years, but you're what, twenty-six?"

"Twenty-eight."

"So what made you choose wedding photography? What did you do before?"

Her brow furrows as she processes. "Before wedding photography?"

Growing a tiny bit frustrated, I sigh. "Look, Reverie, you seem incredibly intelligent, but catch up, beautiful."

That jump starts her brain, and her face transforms into frustration. "That's rude."

"Yes, yes," I say impatiently. She's way too dedicated to misunderstanding me, which tells me it's a resistance to attraction and not because she outright dislikes me. "You like it when I'm rude. Anyway; photography; why?"

She pinches her lips so tight, I'm tempted to make a sex joke, but I dig a claw into my thigh; she might very well kill me if I joke how her mouth resembles an anus. Finally, she speaks, but with no shortage of mental pain in her tone. "Since I was a kid. My father bought me my first camera when I was seven."

"Nice gift for a kid."

She nods, her eyes far away in a memory. "It's because I was so alone." Her eyes flick to mine, then away. "I wasn't liked at school, so my weekdays were hard. Feeling bad for me, he bought me a camera and took me to Leniar Falls for the day." She spins the straw in her drink, her voice quiet. I lean in, soaking in every detail. I'm afraid that if I speak, she'll clam up entirely.

Smiling to herself, she says, "I took so many photos that day." She looks up. "Have you been?"

I shake my head.

She hums, breaking eye contact, but keeps that little smile. "There is a species of bird there called a Lunite. They're native to Glyridite lands, at Cilyestia Pools. I've never been — my father doesn't like his lineage — but a few accidentally migrated to the falls." Her voice is barely above a whisper. "They are so beautiful. All reds, purples, and blues. Around their eyes is a white circle, so they look perpetually shocked."

She laughs to herself with tears glistening. "It was the first time I had smiled in over a year. Dad let me take thousands of photos, complimenting every single one. I still have one; it's taped next to my bed. It reminds me that when I feel lonely, there's beauty out there I need to find." She pauses, searching my face for something. "So that's what I do ... I go find the beauty."

I ache so deeply to wrap her in my arms, to take away that pain. "I'm sorry you've felt alone," I murmur, lost in her sunshine eyes. "Do you feel better now?"

She's been hurt so much, and I'm a part of that hurt. The fight goes out of her, like a match blown out. This is the saddest I've ever seen her.

"No."

The word stands between us like a door half-ajar; whatever happens next will decide everything. "I can keep you company if you'd like."

I swing the metaphorical door open, praying to the twelve goddesses that she walks through. The indecision is plain on her face, a battle between a heart and mind. So much passes through those eyes, it's like she can see everything bad that has ever happened to her.

Finally, with no small amount of regret in her eyes, she says, "I think it's time for me to go home."

She didn't close the door; that's all that matters. Sliding corals onto the bar top to settle the tab, I grin. "Let me at least walk you to the cloudavator."

15

Reverie

This man is so infuriating. He knows he's undercutting colleagues, but appears to have no remorse about it. Then he offers to keep me *company?* After listening to my story?

Ugh.

Luca unfolds his towering frame, peering at me as he stands. My eyes track the corals he puts onto the bar, and I'm torn. One part of me is irked that he thinks he can pay for me; the other part thrills at the decision.

"I can pay for my drinks," I say quietly.

His smile dazzles. "I know."

It's difficult to ignore the flip-flop of my belly.

I stand, waving goodbye to Prestley. I ignore the knowing look he gives me. He doesn't know what he *thinks* he knows.

Luca steps back, allowing me to walk forward so his wings don't knock me off into the sky.

I'll always catch you.

The knowledge that he would leap from this puff bar to save me gives me butterflies. I grind them into dust, refusing to entertain those feelings. What else was he going to say? *I'll let you plummet to your death.* No, he said the right thing. The right thing to say and what's true aren't always synonymous.

A cloudavator is already waiting, so I step on, giving Luca room to stand. He's still holding our gear effortlessly, wearing a dopey grin that unnerves me.

As I gaze out at the millions of stars and two moons lighting the cloudy sky, I fight the urge to fidget. It's a struggle to act like I don't care about how much I shared. Why did I go into detail in that story? Why did he watch me like I'm his own private constellation?

Luca places the gear at our feet and faces me. My body tenses, ready to fight off whatever thing is about to come out of his beautiful mouth.

"Reverie, can we start over?"

I jerk my head up. "Start over?"

"Yes," he answers patiently. "Start over. I know I fucked up all those months ago, but I'd like to start fresh. I'm not your enemy." He steps closer. I inhale sharply, my eyes fluttering at his imposing presence. Why is he so *big?*

"I don't know if we can start over," I admit. "You hurt me, Luca."

"I know," he murmurs, face full of regret. "I'm so sorry for that. I would never hurt you on purpose. I promise there was a good reason."

"Is it because you're gay?" I blurt out, then slap a hand over my mouth. I don't want to force someone to reveal their orientation without consent.

Luca's square jaw drops, his face contorting into a comical expression of bewilderment. "Gay? You think I'm *gay?*"

I motion to his arm, where the purple dick was. "You didn't care about a dick on your arm. You kissed me, then disappeared. You actually listen to me when I talk, and straight guys don't usually do that. I figured you're going through some late-in-life exploration of your sexuality. I don't blame you; life is confusing. I'm okay with your being gay, I promise."

"Reverie." He breathes my name on the tip of his tongue like a prayer.

Cheeks burning, I lift my gaze to his. What I find there dries my mouth and sends shivers down my spine. Luca is watching me like a man starved, desperate for a snack.

I've just now realized ... I'm the snack.

Without warning, he's tugging me flush against his broad chest. I let out a squeak of surprise as his mouth descends on mine. His other hand cups the back of my head. For a moment, I'm brought back to the other time he kissed me, under the same night sky. With two moons and thousands of stars as witnesses.

"You taste like dessert," he whispers.

A thousand floating bubbles fill my belly at the words. With a teasing smile, I murmur, "But you haven't had your dinner yet."

"Then let me feast," he growls, consuming my mouth like it's a four-course meal.

Like in that moment, his lips are demanding now. His rough tongue flicks against my lips, a silent plea. I obey, parting my mouth to let him continue lighting me on fire from head to toe.

There is absolutely *nothing* gay about him right now. The evidence presses against my stomach, thick and insistent. Warmth pools low in my core, feeding the sudden desperation to wrap my legs around his waist that is almost too much to bear.

I allow my hands to press against his muscular chest. They skim along his torso until my fingers find his plump ass. My thumbs brush against the base of his tail; he groans. Something tickles my calf. His tail lazily wraps itself around my leg, giving it a gentle, tortuous squeeze.

This man is clinging to me like he's drowning and I'm his lifeboat.

There's a jolt, breaking us apart. I'm temporarily stunned at the interruption. We're at the launch platform, stopped right in front of a long line of people waiting to ride a cloudavator to a puff bar. Some of them jeer; others clap in encouragement.

My body, already on fire with desire, burns with embarrassment. The tail disappears as Luca steps back. With eyes full of swirling mercury, he grins from ear to ear. Leaning down, he grabs our gear and leads me off the cloudavator. I refuse to make eye contact with anyone, but I hear a *"Good goin', girl!"*

Grimacing, I duck my head and cross my arms, because someone in the crowd whispers, *"I wonder if she sang him into liking her."*

He knows I'm a siren and has said nothing about it. Loosening my hair, I cover my brand as I follow two massive wings through the crowd. We have to talk about it. All of it.

Just not tonight.

16

Reverie

Luca: So … Do I kiss like a gay man?

Reverie: I haven't kissed many gay men, but I think I tasted a love of brunch somewhere in there.

Luca: Damn. I do love a good brunch.

Reverie: Same. Where's your favorite spot?

Luca: Itty Bitty Tiddy.

Reverie: Excuse me, my breasts are not itty bitty. That's rude.

Luca: I agree; they're pretty magnificent. As much as I'd enjoy discourse over your breasts, Itty Bitty Tiddy is a restaurant owned by a Tiddy Mun. Take your mind out of the gutter.

Reverie: I thought you'd want my head down in the gutter.

Luca: I'd like your head down, but there are better places than a gutter.

Reverie: I'm going to block your number.

Luca: Please don't. Wait. We can talk about your breasts if you insist.

Reverie: Sorry, but this number is no longer in service. Go to brunch on your own.

Luca: Tomorrow at 10?

Reverie: Fine, but I'm bringing a friend.

Luca: I'll bring one, too. You might've heard of him? Kahlo?

Reverie: He's walking again?

Luca: No. He's in a wheelchair and can use one arm.

Reverie: I can't wait to see that. Tomorrow at 10. Don't be late.

Luca: Wouldn't dream of it.

***

Itty Bitty Tiddy is a quaint restaurant, created to resemble a bog. Under the glass ceiling, wooden tables sit on raised mounds, connected by grass pathways. Smokey bog water separates each table in ominous swirls. After studying the images online, I can't fathom why Luca loves this place. It smells of fresh grass and musty mud.

But after the other night, I want to give Luca a chance. Especially after that kiss. Just thinking of it heats my blood. After the kiss, we went our separate ways, and he texted me within five minutes, wishing me a good night. He hasn't stopped texting me, as if determined to prove that things will be different now.

I'm pleased to see Luca waiting. Apparently, he likes to be early, too. Another point in the Maybe Trust Luca department. He spots me, and a dimpled grin splits his face.

A loose bun holds half of his long white hair. He's wearing a white button-up shirt, with the sleeves rolled to his elbows. Fitted khaki shorts wrap around his thick thighs. My eyes linger on the rest of his legs; he keeps his claws polished.

A man who indulges in self-care. I can appreciate that.

For a split second, nothing exists but him and the way his eyes run over me with appreciation. I'd chosen to show off my veins and brand today. I'm wearing one of the few pieces of non-black clothing in my closet. It's a white sundress, with modest shoulder straps, a low neckline, and a knee-length hem that bares my body more than I'm comfortable with.

I brought a sweater to cover the brand if it comes to it, but I'm hoping to have a normal moment at a normal brunch with normal friends. However, there's never a time where I show both off and there isn't some form of negative attention.

It's all but guaranteed, and a small part of me is curious about how Luca will respond.

Hopefully, he doesn't disappoint.

Next to him, in a motorized wheelchair, is Kahlo. How Kahlo is going to move that damn thing across the bog grass, I have no idea.

He's a smaller Gargoyle, not nearly as humongous as Luca, but his wings are still large enough that the specialized wheelchair can't prevent them from scraping against the ground. He's taped tattered socks on the bottom bone points and towels on the soft, leathery membrane.

Kahlo looks ridiculous, and I'm glad of it. Anyone stupid enough to ride a Slogoth deserves socks on their wings.

"You're stunning," Luca murmurs, giving me a chaste kiss on the cheek. One of his hands grazes across my bare back as we hug. My heart skips a beat at the touch. I resist the urge to inhale his scent too deeply.

"Thank you," I whisper back.

Kahlo clears his throat, and my upper lip curls. *Some* normal friends.

I point a finger at him. "You have some apologies to make."

Kahlo's dark red eyes shine with mirth. His black hair curls over his shoulders softly. When he laughs, the lone earring hanging from an earlobe sways. "What? There was a pretty woman I was trying to impress."

I smirk at Luca. "Don't get me too drunk, or I might fire him."

Kahlo sputters a sound of protest. To his credit, he looks actually hurt. "You can't live without me, and you know it!"

I jerk a thumb at the towering Gargoyle next to me. In the corner of my eye, I see Luca's chest puff out with pride. "Seems like that might not be true."

Luca beams, giving a smug smirk. "Told you."

Kahlo pouts. "Whatever."

Luca brushes a hand on the small of my back, offering a small, intimate smile before approaching the hostess stand. I watch him walk away, feeling both giddy and confused.

I'm scared to admit the level of desperate belief anchoring me to reality.

"He really likes you, you know."

Kahlo's voice breaks my trance, and I give him a curious look. "And how would you know?"

"Because he told me about you after that first time." Seeing my stunned expression, Kahlo nods thoughtfully, glancing to make sure

Luca isn't nearby. "He told me he'd met a woman who made him feel like gravity didn't exist." He gives me a lopsided grin. "Which is impressive considering what we are."

"And you didn't realize it was me when he described me?"

Kahlo grimaces. "We aren't the type to share details like that. I mean, maybe I would've, but not Lucky."

Frowning, I ask, "Why?"

Kahlo lifts a hand — his only working hand — to the control stick of his wheelchair, spinning it toward a waiting Luca. "Lucky doesn't care about those kinds of things. He's not one to buy into bigotry or fear. So, it wouldn't be natural for him to bring it up."

Maybe Luca doesn't actually care about my Glyridite or siren side. The thought blooms warmth in my chest, making my skin tingle. I'm overcome with the urge to shimmy a happy dance. But that would be ridiculous, so instead, I stuff my hands into my pockets and try to maintain my composure.

"Well, we're just ..."

Kahlo raises an eyebrow at my inability to explain what Luca and I are. "Whatever you're *justing*, be nice to him while you do it."

It's my turn to raise an eyebrow. "I can be nice."

My second photographer, who I've spent countless hours with over the years, huffs out a disbelieving laugh. "Ree, I've seen you verbally destroy a drunk Orc at Prestley's who tried to grab your ass. You told him his face resembled the offspring of a Minotaur's nutsack and his mother's left tit. He cried, and you *laughed* at him."

We share a chuckle, because I'll never forget the look on that Orc's face. Kahlo gives me a knocking smile. "You're a good person, but you're not necessarily a nice person." At my curled lip, Kahlo says quickly, "No need to prove my point. I like it about you. But Luca is my best friend — he deserves to be happy."

I'm speechless. He's not wrong, but he's not normally so candid. Or serious.

Most likely in an attempt at a dramatic exit, Kahlo spins the wheelchair and scoots over next to Luca.

"Ree!" Malona's melodic voice has me spinning on the balls of my feet with a grin. She's a vision, with her hair in chunky curls, styled to the side, baring her long neck. Wearing a bright red gingham top, with puffy sleeves hanging on her shoulders, her short legs work furiously as she speed walks.

We have an almost six-inch height difference, so when she hugs me, she kisses my sternum. I laugh. She steps back, examining my outfit. "Friend, *what* are you *wearing?* What is this absolute *magic?*"

I motion to her flowing red skirt. "You dressed up, too. No paint anywhere; who are you and what did you do with my best friend?"

She slaps my arm with the back of her hand, giggling. "I wanted to color coordinate with my wings, silly. Plus, you said your guy is bringing a friend?"

"He's not *my* guy," I rush out. "Luca and I are ..." I trail off because the way we kissed, we definitely aren't friends. Clearing my throat, I clarify, "He's not mine."

Malona's eyes shift over my shoulder, and her face brightens with understanding. "Is this him? Are you *the guy?*"

I close my eyes and count to five, because I know he heard me. Behind me comes a rough chuckle. "Yes, I'm Reverie's guy."

I whirl around, ready to give him a piece of my mind, but the dung-eating grin on his face tells me he's spoiling for a heated debate. Unwilling to give him the satisfaction, I growl and cross my arms. He smiles wider and offers a hand to my friend.

"My name is Luca."

Malona's light pink eyebrows raise as her eyes go up, up, and *up* to his face. "Well, Luca. I hear you've been driving my best friend crazy."

"Can't drive someone where they already live," Kahlo mutters.

Luca swings a wing back, revealing my sullen second shooter. The moment he sees Malona, his entire face transforms, as if Malona is Cupid, stabbing him with a dozen love arrows. "Oh," he says dumbly. Even Malona looks taken aback.

"Do you two know one another?" Luca asks, glancing between the two of them with a bewildered expression.

Kahlo shakes his head, unable to peel his gaze from my best friend's face. "No. But I need to."

Malona titters — *titters!* — and tucks a non-existent loose curl behind her pointed ear. "I'm ... Malona." She holds out a small hand, but unfortunately, its opposite is the arm Kahlo can't use yet.

With an eggplant-colored blush, Kahlo appears to be ashamed. "Sorry, I can only use this arm." He raises the good hand, nibbling on his lip with a fang.

"Oh!" Malona's face flushes tomato red, flustered as she switches hands. "I had no idea. Reverie didn't tell me." She steps closer, resting her hand in his. "Are you okay?"

"Yes ..." Kahlo gives his cousin a pleading look, and it takes every inch of self-control to not burst into laughter. Now he has to explain his stupidity.

With a pathetic grimace, he admits, "I tried to ride a Slogoth the other day and ... it didn't go well."

"Oh, you poor thing!" Malona touches the arm laying lax at his side. She fusses over him, asking questions about his wild ride that cost him an entire month of being my second shooter.

Luca and I exchange similar expressions of shock. Did we somehow accidentally create a meet-cute?

"Destau? Party of four?" The hostess calls from within the restaurant. All four of us turn to the voice. Luca smiles, holding out a hand. A simple gesture that makes me pause, but I'm not sure why. It's not like holding hands will get me pregnant or anything. It's only hand holding.

Maybe he has an excellent reason to not call me. So far, since we've been spending time together, he's been kind, thoughtful, and funny. Like he was that night. There's no clear reason as to why he's reticent about sharing, but he'll tell me, eventually. And honestly, I'm tired of fighting whatever this is between us.

I'm more exhausted with how the world never stops objectifying me; the opposite of Luca. But if I don't keep giving men so many chances, then I have no choice but to go through life without a partner. A bone deep ache throbs at the thought of being alone forever, allowing my past traumas prevent me from experiencing anything good.

I glance from his hand to his face, realizing I've been staring at his hand, processing my thoughts. He hasn't flinched or shifted; just patiently allowing me to work through my thoughts.

Okay, I'll give him one more chance.

Pushing aside my terror and anxiety, I break every personal vow about men and put my hand in his.

17

Luca

I did not expect Kahlo to become enamored at brunch with Reverie's best friend, but the way he and Malona already dote on one another, it wouldn't surprise me if his first-born arrives in a year with my namesake. During the meal, they ignore us entirely. Despite how my cousin annoys me, I'm glad for him. Everyone deserves a love story.

Reverie keeps sneaking glances at me, thinking I don't notice. It's as if we've silently agreed to watch the show unfolding right in front of us, but it's more than that. We're comfortable in silence and don't need to fill the air with needless words.

When she appeared, wearing white, it made me wonder what she'd look like in a wedding dress. I immediately batted away the vision, chalking it up to my career influencing the way I see the world. For men, it's not normal to see a woman wearing white and wonder what her favorite flowers are and how they'd decorate the aisle. How would she decorate the reception tables? Would she let me help decide, or would she want to be fully in control?

Turning to her, I ask, "What are your favorite flowers?"

Scrunching her freckled nose, she asks, "Yellow poppies? Why?"

Yellow poppies would be stunning on a ceremony arch. We could match the smaller details to the flowers, in different shades of yellow and orange. It could—

"Are you okay?" Reverie watches me, concerned.

I take a moment to chastise myself. I barely know this woman; planning our wedding is absolutely ridiculous. I'm acting like a lovesick adolescent and not a thirty-three-year-old male Gargoyle.

"Just curious," I say, giving her a smile that hopefully doesn't lead to more questions. If she knew what I was thinking, she'd run so far away, I'm not sure leaping off of Avalon's continental edge would be enough for her.

"This is wild, right?" She whispers, giving our friends a pointed stare.

I lean closer, inhaling her scent of raspberries. "Is Malona normally like this?"

"She's always a bit of a flirt, but never like this," Reverie admits. "And we know how Kahlo is."

"Maybe they've met their match," I joke. *Would you wear a veil or would you let me see your pretty face as you walk down the aisle?* "Crazier things have happened."

She hums in agreement. "Why are *you* a wedding photographer?"

Unlike her, the question doesn't take me by surprise. "Blood."

"Blood," she says flatly.

I grin. "I was a professional boxer until a few years ago. Now, I do it for fun, to let off steam."

Her eyes flick over my body. I can't help but wonder if she's envisioning my ridiculous boxing outfit, the loincloth. It was a half-drunk decision when I was twenty-three, and the gimmick stuck, especially after I won fight after fight. The crowd loves it, and I love the sound of their cheering.

"Okay ..." She plays with a napkin, appearing to process the words. "So you started using a camera as a weapon, took a photo, and liked it so much you take photos now?"

I let out a loud laugh. "No. My cousin got married, and the photos were beautiful. Since I didn't want to keep breaking my nose in the arena, I figured a career change would be good."

"You're very good," she says quietly, squirming like the compliment costs her. It makes my heart skip a beat.

"So are you." She blushes at the returned compliment.

Is it terrible that I want to lick her pink cheeks?

There's movement in the corner of my eye, and I break our connection to see what's drawn my attention. It's a group of male Elves eyeing Reverie. Not eyeing — leering. My instincts rise, ready to tear apart the world if they even think of making her uncomfortable. Maybe it's because of her beautiful glitter veins; it could be the delicate brand under her collarbone. Either way, she was brave enough to wear this sundress, and I'd rather fight a Minotaur than let any of those Elves hurt my girl.

Reverie catches the object of my attention and grabs the ridiculous sweater hanging from the back of her chair.

I put a hand on her shoulder. "Don't."

Eyes the color of tropical oceans meet mine, filled with fear. "I don't want to make them uncomfortable, Luca. Just let me—"

"Absolutely not," I growl. "It's too damn hot for you to put that on. If they say anything, I'll take care of it."

Her blunt teeth worry at her glossy, plump lip. "It's such a nice day; it's easier for me to put it on. It isn't a big deal."

"Dimming your sparkle would be a travesty." I brush a strand of hair behind her ear, revealing the delicate lines of rainbow branching along her throat. Goosebumps break out across her porcelain skin.

Reverie's eyes search my face. "Why do you care so much?"

"Because."

Irritation flickers across her face, eliciting a smile from me. "'Because' is a terrible answer."

"Fine," I mutter, leaning in closer to the shell of her ear. She shivers as I whisper, "Because even if you don't think I'm yours, you're wrong.

I was yours the moment I saw the sun lighting up your colors and filling your face with wonder."

She inhales sharply, and I straighten in my chair, reaching for my drink. Let her stew in the words. I have no expectation of her suddenly declaring her devotion or that maybe she wants to go on a date. While she learns to enjoy holding my hand, I'll plan our future together, with plenty of space for her input when she accepts this magnetic pull between us.

I'll wait however long it takes.

Taking a bite of a muffin, I ignore her staring. Instead, I watch the Elves. When one of them catches my stare, his ears flick back in threat. Knowing it'll earn disgruntled glares, I flare my wings slightly; a subtle, but clear message.

Behind me, someone makes a sound of surprise. Our waiter, passing by with a platter of drinks, sends me a nasty glare. I don't care; the point's made. The Elves avert their gazes and don't look back for the rest of the meal.

18

Luca

Reverie is quiet for the rest of the brunch. She doesn't put the sweater on, so I count that as a win. No one says anything to her, and some of that is probably due to my display, subtle as it was.

Malona and Kahlo start sucking tongues by the time the bill is settled, and she offers to bring him home. I happily shirk my cousin's care duties, clapping him on the shoulder in congratulations. She's not my type, but Malona is a beautiful woman. She seems to truly care about Reverie. That's all that matters.

Stepping out of the restaurant, we both pause. She gives me an uncertain look, nibbling on that lip again. I can see the wheels spinning in that brilliant brain of hers, her eyes flicking to my mouth. Does she want me to kiss her? I'd kiss her for the rest of the day if she'd let me.

"Well, thank you for brunch," she says awkwardly. Money is tight, I don't care — she won't pay for anything as long as I'm around. If anything, it's an investment in my future.

I invade her space, curling my wings around us for privacy. Her chin lifts as she tries to step back, running into my self-created cage. I grin. "You're not going anywhere yet."

Her throat bobs as she swallows. "You can't keep me here forever."

"What about for three minutes?" I rasp, fisting my hands to prevent doing something that would be incredible in the moment, but scare her off forever. I'm desperate to have those glittery veins under my palms.

"How about for two minutes?" To my absolute delight, she moves forward until her breasts almost brush against my chest. My cock throbs in response. Questions race through my mind. What color are her nipples? Will they taste like raspberries? What will she feel like in my mouth?

Unable to resist, I playfully tug on a strand of pink hair, smiling. "What about two and a half minutes?"

"Thirty seconds have already passed. You better hurry up." Her voice is melodic; hypnotic. A tiny voice in my head demands, *hurry, hurry!*

Her eyes widen. I know she's accidentally used a touch of her siren's song.

It's an interesting experience, feeling that pull. But I'm able to resist the command because there's no real force behind it. She doesn't mean it, but even if she did, she could sing me to the depths of the deepest sea, and I'd happily inhale the water.

"I-I-I'm so sorry," she whispers, stumbling back.

I grab her elbows to steady her. "It's fine, Reverie. Truly."

Her crystalline eyes dart around, as if checking to see if anyone heard her sing, despite the privacy of my wings. "I didn't mean to, Luca. Please don't—"

Her fear hurts my heart, but she needs to know how little I care about her siren side. Ignoring the world around us, I weave fingers through her long hair and tilt her mouth up.

"Reverie, I don't want to waste more time. Can I kiss you please?"

Conflicting emotions flicker across her face. Just as I'm about certain she's going to say no, she nods.

Bliss feels like sinking my lips to hers. She's tense at first; frozen from surprise. Then she melts in my grasp, letting out the tiniest sound.

Reverie's whimper is the sweetest treat.

Her hands flutter against my chest, explorative in their touch. When her bare palm slides around my neck, every particle of my body becomes an inferno. My cock throbs painfully, jerking my hips forward. If her hands do this to me, what in the Hells will her entire naked body do?

It'll be an absolute extermination of self, is what.

Each swipe of her tongue licks heat down my spine, curling my tail. Shifting my free hand, I grip her hip like it's an anchor to this world. Otherwise, I might float away from this heady feeling of having her close. Digging my fingers into her curves, I press her closer.

Which is, apparently, a step too far.

Reverie's hands freeze. The world comes back into focus as she rips away from my hold.

Her pink lips part as she catches her breath, plump from my kiss. I like seeing her mouth freshly kissed like this. It should be a daily occurrence.

But her expression extinguishes my desire, replacing it with concern. Her eyes are unfocused, as if the kiss left her dazed as well.

"I-I have to go," she stammers, her hands shaking as she tucks a loose strand of shimmering hair behind her ear.

She whirls around, but I snatch her wrist before she can bolt. "Reverie — it doesn't bother me."

"You don't mean that. Trust me, you really don't." She tries to tug away from my hand, but it's physically impossible for her to do so. I won't hurt her, but I won't let her bolt until she hears my words.

"Please don't insult me by assuming you know me better than I know myself."

Her control shatters, panic pinching her expression. My wings twitch. It makes me want to fight whatever invisible battle she's enduring.

This time, when she yanks against my hand, I let go, unwilling to make her feel trapped. I open my wings, letting the city invade our world again. Face twisting in anguish, Reverie's eyes fill with tears. I sense the stares, and with the way her eyes dart around, I know she can, too. I'm tempted to bring my wings around her once more, to shield her from any judgment.

"I-I don't know what you're talking about," she whispers. "I d-didn't use it."

I tilt my head. She's lying, but I understand why. Using a siren's song without consent is not only an egregious insult; it can carry a prison sentence if a judge is particularly venomous.

"Either way," I say smoothly. "I don't care."

"They all say that," she whispers, her voice cracking. "Until they start to feel ..." Her voice chokes. She inhales a shuddering breath. "And they don't believe me when I tell them I never used it at all."

This time, when she whirls around to rush away, I don't stop her. Maybe I should follow, but the way she clutches her elbows, shoulders drawn tight, and the pungent scent of fear in the air, I know there's nothing I can say to make it better. Not now, at least.

But one day, if I'm lucky, she'll let me soothe her worries.

19

Reverie

Two hundred years ago, sirens were almost hunted to extinction. It was primarily fear-based, although some with ill-intent manipulated themselves into positions of power. They never told anyone what they were, so when it was revealed through a broken promise of silence, all Hells broke loose.

Said manipulators were sentenced to death. Almost every siren was caught and silenced through the destruction of their vocal cords.

As time passed, society realized that muting sirens for something they didn't actually do was cruel. In an effort to compromise, and to prevent the manipulation of others, a law now enforces the branding of every baby within thirty days of their birth. Because newborns are dangerous — said no one ever, except maybe a Gorgon's mother.

My mother drilled into my head every single day that to use my song is to hurt others. While they taught me control of it, and how to use it properly to avoid accidentally using it, my parents have never encouraged me to embrace this side of me.

Today, my control slipped. So absorbed in everything that is Luca, my song activated. I don't even understand why; he clearly doesn't require any encouragement to want me. That should thrill me, but what if one day he doesn't believe me?

I cover myself with the sweater and keep my head down, rushing back to my apartment. Sometimes, I feel like a ghost moving through the city. The only time I'm seen and alive is at work; even then, it's my job to not be *seen*.

As I hail a Dragxi, I check for missed texts. There's nothing. A lump forms in my throat.

You saw him two minutes ago. Still, I'm dying inside, not knowing if he'll ever speak to me again. Will the wedding tomorrow be awkward? Goddess, I hope not. After receiving his protection and kindness, I won't survive his rejection. *Again.*

The green Dragxi lands, smoke curling from her nostrils. Barely able to speak without crying, I give my address and load onto the seating compartment.

While we zoom past buildings and through mist, my photographic memory tortures me. His stubble on my chin. Hands fisting my hair. The heat of him. The way he flared his wings as a threat to those Elves. His scent of petrichor. The concern in his eyes as I exist in a prison of the world's making.

Inhaling slowly, I try to stave off the tears. Every memory continues to chip at my heart. I've kept it locked away for safekeeping to protect it from further harm. Luca is wearing at the metaphorical chains, and it's terrifying.

He's proven repeatedly that if I allow it, he'll protect me. But my history with men won't let me. Right now, that's in charge.

The Dragxi drops me off at my apartment's landing platform, and I rush to my floor, relieved when the deadbolt locks behind me. Leaning against the door, I slide to the floor, holding my head in my hands.

And let myself cry it out.

While crying has never truly solved anything, it's the release I need. Reliving those few moments where men have been awful and society has scorned me brings up old, festering sadness that's been eating me from the inside out.

Leaning back against the door, arms resting on my knees, I stare off into my apartment, lost. How can I possibly overcome this fear? Searching inside myself, I know I'm losing the capacity for more heartbreak. If Luca hurts me, like truly hurts me, it might very well be the last time I ever try. Maybe I'll buy eleven sphinxes, go live in the mountains, and learn how to garden so I don't starve.

Somehow, imagining this alleviates some of my devastation. Taking advantage of the emotional reprieve, I push myself to stand. Something sticks to my hand. It's a white envelope with my name on it. Someone has slipped it under the door.

Bringing it over to the kitchen counter, I lean against it as I open the letter. Wiping the tears from my face, I skim the contents.

Then start crying all over again.

Dear Ms. Songlight,

As a courtesy, we're informing you that your rent will increase next month. It's come to our attention that you're an undisclosed siren and as such, we're considering filing a grievance with the city. However, the raise in rent will be sufficient.

If you agree, we will proceed with the rent raise. If you would like to dispute it, please inform us immediately, and we will proceed with the grievance to recover any damages.

Sincerely,

Horoscope Management

The rent payment is thirty percent more. Money I don't have because of *Luca* and the chaotic market that has been Hells on my income.

Crumpling the letter, I throw it in the trash. Studying my cozy apartment, with its dim lights, dozens of pillows, and my plants, I know there's no alternative. The city would crack down on me. I truly didn't think my landlord needed to know I was a siren and, technically, they probably don't. But the litigation of it all would deplete my savings.

Needing a distraction, I go walk to my little desk, covered in rainbow decor, and decide to edit my most recent weddings. Sometimes, a beautiful moment captured can make everything better.

Opening the editing program, I scroll through the images Luca took. My eyes pause on the first one of the day.

It's a photo of me.

I'm in the arena with the groomstuds. My hair is windswept, shimmering in a sunbeam. An uninhibited laugh brightens my face. The camera hovers in front of my nose, as if I'm searching for the next beautiful moment to capture.

It's probably one of the prettiest photos of me ever taken. Luca caught me at my most free and vulnerable.

Huffing with reluctant appreciation, I do a quick edit and print it out. It takes a few moments for it to develop, but once it's done, I grab it and walk over to the collage of images by my bed.

Next to the image of the Lunite bird, I tape this photo of me. It's beside all of my favorite photos throughout the years. I give it one last lingering stare, irritated with how it makes me feel. Like falling through the sky, without a worry in the world. It's dangerous to feel this way — an emotion that, once you get used to it, is all the more devastating to lose.

I continue through his images, grumbling to myself about how good he is. He finds the smaller moments, like tiny tears or brief hugs. He's always so incredibly observant, and though it unnerves me, it makes him very good at his job. Even better than Kahlo.

I find the photo of Luca discovering my brand. Dappled light spots his enormous purple form; the camera barely lowered below his chin as he gazes at me.

Realization draws his expression tight, but it's not disgust. It's ... surprise mixed with sadness. Sadness for me? After his reaction to my fuck-up today, I don't think it actually bothers him.

The sadness, though ... for whom? Me? Him? Us? Dating a siren will absolutely earn him glares and comments. He doesn't understand what he's agreeing to. They never do.

Frustrated, I turned off my computer. The images can wait for another day, another time when I'm not so raw.

Pulling out my phone, I text Malona.

Reverie: What'd you think of Luca? You seemed enamored with Kahlo, which is impossible since he's an idiot.

Malona: Luca seems nice. I'm with Kahlo right now, actually.

Reverie: You're kidding me, right? The guy tried to dance with a Slogoth.

Malona: I think it's endearing that he tried to dance at all.

Reverie: So what? You're carrying him around since he can't walk?

Malona: Of course.

I stare at the text in disbelief. Not because she can carry him, since Cherubs are incredibly strong despite their stature, but because she makes it sound like it's natural to carry around a half-paralyzed male Gargoyle.

Reverie: I love you, Mal, but you have terrible taste in men.

Malona: I love you Ree, but you're being incredibly stubborn about Luca.

Reverie: You're mean.

Malona: You're mean.

Reverie: Love you.

Malona: Love you.

Putting my phone down, I lay back on my bed and twiddle my fingers and stare at the ceiling. Before Luca swept into my life with annoying quips and dimpled smiles, my life made sense. It was lonely, but it was predictable. Drinks at Prestley's, weddings, and sitting in my tiny apartment, editing photos until the next batch. Rinse, repeat every single week.

Now, this towering purple giant has clobbered his way into my days, my mind, and my heart.

I hate that I like it. No, I don't just like it. I *crave* it. Despite myself, I think of the way he kissed me on the cloudavator after being accused of being gay ... and a smile spreads across my face.

20

Luca

Adjusting the purple tie in the mirror, I inspect my reflection. I'm wearing my normal consultation suit, a black Sunaysian wyrm silk. It cost me an entire wedding's paycheck a couple of years ago, but the investment has been worth it. It's impressed enough clients that I'm able to afford this beautiful apartment and give Reggie the best quality food.

Speaking of a picky chimeragon, behind me, Reggie whines. He's laying at the foot of my bed, splayed out on his side, leathery wings laying haphazardly across his throne of pillows.

"What?" I raise an eyebrow as I slick back my hair with a comb. "You already had two walks today, a bone, and I applied oil to your scales. What else could you want?"

He whines again. I roll my eyes, pulling a piece of lint off my black jacket. "Sit tight. I'll close this deal, and we'll go visit Mom."

Reggie's scaled tail thumps with pleasure. I scruff his dark mane before walking out of the bedroom. My apartment's connected to my studio, so it's a quick jaunt from the front door to the entrance of my office.

My couple, a pair of Cyclops, are already waiting. From checking my notes earlier, I know their names are Finley and Venerin. Finley wears a sharp-looking suit as well. From the inquiry form, I know he's an accountant.

Venerin works as an influencer in the fashion industry, which explains the pin-stripe jacket and pencil skirt. Her hair is a riot of neon green curls, with matching eyeshadow above her mascaraed eyelashes.

Taking a deep breath, I brandish my most personable grin and hold out a hand to Venerin first. "Hello, I'm Luca. You must be Venerin."

She grins, showing perfect teeth. "Yes, it's so good to meet you."

"And you must be Finley," I shake his hand, the pressure commanding. Opening the door to my office, I wave them forward.

"Please come into my office and have a seat. I can't wait to hear about your wedding."

My office is a balance between austere and stylish. Lit candles decorate every surface, with low music playing on an overhead speaker. In one corner is a viewing area with an overstuffed forest green couch, a large holographic screen to show a client's images, and a coffee table made of dark wood with album samples.

In another corner are my desk, computer, and a gear station.

The gasp from Venerin is amusing. It's important to set the tone for their ongoing experience with me. These two are having a very high-end luxury wedding at one of the top venues in the city — I *need* to book this wedding. Bills are accumulating, and my mother's hospital care is becoming more expensive.

While they get situated, I walk over to the wet bar in the last remaining corner of the space. "What would you like to drink?"

"Water is fine," Finley says.

Venerin meets my smile with one of her own. "Do you have any wine?"

"Red or white?"

"White, please."

"Of course," I say smoothly. "Coming right up."

While I pour the wine, I watch them peer out the floor-to-ceiling windows overlooking the far-off mountains. My apartment is high enough that the ground's visible only using binoculars.

"Your view is incredible," Finley observes. "I've heard it's difficult to find an apartment in this building because of it."

"It is." I grab their drinks, careful not to spill a drop. "I was on the waitlist for three years before this unit opened. I knew I wanted one with an attached office, so it took longer than most."

"Appears to be worth it. Thank you." Venerin accepts the wine, grasping the stem delicately. "Have you lived in Gondora your whole life?"

"Born and raised," I hand Finley his drink. "My parents moved here from Oasha about forty years ago."

Venerin's eye lights up. "Oh! Oasha! I hear the desert is perfect for fliers."

"It is," I agree, sitting in the chair across from them. "The desert dunes are stunning, as are the oases. I haven't been back since I was little, but my mother still speaks of it fondly."

"Oh, Fin, we should go someday!" she says with excitement.

Finley frowns. "You hate sand."

She playfully swats him on the arm. "We don't have to lie in it, silly."

I grin, already loving their banter. "Where do you plan on honeymooning?"

Finley looks at his fiancée, which is a good sign. A man who defers to his partner usually means a happier, healthier relationship.

Venerin, not even noticing, gushes, "We're going to the Weeping Pools of Berath. Fin booked a cabana overlooking the seventh pool, where the mermaids live."

"That sounds amazing," I say, impressed. It's not a cheap vacation, which could indicate their budget. *Please have a high budget.*

"Yes, it is!" Venerin beams. "We'll leave the day after our ceremony."

Perfect segue. "Speaking of the ceremony, I'd love to hear what you have planned. I've heard Cyclops have very particular ceremony aspects; I want to make sure I capture every moment."

We spent the next thirty minutes discussing all the details. It sounds extravagant, but that doesn't mean their photography budget will match their bloated imagination. I'm patient, biding my time, smiling at all the right times.

When it appears Venerin has gone through most of the overarching details, I ask, "So what are you hoping for in a wedding photographer?"

They exchange a glance. "Well, you know I'm a fashion influencer, right?"

"Yes, I looked up your socials. You have quite a sense of style."

Venerin preens at the compliment. "Thank you so much. Well, unfortunately, Finley's firm prefers he isn't all over the socials, so we've had to compromise. I can use five photos on my socials, pre-approved by his marketing team. We heard you focus on being discreet. There aren't even photos of you on your website."

Ah. Bingo. "Yes, of course. I pride myself on being discreet with clients. I have an NDA and model release built into my contract, but there is also a privacy clause. Whatever you'd like to keep private is for you to decide."

"Perfect." Venerin claps her hands, diamond rings glistening on her fingers. "I think we could work well together!"

My heart races with excitement. Keeping my voice as even as possible, I ask, "So what kind of budget were you considering for a wedding photographer?"

They exchange another look, and my heart sinks. Venerin says the absolute worst thing possible. "Well, we were considering Edges of Glitter, and she sent over her pricing guide a few days ago. We met and enjoyed spending time with her, but we think she may be a bit more ostentatious than we'd want. We're also on a tighter budget. Do you think you could work with us?"

The blood in my veins runs cold. The goddesses have a twisted sense of humor, forcing me to choose between the woman I'm falling in love with and ... my mother. Just this morning, I received another bill from the most recent hospital visit. One thousand corals, due next week. This wedding would cover that expense.

The simplest solution is to be honest with Reverie. Tell her about my predicament. She might even have a solution.

But if I tell her some of it, she'll want to know all of it. We've only kissed twice — it's far too soon to tell her about my mother. She'll run away screaming to the continent's edge.

A sick sense of dread sinks roots into my heart, and I break out in a cold sweat. She'll never forgive me. I know this without a single doubt in my mind. Yet, it's a simple choice, regardless.

My mother's dying, and I'm all she has.

Recovering quickly, I smile. "We may be able to work something out."

Forgive me.

21

Reverie

Today's wedding is for a pair of Vampyres. Personally, I love Vampyre weddings because they lean toward dark and maudlin, which is a fun change of pace. These two have been together for over five hundred years; why they've taken this long to tie the knot is beyond me.

We're already well into the day; Luca is with the groom, and I'm with Bella, the bride. She's stunning in front of the large ornate mirror, its edges decorated with black filigree. A stunning dress made of black chiffon drapes across her narrow frame, complementing her translucent skin. Her red eyes meet mine in the reflection after I take a photo.

"Do ju think it's okay?"

Taking in her ornate braids, diamond-flecked fangs, and the dozens of piercings in her ears, she resembles a goddess. I nod enthusiastically. "Azmodeus is going to be thrilled to finally see you walk down the aisle."

Yet, she's too insecure for a bride about to commit to forever. Because that's what Vampyres promise: forever. It involves old magyck and an exchange of blood. You'd think after five hundred years, one would know if someone is The One, but Bella is as uncertain as if she were marrying someone on their first date.

Her maid of honor floats into the room, a gorgeous phantom carrying a jewelry box. While the maid of honor helps put the complicated necklace of blood diamonds on, I text Yureka and Luca.

Reverie: Bella is almost ready. How are things?

Yureka: We have a problem.

Reverie: Do you have a solution?

Yureka: The groom's mother is wearing a gray dress.

Reverie: WHAT.

Luca: I need to see this. Where is she?

Yureka: The reception hall. An aunt is trying to get her to change, but she's refusing.

Reverie: For fuck's sake. I can't tell Bella ... she's already freaking out.

Yureka: Is it because her mother-in-law still hasn't cut the umbilical cord after eight hundred years?

Reverie: Could be.

Luca: Oh good goddess, I can't believe she's wearing that.

Luca sends a discreet image from the sky; the mother of the groom is wearing a smokey dress with a modest train. The traditional color of virgin brides. I bite back a groan, not wanting to lead Bella into assuming something is wrong.

Reverie: She needs to change.

Luca: Azmodeus is on his way to Bella.

Reverie: WHAT! NO! STOP HIM.

Luca: I tried. On my way.

Panic thrums in my blood. Bella might very well bolt if she finds out, especially if her nerves have anything to do with the conniving woman in the reception hall.

"Vhat's Vrong?" Bella's ruby-red lips purse. "Your heart rate jast skyrocketed. Iz everything h'okay?"

Fuck. Inhaling, knowing I can't slow my pulse, I nod. "Yes, there seems to be something happening at the reception hall. Luca informed me that Azmodeous is on the way."

Bella shrieks. "He cannot! Zit ez bad luck!"

Inwardly, I cringe. Luck has nothing to do with a mother-in-law like that. "If he needs to talk, maybe you can do it through the door?"

Thankfully, this appears to mollify her. "Jes, that vould vork." She wrings her hands. To her maid of honor, she asks, "Hanora, could ju please go see what is vrong?"

Hanora nods and floats out of the room. Bella refocuses on me, imploring for an answer I can't give. "Vhat do ju know?"

Cringing, I tuck my phone into my back pocket. "Your mother-in-law apparently has chosen a less-than-optimal dress."

"Meaning?"

"Meaning ..." I sigh, resting my hands on my cameras. "She's wearing a gray dress with a train."

"VHAT!" Bella's shrill scream is so high pitched, my hands fly to my ears and the nearby mirror cracks. I check my cameras and lenses. Luckily, I was far enough away that they're still safe.

She peers at the crack and deflates. "I am very sorry." Giving my gear a worried look, she asks, "Is jur camera okay?"

I tap one of them. "Everything is okay."

My smile fades when there's a knock at the door. I hear it open, and Hanora murmurs. Glancing over my shoulder, I see Azmodeous at the threshold. No one grants him permission to enter, so he waits, rocking on the balls of his feet.

Seeing my face, he pleads, "Please, Reverie, have my bride come speak to me immediately."

I raise my eyebrows. If she can hear my heartbeat, she can hear his words. Walking to my side, but right behind the wall, she yells, "Vhat has jur matder done, Azzy?"

My head is on a swivel as they exchange words. Digging my nails into my palm, desperate to keep my heartbeat calm. It's difficult to maintain an even breath. This is the most annoying thing about working with blood feeders — they can sense a pulse point half a mile away.

Where is the damn wedding planner? It's my long-time friend Euresta; she's excellent at her job, so she's probably doing wedding-related things. Which means it's my job to calm the scene.

Azmodeous opens his big fat mouth. "My mother requested to wear a gray gown today. I did not believe it would cause an issue because she is not the bride and you are wearing black."

He knows damn well gray dresses at weddings signify maidens. As in virgins. Seeing as that's impossible, since he's breathing in front of us, this means his mother is being an intentional bitch because she knows Bella can't wear gray today; it'd be considered a lie, which violates their marriage contract. All standard Vampyre laws and beliefs. So yes, this mother deserves a public flogging, at minimum.

I'm running a hand over my face in disbelief when the worst thing happens: Bella begins to cry.

"Vhy is jur matder like this, Azzy? She cannot give me vone day. Not vone!"

Azmodeous runs a hand through his colorless hair. "Why can you not move on? Is it really that big of an issue?"

Bella sobs, mascara running down her face. This is devolving rapidly. Time to stop this. I clear my throat. "Erm, look. Azmodeous, please go speak with your mother. Bella told me she's so excited to marry you, so let's make sure it's a special day, okay?"

Azmodeous presses against the invisible barrier created by a lack of invitation, then hisses. Not at me, but at the barrier. "No. This cannot continue. My mother will not see reason, and I will not spend energy trying to convince her otherwise."

Bella falls to the ground dramatically, clutching the door frame with black-colored claws. She wails as if someone has died. "I cannot, Azzy! Eet iz too much! I cannot!"

My phone buzzes, and I discreetly pull it out.

Luca: I'm outside the door. Sounds serious.

Reverie: Azmodeous is being unreasonable, but so is she.

Luca: Vampyres are incredibly dramatic. It's how they entertain themselves after hundreds of years.

Reverie: I haven't photographed a Vamp wedding in a couple of years. I totally forgot.

"Fine. I shall go speak with my mother, but no promises, Bella. You must put yourself back together. We will be married on time."

Azmodeous stalks away, muttering to himself. At my feet, Bella wails. I'm taken aback as she latches onto my calves, almost making me fall as she shakes me.

"Revaree! Please! Halp me!"

I kneel, prying her hands from my body. In a quiet tone, I ask, "Help you how?" I know how; she approved the siren song addendum. Some clients hire me to calm their nerves. It's entirely consensual, but it still requires a few questions for legal purposes.

"Thee song, Revaree. Sing it!"

At the bridal suite entrance, I see Luca appear. Halona steps back, eyes wide. I wave her over. "Hey, Halona. I need you to be a witness, please."

Halona obeys, coming to our side with preternatural speed. Luca ducks into the room, rounding his wings to fit. I'm terrified to let him see this. We've barely spoken since I bolted from brunch. From that moment I broke the law and lost control. He claims to not care, but will he feel that way when he sees what I can do? The power I hold?

Balling my fists, I press them into my thighs to hide the shaking. To Halona, I ask, "Are you the witness to this siren's song?"

"Yes."

To Bella, I say, "Are you consenting to the siren's song?" Bella shakes her head furiously. "You need to say it, Bella."

"Jas! Jas!"

I squeeze my eyes shut, willing the stares away. *His* stare. Digging deep into myself, I find the siren. She rests right above my heart, made of oceans, hurricane winds, and the soft scent of brine. The color blue fills my vision as I begin singing.

22

Luca

I dislike Vampyre weddings. All of them are dedicated to drama, and this wedding is no exception. That mother-in-law knows exactly what she's doing. Azmodeous is her fifteenth son out of thirty kids. This isn't her first, nor last, wedding.

I'd be more furious, except it allows me to see Reverie release her siren song. She sits across the ornate bridal suite, all of its white upon white offering a stunning contrast to her colors. On the floor next to who I assume is the bride is the most striking creature I've ever seen.

Reverie's wearing her typical black outfit and those hideous pink shoes. Her face is devoid of makeup, and her hair's piled on top of her head, random strands trailing to the ground in colorful ringlets. Her siren brand is easy to see, and all I want to do is lick each squiggle.

When Reverie begins to sing, the Heavens part.

There are no lyrics to a siren's song. It's not quite a musical song, either. It's more of how a feeling sounds, yanking your senses toward her, every sensible thought reaching toward each note. My body tingles and vibrates, preparing my instincts for whatever she commands. Bella is hearing something different; the song is intended for her, so it only works on her.

Other than the breathtaking sounds coming from her lips, there's no other sign of her song. No bright light or glowing eyes. If she wanted to whisper it, she could. It's what makes people believe sirens are dangerous. Personally, I find the power fascinating. Being able to make everything in your life happen with a few choice sounds? Incredible.

Yet, it's clear Reverie doesn't. There's nothing she's done or said on the topic to make me believe she accepts the talent as something positive. Aside from this. I'm just now finding out she offers a clause of service in her contract; smart, but risky. It's not illegal with a witness paired with clear consent, but people behave differently at weddings.

When the song is done, tears simmer at my lashes. Her talent is so mesmerizing. When her eyes find mine, they soften. She mouths "Hi" and I do the same. The hands squeezing hers release their hold, and Reverie flexes her fingers with a grimace. She stands with some difficulty, and I rush forward as she stumbles through the door.

Her eyes widen. She laughs nervously as I grab her elbow. "Whoa."

"Easy," I murmur. "Does using your power exhaust you?"

Her eyes are slightly unfocused. "I'm fine. It's just been a while."

I curse under my breath, earning a glare from Bella. The Vampyre has the audacity to hold her arms up, like I'm expected to lift her like a baby.

Holding back a sigh, I help the dramatic bride stand. "I'm going to help Reverie take a seat. Halona can help freshen you up."

Bella nods, wiping away snot from her nose. "H'okay. Thank ju."

Wrapping an arm around Reverie's waist, I guide her to the couch. Shoving away the piles of clutter, I help her sit. Kneeling at her feet, I lift her chin with a finger. She gives me a weak smile.

"I forgot how much it takes when I don't practice."

Swallowing a growl of frustration, I pull out a homemade granola bar from my satchel, fresh from my oven this morning. "Here, have a snack."

As she takes a bite, I place a bottle of water in her lap. After using it to swallow her bite, she gives me a wry look. "I thought you only carried nuts around."

I whisper, "Always. But I have to keep things interesting. Would hate for you to get bored."

Amusement twinkles in those tropical irises. "I liked those nuts."

"I've got good news, then." My mouth quirks, and I love the way joy seems to radiate from her.

"Incorrigble."

"Dedicated."

"Dedicated to bad sex jokes?"

I shake my head. "Dedicated to making you laugh."

She chews thoughtfully. I can tell my words have rattled her. Behind us, Bella's in a panic *again* because her makeup isn't perfect anymore and the makeup artist is already long gone. Wasting the song, all because she loves the drama.

This wedding could not be over fast enough. We haven't even reached the blood goblet ceremony, where the groom's mother is sure to cause some kind of disturbance.

When the granola bar is all gone, I make sure Reverie has a couple more sips of water before helping her stand. She's stable, giving me a grateful smile before exhaling loudly. A small little reset before her wedding mask appears.

Weddings wait for no one.

***

I'd like to say the rest of the wedding went off without a hitch, but it'd be disingenuous. Vampyre weddings aren't successful without at least three breakdowns, one showdown, and one messy teardown. Blood; there's always so much blood.

During the reception, Vamps get blood-drunk, where live donors lay on tables, munching on donuts while their clients wet their teeth. The fresh source activates a chemical in their brains that makes them deliriously happy and ... horny.

Typically, when this occurs, wedding photographers leave. It can get dangerous when bloodlust appears for Vampyres. For reasons I cannot comprehend, Reverie did not end her contract after the cake cutting.

Which is why I'm forced to stand on the outskirts of the dance floor, the black-and-white tiles slick with blood, trying to not appear territorial. But Bella and Azmodeous are fucking on the dance floor, her blood diamond necklace swaying with his every thrust. The bass from the DJ's setup thumps in the room like a pounding pulse.

Across the room, Yureka looks both fascinated and nauseous. The corner of my mouth quirks. She's clearly never been to a harpy wedding. They actually sacrifice creatures to their gods between dances. The smell is unspeakable.

I scan the graphic scene for a colorful head of hair. Reverie's loose strands of hair swing as she squats closer to the dance floor, getting an angle that would make an Angel blush. I have to admire her commitment. When her camera lowers, she catches my eye, and flashes me a grin. Still not the one I'm aching for, but breathtaking enough to kick start the anxiety in my chest.

I need to tell her what I've done, but I can't. Not yet. She may never smile at me again. It makes me selfish, but I want to delay the oncoming slaughter of our connection for as long as possible.

It's a dedication to folly, falling in love with her. For those eyes made of summer, I'll become the biggest fool of them all.

She stands with a wince, bending over to rub her knees before gingerly making her way over to me. Sidling up against my arm, she shouts, "I probably should've cut the contract short."

I nod in agreement. "You mean you don't enjoy watching Vamps fuck in pools of blood?"

She laughs; it reminds me of wind chimes and a spring breeze. It's a part of her siren side, and it's wonderful. "I'm not normally one for watching people fuck in the first place."

I raise an eyebrow. "Not even in a mirror?"

Instead of the offended glare I fully expect, her full mouth twists into a mischievous smile. "Can't say that I've tried. Maybe one day. With the right person."

Is she ... actually flirting back? Without a fight? The surprise leaves me speechless. Seeing my loss for words, she tosses her head back and laughs. It's a stunning sound, filled with amusement. I want to swallow it up so I can shove it into my soul.

The wedding planner, Euresta, appears at Reverie's side. Euresta's a dark-skinned Dimension Witch, capable of hiding and holding things in alternate dimensions. It makes her fantastic at her job, capable of carrying anything she wants anywhere she desires. Her hair is streaks of white and red, slicked back into a tight braided bun. She wears all black, minus a gold chained locket around her slender neck.

She whispers something into Reverie's ear. They share a smile, and Euresta pulls out the timeline, pointing to the end. The grand exit. It's supposed to be with sprite lights, but when Eureka shakes her head, my excitement spikes. Maybe we'll get out early.

Reverie beckons me to follow her. I obey, trailing behind her out of the reception hall into the quieter hallway. The pulsing bass fades as the metal doors close behind us.

I sigh with relief, gaining a chuckle from Reverie. She tucks stray hairs behind her ear. "This is a little more intense than expected. I cannot believe they're actually fucking in the middle of the dance floor."

I nod, leaning against the dark blue wall. "Did you see the envy on his mother's face? I was sure she'd ask to join."

"Do we keep taking photos?" Reverie wonders, tapping her chin in a farce of contemplation.

"Or do we join?" I tease.

Reverie shakes her head and in a serious tone, she says, "Azmodeous isn't my type."

"Who is your type?" The question comes out nonchalantly, but I'm feeling very 'chalant' about the answer.

To my delight, she gives me the most delicious perusal, biting her lip when her eyes pause below my belt.

Who in the twelve Hells is this woman? Surely not the same one from three weeks ago. As much as I'd like to trust her flirtatiousness, I can't help but wonder if she's affected by the bloodlust, even if it's impossible as a non-Vampyre.

She pulls out her phone to send off a text. "Follow me."

Dumbfounded, I obey, willing to follow her to the ends of the earth if she commands.

Reverie marches down the mostly empty hallway, checking doorknobs until one door finally opens. With a mischievous grin, she steps into the room.

Okay, the term "room" is generous here. It's a closet with cleaning supplies. I barely fit, especially with my wings. When I hesitate, she yanks me inside.

"Reverie, what are you doing?" I whisper, grunting when a mop handle jabs into my ribs. Just as I'm turning to face her, something clatters to the floor behind me. Hopefully, it's not a lamp.

When the door closes behind me, the room electrifies with tension. Of what kind, I can't tell yet. "Are you okay?"

"More than okay," she promises, unhooking her cameras and carefully placing them in her gear bag. My heart picks up its pace. When she slides off her camera harness, letting it drop to the floor, my mouth goes dry. Pushing cleaning supplies out of the way, she hops onto the counter situated on one side of the space, spreading her thighs, and every thought in my mind disappears.

23

Reverie

Maybe I've lost my mind, but between the way he watched while I sang the siren's song, and then watching the Vampyres screw each other's brains out, I'm desperate to press Luca against my body. Wedding reception be damned.

After texting Yureka that we're taking a quick break, my ache for Luca becomes unbearable. I'm so tired of resisting him when all he's done is prove repeatedly that he wants to be there. Next week, we're headed out for a destination wedding, and a small part of me hopes we can make it more romantic.

Nerves shake my legs as I hop on the counter, terrified he's going to reject me. To tell me it's unprofessional to make out in a closet while working.

I see his focus home in between my thighs. His dark blue tongue flicks out to lick his thick lips. No, he won't reject me. Emboldened, I lean back on my hands and playfully swing my feet.

He's so massive, it's half a step forward before his hips are flush with my pelvis. Two large hands grab my ass to press us together. Already, the hardness of his cock strains against his zipper. I whimper as my hips lift, craving the friction.

His forehead rests against mine. The only sounds in the room are the pounding pulse in my ears and our heavy breaths mingling.

"Is this real?" he rasps. "Before I continue, I need to know this is real. That you're in your right mind?"

His words have me hiccuping out a laugh. It feels sudden, yet a voice in my head mutters, *Finally.* I've been so hurt by his disappearing, although the anger truly comes from my bitterness at the world. I've been so angry and afraid for so long, it felt more natural to be that way around him.

But I don't want to be angry all the time. Maybe with Luca ... Maybe I can be soft.

I bring my hands to his jaw, loving the rough stubble against my soft palms. Hovering my lips close enough to feel the heat on his, I whisper, "Around you, I'm never in the right mind. Let's be delusional together?"

A deep, rumbling growl vibrates his chest as he snarls, "Fuck yes," before slamming his mouth to mine. Keeping one hand on my ass, he brings another to my head, taking a fistful of my hair to yank my head back. He takes advantage of my gasp, invading my mouth with his insistent tongue.

Fire licks up my spine, and I moan, pressing harder against his thickness. What would that feel like inside me? We definitely aren't fucking for the first time in a closet during a wedding, but curiosity gets the better of me. My hand slides between us, allowing my fingers to rub against his cock, and he jerks forward, breaking the kiss to make a choking sound before panting out, *"Reverie."*

My name is both an admonishment and a plea. Stroking his length, my core tightens, aching to be filled. Every inch promises pleasure worth breaking myself apart for.

Luca's hand releases my ass to trail along my rib cage with a clawed finger. I moan as the claws retract and he palms my breast roughly. His fingers curl around the edge of my top, teasing me until I whimper. At the sound, he yanks downward, baring my breasts. I inhale sharply as he dips his head to latch onto my iridescent nipple.

An obscene moan rumbles in my throat, and he slides his other hand over my mouth, cutting off the sound. When his tongue flicks the peak of my nipple, I pant like a hound. More. I need *more.*

Bringing my fingers to the juncture of his wings, I drum nails along the soft flesh. He snarls, breaking away from my nipple to give me one of the most fierce glares I've ever seen.

"Do *not* do that unless you want me to fuck you raw right here in this coffin of a closet. Because *I fucking will*, Reverie. I swear it to the goddesses. Do *not* test me."

I giggle. "Promises, promises."

The masculine ferocity in his expression morphs to one of dangerous vows. "You like to play games, *Bilaste?*"

With precise intention, Luca straightens and adjusts my shirt back into place. I'm left splayed out in front of him like a wanton lover, frowning at the abandonment.

"Where are you going?" I whimper, inwardly cringing at the hurt in my voice.

The most diabolical smile curves his mouth. Bringing his lips down to graze mine, one of his thumbs lovingly brushes against my jaw as he whispers, "Tonight, when I get home, I'm going to fist my cock, thinking of your perfect breast in my mouth. I'm going to cum all over my fingers and imagine you licking it with that sweet little tongue of yours."

When I inhale sharply, he nuzzles my cheek, trailing a warm breath to my ear. He whispers, "And you're going to remember that the next time you touch my wings, you better be ready for me to claim every inch of that sweet cunt."

Grabbing my hair roughly again, he tilts my face, the intensity in his expression making me gulp. "Am I understood?"

I try to nod, but he holds my head in place. "Say it," he rasps, and it hits me how much restraint he has right now. This tension between us is a frayed tightrope, barely hanging together by a thread.

"Yes," I whimper again, wishing we were anywhere but a closet. "I understand."

He releases my hair. We hold our stares, both of us still heaving for breath. The blood in my veins is on fire, and I know my power is clamoring for release. Not breaking eye contact, Luca grabs my gear, placing it on the counter beside me.

"I'm going to walk out now, and you can follow shortly after to not raise suspicion, okay?"

I nod, not able to speak yet. The way he gazes at me ... I want to take a picture and tape it near my bed for the next time I'm touching myself. It's that fucking delicious.

"We're going to spend the rest of the evening as professionals, understand?" He taps a finger on my temple. "And if your brilliant mind tries to convince you that I don't like you or want you, make sure to tell it to shut the fuck up. Because I've wanted nothing more in my life. Understood?"

"Yes." The word is barely a whisper. It's hard to breathe after that declaration.

With one last nod, satisfied that I'll obey, he opens the closet door. As he closes the door, my body slumps into an exhausted, strung out heap. This was an impulsive decision on my part, but I don't regret it. Whatever's blooming between us is indescribable, but monumental. Luca isn't a random hook-up from a club — he's far more.

At that realization, a shard in my heart thaws, filling with optimism.

Things can be different. I know they can. Luca might very well be my forever.

The thought makes me giddy.

24

Luca

The scent of raspberries fills my nose on the too-long flight home. Landing on my balcony, I shuck off my gear and stalk to my shower. Shedding every bit of clothing, I turn the shower on and step under the icy spray.

Even with the freezing water, it's not enough to dampen the burning desire swelling my cock to the point of pain. Fisting its length, I jerk against myself roughly, bracing a hand against the wall as I let myself grunt as loud as I need. It takes less than a minute for release to tighten the base of my spine and for pleasure to blur my reality. A too-short liberation from the torment that is Reverie Songlight.

I'm still recovering from the shock of her initiating that whole thing. It was like a dream come true.

As I dress and go through my post-wedding routine of playing with Reggie while listening to relaxing music, I replay the memory of her body in my hands. In my mouth. She tasted of lashing winds and lazy summer days. Kissing her felt like skimming the highest thermals. I will do anything possible to have another opportunity.

You need to tell her.

I need to tell her *everything.* There's no way we can move forward until there is full transparency. There's no way I can let us get more serious than we already are without telling her about my choices.

Not only about taking another client from her, but about my mother. About my future of being alone. Once she knows it all, there's a high chance she'll think I'm both duplicitous and that my mother is too much work. She already has so much to worry about in this world; I don't want to add to it.

Yet, I can't stay away. Yes, I'm committed to photographing the weddings, but there was no reason for taking her rock climbing or brunch ... I just enjoy playing with fire.

Tucking Reggie into bed with one last treat and hug, I crawl into my bed and grab my phone. Wrapping the soft sheets around my still-humming body, I shoot off a text.

Luca: Did you get home safe?

Reverie: We're still at Prestley's, but about to leave.

I'd been tempted to join them, but Reggie needed to be let out.

Luca: Text me when you're home.

Reverie: Yes, Sir.

Luca: You're playing with fire, *Bilaste.*

Reverie: What does that word mean? You called me that in the closet.

Luca: It means text me when you're home.

Reverie: I'm going to stroke your wings next time I see you.

Luca: Be prepared to spread those beautiful thighs.

Reverie: Yes, Sir.

Luca: Do not tease me. Gargoyles don't handle teasing with decorum.

Reverie: Oh, I'm well aware. I took my multi-cultural class in school like everyone else.

Luca: Remember that I can fully control my tail.

Luca: Reverie?

Luca: Hello?

Luca: Text me when you're home.

As my mind begins to drift off, my phone dings. Her words have me shooting upright, heart thundering and cock instantly hard.

Reverie: I'm home. Touching myself.

Luca: Prove it.

Reverie: There's glitter everywhere.

The conniving Glyridite sends me a photo of her fingers covered opaque white glitter. I groan, my cock hard as stone. *Again.* For the third time since getting home, I clutch the length for dear life. The image of soaking myself in her sparkling wetness is enough to break my control within seconds. I'm an adolescent all over again. If there were witnesses, I'd hibernate in stone for millennia.

Sending her the photo of my fingers covered in cum, I wipe off the wetness with a tissue. Her response is almost immediate.

Reverie: There's no one there to lick it off, right?

Luca: There's no one there with a cock covered in glitter, right?

Reverie: Not yet. I could make some calls.

The suggestion of anyone coming near her right now almost sends me into a frenzy. I'm more possessive than I've ever been, or have any right to be. It's a sin to covet what you shouldn't have — Reverie has made it clear how she feels about me.

But now that she's allowed me to do far more than kiss her, it feels meaningful. And any man that tries to hurt or have her will have to answer to me.

Luca: I'm visualizing ripping off cocks and flinging them into a tornado.

Reverie: So territorial.

Luca: Does it bother you?

Air freezes in my lungs, terror locking up my muscles. What if she says yes? She would have every right to lay down another boundary. But maybe we're on the same page here, for once.

Reverie: You get a taste of my tit and now you want me all to yourself?

I scoff and give Reggie's sleeping face a dry glare. "Is she for real?"

Luca: Baby, I wanted you all to myself since you offered me a glass of femire at Prestley's.

Reverie: I didn't *offer* it. You showed up and bullied me into having a drink.

Luca: Yeah? Well, I'd do it again. Best glass of femire in my life.

Reverie: Me too.

I stare at those two words. It was the best glass of femire for her, too? The revelation has me grinning so wide, my lip almost splits against a fang.

Reverie: Thanks for not freaking out about me singing. It's not something I do very often.

Luca: I thought it was beautiful. Today was intense. You did great.

Reverie: Thank you. It was intense. Sorry I dragged you to the closet.

Luca: It's okay. I didn't expect my first threesome to be with a broom handle, though.

Reverie: If the broom handle can count as a partner, what does that make your tail?

Said tail thumps against the mattress. Involving my tail with her in any capacity sounds transcendent. In Gargoylian culture, touching another's tail is almost completely taboo. Saved for those tied together with deep intimacy.

The thought of her mouth anywhere near it makes my mouth water.

Luca: It can be whatever you want it to be, *Bilaste*.

Reverie: I'll keep that in mind. And I've decided it doesn't bother me.

Luca: What doesn't bother you?

Reverie: You ripping off the cocks of creepy men and flinging them into storms if they come near me.

Luca: Good, because I'll do it. If there's a hurricane nearby, I'll throw some in there too.

Reverie: I don't want anyone near you, either.

I slap my arm, checking to make sure I'm awake. It feels like the Oasha desert under my skin, heating me from the inside. What I wouldn't give to have her right here, sharing a smile with me. It really feels like we've turned a corner. It makes me giddy.

Luca: Then it's a deal. I swear to have only thoughts of glitter on my cock and rainbows in my mouth.

Reverie: You remember that?

Luca: I remember everything. Including the way your tit tasted. I've never seen such pretty nipples.

Reverie: Goodnight, Louie the Lamentation.

Luca: Sweet dreams. *Bilaste.*

25

Reverie

We're going to the Orc wedding in a few days and, admittedly, I'm half-way to a panic attack at any given moment. This wedding season has been busy. Between the weddings with Luca and the engagement sessions I'm shooting during the week, *plus* all the editing, it's been non-stop.

Now, I'm standing in front of my closet, trying to figure out what to pack. We leave in three days, and I'm tempted to grab everything off the hangers and stuff it into the suitcases. Can't forget anything if I bring it all, right?

With a sigh, I grab my nicer pieces of clothing and begin folding them into a pile. Most of them are conservative, with long sleeves, but I cave to the temptation of bringing more revealing pieces. Luca will join Yureka and me for all dinners, at a minimum, since it's all a business expense for me. It's *not* a date, but I want to look nice regardless.

After our long text conversation the other night, hyper Pegasi rattle around in my chest every time I think of Luca. It shouldn't warm my belly when I remember how possessive he acted, but it does. A therapist would have a heyday analyzing why I can't stand being treated like an object, but Luca threatening to tear off dicks from rude men made me squeal and kick my feet in bed.

It's ... it's nice to have someone care about my feelings. Not what they think I should feel, like my parents, but what I actually feel.

Optimism is a dangerous thing, a temptation of Fate's attention. After Luca ghosted me, I'd thought my instincts were broken because he had filled me with nothing but optimism, only to disappear right after.

There's still a tiny niggle of doubt plaguing my thoughts, but the die-hard romantic in me desperately wants this to be different. Because if he's not who he claims to be, if he ends up dishonest, it might break me.

As I'm grabbing a pair of sandals, my phone lights up. Seeing Luca's name, I grin.

Luca: Is it okay if I wear a bikini to the thermal pools?

Reverie: No, because you'll probably look better than me.

Luca: Doubtful. What are you doing?

Reverie: Also trying to figure out what to pack. Wishing I owned a bikini.

Luca: Want to come over? I'm currently ironing my underwear.

Reverie: Please tell me you're kidding.

An embarrassing chortle snort escapes when a photo loads. It's of him holding up a very flat, wrinkle free sock.

Reverie: Diabolical. You're a serial killer, aren't you?

Luca: I do love a good bowl of cereal.

Reverie: Hah. You want company for ironing your under-wear?

Luca: And my T-shirts.

Reverie: What an irresistible offer. I'll be there in twenty.

Looking down at my outfit, I decide it's good enough. I'm wearing a fuzzy light blue sweater, black leggings, and calf-high white socks. I haven't washed my hair in a couple of days, so it's piled high in a messy bun.

Checking my reflection, I grimace. Weariness darkens the circles under my eyes, and without mascara on, my pale eyelashes might as well not exist. Maybe make-up would be a good idea. My eyes flick to my collection of makeup on a shelf. The energy required to apply it feels like too much to ask of myself.

Fuck it. I've already put Luca through his paces — what's one more litmus test? Either he likes the unwashed hair and natural face, or he's not long-term material, anyway.

Within three minutes, I have my purse in hand and a Dragxi whisking me to Luca's apartment. It's impulsive, but it's impossible to resist the invisible pull toward Luca. Never in my life have I spent time with a man who is ironing his undies, but there's a first time for everything.

Eighteen minutes later, I'm knocking on his apartment door, jittery with nerves. When the door swings open and Luca's dimples greet me, a sense of calm settles over me. Even as those silver eyes skim over me, I feel confident enough to raise my chin and return his smile.

He's wearing a white tank top, revealing all the muscles I haven't seen since the battle arena. Even then, I'd tried really hard not to look at him. Now, I can look my fill. Gargoyles are naturally muscular, but Luca stays active enough for him to be larger than most.

My eyes trail down his stomach, pausing when I see the bulge resting under his gray sweatpants. My mouth goes dry.

Thank you to all twelve goddesses, because I don't think he noticed my lingering stare. Or the way my eyes flare with greed.

"You look gorgeous," he murmurs, leaning down to kiss my cheek. For a split second, I'm brought back to that moment in the closet. With his mouth on my breast and hungry lips devouring mine. My core clenches with the vivid memory.

I inhale his fresh scent, relishing the warmth of his lips. "How do you sleep with all of those boulders attached to your body?"

His chuckle is all warm honey and smoke. Luca straightens and motions for me to step inside. Glancing at his layers of muscles, he raises an eyebrow. "These old things?"

"So modest," I tease, scanning his apartment. It's organized, but overloaded with the typical bachelor colors of black, white, and gray. Not nearly enough glitter. It smells like him, with hints of sandalwood, presumably from a lit candle flickering on his kitchen counter.

Near the wall of windows are an ironing board and a steaming iron. Piles of neatly folded laundry rest on his black leather couch. Sure enough, the pile of T-shirts looks starched within an inch of its life.

What is noticeably absent is a chimeragon. "Where is Reggie?"

"Groomers. Would you like something to drink?" Luca walks over to his refrigerator, glancing over his wing at me. "I have water, wine, femire, beer, and I think a rogue can of seltzer if you're feeling bubbly."

Pushing away my disappointment because I really want to meet Reggie, I say,"Femire, please."

"One blackberry femire coming right up."

Does he remember ... ? No, surely not. It's a coincidence. Right?

Just in case it isn't, I ask, "You like blackberry femire?"

Mercury eyes flick to mine while he pours us both a glass. "It became a favorite a little over a year ago."

So, not a coincidence. "You really remember everything?"

An emotion I can't quite place flickers over his face, then disappears. "Yes."

The nervousness returns as he hands me a glass. I'm still so confused as to why he ghosted, if he coveted so many moments from that evening. It doesn't make sense.

Today isn't the day to push, though. Instead, I jerk my head over to his laundry. "Show me how you starch, big guy."

Luca grins, flashing me fangs. "Come along then, Rainbow Menace."

Trailing behind him, I grunt a sound of protest. "Excuse me, but I am *not* a menace."

He points a finger at the dish towel I'd turned into red glitter when he wasn't looking. Or at least I thought he wasn't looking. "Prime example number one."

My cheeks flush. It had been an impulsive joke. Taking a step back, I say, "Sorry, I'll fix it. It was just an innocent prank."

Luca pauses by the ironing board and glares. "Don't you dare."

There goes the Pegasi making a racket in my belly. "You sure? I can change it back without an issue."

He sweeps a hand across the room. "I could use a little color in here, don't you think?" Placing his glass of femire on the coffee table, he taps his chin. "In fact, I've always wanted a sparkling couch. Can you make that happen?"

The sip of femire in my mouth almost chokes me. Coughing, I sputter out, "Y-you want me to *change* your couch?"

Luca shrugs, grabbing a wrinkled T-shirt from a laundry basket. Placing it on the ironing table, he says, "I'm partial to turquoise, the color of tropical waters."

It would be a beautiful color to drown in.

This man has me questioning everything I've ever thought about men. "It won't really go with your, um, decor."

Luca shrugs again, pressing the steaming iron to the white T-shirt. "Then I'll change my decor."

Apprehensive, I approach the couch as I take a deep gulp of the femire. It's easy to reverse when he changes his mind — because once he sees it, surely he'll ask for it to be reversed — but I'm still a bundle of nerves when my finger touches the cool leather.

Within seconds, the entire thing is the same shade as my eyes. It's almost too bright for the room, but when I check his expression, Luca's eyes are shining with bedazzlement.

"Fabulous," he breathes, sounding awed. "Now make the coffee table match."

This command makes me bark out a laugh. Sitting on the couch, I curl up with a black pillow. Grinning, I turn it hot pink, thinking that will be his breaking point.

Instead, as he gingerly folds the stiff, wrinkle-free T-shirt, Luca says, "Make sure they all complement one another, *Bilaste.*"

A surge of pride fills me as I snatch each fluffy pillow and turn them different colors. Luca watches with amusement. Each time I pick a bright, obnoxious color, I'm confident he'll demand something different.

But he never does.

By the time I'm done with my glass of femire, his couch is blue, the pillows are neon colors, and the coffee table is a soft glittering lilac, similar to his skin tone. My skin flushes with pride, and my veins glimmer from the pleasure of using my power.

"You're beautiful when you use your power," Luca says, acting nonchalant as he organizes the piles of his finished laundry. He's not even looking at me, acting like his compliment couldn't possibly affect me.

No one has ever said that to me. Not even my parents. It makes me want to pull down my sleeves and hide my hands.

"You're just saying that," I mutter, staring into my empty glass. Claws click on the tiled floor, and Luca's hand enters my vision as he grabs my glass. I look up into his stern expression, battling with the doubt trying to shrink my insides.

"I am not in the habit of saying things I don't mean, Reverie," he chides, walking over to his kitchen to refill my glass. I watch the way his ass shifts in the sweatpants, that purple tail swishing and curling with contentment.

While he pours the blackberry femire, Luca asks, "Are you hungry? I could make you something."

Wait. This man irons his clothes, has a clean home, a full-time job, is physically fit, *and* cooks?

"What's the catch?" I blurt out.

Luca looks up sharply, almost spilling the femire. "Catch?"

I motion to every glorious inch of him as he brings back my now-full glass. "You appear to be every woman's dream. Career, skills, and knows how to iron clothes. There has to be a catch. Why are you still single?"

A darkness I don't understand crosses his face, then disappears, replaced with an easy smile. "I'm actually bad in bed."

Now *that* I refuse to believe, but I play along. "*Pfft,* easily fixed with training."

"I'm *very* interested in on-the-job training," he agrees, sitting next to me. His wings hook over the back of the couch, stretching out lazily. "Are you offering me a position?"

There are so many things worth and not worth saying in this instance. After considering my plethora of options, I grin. "I'd like to offer you the position of Official Undies Ironer."

"Do I get a name tag?"

"Yep. I'll even make you a business card."

Luca chuckles, taking a sip of his drink. "I'm really moving on up in this world."

"Don't let it go to your head," I warn, loving this easy camaraderie. "I'd hate to fire you."

Resting an arm along the back of the couch, one of his fingers plays with a strand of my hair. "Is there an opportunity for promotions?"

"You can work your way up to Head Dishwasher Extraordinaire."

The most charming Gargoyle I've ever met leans closer, the heat emanating off his chest caressing my skin. "Whose body must I dispose of to achieve the title of CEO of the Kiss Management Department?"

My tongue flicks out to wet my lips, and his eyes home in on the movement. His gaze darkens as he smirks.

Inhaling a steadying breath, I say, "Good news. The position was recently vacated."

Moonstone irises narrow with displeasure. "*How* recently?"

"Those kinds of questions are unprofessional, Mr. Destau," I murmur, shifting forward and tilting my head up an inch. A silent offering.

It becomes impossible to breathe when he hovers his mouth right above mine. "Are there any tryouts I need to prepare for?"

He's so close to kissing me, it makes my chest ache. "Well, you did mention needing training."

"Mmm," he hums, nuzzling his nose against mine. "May I show you some of my skill set, and you can decide whether it's worth all the paperwork?"

Goddess, why won't he just kiss me?

"Excellent idea."

The kiss is feather light at first, enough to pull me toward him like a magnet. The urge to crawl into his lap is overwhelming. Maybe it's the femire, although a single glass won't make me want to climb a man.

When Luca breaks the kiss, I whimper, chasing his disappearing mouth with mine.

He's breathing hard, searching my face for something. "I didn't bring you over here to do this, you know."

"I know," I murmur, desperate for another, deeper kiss. "I'm taking advantage of a lonely man right now."

"I'm very lonely," he agrees. "But wouldn't you prefer some food? I make an excellent omelette."

"Unfortunately, management needs one more example of your kissing skills before a decision can be made on who to hire."

"So, I better make it good?"

"You better make it damn good."

The space between us charges with tension. Just as I'm about to pounce, he growls, "Fuck it," lifting me to straddle his lap.

I squeal with surprise, then let out an ungoddessly moan when my pelvis brushes against the hard length barely concealed under these maddening sweatpants. Luca lets out a shuddering breath at the sound. Thick fingers dig into my ass as his mouth crashes against mine. It's an instant inferno, and our first kiss not in public. There are no eyes scrutinizing us; no one around to catcall. The broom closet certainly didn't count, with guests milling around outside.

Right now, my sounds are uninhibited and all for him. Raking my nails over his scalp, I fist his loose strands of pale hair and yank voraciously. Luca's hips buck and his hands jerk me forward into his stomach, rubbing my clit over his hard cock. Pleasure skitters up my skin, and my head drops, overwhelmed with the sensation.

A fang rakes along my neck, Luca's hot tongue trailing along my veins. When he nips my pulse point, I whimper. With a mind of their own, my hands skim down his neck and shoulders, grabbing the muscles. His skin is soft suede; I want to rub myself all over it.

"This fucking sweater covers too much," he complains, sliding a hand up my shirt and along my spine. Goosebumps pebble my skin.

"You can take it off," I pant. "It could be part of the audition."

"It could," he agrees, kissing my skin between words. "But again, that's not why I brought you here."

With that, his hands still and the kisses stop. Pouting, I pull far enough away to look him in the eye. "What's wrong?"

I adore the way his expression softens. "Nothing, *Bilaste.* I want this; don't misunderstand. But if it's alright with you, I'd like this afternoon to be more about spending time together." I open my mouth to protest, but he interrupts me with, *"Clothed."*

My mouth snaps shut. It's disappointing and thrilling at the same time. Once again, Luca is proving that he's different.

With the heaviest, most dramatic sigh possible, I say, "Fine. I suppose an omelette could tide me over."

He nips my chin, grinning. "Does that mean I got the job?"

Pressing a finger to his nose, I tap it twice. "You're officially hired as the CEO of the Kiss Management Department."

"I'm adding it to my resume immediately."

"Not before you make me food," I warn. "You're still on probation."

With minimal effort, Luca holds me around his waist as he stands. Carrying me to the kitchen, he whispers in my ear, "I like probing."

"Incorrigible," I mutter, chuckling despite myself.

Luca places me on the counter, allowing me to sit there while he pulls out eggs. "Well, Miss Nonya, what would you like in your omelette?"

"Bacon, cheese, mushrooms, and spinach?"

"I can do the first three. No spinach on the menu today."

"I'll survive."

While he cooks the omelette, I discover a new kink: muscular men cooking in gray sweatpants.

26

Luca

The afternoon with Reverie was domestic bliss. She clapped with delight when I placed the omelette in front of her. Watching her eat something I made and provided fills me with a level of masculine pride I've never experienced before.

It's like tasting my dreams, savoring what could be.

Unfortunately, in reality, I'm plagued with nightmares, where Reverie finds out from someone else. She slaps me before running away, refusing to speak.

I have to tell her.

From the moment I wake in a cold sweat, it gnaws at me like Reggie working a bone. I'm not a dishonest person; I may make certain choices that require a lack of information for others, but I never go out of my way to downright lie.

But I'm lying to her.

The catch of it all is that from the moment I saw her iridescent soul, I never wanted someone like I've wanted her. *Needed* her. Seeing her in that puff bar was a taunt from Fate; reality pommeled me back into submission the very next day.

She'll never want to be with someone in my shoes. Everything with my mom is so much.

I spend most of the day berating myself for not having more self-control. For being selfish. Even as I try to tackle my to-do list, it isn't enough to distract me.

We're going to the wedding tomorrow. We'll be spending whole days together. Our reservation is for two rooms, since Yureka is going, but we'll have multiple meals together. Probably do one activity.

After last night, I have no doubt things will escalate, at least a little. If I tell her now, will it ruin her focus on the wedding? If I don't tell her, will we fly past the point of no return? Only to end things in a more painful break?

There's no reasonable answer here.

But I want her. Ever since that night at Prestley's, when I experienced that very first flicker of sarcastic humor, Reverie has taken up more of my thoughts than is reasonable.

Spending so many days with her, having her in my arms ... my feelings for her are unquestionable. We might be done working together in a few days, but I'll never stop wanting her. Even if she forces me to do it from afar, there's no way I can move on.

I need to see her. I need to know if she feels the same. Even if she doesn't, I want to make a lasting impact on her life.

After a shower, I dress in casual clothes, tying my wet hair back and inspecting my reflection. Dark circles crescent my eyes, emphasizing their dull silver irises. Being dishonest feels disgusting.

Behind me, Reggie whines, sensing my despair.

"It's okay, bud." I ruffle his mane with a weak smile. He flops over, showing his silver belly. Rubbing his soft fur, I smile. Reverie will love meeting him.

An idea appears, brightening my grin. "In the mood for some outside time?"

Reggie whips his serpentine tail in agreement, pushing his head into my hand. Pulling out my phone, I dial Reverie's number. She answers on the third ring, her voice lifting my spirits despite all odds.

“Hey, you.” Her voice is so different from all those weeks ago. Right now, she sounds full of light — as she should — filling me with bitter-sweet longing.

"Hey beautiful. How are you?"

She sighs. "Bad news. Yureka can't go to the wedding."

My heart leaps into my throat. "Is she okay?"

"Yeah, she's fine, but she can't leave the city. So it's just you and me."

Excitement flutters in my stomach. "So I get you all to myself, then?"

Reverie laughs. "Well, we're still in separate hotel rooms, but I guess you could take me to dinner at least once."

"Once is enough," I say quickly, thoughts already racing with all the things we could do without Yureka there as a barrier. "We'll have a great time."

Her voice is so sweet when she says, "I know. Somehow, I always have fun with you."

Rubbing the pang in my heart, I walk out onto the balcony to study the weather. My Gargoyle instincts tell me it’s going to be a beautiful evening, with a slight breeze. “What do you say to an adventure? The sun will set soon, and I want to show you something.”

“Oh!” She chirps. “That sounds lovely. Have you already packed?”

I glance at the suitcase by the front door, half-full. My gear’s prepped — I simply need to find more socks. “For the most part. You?”

She laughs. I’ll never tire of the sound. “I’ve been packed for days, but I can’t decide on exactly what to wear. Checking the schedule, we’ll have time to relax. I’m tempted to bring my entire closet so I’m not under-prepared.”

The thought of her being a heavy packer lightens my mood further. I’ll carry every suitcase without complaint. “Sounds like we’ve both earned an evening to relax. Want me to come pick you up? I have someone you’ll want to meet.”

Her tone is full of happiness as she asks, “Is it Reggie? Please say yes.”

“Only one way to find out,” I tease. “I’ll be there in twenty. Meet you at the platform?”

“Sure. Do I need to pack anything?”

This woman will learn I'm always prepared. "Keep it light. I'll have all the supplies we need."

"Including the nuts?"

"Always the nuts."

She giggles before hanging up. I close my eyes, cementing the sound in my mind for when I never hear it again.

***

"I didn't realize you were going to carry me," Reverie says, aghast when she sees me land.

"Hello to you too," I say, tone dry. "I brought you a surprise."

Behind me, still in his backpack, Reggie chirps. She squeals, rushing up, grabbing my elbow to spin me. I'm careful to avoid toppling her over with a wing as she coos over Reggie. "Oh, aren't you the *sweetest!* I've been dying to meet you, Reggie. I hear you turned his aunt into stone."

"For only three minutes," I grumble, smiling.

She speaks to him in gibberish baby talk. "Who is the cutest itty bitty chimeragony sweet boy? You are! Yes, you are!"

Reggie purrs and mewls, preening under the affection. A burning frustration scalds my skin; I'm jealous of my chimeragon. *Grow the fuck up.*

Except the feeling grows. My minutes are running out. Trying to act natural, I face her. She pouts, and I resist the urge to nip at that plump lip.

"Come on, I want to make sure we get there in time."

She frowns. "In time for what?"

My arms open as I kneel. "Come on, *Bilaste.*"

Reverie crosses her arms, narrowing those stunning eyes. "What does that mean? Tell me now."

Behind me, my wingpal whines, eager to be let out of his mesh backpack. I cock an eyebrow. "Are you going to torture my son because I won't translate a Gargoylian word?"

Practically stomping her heel in frustration, she eases into my grasp with a stubborn huff. Scooping her into my arms, I inhale her scent. Raspberries.

It's as if the Fates instantly align with her here, in my arms. She's been in my hold before, but this time, it's entirely willingly. She watches me with such trust; it borders on devotion.

I need to tell her tonight. Tell her everything. What's going on ... The way I feel ... it all needs to be out in the open before we head out on this trip together. Otherwise, I won't be able to look myself in the eye.

There must be some bit of self-loathing appearing in my expression because her brows knit together. Raising a hand to my cheek, she murmurs, "What's wrong?"

I close my eyes, pressing into her warm fingers. Her simplest of touches has always been enough. A simple palm to my face is better than any caress to my cock.

Opening them again, I pretend I'm not about to break her heart. "I never told you the fare cost of a Gargoyle ride?"

Her face splits into a brilliant smile. *The* smile. The one I've spent every moment aching for. It's more beautiful than a sunrise on the highest mountain peak. If someone asked me in the last moments of my life what I'd want to remember before returning to the Heavens, I'd say this one.

"What's the cost?"

I playfully make kissy noises, and she giggles. "A kiss or two, *Bilaste.*"

Moving her hand from my cheek to the back of my head, she pulls my face to hers. It's a sweet kiss, languid, and full of unspoken emotions.

Another memory to look back on.

27

Reverie

Kissing Luca is unlike kissing anyone else, ever. I'm twenty-eight; I've had plenty of partners. Well, the term "partner" is generous. I've been involved with all types of people, from genders and species. For me, it's about what's in their heart and not what's between their legs.

Or rather, what I've perceived their heart to be, because clearly, my choices haven't been working out. Each time, it felt like something was missing. A gaping hole in the puzzle that is my life.

When I kiss Luca, it's different. Like that missing piece slots right into its destiny. He's always seen past my vicious exterior.

Today, I'm grateful he has.

As we fly in the sky, heading to wherever he's taking me, I close my eyes and rest my head against his chest to feel his heartbeat. It's steady, thumping against my cheek. The warmth of his body protects me from the chilly mist as he sweeps through the sky.

When I peek an eye open, I see towers of pastel clouds reaching into the golden sky like fluffy mountains. There's some air traffic, but mostly, it's just the two of us. Closing my eyes again, I nestle closer. His hold tightens, as if he's afraid of something forcing him to let go. I know he'd never.

I've decided that when we land, wherever it is, I want to tell him how my feelings have changed. I have this burning need to tell him how much he's already altered the way I view myself in this world. He makes me want to be the best version of myself.

Suddenly, a sound vibrates against my cheek, startling me. Luca's humming. It's a familiar song, popular in party spaces. Biting the inside of my cheek, I worry about what will happen if I join in. It's impossible for a siren to sing normally. I'm a half siren, but I'm no exception.

But Luca has made it clear he doesn't care about my singing.

It's tentative at first, and I sense his eyes on me. Too nervous to discover what I might find in his face, I continue singing. There's no purpose or command in the sound. It's noise that would catch someone's attention, ready for instruction. His hands tighten into my curves as he continues humming. For the first time in my life, I'm able to sing without judgment. It's a privilege for a siren to engage in their talent without fear.

Of course, Luca would be the one providing that privilege.

Another frozen sliver in my heart thaws. He's chipping away at it, bit by bit.

My mind drifts, lost in the song. I don't even notice we're descending until Luca's voice rumbles like thunder in my ear. "Open your eyes, *Bilaste.*"

With eyelids fluttering open, it takes a moment for me to process what I'm seeing. When it finally hits where we are, I gasp.

Cilyestia Pools. The most sacred place for Glyridites.

It's a place I've always wanted to visit, but never had the gall to do it alone. My mother refused, claiming it wasn't her place. My father, despite being a Glyridite, also refused, citing that it was nothing of interest.

Tears shimmer in my eyes as the colors — oh, the *colors* — fill my vision.

Cilyestia Pools is a series of interconnected waterfalls, the tallest one being hundreds of feet high. I've heard that during the day, rainbows never leave the mist, regardless of the sun's angle. At night, instead of rainbows, there's glitter. It pours from the largest fall into a dozen others, each a different height. All of the water coalesces into a larger body of water. My mother once told me that at the height of the sun, you can see to the bottom, dozens of feet down.

My whole body breaks out in goosebumps, the glitter in my veins immediately throbbing against my flesh, clamoring for release. It's pure instinct, one I won't be able to ignore once we land.

"I hope this is okay," he murmurs. "I know technically I'm not supposed to be here, so tell me to turn around if it's too much."

"No!" I resist the urge to squirm with excitement. "I don't care about that. This is *amazing.*"

"Then enjoy yourself, *Bilaste.*" Luca's lips linger on my forehead, and my head lifts into the kiss, wanting it to last.

The moment Luca lands, I'm wriggling out of his grasp. A part of me wishes he'd warned me, because maybe I could've prepared for the way thoughts escape into the shimmering mist, leaving only instinct. I don't look at him. I just ... exist.

I inhale the fresh scent of blossoms and moss. Everything about this place screams home. Scanning the area, I pull off my shoes and dig my toes into the moss. It's wet and soft, offering a gentle cushion to my steps.

Hesitating, I peer over my shoulder. Luca is unloading Reggie, but his moonlight irises are locked on me. He ushers me forward with a flick of his hand.

This is the most vulnerable I've allowed myself to be, with anyone. His genuine smile, the joy in his expression, make me feel like I can expose myself in more ways than one. Luca wants me to embrace myself.

So, it's time to do just that.

Within seconds, my shirt and trousers are in a pile at my feet. Heart hammering and limbs trembling, I shed my undergarments. Behind me,

Luca inhales sharply. A burning desire to release glitter hums through my skin. This place is so beautiful, and so completely Glyridite, it takes my breath away.

Why was I raised to hate this part of myself? How can a place be this beautiful and I'm still considered ugly? A freak? An anomaly? Everything in my blood screams in recognition, which means all of this stunning scenery is *me.*

I'm this beautiful.

The waterfalls are so amazing, I can't help but bolt for them. With a wild scream to the darkening clouds, I hold my arms out, releasing my glitter. It bursts from me in every color imaginable, leaking from my veins like rivers. It spans dozens of feet in every direction, coating anything in its wake.

A stream of glitter trails behind me as I laugh, loving the sensation of moss under my feet. I leap over mushrooms and ferns. Small bioluminescent bugs skitter away. A bird cries out in alarm from somewhere above.

From the trees hang floating orbs. Legend says they're souls of Glyridite fortunate enough to die here. Each is a swirling sphere of iridescent color, lending faint light to my path. Raising a hand, I let out swirling peaks of glitter, letting them lazily twist like mini vortexes. It rises high enough that it touches an orb. I giggle when the orb brightens, accepting the offering greedily. Maybe they really are souls.

Just in case, I send glitter to a dozen of them, delighted as each brightens in gratitude.

This is incredible.

Tears stream down my face as I openly weep. The need inside me is frantic, propelling my feet forward. Pure instinct has me leaping into the water with a gleeful cry, arms wide and soul alight.

The pool's warmth embraces me. I let out another burst of my power, my mouth split in a smile so wide, it's almost painful. Opening my eyes underwater, it's a delight to see bioluminescent fish watching me with curiosity. Glitter shimmers everywhere, swirling with the currents of water.

For the first time in my life, I truly belong somewhere.

Breaking the surface, I laugh again. My tears mix with the water as I tread in place, enthralled with everything.

A chirp breaks my fascination. Reggie sits at the edge of the pool, his wings tucked into his round belly as he eyes me curiously. Swimming over to meet him, I boop his nose, leaving a shimmering dot. His forked tongue swipes out to lick it up.

"Hey buddy," I coo. "Where's your dad?"

Resting my arms on the soft moss, I search for Luca. He's in the same spot, except he's on his knees. His wings sag against the ground, and something about him seems like it's cracking in half as he watches me with unadulterated reverence.

Luca is beautiful. Every carved muscle holds power he never lords over others smaller than him. His white hair absorbs the glimmering colors, like he could be part Glyridite. His big hands rest on his powerful thighs, as if in supplication to the goddesses.

Like *I'm* the goddess.

Since we've met, he's never treated me as anything less. At every turn, he's encouraged me to live fully, without apology. He makes me laugh and is protective, but not domineering. Plus, he's an excellent kisser. Probably an even better lover.

But even if I never find out, I'm still incredibly grateful to have met him. To find someone who advocates for me, even if that means teaching me how to advocate for myself.

I've experienced so much unkindness, I know exactly how special that is. I want to bottle it up like an elixir. Guzzle it when I'm most starved. Fatten myself on the way he loves me.

Awareness is like a lightning strike splitting my soul. It's a shock the world itself doesn't tilt on its axis as I realize something vitally important.

I'm in love with Luca.

The realization is both a relief and terrifying. He holds my heart in a lilac, oversized palm, but I know he won't hurt me. Which means I have a choice: Do I let him continue holding it, becoming familiar with it in his grasp?

Or do I snatch it back and run away forever?

28

Luca

If a goddess split the Heavens to step from between the clouds, demanding worship, I'd promptly tell her to fuck off because I have my own deity.

It was a spontaneous idea, bringing Reverie here. While I don't know a lot about the history of how her parents handled her being a Glyridite, it's painfully clear how much she loathes this part of herself. I've spent the last few weeks researching Glyridite and siren powers, their beliefs, and anything else that will allow me to support her.

Technically, I'm not welcome here, but I'm positive the goddesses would understand. How could they not, when Reverie sprinted for the pools as if they held the secrets to her universe? The stream of glitter behind her was like wings, taking her to new heights, even if only in her mind.

When she undressed, gold glitter swirling around her, I fell to my knees in awe. Not because she has the most perfect body, all luscious curves with long legs. It's more the way she lights from the inside out, commanding her power with newfound appreciation. Each vein of glitter glowed, leaking her power into the night sky.

It's an honor to do this for her. Even if this is all our friendship becomes, I'm okay with that. Because seeing her filled with jubilation is something I could never forget. It solidifies something I've known, but struggled to admit: I'm so in love with Reverie. So completely, utterly, and totally in love.

Since we met, Reverie has shown me alternate layers of herself, reticent and fearful, but brave enough to do it, regardless. From the first words she snarled, to this moment, I've witnessed her anger, shame, and fear. But I've also seen her bravery, brilliance, and beauty. I ache to experience more of her, no matter what that looks like.

I watch her step out of the pool, shimmering water sluicing over her limbs in rivulets. Setting aside my honor for a single moment, I allow myself to memorize her naked body. The way her full breasts sway as her ample hips swing. The softness of her belly. The powerful strides of her thick thighs. Even her feet are adorable.

Catching my perusal, she smirks, and lifts her hands. Golden, iridescent glitter bursts from her hands. Sweeping her hands alongside her body, a dress appears, offering unexpected modesty. I bite back a groan, but also grateful. There's no way my restraint would survive her bared iridescent nipples.

She approaches with slow steps. My entire world narrows in on her sparkling face and glowing eyes. They are no longer blue; they hold every color this world offers. Blood pounds in my cock, throbbing with an unquenchable ache. Every nerve in my body crackles — no, *burns* — with the demand to claim her. She is *mine.* Every speck of glitter flowing in her veins is mine, if she'll let me have it.

"You look like you've been visited by a goddess," she teases, using her siren song. All air leaves my lungs as my body lurches, pulled toward her magnetism.

My tongue barely remembers how to work as I rasp out, "I am."

Every muscle in my body weakens as she stops right in front of me, wet and shimmering. Like a benevolent deity, she rests a hand against my cheek.

Needing to know this is real, I lift her hand and kiss her palm. She hums with contentment, and my rapture shatters right along with my restraint. My hands are on her hips, pulling her down with a possessive growl. She inhales sharply as I settle her legs around me. To my distinct pleasure, she scoots her hips closer, rubbing against my hardness.

The glitter has no actual substance, which means her body is naked in my embrace. Mindful of the position I've put her in, I'm able to rasp out, "Is this okay? Tell me to stop if you need me to."

"Don't stop," she whispers, bringing her lips to mine.

My remaining vestiges of self-control snap. This is everything I've dreamed of, everything I've wanted. Our hands rove over each other, touching anything available. One of her hands runs through my hair while the other seizes my jaw. Even through my trousers, she feels divine as she rides me.

One of my hands brushes past her hips. She whimpers against my mouth when my fingers slip into the crack of her delectable ass. The other kneads a breast, and I'm ecstatic when her nipple hardens against my rough palm. I'm becoming mindless with need. Our kiss deepens, becoming ravenous. I'm scared of catching her lip with a fang, but she doesn't seem to have the same concern.

Bringing both of my hands to her hips, I imagine myself already inside her, moaning into her mouth at the zing of pleasure hitting straight into the base of my spine. This is *without* being inside her?

The thought of sinking into her is almost unfathomable.

"Luca, I *need* you," she whispers, wrapping her arms around my neck. Keeping her legs alongside my thighs, I help her lay on the welcoming moss. Spreading her out in front of me like a buffet.

"Let me see you, *Bilaste.*"

Without another word, she dissolves the glitter, revealing every glorious inch of her luscious body. Shyness softens her eyes as she dips her chin, bringing her arms to her breasts.

"No, *Bilaste.* Not with me." I gently separate her arms; my heart nearly breaks at the sweetness in her smile. Her breasts part, ready for adoration. I allow myself to study the treasure between her thighs. She's already swollen, with wetness glittering on her thighs. She wants me as much as I want her.

"Let me worship you?" I plead, not giving a damn about sounding desperate..

A beautiful blush pinkens her cheeks, barely visible in the faint glowing lights from all around us. "Luca, I want to tell you something."

My heart stutters. "Can you tell me after I coat my mouth with your glitter?"

She huffs out a laugh, giving me an inviting expression. "Are you sure? I mean, I can remove it later. It won't stay on you forever, I promise."

Scooting back, I spread her thighs. "*Bilaste,* I don't give seven flying hippogriffs if you cover my entire body with glitter and keep it there until the day I ascend to the heavens. Mark me as yours."

"If you insist," she says in a teasing tone.

As I dive toward my feast, a finger touches my forehead. I study her from between my lashes and grin as purple glitter slithers across my skin in a playful caress. Within seconds, not a single inch of me is glitter-free. If the sun were shining, I'd be a blinding sight.

Eager to show her how much I don't care, I give her core a slow, lazy lick from top to bottom. We moan in tandem. The taste of her is ... transcendent. The tang of raspberries and something else that is distinctly Reverie. When my pebbled tongue finds her clit, I give it a flick to test out her responsiveness.

Her back arches as she lets out the most beautiful sound. When I do it again, I'm rewarded with the same reaction. Sticking with that motion, I bring a hand to her breast, tweaking the raised peak of her nipple. Her hands reach above her head, digging into the moss as her hips buck. Glitter leaks from each vein in lazy rivulets, covering the ground. Does she do this every single time, or is it because of this place?

Either way, it's a sight to behold.

When she's panting and mewling for more, I bring a finger to her entrance, pressing until it sinks into her body. I pause, gritting my teeth at the silky tightness. My cock throbs, an aching annoyance. Her perfection is not helping.

Frantic fingers dig into my hair, making a mess of the strands. "Lu-Luca."

"Yes, *Bilaste?*" I purr the nickname against her pussy, letting the word rumble over her clit.

"M-more. I need more." Her thighs tighten around my ears, almost crushing my head. Perfect. I pump my finger, allowing the friction to build. She's a writhing mess, moaning my name repeatedly.

When I add a second finger, Reverie's entire body glows as she cries out, back bowing. I increase the pace, single-minded in my goal. I *will* see her cum. I *will* see her undone.

"Come on, baby. Give it to me." I whisper as my fingers sink up to the knuckles. They aren't nearly thick or long enough to prepare her fully for me, but this is a sublime start. "Be a good girl and give me everything you have."

"Luca," she sobs.

Tears shimmer in my eyes, the love I have for her so overwhelming, it rends my soul apart. It's excruciating loving someone this much. No one tells you that love is an agony of the sweetest kind.

Giving her clit one last suck, she shatters. Her pussy clenches around my fingers so tightly, I can barely move them. I murmur praises as she unravels, her sweat-slick body shaking.

As she comes down from the orgasm, I slow the pace of my fingers, still watching her every little reaction. She's ethereal, with the soft glow of her skin and the faint lights all around us casting a golden hue.

She looks dazed as her eyes flutter open, still gasping for air. I sit up, memorizing the curves of her body. When her gaze finds mine, I stare deep into her eyes. Without blinking, I stick my glittering fingers into my mouth and suck.

Hard.

29

Reverie

There aren't enough words to explain how I feel right now. No one has ever asked to worship me, let alone redefine the word. Luca watches me with shining eyes. Are those actual tears? The realization splits me open, baring me in the most terrifying way. Who is this man?

His hair's mussed, thanks to my frantic fingers digging for an anchor to reality. Glitter covers his skin. Luca's lopsided smirk, revealing half of a fang, brings out that little dimple in his right cheek.

I point to my face, indicating a shimmering spot on his cheek. "You have a little something right there."

A devastating smile splits his rough-hewn features. "Perhaps I should go hunting for more?"

I giggle, popping my hips forward. His gaze homes in on the mess he's made. The glitter in his eyes makes him look so innocent, like he's never seen a naked woman before. I'm actually unsure how many partners he's had.

Instantly, I'm alarmed. What if he's a virgin?

Panicked, I blurted out, "Are you a virgin?"

The intensity in his gaze disappears as he snaps his head up. "What?" he barks, then recovers, shaking his head. Chuckling at himself, he says, "Apologies, that took me by surprise."

"Is it because you've never seen one?" I ask, worried. Sleeping with virgins isn't my thing. He *acts* like he's definitely done this *at least* three times, although my instincts tell me it's much, *much* more.

Luca stares at me like I've grown seven Hydra heads. "Where in the twelve Hells did that come from?"

"The way you're looking at ..." I motion between my legs. "... *me* ... makes me think you haven't seen one before."

He presses a hand to his chest in protest with a playful smirk. "Miss Nonya, are you asking how many partners I've had? Right now? With your glitter coating my ear canals?"

"That's a show of *my* prowess. Not just anybody can coat ear canals."

He makes a show of puffing out his broad, muscular chest. "You know, I bet I'm the first glittering Gargoyle."

I laugh. "You know what? I bet you're right."

Falling forward, bracing an elbow by each of my ears, Luca hovers a couple of inches above me; close enough to feel his heat everywhere. "I'm *desperate* for you, *Bilaste*. But I fear my chimeragon is staring at us, begging for attention."

I peer past his massive forearm to find a very irritated Reggie. His scaled tail flicks angrily as he sits primly, ears flat. "Does he always look like that?"

"No," Luca laughs. "He probably thought he'd get to play fetch or something. Not watch his dad turn into a disco ball."

Reggie meows as if agreeing. I let out a laugh that devolves into a fit of giggles. Luca could absolutely pass as an enormous purple disco ball. His nose nudges mine.

When he speaks, it's full of yearning. "I love your laugh."

As I grin at the compliment, his head jerks back to fully see my face. "And that smile." He groans as he nuzzles my neck. "*Bilaste*, I love your smile."

He shifts, bringing his head to my chest. My muscles seize when I realize what he's about to do.

"Please don't," I whimper.

Luca presses his mouth to my brand. *No one* touches my brand. It's a flutter of a kiss, full of reverence and ...

With a heartbreakingly soft expression, he says, "I love you, Reverie."

The world freezes. Time stands still. My heart actually stops beating for a couple of seconds. Did he really say that?

"What?"

How? Why?

Pulling his head back to study my reaction, his expression is so sweet it makes my heart ache. "I love you."

Such quiet, confident words that make no sense. Me? *Why?* "You barely know me."

"I know you. I might not know everything about you yet, but I know enough to feel this deeply. I know you're desperate to see beauty in the world, because you don't feel it in yourself."

I inhale a shaky breath. It's my greatest truth, *and* greatest shame, laid bare for someone else to see. To judge. To reject. He has the power to destroy me with this knowledge.

"Do you want to know what *bilaste* means?" The raw vulnerability on his face cleaves me in two. Why does this hurt so much?

Despite my apprehension, I nod my head.

"It means..." He exhales slowly. "Bliss. *Bilaste* means bliss in Gargoylian."

Bliss. He calls me Bliss. As if I'm *his* bliss. Is this a dream? I halfway want it to be, because this is inexplicably terrifying.

"Luca." My throat seizes. No one has ever said those words to me before except for my parents. Even then, it wasn't often. Terror like never before grips my ability to speak. How can someone like him love me? It doesn't make sense. There has to be something disingenuous here. Something he's not telling me.

"You don't have to say it back," he promises, kissing my neck, lingering at my fluttering pulse. I tilt my head to make it easier for him. "My love has no expectations."

He calls me Bliss. My thoughts are reeling. Am I bliss? I don't know.

I'm cracked and peeling on the inside. Like a worn down home in dire need of rehabilitation. For the first time, though, there's a surety inside my heart, a knowingness that I'm finally strong enough to renovate.

I'm finally strong enough to be vulnerable.

Confident in my feelings, I say, "Luca, I—"

And that's when his phone rings.

30

Reverie

Luca jerks back like he's on fire and, to my dismay, scrambles for his phone inside his backpack. When he sees the caller, the joy on his face disappears, replaced with fear. It's impossible to not meet his fear with some of my own. What could make him this afraid? Luca is never afraid.

"I'm so sorry, *Bilaste*," he rushes out as he stands. "Give me one moment."

Frowning, I sit up to cover my exposed body with glitter. Reggie bounds over to bump my shoulder with his head. I plant a kiss on his soft snout and rub one of his ears.

"Hey cutie," I murmur, watching Luca pace, too far away for me to hear his murmured words. The concern on his face has me frowning. What could cause this type of reaction from him?

There's no way we'll return to the lighthearted mood as before. The floating sensation in my body fizzles away. Dread sinks its claws with each frustrated flick of his tail. Occasionally, he glances at me, but for the most part, I might as well not exist.

Even though whatever is going on appears important, it still stings. I was just about to admit that I loved him, too. But there are too many memories of men walking away when they're done. My hands turn clammy.

Luca's not the same.

Right after that thought is a mean voice whispering, *Are you sure?*

No, every time I've felt sure, I've been wrong. Doubt nibbles at my confidence.

While he murmurs to someone on the phone, I walk over to my clothes. As I dress, Reggie runs circles around me, using his wings to hop and fly, snapping his jaws at flickering bugs. He's absolutely adorable, even if he could turn me to stone.

Settling my shirt over my torso, I take another look around Cilyestia Pools and braid my wet hair. Was it only minutes ago that I leapt into the water?

Everything appears to glow from within itself, as if the glitter's alive. Maybe sometime soon, Luca can bring me during the day so I can release my rainbows. I'd love to see the water in the sunlight.

If he sticks around that long.

The thought trembles on my lower lip. Sucking it into my mouth, I bite down.

Luca's frozen in place now, silver eyes staring at the moons. The broad mountains of muscle in his shoulders are tight. I frown at his collapsed wings. It's as if they're a signal of how he feels inside. Whatever it is, it must be pretty bad. Concern flickers through me as he runs a hand through his already-mussed hair.

I'm about to round his wing when he spins, tucking away his phone. Anguish yanks at the corners of his eyes, weighing down the frown at his lips. Gone is every bit of joy from moments ago.

I reach for his hand, about to ask what's wrong, but he rushes out, "I'm so sorry, *Bilaste,* but I need to go. There's an emergency I must attend to."

My heart flutters, knowing what the nickname means, but then plummets to my toes. "Is everything okay?"

Something I can't decipher flickers across his expression before being schooled away. "No, but I can't talk about it." He snaps his fingers at Reggie and points at the backpack on the ground. "Come on, buddy. We have to go."

Reggie's reluctant as he steps into the backpack. Tucking his wings flat against his round furry body, Reggie ducks his head as Luca zips it closed. Luca slings it over his head, then snaps the straps at his chest.

"Luca ..." I'm shrinking on the inside. Normally, if I hesitate, he's there to catch me with a kind word. When he says nothing, something curdles in my heart. He holds out his arms, impatience rolling off him in waves. Everything within me turns small.

Without another word, I step closer so he can scoop me up.

"Hang on, *Bilaste*," he murmurs in my ear, nuzzling me with his forehead. The affection lightens my worry a little, but not enough. He launches himself into the sky with one powerful downward sweep of his wings. As we gain height in the sky, his body vibrates with ... *something.*

I press my head against his chest; his heart beats erratically. What could have this strong pillar of a man reduced to a nervous ball of silence? I've never seen him scared, but that's how he feels: scared.

Not knowing if it will help, I run my fingers over the back of his neck, hoping to bestow some semblance of calm on him. He kisses my forehead after a few minutes. I inhale his scent, wallowing in indecipherable surety that something bad is about to happen.

Against my best efforts, tears pool at the corners of my lashes. The wind eats the ones that fall.

I'm so lost in my worries, I only realize we're at my apartment building by the jolted landing. "Sorry," he says roughly, setting me on my feet. I stand, my legs like jelly. I face him and reach for his hand. It's damp, shaking under my hold.

"Luca, what's wrong? You can tell me about it, I promise."

His platinum eyes search my face as if there are secrets to discover. The pad of his thumb wipes away the lone tear as pain twists his features. He opens his mouth, closes it, then opens it again.

"I need you to remove the glitter, *Bilaste.*"

Remove the glitter? But he said ...

His lie, the betrayal, slices deep in the softened spots of my heart. My concern for him is crushed under the weight of his abandonment. No explanation. No reassuring words.

Nothing.

Within a breath, it's all sucked back into me. Not a fleck left on his body. Not even his ear canals — I made sure of it.

Voice bitter, I announce, "Done."

We hold our stare for too many heartbeats, and I feel like the Hells are swallowing me up. Is he running off to see someone else? Someone more important? After telling me he loves me? Was it all a ruse? Did he *trick* me?

Is there actually anything wrong at all?

The insecurities rage inside me, overwhelming every attempt to placate them. Unable to handle this raging river of suspicion in front of him, I cross my arms. His mouth firms into a thin line, like he knows exactly what's happening between us now.

"Reveric—"

I motion toward the sky. "Go on. You clearly need to be somewhere else. Don't let me stop you."

I didn't think anguish could be so painful to see on someone's face. He steps forward. I step back. The movement deepens the worry lines on his forehead.

Throat aching with unshed sobs, I say, "Go on. I'll see you tomorrow at the transport."

"Reverie, please. I don't have time to explain right now. Please wait until tomorrow?"

Maybe he's right; maybe this is easily fixed over coffee. I'm being hypersensitive because vulnerability is already terrifying for me.

"Fine."

This time, when he steps forward, I stay in place. He gives me a heart-wrenching, reverent kiss on my lips. My fingers curl into fists, resisting the urge to cling to his shirt and beg for an explanation.

Too soon, the kiss breaks. Forehead against mine, he says, "I love you, *Bilaste.* Please don't forget that."

I drop my gaze, trying to hide the whimper fighting for release.

Just say it back.

No, I can't. Not while he's leaving like this. He's hiding something.

Say it back!

This time, I grind the foolish thoughts into dust as I choke out, "Be safe."

One half of my heart steps back, looks toward the shimmering night sky, and takes to the clouds. Leaving me watching his shadow disappear into the darkness.

***

I slept like Slogoth shit. Tossing and turning all night, checking my phone obsessively. There are no missed texts. No missed calls. It's like Luca disappeared from the continent, leaving behind a wreckage inside of me.

Again.

I've texted repeatedly with no response. My imagination runs wild, considering everything that it could be. Maybe it's a gambling debt, and the mobsters threatened Kahlo. Maybe his apartment was burning down.

No, he'd tell me if that were happening.

This was something he didn't want to talk about. My instincts tell me it's tied to why he disappeared for a year, although I can't prove it. Yet. Today while we travel, I'm going to pester him for answers. He was patient and consistent with me; I can do that same.

I'm wide awake by the time my alarm goes off, already feeling like a ghoul. Sitting up, I rub my face. Checking my phone again, despite checking it twenty minutes ago, I'm disappointed to see no missed texts. But there is an alert for a new email from potential clients I met with last week. My aching heart flickers with excitement.

I've been hoping they'd hire me. It's a high-profile wedding, with a fashion influencer. It would boost my portfolio and maybe even help introduce me to other high-end clients. With the landlord breathing down my neck, and taxes due, every coral matters right now.

Opening the email, I skim the contents. The anticipation rots into confusion, anger, then rage.

Dear Ms. Songlight,

We were quite pleased to meet you last week and really love your work. Unfortunately, after meeting with Stone and Skies Visuals, we've decided to go in another direction. He was willing to work with our budget, and during our discussion, you were very clear about your pricing. We respect that; our budget is very specific. We know your work is worth a lot; it's unfortunately not within our reach.

Thank you again for meeting with us. We'll be sure to tell all of our friends about your work. Have a wonderful day.

Best,

Venerin

He lied to me. Luca *lied* to me.

With shaking hands, I place the phone on the nightstand. Staring at my wall, I draw my knees to my chest. A lone tear rolls down my cheek. I met with them last week, which means he had to have met with them in the last handful of days.

Which means he lied.

I'm not sure I can forgive this. Luca knows I've been hurt repeatedly with lies. Maybe he doesn't know the specifics, but he still *knows.* How can I trust his words ever again? Does he actually love me if he lied to me? Love isn't built on lies.

No, there's no way Luca Destau loves me.

This isn't love.

31

Luca

Stepping out of the hospital, feeling like decomposing dung, I vigorously rub my face, trying to clear away the exhaustion. I was up all night wondering about Reverie. My mother. The future.

I was so fucking selfish, telling Reverie that I love her without being completely honest. I was going to, but that doesn't matter now. Because I saw her tearful eyes. I'm under no illusions that when I see her today, the dynamic will have shifted back, at least a little. I'll have to re-earn those smiles ... if she'll ever let me.

I remember her face when I asked for the glitter to be taken away. The hurt was plain as day. But there was no way I could waltz into the hospital sparkling from head-to-tail tip. It would distract everyone who should be doing their job, like keeping my mother safe.

But I never thought I'd be desperate to become a disco ball again. It's a bewildering realization.

My phone rings. The hospital is a dead zone, so it's been silent all night. Sighing, I answer. "Yeah?"

"How is she?" Kahlo sounds worried.

"The worst she's ever been."

I hear someone, a female someone, whispering from the other side. Kahlo asks, "Is she better?"

"No."

He exhales a sigh of frustration. "I'm sorry, Luck."

"I hate that fucking nickname, Kahlo. I'm not lucky. There's nothing lucky about any of this."

"Look, you can't—"

"I told Reverie I loved her last night."

There's silence. More whispering. I swear it's Malona's voice, but that would require him to actually let a woman stick around. Finally, he says, "And?"

"There was nothing to say because the hospital called and I had to fly her home, Kahlo. Left her there without an explanation."

"Explain it to her, man."

The phone almost shatters in my hand; I'm so furious at the ignorant, simplistic response. "Oh sure, let me tell her exactly who she's falling in love with. I'm sure that will go over well."

"It could," he says in an uncharacteristically soft voice. "If she loves you, she won't care."

Reverie was about to say something last night, and my gut tells me it was a confession of her feelings. Interrupted by the worst news possible. It'll be a miracle if she opens up like that again any time soon.

"And if she doesn't love me?" Kahlo is silent long enough that I think he hung up. I check the screen, confused to see the call still connected. "Hello?"

"Luck, how could she not love you? What is there about you not to love?"

His kindness whittles me into a pinpoint of agony. "Too much, cousin. Too much."

"Tell her."

"Maybe." I glance at the clock. "I have to go. We're leaving for that destination wedding today to Miryath."

He swears. "That's today?"

"In three hours."

"Well, good luck. Talk to her, okay? Enjoy the caves. Send me pictures."

"Yeah, okay."

I'm about to hang up when he says, "Luca?"

Stunned at the normal use of my name, all I can say is, "Yeah?"

"You're my best friend, and I love you. Everything will be okay."

Emotions squeeze my throat, making it hard to believe. "I wish that were true, Kahlo. I really do. I love you, too."

***

The transport station is bustling with activity. All forms of transport leave from this station at all hours of the day, so it's always hectic.

I land on the launch pad and seek my favorite head of hair. I need to tell her today. All of it. No excuses. Hopefully, if I lay myself bare, she can forgive me. If I'm actually lucky, she'll continue to love me, even if she can never say it. I don't care if she ever does, as long as she keeps smiling at me.

Finally, I spot her in a transfer station line, standing with Yureka. The latter's here to drop Reverie off. They're chatting with excitement, but something is off with Reverie. Her shoulders are tight, and her smile doesn't reach her eyes. Her brain is probably being cruel right now.

Smiling to myself, I walk over to them. I can fix it. I've done it before; I can do it again.

Except when she spots me, there's nothing but absolute venom in her expression. It feels like a giant boulder punching my chest repeatedly, pommeling me into dust. Is she actually furious at my abrupt departure? I know it wasn't ideal, but I tried to reassure her before I flew off. She said we could talk today. What happened in the last eight hours?

Nervous, I come to a stop in front of them and shove a bastardization of a smile onto my face. "Morning, you two."

Yureka does a double take. "Are you okay? You look exhausted."

I nod, looking at Reverie. "It was a rough night. How did you sleep?"

Reverie purses her lips and for a second, I think she's going to refuse to respond. "Fine."

That's it. *Fine.*

"I barely slept," Yureka announces, not noticing the tension. "I'm so sad I can't go with you both. I've never been to Miryath. You both are going to have so much fun."

Reverie glares at me like I'm dung under her shoe. I search her face for clues. I expected perhaps a few steps back, but this is more than a few steps. This is square one. No, this is further beyond square one. The hate in her eyes makes little sense.

I resist the urge to invade her space as I ask, "Are you okay? What's wrong?"

Her brows lift in mock surprise. "Are you sure you care?"

"Of ... of course I care," I'm incredibly lost. Has she somehow gained amnesia overnight and forgotten my words? Care isn't even in the same realm of the words I'd use to describe my feelings for her. "Why would you think I don't?"

"Actions aren't quite matching words, Lucasta."

Why is everyone using my name differently today? "Are you really that mad at me? I'm sorry I had to leave, but I want to explain—"

"Don't. Bother." She turns away from me.

What the fuck?

The three of us look at the ceiling as our transport is announced. I'm wearing my travel gear setup, which consists of two backpacks carefully attached to one another on my back, with my light stands cinched against one of them. In front of Reverie are three suitcases. She really is an over-packer. Trying to appear nonplussed, I motion to two of them.

"Do you want me to take those?"

Reverie ignores me, struggling to direct all three. I step closer. "Reverie, let me take one." When I go to grab a handle, she slaps my hand away. I jerk it back, experiencing the sting more in my heart than on my skin.

Her eyes narrow into hateful slits as she hisses, "Don't touch my shit, Luca."

The foul words hit like an open-palmed slap. Yureka pauses, finally sensing something is very wrong. She inches toward Reverie, like I'm about to attack her friend.

Trying to keep the hurt out of my voice, I say, "I'm trying to help."

She sneers, eviscerating a part of my soul. "Your help is required at the wedding. No where else. Am I clear?"

"No," I say quietly. "I don't understand what happened. I'm truly sorry I had to leave last night, but—"

"We're professionals going to a gig, Lucasta. Nothing else. Am I understood?"

Her words are blisters on any remaining hope I had of being able to move forward with her. I might not know what's going on, but whatever it is, I probably deserve it. Maybe she found out about my mother and is rejecting me outright.

I don't know how she would've found out, but it's the only thing I can think of that would earn me such hate.

She turns away *again*, struggling with her suitcases.

I stand there, lost and broken as I watch the woman I love walk away.

32

Luca

The Pegasi carriage ride consists of the worst six hours of my life. It's a full carriage, with about twenty passengers. My wings relegate me to one of the specialized chairs, which Fate has cruelly ensured is on the opposite side of the carriage from my girl.

For six hours, I endure being ignored by Reverie. I'm sweaty and panicked. Every terrible outcome possible has raced through my mind, settling on one conclusion: Fate is telling me I deserve to be alone. To desire love is to be selfish. This is my punishment for thinking it was a possibility.

By the time we land in Miryath, I've mentally shredded myself to pieces. As we disembark from the carriage, I wait at the bottom of the stairs, but Reverie breezes past me.

At the front of the terminal, we're welcomed by a team of Elves wearing suits. One of them greets Reverie, taking her suitcases as he explains her clients arranged private transport. I load my bag into the back of the small train. It hovers off the ground, powered by light magyck.

This ride feels longer because she's forced to sit next to me. Our hips press together, but she's subtly leaning away. I watch in silence as she laughs with one of the male Elves, asking questions about the caves. Every smile she gives him, I want to rip from his eye sockets. He doesn't even know her. He doesn't know what her best smile looks like or how she shines in the dark.

She doesn't catch it, but I see him checking out her brand and even licking his lips once, like he wants to place his mouth where mine was only hours ago. I don't like it. Mid-conversation, he catches my glare. I dip my chin and reveal a fang. He lets the conversation naturally peter off.

It's becoming painfully clear that my hope of spending quality, wonderful time with Reverie will not be happening. When we arrive at the cave resort, she allows the Elves to take her bags and marches up to the check-in desk without a glance my way.

While she stews in righteous fury, I examine the space, searching for ideal spots for photos if the need arises.

Orcs always aim to bring the outdoors inside, so for the main entrance foyer, a large hole was bored through the rock, allowing a misty stream of sunlight to beam onto a large pool of water. That's the main source of light, casting everything into darkness.

The lounge chairs are plush, in different shades of gray and black to match the carved rock walls. The walls crawl with colorful, bioluminescent moss. Glowing bats flit around the tall ceiling. My wings twitch at the lack of sky; we haven't even descended into the depths of the mountain yet. This will be my last bit of sunshine for three days.

Dozens of people loiter in the entrance, most of them Orcs. With this wedding being so large, it's no surprise that the check-in desk has a long line. However, because the clients are Orc royalty, there's a private check-in area, which is where I find Reverie. The harried hotel concierge watches her with a lost look.

Heaving an exhausted sigh, I walk to the desk, only perking up when I realize Reverie is arguing with the check-in clerk.

"No, there must be some mistake. I didn't cancel the second room."

The Forest Sprite frowns, her long fingers flying over the keyboard as she double checks the computer screen. "I'm so sorry, ma'am, but your clients canceled the second room. They were under the impression your assistant wasn't coming."

Reverie exhales slowly, finding her patience. "I informed them my assistant wasn't able to come, but there were three of us. One room for me and my assistant, and one for my second shooter. That reservation was set months ago."

The Sprite, whose name tag reads Kaetlyn, gives Reverie a pained expression. "I'm sorry, but the reservation was canceled."

Shifting to lean on a hip, Reverie waves a hand in the air. "Is it possible to book one on my own? I'll pay for it myself."

Kaetlyn looks between the two of us. "Again, I'm deeply sorry for the inconvenience, but all the other suites are booked. As I'm sure you know, this is a rather large event, and the room block—"

"Fine," Reverie says abruptly. "Please give me the key."

While Kaetlyn registers us for the room, I whisper to Reverie, "I'll sleep on the floor."

Without looking at me, she mutters, "Yes. You will."

My bones feel hollow and my steps heavy as I follow her to the elevator, forced to watch her perky ass walk away from me as fast as possible, like we aren't headed to the same destination.

The elevator ride to negative-floor ten is torture. Without her suitcases, she clutches her elbows, shoulders bowed. Like it hurts her to be this mean to me. So why is she doing it at all?

"Reverie, can we talk—"

The elevator doors open, and she rushes down the hallway. Stabbing a fang into the inside of my lip, I bite back tears. This has easily turned into the second worst day of my life, the first being Mom's first hospital visit when she received her diagnosis.

Walking into our room might as well be like stepping into a dungeon cell, even if it's easily one of the most beautiful hotel rooms I've ever seen.

The pale rock floors are installed with up-lighting, offering a glowing source of stylish lighting. A fake window is installed in the wall, showing the outdoors on a projection. Perhaps to make people feel less claustrophobic. There are warmly lit lamps in every corner — I need to avoid those — and a decently sized bed in the center. No couch.

Behind the bed is a collage of different colored green moss, with hanging strings of moss over the mattress. The bathroom itself is a highlight. Even though I'll never get in it, there's a small thermal pool fed from the hot springs inside the mountain. The water glows from blue lights installed in the pool's wall. Thank the twelve goddesses that the nearby shower is big enough to fit me.

Overall, it's a comfortable, earthy aesthetic.

Except for the simple fact that I'll be sleeping on the chilly stone floor. The irony increases my self-hate. Perfect for a doomed man made of stone.

Our bags lay nestled in the suitcase holders. Reverie marches over to the titanic bed and snatches off a pillow. Throwing it at me with impressive vitriol, she seethes, "I'll ask for an extra blanket. Sleep anywhere but in the bed. I don't give a fuck if it's in the damn bathtub; it's just not near me."

"Okay."

My simple answer turns her face the color of a tomato. If she isn't careful, her head might actually implode from rage. Letting out an impressive growl of frustration, she furiously unzips her suitcase. Tossing out various pieces of clothing, she mutters under her breath.

"I can't believe I'm in this situation. It's my luck that at the biggest wedding of my career, I'm stuck in a hotel room with ..."

That last part is said too low to hear, but I suspect it isn't flattering toward me. All I can do is stand there, adrift from my normal confidence. From last night, when I bared my heart to her, to this hateful behavior ... it's the meanest I've ever seen her.

What happened?

When she brushes against me, her shoulder slams into my arm. I move with her so my tense muscles don't hurt her.

Behind me, I hear her pause. With the most venomous tone imaginable, she says, "Don't fucking touch me, Luca."

It would be stupid to point out that she ran into me, so I say nothing. Maybe I can go downstairs and turn on the charm; beg for a different place to sleep. At this point, a broom closet would be better than being assaulted with the hate intent on shattering my heart into unfixable pieces.

33

Reverie

I've never been so angry in my life. It's consuming. Deep down, I know it's not actually hate; it's heartbreak. He lied to me. And has the audacity to act not only like he's clueless, but like *I'm* the one breaking us apart.

He did that the minute he kept that contract a secret. Did he think the clients wouldn't reach out? Sometimes they don't. The email was far more transparent than others; that's certain. However, some potential clients feel the need to assuage their guilt at denying a vendor by giving an, *It's not you, it's us* spiel.

It wasn't just me, though, was it? It was *him*. Undercutting again. For what? Money? Is money that important to him?

It wouldn't be for me if I weren't in such a precarious position. Maybe I should've told him what my landlord is doing, but until recently — until *last night* — it wasn't something to tell him about. We've been finding a new equilibrium; figuring out this magnetism between us.

If he had just been honest when they decided to book him. Transparent. I would've been disappointed, but I would've understood. But no, he had to be deceitful.

Now, it's all gone to shit.

Which is why I'm in the bathroom getting ready to head to the bar. I'm going to drink my anger away. The wedding doesn't start until late afternoon tomorrow, since Orc weddings don't revolve around the sun. Plenty of time to nurse a potential hangover.

He can stay here, resembling a kicked chimeragon, doing whatever private pity party he's engaged in. It's not my concern.

After slipping into the shower to rinse off the scents of travel, I quickly slip on a tight-fitting dress. I refuse to acknowledge it, but I've chosen a dress that reveals more of my cleavage than ever before. I thought Luca would love it. It's a favorite, the color of Malona's pink wings. It exposes my veins and brand. Losing myself for a minute, my fingers flutter to the brand, the invisible press of Luca's lips lingering.

No.

Balling my fists at my side, I check my reflection. Slathering on lip gloss, I test out a smile. It's too tight across the tension in my face, like an ill-fitting mask.

Stepping out of the bathroom, I ignore his sharp intake of breath and march over to one of the purses I'd brought. Grabbing the white leather strap, I sling it over my bare shoulder. Taking my phone off its charger, I shove it into the bag and zip it shut.

Grabbing a pair of white heels, I slide them on. I take a second to admire my white toes; Malona and I'd gone for pedicures a few days ago in anticipation of me spending time in the thermal pools during this trip.

Frowning, remembering I'd pictured Luca there with me, I head to the door.

"Where are you going?"

Hand on the door handle, I pause, ready with a verbal blade to slide between his ribs, hopefully nicking his heart.

Something stops me though.

The painfully vivid image of the wonderment on his face last night seals my lips shut. For that version of Luca, the one I thought was real, I stay silent as I open the door and shut it behind me.

***

Having a photographic memory can be handy at times. When remembering a timeline or shot list. Perfect for winning arguments. I remember the words of every book I've read. Special dates for celebration? My mental calendar has it scribbled down forever.

Then there are times like these, where the memories are like an assault, stabbing me obsessively.

Luca catching me when I fall.

Him defending me to the DJ.

Kissing me under the stars.

Luca's worshipping touch under the glow of iridescent orbs.

His confidence as he reveals the depth of his emotions.

The scent of skies and earth enveloping me like a warm hug.

With each memory, I take a furious sip of my wine. There are a lot of memories; I've taken *a lot* of sips.

Already on my third glass, I stare at the stone bar top, wishing I was at Prestley's. He'd listen to me rant. Maybe toss me a bone in the form of a free thunderstorm foot massage with extra lightning.

The bartender here isn't much for conversing. He appears to be part Orc, part Goblin. It makes him terrifying to look at, being almost seven-feet-tall, with ears a foot long and jagged teeth overlapping his lips.

The bar itself is gorgeous, though, with the pale stone lit by ambient lighting, chandeliers, smooth music playing over a speaker, and a wall dedicated to stylish bottles of alcohol.

A pretty backdrop to my personal pity party — yes, I know, not unlike *Luca the Liar* — but I know where I'd rather be. If two pity parties joined forces, would it just be a party? What would Luca be like at a party? I bet he's fun. We'd have a blast together. I love being —

Shut up, brain.

I take another sip of white wine, crushing the rogue thoughts.

"Is this seat taken?"

For a split second, I'm taken to that fateful moment over a year ago, when a different, deeper voice had asked the same question.

I look up to find a very handsome Elf smiling at me. The same from the train transport. He'd been nice and a little funny. Not as funny as Luca, but enough that he could be a decent drinking partner.

I motion to the empty seat. "By all means."

The Elf sits. He's wearing the same outfit as before — a crisp white suit with a green pocket square. His black hair's slicked back, revealing pointed ears with simple diamond earrings in each lobe. He's too slick to be my type, but again, I'm not searching for love — just a drink.

"My name is Zkiel, by the way."

"Reverie."

"Reverie ..." he purrs. "What are you drinking, Reverie?"

I shrug, staring at my drink. "House wine. Not sure what it is."

Zkiel waves over the bartender and asks for the same. A flash of irritation curls my lip.

"I'm not going to sleep with you."

The Elf's unperturbed as he purrs, "Never say never."

My sour mood shifts to something darker. A muscle works in my jaw as I grind my molars. So that's how this is going to go. I see his eyes flick to my brand. My hands curl into fists at the urge to slap him. I'm a battleaxe desperate to be swung; this Elf is playing with a blade and doesn't even know it.

I'm so tired of men. It's exhausting to be reviled and revered for the same things. No one can trust a siren, but everyone wants to hear a song. No one likes Glyridites because it's a useless, messy power, but they want it as a party trick.

This man is like all the others. Especially with the way he licks his lips. It's not like how Luca watches me — like I'm something special. No, Zekiel studies me like I'm an exotic meal to take a bite out of.

"Well, I'm going to say never," I snap. "And if that's your intention, fuck off. I'm taken."

I freeze as that last part comes out. It was an unintentional admission, and I'm unsure if it's the truth. My fury makes it impossible to be objective.

The Elf's brows crease. "Is it that enormous Gargoyle? The one who glared at me the entire ride?"

Luca glared at him? I shove away the warmth that information gives me. "Yes. That one."

Zkiel makes a show of looking around. "Really? Where is he now? Leaving you all alone at the bar, too pretty to be ignored?"

Taking a slow sip of wine, I think of all the ways I could answer the question. Finally, I settle on, "He's occupied."

Zkiel's wine arrives, and he downs half the glass, those creepy blue eyes settling on my breasts. Licking his now-red lips lasciviously, he croons, "Well, if you were mine, I'd only be occupied with you."

"But she's not yours. So kindly go the fuck away before we have any issues."

The words, said in a low growl, take us both by surprise. Luca stands mere feet away, vibrating with fury. He wasn't there a second ago, which means he just now rushed up. His eyes scan my body, checking I'm unharmed — no, my pussy does *not* clench at that — then directs his frosty glare onto Zkiel.

"Sorry, I didn't know," the Elf responds smoothly, standing, leaving his wine. "She's a bit of a cold fish for a siren, anyway. She's all yours."

Luca's wings flare, and he takes a menacing step forward. I don't need him to defend me right now, though.

Before he can do anything, I say, "Hey." They both look at me. I grab Zkiel's wine. "You forgot your drink."

I toss it in his face.

Wine drips from his formally pristine facade. Rising, wobbling on my too-high heels, I hiss, "If you ever speak to me again, I'll report you for harassment. Am I clear?"

Zkiel gives me a disgusted snarl. "I should report you for singing to me against my consent."

My bravado falters as fear locks in. I'm too drunk for this confrontation. He could put me in prison for years. It's his word against a siren. "Please—"

"If you do that," Luca says quietly, "I will hunt you through these caves like your personal executioner until I find you. I'll cut the points off your ears, rip out your fangs, and let you discover what it means to choke on your own dick."

Zkiel pales and sputters, "Y-you wouldn't—"

Luca's claws shoot out from his fingertips and his fangs lengthen as he hisses, "You have *no fucking clue* what I'd do for her. Now get the *fuck* out."

The skeezy Elf scurries off without a backward glance, leaving me with the man who has both hurt and healed me.

Curling my lip with disgust, I point at him. "I had it handled."

His mouth twists in anger. "I will not be visiting you in prison, especially for something you didn't do."

"If I go to prison, you won't be on the visitor list."

"I'll literally claw my way through the stone to see you."

"Maybe I'll want to go to prison to be free of you."

He gives a flat look. "Even in prison, I'll continue to love you."

"You make love feel like a prison," I spit out. The regret is immediate, because it's the biggest lie I've ever told.

The blow lands. He visibly jerks back like I punched him in the gut. Right in front of me, this towering giant wilts. Even his wings droop.

"Fine." The word is excruciatingly quiet. "I'll never be a prison for you, *Bilaste,* ever. After this trip, we never have to see one another ever again, if that's what you wish."

"I do." *I don't.*

Luca holds my stare for a few tortuous seconds. Nods. "Okay."

He walks away. Leaving me feeling like the biggest dunghole to ever exist on this cursed continent.

34

Reverie

After another hour of stubbornly sitting at the bar, I go back to the room. It's quiet as the door snicks shut. A lone light on my side of the bed is on. Luca's laying flat on his back on the floor, pillow under his head, staring at the ceiling. Big, lavender hands rest on his chest, but his twitching tail betrays his silent turmoil.

His deadened silver eyes find mine. I avoid his gaze, filled with shame.

You should apologize.

Yeah, well, he should've been honest with me. This *isn't* my fault.

Silently, I pull pajamas from my suitcase. Not realizing I would share a room with him, I'd packed a rather revealing cotton ensemble. Cringing, I head to the bathroom and change out of the dress, leaning against the sink so I don't fall over.

Four glasses of wine were too much.

All of it's *too much.* Too much anger. Too much sadness. Too much confusion.

After going through my skincare routine, I examine my reflection. The fury has taken a toll; the light in my eyes is dull with grief.

I can't believe I said that to Luca. My cruel mind repeats his reaction; the way my words made him stumble, hitting like poison-tipped arrows.

Placing my hands on the counter, I hang my head, focused on breathing. Squeezing my eyes, I try to stave off the burning in them. Tears help nothing right now. I want to march out there and *demand* he tell me everything.

But when I swing the door open to check, his eyes are closed. His breath is steady. No twitching of the tail. Is he actually sleeping? Or is he pretending so as to avoid confrontation?

Tip-toeing to the bed, I quietly remove the excess pillows. Unwilling to examine why, I place them at the foot of the bed. Just in case he needs some.

As I'm about to crawl between the sheets, I glance at him again. His eyes are on me, face devoid of ... anything. The pain of seeing him so guarded shreds something in me. He's always full of life; this alternate version of Luca is excruciating.

Why couldn't you be honest with me?

I want to weep out the words, grieving for what he ruined with his duplicitous choice.

Swallowing the tightness in my throat, I slide between the sheets, pretending I don't care. Laying on my back, staring at the mossy strands, I can't help but wonder if he's still watching me. If I peeked over the edge of the mattress, would his eyes still be waiting for me?

My heart tells me yes.

So I tell it to shut up as I turn off the lap and roll to my side, glaring at the shadows until sleep sweeps me away.

***

"You sang me into liking you. I know you did!" Toro gave me a furious glare, his green pointed ears flattening. He shoved a finger at me. "I should report you!"

I sat on my couch, crying. "I didn't, I promise. Why would I do that?"

"Everyone knows sirens can't help themselves."

Lifting my phone, I pointed at the evidence. "Are you doing this because I found out you're cheating?"

Toro's disgusted, refusing to look at the photos of him at a nightclub last night, sucking tongues with a Sprite. "I can't cheat if you tricked me, Ree."

"I didn't trick you," I pleaded. "Why are you saying that? You knew I was a siren when we met."

"Maybe you sang me into being okay with that."

Feeling hopeless, I sagged. It would be impossible to fight against something I could never prove. I thought he was different, but I always thought that. They never were. My siren side was a failsafe against men's cruel behavior. Don't want to stick around? Throw around some accusations, cowing me into never speaking up.

Toro's face transformed, and the pit in my stomach deepened. My muscles tensed as he came to sit next to me. Alarm bells rang as he faced me, face sad.

"Ree, I don't know how I can believe you. How can anyone believe a siren?" His clammy hands brushed against my cheek, then trailed down my shoulder. Goosebumps prickled as my instincts told me to run.

But instead of bolting out the door or telling him to fuck off, I froze as he leaned in. His breath was hot on my face, wrinkling my nose.

With a tone meant to console, Toro says, "Let's have our break-up sex and be done with it."

I gave him an incredulous look. "You cheated, but you expect me to fuck you?"

"If you don't, I'll tell everyone what you did."

His green eyes darkened. The smirk I loved tilted his cheek, revealing fangs. Reminding me of a sphinx holding its still-squirming prey. I couldn't believe I'd trusted him.

He was forcing me to do something I had no choice in. This curse of flesh and sound has always been my demise.

So, I quietly closed my eyes, surrendering. If I didn't, who knew what else he'd do?

***

"Reverie!"

Sobs rip from my throat, yanking me from the nightmare. Barely aware, I curl into myself, horrified by the memory assaulting my mind. The scents; sounds; touches. My body shakes with residual fear. So many nights after, waiting to be arrested. It took weeks for me to feel safe again. The shame dug deep into me, turning my insides to ichor.

"Reverie." Big, warm hands gently rock my arm. A quiet, velvet voice murmurs, "It's okay. Shhh, you're okay. It's a bad dream."

My eyes bolt open, fear shooting through my veins. I smack the hand away, scuttling backward. "Don't. *Stop.* Please ... *Don't.*"

I choke on the last word, grabbing a pillow to hide my body. The hands pull away, leaving me cold. Shivers shake my whole body as a headache throbs in my skull.

The lamp on my nightstand is on again, casting a glow over Luca's shoulder. His concerned expression has me wanting to curl up in his arms. My body twitches, ready to do just that, but then my brain catches up.

The email.

His lies.

My determination is to burn this bridge so wholly, it's ashes.

Another keening cry rips out from between my lips. I curl into the pillow, trying to muffle the sound. That he's witnessing this rawness is almost too much to bear. Newfound shame heats my skin. Toro isn't here for me to scream at, but Luca is. The two are not the same, but somehow, Luca's betrayal hurts worse.

He rests both hands on the spot where I'd been sleeping. Those powerful wings are half-spread as if he'd be able to fight my nightmares.

Luca was supposed to be different, but he's a liar, too. How can I trust him again?

"Why did you have to lie?" I whimper, unable to look at his distraught expression. The agony splices me in two, and I cry out again into the pillow.

"What?"

The confusion in his tone makes me scream. Without the pillow, someone would surely call security. When the feral release is over and my throat is raw, I furiously blink away tears as I give him a scathing glare.

"Go back to sleep, Luca. Leave me alone. I just want everyone to leave me *alone.*"

His wings slump further as he sits back, appraising my demeanor. It makes me want to scream again.

Why did you have to lie?

Luca stares so long, I almost march into the bathroom to sleep in the shower. Before I can, he returns to his spot on the cold stone.

Leaving me to cry myself to sleep.

35

Luca

I still don't understand her fury. I've laid on this cold floor, the single pillow under my head, staring at the ceiling as I run over everything I've ever done or did that would warrant this treatment.

Her words repeat in my head, trapping me in my personal hell.

You make love feel like a prison.

Why did you have to lie?

I've never intended to make her feel trapped. Have I done that? Am I so desperate for her love that I've been suffocating her this whole time?

And that nightmare? I'd rather shred my wings with a dull knife than ever hear her cry like that again. I'd been dozing, woken by the most wretched sob. When I realized it was from her, I decided waking her was more important than respecting her space.

Anguish twisted her face into an unrecognizable expression when she demanded that I leave her alone. She'd rather be alone in bed than receive any form of comfort. It makes my body heavier than a pile of boulders.

Sleep came in brief spurts. Every time she moved, my eyes flew open. She tossed and turned so much, she gradually came to stillness at the edge. I haven't taken my eyes off of her since, soaking in every detail. Despite the ragged exhaustion tightening her face, the colors of her body twinkle. I'm grateful that her breath is steady; I hope she's able to get some rest.

As the fake sun rises outside the simulation window, I've concluded that she's somehow either found out about my mother or ... she found out about the wedding I booked, by undercutting her. Clients don't always email past vendors written rejections, but if they did that ... it could explain everything. It could explain why she asked me why I'd lied.

The more I consider it, the more I think that's the reason. Finding out about my mother wouldn't be beyond the realm of possibility, but it's extremely unlikely.

If she discovered my deceit, my horrible but necessary choice, it would explain why she looks at me as if she wishes she'd never met me.

But would she truly throw away everything because of money? Or is it because I failed to inform her immediately? Would she take it as a lie? Was it a lie?

Who the fuck am I kidding? Of course, it was a lie.

When her eyes flutter open, there's a split second where I can tell she's forgotten her hate. A smile plays with her sweet mouth; it cuts deeper than her cruel words because it's not real.

Seeing the pain on my face, understanding dawns. Her whole expression twists into the familiar, expected anger. She rolls away, robbing me of her beautiful face.

Even if her rejection scrapes my heart from between my rib cage, she needs to know some of it.

"Reverie." I whisper her name, but I know she hears me when she shifts under the comforter. "Reverie, we need to talk."

"No."

"We can't go the whole day without talking."

She stuffs a pillow over her face, muffling her words. "Yes, we can, because we're professionals."

I sit up, grimacing at the crick in my wing. Sleeping on the floor was Hells on my wings. "No, I think we need to discuss what you found out."

With a deep, unearthly growl of frustration, she throws the pillow away from her face. It flies through the air and hits a lamp. It shatters. She bolts upright, eyes wide at the mess.

I crack a weak smile. "I have a lamp budget. I'll pay for it."

Incredulous, she hisses, "What?"

I sigh, not about to spend precious time explaining my necessary lamp budget. "Never mind. We need to talk about what you found out."

Her expression's icy, her bright eyes like chips of ice. She's more stubborn than most Gargoyle males I know. "What do you think I found out? Please. Enlighten me; tell me what you should've told me days ago."

Okay, so my assumption is correct. "Reverie, I know you're mad that I got the contract, but—"

"It's not about the contract!" She shouts. I flinch. She jerks back with wide eyes. Reverie lowers her voice, hissing, "It's *not* about the contract. It's about you not telling me about underbidding." Her voice wavers. "It's about you telling me you *love me* while *lying* to me."

Hearing it from her lips, all of my deepest fears are realized. I've been so afraid of her hating me, I've refused honesty. The avoidance of conflict has destroyed us. This is all my fault, even if my reasoning is sound. What's logical on paper rarely aligns with what's logical in our hearts.

"I'm sorry, I needed the money, Reverie," I plead, hating the desperation braided into the words. "Please believe me, if I had another choice—"

She prowls to the edge of the bed, her movements resembling a mountain cat about to claw my face off. I'd let her if it meant she would touch me. Talk to me.

"Money is more important than love? Is that what I'm understanding? Piles of corals stashed in your high-rise apartment and your private office and your high-end clients are more important to you than *loving me?*"

A sparkling tear trails down her cheek. I move without thinking, rising onto my knees. "Reverie, I—"

"My landlord has threatened to evict me, Luca. They're threatening to throw me out on my ass until I come up with hundreds of corals for some Pegidung made-up clause or whatever. And you know what?"

Her voice cracks, right along with my heart. "I have to figure it out because being a siren is a *curse.* They said it was some bogus siren fee. They threatened to turn me in for Singing them into lower rent. My nightmare? Was just another man taking advantage of it."

Her next words are barely audible, but I catch every word. "My bloodline *haunts* me, Luca."

The shame, already leeching off my sanity, purrs at the fresh slice of knowledge of how I've hurt her.

Just as much as the world has.

I can't let her think it's about the money. I'd give up every coral if I could, if it didn't hurt my mother.

Closing my eyes, I brace myself. Once I tell her everything, there's no going back. She'll either continue hating me, or she'll ... I don't know what she'll do. She's more unpredictable than a rabid griffon.

"My mother is really sick, Reverie," I plead, lacing my fingers together in prayer, hoping she'll listen. I feel both dread and freedom as I divest myself of half a secret. "She's in the hospital. The fees are astronomical because of her ailments. I'm trying, but it was an impossible choice."

For a split second, I straddle the line between confession and realization. Time stands still as her eyes search mine, the words processing.

When their meaning sinks in, she reels back like I've punched her. Her voice is barely audible when she says, "What?"

I nod furiously, grasping for the sliver of understanding she's showing. "She was diagnosed the day after I met you. It's one of the reasons I never called. Her required care is consuming. It costs money for me to have someone watch her at home if she isn't in the hospital. I'm barely staying afloat as is."

My chest heaves as I try to calm my hyperventilating breaths. I can't live with myself if she won't listen to this. I should've told her about my mother before now. She's a beautiful soul — she would've led with empathy. I know this; yet, fear kept me in a chokehold.

Sitting back on her heels, she absorbs my words, stunned. Her anger visibly drains away. Every bit of its disappearance fills me with foolish hope. She places her hands on her bare thighs.

Face drawn with devastation, Reverie's mournful as she says, "Luca, that's awful. Why didn't you *tell* me?"

"Because I'm a fucking idiot, that's why," I say bitterly, staring down at the stone, too full of shame to look at her. "Because I've been terrified you'll reject me."

Her jaw drops. "You think I would reject you over a sick mother?"

"No," I say quickly. "It's not that at all."

Silence hangs between us, devoid of everything else I should say. I'm not strong enough. Nausea rolls through my stomach, my body preferring to spill vomit instead of words. Sweat trickles down my spine. It feels like my heart is about to burst with terror.

Reverie cocks her head like a predator, homed in on my micro-expressions. The hair on the back of my neck stands up. For the first time in my adult life, I want to fly away and never return.

"What's the other reason?" The words are smooth like the flat of a knife.

The question takes me by surprise. I blink furiously, trying to understand. "What?"

With an even tone, Reverie says, "You said your mother is *one* of the reasons you disappeared. What is the other reason?"

And there it is.

Vomit burns up my throat. I can't tell her right now. Not only is my body refusing, but this is the worst timing possible. The worst mindset possible. With her hair still tousled from sleep and me, with tears in my eyes? It's wrong. This isn't a discussion for an emotionally charged moment.

When I shake my head, disgust fills her face. Rushing out the words, I say, "This isn't the right time to discuss it. After the wedding, Reverie.

We have too much to focus on for us to have an even deeper conversation right now."

Scoffing, she blows me off with a roll of her blue eyes. "Fine."

Scooting off the bed, she stands. I remember the last time she stood before me, swathed in glitter. The dichotomy is devastating.

With an impassive cadence and flat expression, she says, "Until you have the courage to be fully honest with me, we're over. We'll work together today, and *well*, because my clients deserve it. But when we go home in two days, if you haven't told me, know I won't be interested ever again." She leans over, condescending as she snarls, "Am I clear?"

I swallow hard, almost choking on the twisted pain filling me up. "Very."

***

We eat breakfast at the restaurant at different tables. We prepare our gear in silence. We rarely make eye contact. As we professionally discuss what needs to be done today, I keep my tone detached. She does the same. It's like we're two strangers forced to work together.

Focusing on any one thing is impossible. My mind's split in so many directions: my mother; Reverie; my job. What's left stews in my inevitable future of being alone.

The wedding begins in an hour. Reverie's already left, demanding staggered arrivals. I'm staring at myself in the suite's mirror, full of hate for the man in the mirror. He looks back at me, haggard and gaunt with grief.

"You fucking did this," I hiss at him. Turning away, I stalk over to my gearbox. My cameras used to give me joy, but right now, they're merely anchors to survival. Mine; my mother's. If I sell them and my apartment, I can keep Mom in her home until she dies. Maybe I can find some office job to help pay for Mom's care.

But that wouldn't prepare me for my own future. The fallout after she finally dies and I'm left to pick up the shattered pieces.

Now is not the time.

Time to spend hours suffering while I have a few last moments with the woman I love. Because once she knows the whole truth, she'll run in the opposite direction.

Anyone would.

36

Reverie

Maybe it's cruel, but I can't stand being around Luca right now. The lies are piling up, and there's, apparently, more revelations to come. I don't know who I fell in love with at this point. Luca having a sick mother is horrific, but why couldn't he tell me that?

I know I'm rough around the edges, but do I really come across as someone who wouldn't care? Or would run away from a challenging time period? I've known nothing *but* challenges. What's one more?

My heart and mind are at odds. My heart wants to rest his head in my lap and let him unburden himself while I play with his hair. On the other side is my brain, furious at the needless deception.

As I roll my gear down the hallway to the elevator, I run through the memory of two nights ago. The way he catapulted off of me to take the phone call. It had to be about his mother. That I could understand, but ... why wouldn't he tell me about her? Has she gone rabid? Cruel to the point of unforgivable? Abuses him?

This question loops in my mind, making me dizzy with anxiety. Why didn't he trust me with the information? What else is he hiding? What is he refusing to share? He's one of the most logical people I know; none of this makes sense.

Knowing there's something worse than his mother that we can't discuss before the wedding has my hands shaking.

What's worse?

What is worse?!

The exhaustion of barely sleeping makes my movements sluggish, even after drinking two cups of coffee. Yet, I'm forced to dig deep to find the dregs of energy left.

As the elevator reaches my destination, I focus on my breath while I close my eyes, counting to five. Weddings wait for no one. Furiously punching down everything else, I allow my wedding mask to appear. A smile forms on my face as I step into the getting ready suite. My rainbows fill the space, announcing that a version of me has finally arrived.

***

This wedding is one of the biggest I've ever booked. The couple, Ulysa and Argot, are Orc royalty, with his father being the king of the Zeplat clan. A client referred me, and if I can pull this wedding off, it could elevate my brand in unanticipated ways.

Orcs often have large-scale events, with this one as no exception. There are over four hundred guests from all over the continent. The wedding party has fifteen on each side, which makes their images take forever. The clients also forewent the First Look, which never bodes well for a day like this.

The downside of this event is that it takes place entirely in caves. Orcs primarily reside in artfully carved out mountains, and while they also indulge heavily in opulence to balance it out, I'm already craving the sunshine. My Glyridite side prefers the outdoors, where my rainbows are the most powerful.

Luca must be restless. This isn't an ideal place for fliers, even if the ceilings are usually at least a few dozen feet high, with the atriums being hundreds.

After I release the rainbows, I immediately dive into hunting down moments worth capturing. Luca shows up about five minutes after me, only hesitating for a split second when we lock eyes. He looks exhausted, but he wipes it away with a brilliant smile when a bridesmaiden appears, ushering him toward the pile of details.

Wedding clients see the best side of wedding vendors — *usually* — which means even if your world is falling apart, you *have* to try to keep it together. It's not perfect, since we aren't robotics, but we're expected to be flies on the wall, occasionally therapists, and get as many stellar photos as possible.

Luca knows this; he wouldn't be one of the best if he didn't. I doubt his life has been so perfect that he's never had to compartmentalize. However, today is more intense than usual, and it's showing.

It starts simply enough. Within the first thirty minutes, he almost drops the entire pile of details, barely catching an ancestral crystal vase before it shatters. My heart catapults into my throat for that one.

During the wedding party images, he knocks over a bridesmaiden with his wing. He's so incredibly cognizant of them, it takes me by surprise. He apologizes profusely, quietly helps her clean the hem of her dress, and increases his awareness ... but it's still odd.

By the time we're heading into the ceremony space, his tail's lashing angrily. I catch him flexing his jaw, as if trying to stamp down whatever it is brewing inside him.

All of it temporarily leaves my mind when we reach the ceremony location. Pausing at the doorless entrance, I gape at the scene.

The cave is the size of four clawball stadiums, capable of fitting up to a thousand guests. The ceilings are at least two hundred feet high, covered in blue glowworms nestled in rainbow colored moss. It's Negla Moss, my favorite kind because it makes me feel less strange with my own colors. From the moss hang vines at least a hundred feet long. Around the vines are Cave Sprite's homes. As the smallest species of

Sprites, no bigger than a small bird, they create multi-level abodes that resemble crystals. They love light and color, so each home glows with warm golden light.

The flooring's made of carefully laid stone with moss as grout. Centered in the cave is the ceremony site. It's a small island, big enough for the officiant, the couple, and the wedding party. Right above the site is an enormous chandelier, about fifty feet in size, that adds additional soft light to the experience.

A small stream surrounds the raised flat stone, reflecting the glowing lights. Smooth wooden chairs make a circle around the ceremony site, so every guest has a good view. They've also skipped a wedding arch to ensure uninterrupted views.

On the cave walls are more orb lights, sconces with flickering fire, and the couple splurged on flickerbugs, a species of sentient insect that floats around, twinkling its butt to a pulsing, silent beat.

Ulysa adores the scent of lavender, so Argot splurged on pumping the scent into the large space. In the corner is a string quartet playing familiar songs I hear all the time at weddings.

The entirety of it all takes my breath away. Sometimes, weddings are difficult, but it's a privilege to witness this level of beauty, curated or not, and take photos of *everything.*

Editing this wedding is going to be so much fun.

I glance at Luca, and I'm pleased to see him staring at the scene slack-jawed. He's never hesitated to enjoy the gorgeousness all around us. It's one of the many things I love about him. My anger toward him softens.

"It's stunning, isn't it?" I murmur, scouting out the best spot for our gear. There are already at least a couple hundred guests picking their seats, so we'll have to be careful where we put it so it's not in the way.

"Yes. It is."

He's watching me with a soft, yearning expression.

It hitches my breath, but I shoo away the butterflies in my belly. "I think over there," I point to a spot not too far away, "will be a good spot for our stuff. What do you think?"

His face goes blank as he glances at where I'm recommending. "Yes. That works." Without asking, he slides my gear bag off my shoulder. "I'll bring this over so you can get started." Luca glances up. "Do you want flight shots?"

The aloofness stings so deeply, I don't have the energy to protest against him grabbing my gear bag. I nod, worrying my lip with my teeth. His detachment worries me; it shouldn't, because we're basically broken up, even though we were actually never together ... *ugh,* why is this so confounding?

Luca walks off without another word, leaving me to simmer in turmoil.

***

The ceremony was beautiful. Ulysa came down the aisle wearing a pale blue dress made of satin, the color complementing her pastel green skin. Argot watches her with tears in his eyes, which might become one of my favorite photos of the day.

Every time I capture the perfection of wedding days, it makes my soul sing, like I've captured the world the way I want to see it: full of beauty.

I know you're desperate to see beauty in the world, because you don't feel it in yourself.

Luca's words echo in my hollow mind, making me stumble. Was that really less than two days ago, in Cilyestia Pools? When he, without even trying, helped me embrace the side of me that holds so much stigma.

When the officiant does the ancient handfasting ritual that involves the entire wedding party, each of them vowing to support the couple in the years to come, it's like a vise around my heart. At my wedding, *if* I ever have one, I'd only have a few people.

I glance at Luca, who's quietly flying above us, getting some of the best angles of the day. He doesn't have a lot of people either. A wedding with him would be intimate. We could—

No.

No thinking about Luca as a groom.

By the time the ceremony is complete, two hours later, I'm ready to sit. Unfortunately, the family portraits need to be done now before the reception begins.

As I'm wrangling the family with the wedding planner's assistance, I hear a loud shatter followed by a chorus of gasps. Alarmed, I search for the sound, dismayed to find Luca staring at the ground. One of his lenses lays in pieces against the moss. He must've dropped it.

His bleak expression softens my anger. Those lenses are not cheap, and since he just admitted he's barely staying afloat, I'm fairly certain I know what's going through his mind right now.

Without a word, I grab one of mine and walk over, handing it to him. I don't have to tell him to be careful — I know he will be. But my concern is mounting. He refused to speak to me about what's bothering him, and we're paying the price.

The only issue is … how steep will this price be?

37

Reverie

The answer comes too soon. We're winding down the family portraits, and it's been Hells. I'm required to be engaging, full of smiles, while I direct the large groups of Orcs. There's always a groomsman with an inappropriate joke, and today is no exception.

Of course, it wouldn't be a wedding without someone there thinking they're my director. It can take the form of a pushy mom, an overzealous maid of honor, or, like today, an incredibly annoying aunt.

Matilda, said aunt, stands next to me, barking orders at her family. At first, I'm polite, hoping she gets bored. When she makes a recommendation, to appease her, I listen. When she screams at everyone *"to look happy,"* I catch myself giving a look of incredulity. She unfortunately sees it before I can wipe it away.

Glaring at me, she challenges, "Do we have a problem?"

Undeterred, I say, "No problem, but wouldn't you prefer to relax and go have a drink at cocktail hour? I hear Ulysa had a custom drink picked out."

The female Orc narrows her purple glowing eyes at me. "Are you giving me attitude? I'm the aunt. You're the photographer."

Now I can't hide my irritation. "I'm also a person."

"You're a gimmick." Her eyes sweep over me dismissively.

Aside from having to ignore any personal problems, a wedding photographer also has to exude excellent customer service at any point. So instead of snapping back at her, like she deserves, I dismiss her by pursing my lips and focusing on my job.

The scent of petrichor announces Luca's arrival at my side. "Is everything okay?"

"Why wouldn't they be?" the aunt snaps, as if he were asking her.

I offer him a small smile, hissing through my teeth, "Nothing I can't handle."

"What do you mean, *handle?* I'm not something to be *handled.*"

The shrill words cause me to wince. I forgot Orcs have excellent hearing.

Before we can respond, Aunt Matilda stalks off, snatching a glass of femire off a waiter's tray.

"Goddess, she's a piece of work," Luca mutters.

I shrug. "Aunts."

We share a knowing smile, a temporary truce over shared celebration struggles.

Then Luca clears his throat. He jerks a thumb over a wing. "Uh, I'm just going to ..."

Face falling, I nod. "Yeah, good idea."

The rest of the photos go well, since Matilda disappeared. The brief photo session with Ulysa and Argot is wonderful. They're so physically affectionate, it's almost uncomfortable, but it makes for glorious images.

When the wedding planner arrives to escort them for a quick break, I head over to my gear to switch memory cards.

I think we were safe from further confrontation, but Aunt Matilda reappears, walking over like she owns the place. Or hired me herself.

She stands a couple of feet from me, glaring at me while I zip up my gear back. Pretending to be focused on checking my lens, I ignore her, but entitled guests like these can be like starving hounds gnawing on a bone until all the marrow is gone.

"Excuse me."

So much for wishful thinking. Holding back a frustrated sigh, I stand, shoving my fists into my pockets. "Yes, ma'am?"

"You were incredibly rude before. You better adjust that attitude before the reception. I'd hate to tell my niece how rude you are."

Schooling my features, I say evenly, "Ma'am, I'm just doing my job."

Her eyes flash with anger. "Well, do it better. Are you new to your job? You appear to be an amateur."

My cheeks warm with anger. What the fuck is this woman's problem?

To make matters worse, Luca stalks over, radiating anger. "Don't speak to her like that."

I hold up a hand, silencing him. Normally, I love his defense of me, but this is *not* the time or place. If anything, he's undermining me.

To Messy Matilda, I say, "Ma'am, you're very welcome to share your thoughts with your niece. I'll address them with my client if she has questions."

Aunt Matilda curls her lip, looking me over before sending a withering glare at Luca. "Maybe I'll do that."

I give the female Orc a saccharine smile. When she's finally out of earshot, I whirl on Luca.

"Don't you ever do that again. I'm the lead photographer, not you. It's my job to deal with these guests and defend myself."

Luca's wings twitch. "She was being rude to you. I'm not about to let—"

His audacity shatters the fragile truce between us. Checking to make sure we don't have an audience, I snatch his elbow, digging my nails into his soft skin. He freezes in place, silenced by my scathing glare.

Keeping my voice low, I hiss, "You need to come with me *right now.*"

Letting go of his elbow so it doesn't look like I'm dragging a toddler across the ceremony site, I march toward an empty hallway. We have about thirty minutes before the reception grand entrance; it'll have to be enough time. Checking doors, I find one unlocked and barge in, ushering him inside.

It's an unoccupied office, with a large desk on the far side of the room. Bookshelves line the wall, and a fake window shines dim golden light into the shadowed space, dust particles dancing in the projected sunbeam.

Locking the door behind us, I stare at the Gargoyle in front of me. He stares at the floor, tail wrapped around his ankle. He might be close to a foot taller than me, but his energy shrinks him.

"We can't continue like this." I put my hands on my hips. Trying to be as calm as possible, I say, "You're going to tell me right the fuck now what you're hiding. Because if you fuck up one more time, I'm going to have to dismiss you. I suspect I don't have to explain how that would reflect on my business."

Dull mercury irises lift to mine, full of sadness. His expression twists into one of anguish. My anger disappears in an instant, replaced with fear. "This isn't a good time."

My hand twitches with the urge to smack some sense into him. "You know what else isn't a good time? You toppling over a guest. Dropping gear. Almost destroying a two hundred-year-old crystal vase. Confronting guests. *That's* not a good time."

Luca peers down at his claws with hunched shoulders and a ticking jaw. "I'm sorry. I'll do better, I promise."

The apology isn't good enough. It's my career on the line right now. It's my heart on the line, too. "I'm serious; I cannot have you continuing this way. *We* can't continue this way. You need to be honest with me, so we can move on."

"Once you know, there won't be a 'we.'" The words are barely above a whisper.

I throw up my hands with a frustrated growl. "You don't *know* that, Luca, because you won't even give me a chance to decide."

His brilliant eyes glimmer through his lashes. The tiny spark of hope in them cracks the center of my sternum. It's so painful, I want to rip out my heart and give it to him, to take that sadness away.

Luca's mouth opens, then closes. His body jerks, as if it's fighting against whatever it is he's hiding.

My restraint snaps, and my desolate, black soul breaks free. His face blurs as tears immediately begin falling down my face. "Why don't you *trust me*, Luca? Let me decide for myself?"

His head snaps up, realization widening his eyes. His wings smack together as he falls to his knees. The floor shakes under my feet as he lands. Reduced to a half-version of the titan I love, I watch Luca fall apart. Fear becomes a writhing, despicable parasite in my chest, thundering my heart to a painful speed.

"Reverie, I—" Luca's voice cracks, reduced to a sob.

This reaction has my unshed tears breaking free. I'm close to hyperventilating, watching him fall apart. All of my anger and hurt are forgotten as I rush to him, falling on the floor in front of him.

Pressing a hand to his heart, I whisper, "Tell me."

Luca's warm hand covers mine. "I know I should've told you, but I'm so terrified, Reverie. I'm scared all the time. My mother ..."

He inhales a shuddering breath, fingers curling around my hand like an anchor. "My mother has Fletchling's Disease."

Time stands still. Surely, I misheard him. Every fiber in my body goes taut, ready to snap. Because it's hereditary, which would mean ...

His free hand miserably wipes at the tears soaking his lilac cheeks. "The doctors estimate I have maybe about twenty years before symptoms show. My mother is only in her late fifties, and she just had her third full-body episode. That's why I had to leave the other night."

My throat burns with unshed sobs. This ... this is unspeakable. Everything clicks into place immediately. I reach up with my free hand and brush a loose hair off his sweaty face. Right now, he needs my strength, not my grief.

"How long does she have?"

Luca sniffles and releases a burdened sigh. "This past year, she's deteriorated rapidly. Right now, she's in the hospital, still turned to stone. They don't know if she'll shift back this time."

I can't think. I can't *breathe.* Fletchling's Disease doesn't make Gargoyles shift into their flying form — it turns them into literal rock. It's irreversible in the final stage, and currently, there's no cure.

This is an unimaginable confession. He was right; we should've waited, but how was I supposed to know?

Because you wouldn't listen.

He tried yesterday, but I rebuked him at every turn. Goddess, the things I fucking said to him. I'm such a stubborn fucking fool. How the absolute fuck are we supposed to go out there with happy faces now?

Luca grabs both of my hands, rubbing his thumbs over the tops. "*Bilaste,* I'm a selfish man. I tried, you know. I tried to leave you out of it by never calling after we found out. Why would anyone want to be with someone who is a guaranteed burden? One day, too soon, I will become stone, leaving anyone who loves me to mourn me for decades after."

Somehow, he shrinks in size as he whispers, "I can't do that to you. I've been *so selfish,* Reverie. Desperate for a sliver of joy with you. I'm so sorry I've hurt you. I'd rather cut off my wings than do it again."

With unparalleled grief, he kisses my knuckles, then says, "I understand if you want to walk away. Truly, I would understand. I'm so grateful for the time we've already had."

My whole body rattles with shared suffering. He thinks after all this, I'd still walk away?

Luca's head falls as he says, "But *I love you,* Reverie. Wholly and completely. I don't care if you're covered in glitter or sing me to my death. My heart and soul are entirely yours to do whatever you want with."

Finally, sitting in front of the decimated man in front of me, everything inside me burns, becoming ash. Because how can this man think he's that unloveable?

I pull my hands out of his grasp and cup his face. He's trembling. "Luca."

He tries to pull away, squeezing his eyes tight with remorse. I hold his jaw firmly. "Luca. Look at me."

Eyes the color of storm clouds focus on my face. It's easy to remember every moment I've had with this man. Luca has been nothing but patient, supportive, protective, and sweet. He's pissed me off, but he's lifted me up far more often. And that's what matters most.

"Lucasta Destau, you are the most kindhearted man I've ever met. You're brilliant and creative."

His lower lip wobbles, and he chokes on a sob. When Luca tries to avert his gaze again, I squeeze his chin, shifting his focus back to me. "*Hey.* Look at me when I'm confessing my love to you."

Dejectedly, he drags his eyes back to mine. Mimicking him, I grab each of his hands and brush my lips across his knuckles.

With a watery smile, I say, "That can be enough, Luca. That's twenty years of bliss. So many don't find that, let alone *twenty years*."

My words appear to break the dam inside him; he's held so much within himself, suffering in silence. I'm filled with shame that he felt afraid to tell me before this. That he thought I'd reject him. But how could he not feel that way? I've rejected him repeatedly at this point.

I've been so afraid of his rejection that I served it first, but he never faltered. He's led with hope, hiding the fear.

Grabbing the back of his head, I bring our foreheads together. "Luca, I love you. I'm so sorry you felt like I wouldn't care or would be furious with you. I'm so sorry that I pushed you away so many times, you didn't feel safe sharing with me. I won't do that again, I promise."

His shoulders shake with horrific sobs; he collapses into my arms. Running my fingers through his hair, I allow my own tears to fall. Has he ever truly faced the forecast of his future? He's right; so many would've rejected him.

But I won't. I can't.

"You're more than a diagnosis, Luca. I know it's scary, but you don't have to do it alone."

It's been a month since he walked back into my life, with that cocky grin and kind eyes. Maybe it's too soon, but my instincts, my heart, tell me that this is right.

Luca is my other half. I'd rather have a couple of decades of laughter and love than to allow fear to force him into a lonely existence.

38

Luca

When my father was still alive, he loved my mother with everything inside of him. I spent my childhood watching them dance in the kitchen and giggle on the couch. They doted on me, but really, their love for one another eclipsed anything else.

Since I was old enough to understand how rare their connection was, I wanted it for myself. Until my father died five years ago.

My mother became a shell of her former self. Secretly, I suspect heartbreak sped up her symptoms. She loves me; I know she does. But when the other half of your soul is ripped away, you become a ghost.

I don't want to do that to Reverie, leaving her behind to be a living ghost. A stronger man would walk away.

Turns out I am not a strong man at all.

Reverie holds me in her soft arms, not judging me for my tears. For my weakness. For my future. She loves me, like I knew she did, but she finally said it. I wish it were under different circumstances, but it's a relief to hear, regardless.

"It's going to be okay," she whispers, running her fingers through my hair. "We'll figure it out. I'll be here every step of the way, Luca."

I will spend every last minute of my life worshipping the ground she walks on. How is she so perfect?

Sniffling, I pull a handkerchief from my pocket to wipe away the mess of emotion on my face. She chuckles, helping me dab the spots I've missed. Glitter coats her cheeks from fallen tears.

"I don't deserve you, *Bilaste.*"

Her mouth quirks to the side. "Never forget that."

I choke out a weak laugh. "Never."

She glances at her watch with a grimace. "I hate to say it, but we have about five minutes until the grand entrance."

A headache clobbers my brain, throbbing against my skull. I rub my temples with a groan. "This is probably the worst part of being a wedding photographer."

"Pretending everything is fine when really, it's all falling apart?"

I snort. "Yes. That."

She squeezes her lips together, the corners of her eyes crinkling. "Well, I expect my second shooters to have the proper decorum. So if you could pull it together, that would be wonderful."

Laughing, feeling lighter than I have in months, I flick her nose. "I love it when you're mean."

"I can tell," she says dryly. "But if you could abstain from provoking me for at least twenty-four hours, that would be wonderful." She hesitates. "There isn't anything else, right?"

I grimace. "Is this a good time to tell you I have a two-inch dick?"

There it is — the smile worth every moment of pain. It blasts through my shame, incinerating it into nothing.

Reverie's face flushes as her eyes flick to my groin. "I suppose I'll have to be *very* careful when I bounce on it later and pray it doesn't fall out."

The thought of finally fully claiming Reverie heats my blood. The vision of her bouncing on my cock — which is certainly more than two inches — almost drives me mad. "You'll have to bounce *really* carefully so you don't break it. My nuts are delicate."

Reverie leans in with a serious expression. Leaning our foreheads together, she whispers, "Can't have the creamy peanut butter without crushing some peanuts."

If I weren't already in love, I would be now. Framing her face with my hands, I kiss her. I'm careful to control the intensity because there truly isn't any time. My tongue dances with hers as she melts against me. She's mine again; I can feel it in my bones.

Elation lights up my nerves; I gather her in tighter. She's here in my arms, not caring about what the future holds. It's the greatest gift, one I won't squander.

Before it gets to be too much, I break the kiss with no modest amount of regret. "I think we have about two minutes."

"Can I have thirty more seconds?" she pleads. Her pupils are large, almost eclipsing the irises. Her scent of raspberries is already starting to drive me crazy.

"Who am I to deny a goddess?"

***

Somehow, with twenty seconds to spare — thirty seconds for another kiss wasn't enough — I'm able to smooth out my hair before we rush out to the grand entrance, only to be informed the event is running fifteen minutes late.

Of course, it is.

It's okay; it allows more time to collect myself. Leaving Reverie in the reception hall, I head to the bathroom to freshen up.

The relief from the confession is indescribable. It's like flying so high that oxygen no longer exists, then plummeting in a free fall until my lungs can have that first sip of sweet air. It's an incredible experience, literally and figuratively.

She *loves* me.

Her love is a baptism, clearing away all of my worries, shame, and fear. My mother is going to be so happy when she finds out I've found someone who doesn't think my death sentence is a burden.

Entering the reception hall, I stand taller. Without telling Reverie, I approach the aunt, ready to apologize.

Matilda eyes me suspiciously. Since Orcs and Gargoyles are distant cousins, she's closer to my height. We're almost eye-level when I stop in front of her.

In a sign of deference, I snap my wings together and bow my head. "My apologies for interfering earlier."

The aunt sniffs with disdain. "Your business associate has so much attitude. You seem far more reasonable than her."

I bite back my irritation at her sexism. "Reverie is wonderful at her job. I wanted to apologize for my rudeness."

Before I can turn around, she stops me with a hand on my arm. "You love her, don't you?"

I pull my arm out of her grasp, irritated to have any other woman but Reverie touching me. "Yes, ma'am. I do. How can you tell?"

Her expression shifts to one of wistfulness. "I've been married six times. I can spot love a furlength away."

The misty-eyed expression makes me shift uncomfortably. "Well, thank you for noticing. If you'll excu—"

"You know, my last marriage was awful. Kirpat was his name, and he was an animal." She winks, and I have to school my expression to not show discomfort. Some guests don't know how to keep things to themselves. "And not in the way you'd hope. He was downright awful."

She appraises me. "You don't seem awful. Will you treat her well?"

I give a stilted nod, unsure where this is going. Some guests treat wedding vendors like we're priests hearing confessions.

The aunt pats me on the arm again. "Good. Good. Talk to her about that attitude, too."

With that, she walks away, allowing me to exhale sharply. Working weddings is not for the faint of heart.

The remainder of the reception passes by smoothly. I'm eager to check the images later, as I'm sure Reverie is as well. Editing is a pain-in-the-ass, but it can also be rewarding.

After the grand exit, where Fire Sprites rain down harmless flames onto the happy couple as they run through the mob trying to touch them, I meet Reverie at our gear.

Kneeling next to her, I remove my camera from my harness. "That was a wild grand exit."

She laughs. "It was. My brain couldn't comprehend we weren't about to be lit on fire."

I chuckle, placing a lens in its case. "Agreed. My wings tingled the whole time, demanding I fly away."

After we zip up our bags, she stands next to me. "I know we can't go to Prestley's, but do you want to go to the bar for a drink or two?"

My gaze darkens with salacious promise. There are many more things I'd prefer to do — namely, her. "You sure you don't want to go to the room?"

A delicious blush warms her pale cheeks. The way her eyes flare in tandem with a sharp inhale, I know we're on the same page.

After chewing on her lip for a moment, she shakes her head. "No. I think we need to ease into things at a more neutral location first."

As much as it pains me to say, she's right. I gather her gear in my hands, thrilled when she lets me. "I'll return these to the room, then meet you downstairs. How does that sound?"

She beams. "I'll save you a seat."

39

Reverie

Am I a fool for not immediately jumping into bed with Luca? Probably. It's not like my body doesn't crave his at an insatiable level.

But we owe it to ourselves to have a rational conversation not restricted by time. Besides, there will be so much time to fuck his brains out later.

For now, a meaningful conversation will suffice.

We've been at the bar for five minutes, rehashing the highlights of today. The pale stone around us, lit with ambient sconces, holds a quiet peace. Despite being carved into the mountain, it's cozy.

Luca is all smiles again; it's impossible to not join him. He's assured me there's nothing else hidden between us now. No buried bodies or secrets. The only thing we have to consider is his turning into a decorative garden gnome. The dark visualization thought has me snorting that almost resembles a chuckle.

Hearing the sound, he grins. "What are you giggling at?"

I stir my drink with the provided umbrella straw. "Oh, just thinking of how I'll decorate you when you become my garden gnome."

He shakes his head, incredulous. "You want me to be a *gnome?*"

I give him a false grimace of regret. "Too soon?"

Luca looks at me with complete adoration. "*Bilaste,* you can make any joke you need to in order to deal with the situation."

"So, would you like to be dressed up every day? Cause I'll do it. Maybe dresses on some days and—"

His expression goes flat as he says dryly, "Okay. Put a cork in it."

I laugh, and he joins in with a chuckle. Grabbing one of his enormous hands, I squeeze. "I meant what I said, Luca. I'm okay with it. I know there's more to learn, but I won't change my mind."

Breathless, he admires me as he tucks a hair behind my ear. "How did I get so lucky?"

I swallow the ball of emotion swelling in my throat. "To be honest, I want to ask myself the same thing."

His face sours into a comical caricature of disgust.

Worried, I squeeze his hand again. "What?"

"Kahlo will *never* stop calling me Lucky now."

I laugh, making the same face. "Does this mean he actually did us a favor by trying to ride the Slogoth?"

Both of us exchange looks of horror. There's no way this won't go to Kahlo's head. Luca perks up. "You know, I called him before we left; I think Malona was there."

I smile, and he narrows his eyes. With a shrug, I admit, "She told me a couple of weeks ago they'd gone on a date. I wasn't sure how far they'd advanced, since I've been swamped, but it doesn't entirely surprise me."

He shakes his head in disbelief. "He's going to be insufferable now."

We sip our drinks with matching expressions of dread. Then he says, "Would you like to meet my mother when we return?"

My heart skips a beat. "I'd really like that." I nibble my lip before asking, "What happens if she doesn't shift back?"

Luca gives me a sad smile. "Actually, I'm not sure. She wants to be buried next to my father under Fhetast Mountain, where most Gargoyles are buried. So I'll probably bring her there. They agreed on it the day they married, and on the day of her diagnosis, she put down all of her wishes in writing. She has no desire to spend eternity apart from him."

"That sounds romantic," I say dreamily, resting my chin on a fist. Realization hits me like a hammer, so I add quickly, "That they loved one another that much — not that she's dying."

He nods, smiling. "I agree." He leans back on the barstool and appraises me. "What about you, Miss Nonya? Are there any secrets in your closet?"

"No, just bodies."

He wrinkles his nose. "I hope you use deodorizer."

"The corpses of my enemies are properly deodorized." I snort with amusement. After taking another sip of my drink, I confess, "I have a photographic memory."

Luca's dark brows shoot up as he leans forward, silver eyes staring at my forehead as if my brain will reveal its secrets. "Oh, really? That's interesting."

I shrug. "It can be amazing or terrible, depending on the circumstances." I pause. "That's how I knew how many days had passed before we met again."

Delight lights up his face. "That's impressive. So you remember *everything?*"

I nod. "Unfortunately."

He glances at the ceiling, thinking. "What were you doing six months, three weeks, and two days ago?"

I sift through my memories, trying to recall the exact day. In my mind, it's like a multi-storied building filled with filing cabinets. It's a matter of finding the right cabinet.

Finally, I'm able to say, "I had toast for breakfast. It was slightly burned because I was distracted with styling my hair. My shoelace kept coming undone, which added to the frustration of not finding the right assistant yet. I had three interviews that day, and it would take another week to find Yureka."

He lets out a low whistle. "That skill must be helpful for shooting weddings."

"Oh, yes," I chuckle. "But it also means I never forget bad days. Mean comments. Lewd gestures. I try to compartmentalize, but it isn't a perfect system."

Leaning forward, he runs a finger up my arm. Voice low, he says, "Do you remember how my mouth felt?"

The question is so unexpected, I'm not able to control the flood of memories overtaking my senses. It must show on my face because he gives me a satisfied grin. "Oh, *Bilaste*, you are in for an experience. Because I have *ideas.*"

I swallow hard, intrigued. With the mischief in his expression, there are undoubtedly salacious plans at work.

"But," he says with a toothy grin. "I need to go to the restroom. I'll be right back."

I laugh as he weaves through the tables. Cupping a hand to my mouth, I say, "I'm waiting on pins and needles."

Turning to walk backward, he winks. "I've got a needle for you."

Bursting into laughter, I pick up my glass and drink the last sips. Eyeing his glass, I wave the bartender over to order two more. Sitting there, I'm unable to wipe the happiness off my face. I can't believe after everything, we're here, after one of the biggest weddings of my career. On top of that, by the time the sun rises, I'll have finally seen Luca naked.

I'm so excited.

"Well, fancy seeing you here."

I bristle at the voice. Without turning around, I murmur, "I highly recommend you walk away."

"Now, why would I do that when a pretty lady is sitting all alone?"

After his threat last night, my patience crisps up under my burning anger. Swiveling, I glare at Zkiel, the idiot Elf seeking death. "I thought I was a cold fish?"

He pouts. "Why can't we play nice?"

Zkiel sits in Luca's chair; I relax. I don't have to do a single thing. Ignoring him, I thank the bartender as he slides the two drinks in front of me.

"Oh, are you not actually alone?" Zkiel purrs. "Has that Gargoyle finally manned up and kept you occupied?"

He smells of something sharp and musky as he leans in. I tilt back, but not far enough. His knuckle graces my bare arm. I shiver, not because I like it but because I need a shower now.

"Do not fucking touch me," I say evenly. "I recommend you leave."

"Or what?" he taunts. "You'll glitter me? Such a shame, being both Glyridite and siren. It's double the ways to get yourself in trouble."

I clench my jaw. He goes to touch me again. I smack his hand away. "I said, *don't fucking touch me.*"

Anger reddens his cheeks. "Listen here, you fucking—"

A large, lavender hand claps on Zkiel's shoulder, extended claws shredding the suit jacket. Zkiel hisses as their sharp points sink into his skin. He tries to get off the chair, but Luca shoves him down.

"No, you'll want to be sitting for this." Luca's furious eyes flick over my body. "Did he touch you?"

Zkiel whines, his hands yanking at the claws in an attempt to remove them. It's like a mouse trying to lift a mountain.

I *did* warn him.

I take a sip of my drink, smirking. "My arm."

Luca cocks his head like a predator. "With which hand did he use?"

Adrenaline pumps through my veins. Luca emanates — no, *commands* — dominance right now. My core clenches so hard, I almost moan.

I point to the offending limb. "That one."

A wicked gleam lights Luca's eyes. "The whole thing or a finger?"

After taking a sip of my drink, I say breezily, "I believe it was the pointer finger, right?"

Sweat beads Zkiel's forehead. "Look, I'm sorry. I was trying to be nice and—"

Luca whispers into his ear, "You touched her; I'm positive she told you not to. Because she's a prickly little thing."

It's incredible to be truly seen and loved, anyway. I'll never doubt him *ever* again. I sit back in the chair, resting an elbow as I take another sip.

Zkiel's gaze turns wild, squirming to loosen the grip of claws. "Why would I touch *her?* She's a Glyridite. I don't want her *disgusting* glitter on me."

For the first time in my life, those words don't affect me. Because as Luca flashes his fangs in a snarl, I realize that there's only one person on this continent whose opinion I truly care about.

Luca holds out a hand to me. "Glitter me, baby."

Momentarily stunned, I blink furiously until his words process. With the brightest, biggest smile of my life, I say, "Gladly."

My body sings with happiness as I allow purple glitter to snake over his body, covering his entire form. There are gasps in the room, but Luca doesn't take his eyes off of me. Zkiel pales, watching with sick fascination as my glitter consumes my partner.

Luca is magnificent as his muscles glimmer with each movement. Someone points at his wings shining in the cozy light. It's a shame that both times I've covered him, it's been in the dark. One day, I'm going to do this in the sunlight.

Zkiel sighs with relief as the claws retract, but it's short-lived relief because Luca snatches the Elf's doomed hand. He forces the pointer finger to extend. "This one?"

With a saccharine smirk, I say, "Yes."

"Look at me," Luca commands Zkiel. The Elf obeys out of fear, sweat pouring from his forehead. "I have to go fuck the love of my life, so I don't have time to play hide and seek in the caves, as much as that would please me." He glances at me. "And her."

Snap!

Zkiel bites back a shriek as Luca hushes him like he's consoling a baby. "Shh, shh. It's okay. Now hold on for one more second."

There's the sound of bones grinding. Zkiel's face is so pale, I suspect he's ready to pass out. Desire pulses between my thighs, forcing me to press them together

Why is this so fucking attractive?

Luca roughly pats Zkiel's hand, releasing the permanently mangled finger. The Elf cradles it, sobbing. "Maybe, before you touch a woman without consent, you'll think real hard about what could be lurking around the corner. Because if I see you again, I'll make this look like child's play."

Luca slaps his back with a jovial grin. Zekiel winces, droplets of sweat dripping from his forehead. "Now. You have a good night, alright?"

Zkiel whimpers like a baby, the chair rattling as his body shakes. Music to my ears. Luca tosses corals onto the bar top and holds a hand out to me.

Ignoring our fresh drinks, he says, "Come, *Bilaste.* We have things for you to memorize."

Heart fluttering, I take his hand. I shriek with laughter when Luca tosses me over his shoulder, one hand on my back, the other on my ass. As Luca stalks out of the bar, I smirk at Zkiel. Holding my fingers up, I lower the middle fingers and stick out my tongue. He's too busy crying over his injury to notice me giving the middle finger.

Still worth it.

40

Luca

Seeing that Elf touch Reverie awakened instincts I normally keep buried. All male Gargoyles do until it's necessary to remind people that we're one of the most deadly creatures in existence. Crushing his finger took no more effort than scratching an itch.

Bones shattering under a tiny bit of my strength, while Reverie watched me with rapt fascination, was one of the best moments of my life. It's unfortunate that the moment included scum like that Elf, but I'd do it all over again to see that smile.

I might not have her photographic memory, but no one can take that smile from me.

Now, with her cackling over my shoulder, the anticipation of sinking into her body, *finally*, has me picking up my speed.

My tail lashes impatiently as I caress Reverie's plump ass with my hand. Pressing the button for the elevator, I think of all the things I'm going to do to her beautiful body. All of the things I'll make her remember. While we wait, I absentmindedly rub her ass, not thinking anything of it until she moans. Surprised, I peer around the hallway to make sure no one heard the moans that belong to me.

I tap her ass lightly. "Knock it off. I've already broken a finger. Don't make me tear off ears, too."

Giggling, she squirms. With a singsong voice, she pretends to be worried. "Oh, no ... Don't ..."

I slap her ass a little harder, earning a squeal. Without thinking, I sink my teeth into her soft hip ... as the elevator doors open.

A family of Orcs, including two younglings, stares in horror. It might also have something to do with the fact that I'm entirely covered in glitter. Not knowing we have an audience now, Reverie says, "You better bite elsewhere later."

Releasing her flesh from my mouth slowly, I give the family a stilted smile. "Reverie, we have small ears present."

"What!" She tries to twist for a better look, but my wing blocks her. Stepping back, I let the family scurry past before stepping into the elevator. As the doors close, Reverie hisses, "Put me down. That was so embarrassing!"

"No. I like your ass near my face."

She slaps my shoulder. "Now!"

"No."

"Now!"

"No. Stop asking."

Her fingers trail along the base of my wing. A shiver blazes from the tip of my tail to the bottom of my neck as my cock instantly fills with blood. My fingers clutch her ass cheek so hard, it'll most likely leave a handprint.

"*Reverie.* Stop that."

"No."

She does it to the other one. I groan, my knees buckling.

I re-hoist her onto my shoulder, securing my hold. "I'm going to drop you if you keep doing that."

"Drop me on your cock?" she purrs, wiggling. I slap her ass, but in response she teases the soft membrane of my wing. The sensation is incredibly overwhelming; my moan is far too loud.

"Reverie," I growl, barely in control of my restraint. Estimating where her hand is, I grab it with my tail. She gasps when it finds her wrist, holding her hand flush against my back.

"Hey!" She uses the other free hand to try again, but thanks to the blessed goddess, the elevator doors open. Bouncing on the tips of my claws, I discombobulate her enough that she's forced to use her free hand for balance. Success.

When we reach our hotel room, I'm so excited, I accidentally slam the door hard enough for the pictures hanging on the walls to rattle with the force.

"Put me down now?" Reverie asks, sounding too sweet for it to be trusted. When I ignore her, walking to the bathroom, she *licks my fucking tail.* I choke, almost collapsing onto my knees.

"You fucking rainbow menace," I hiss, dragging her breasts across my chest as I lower to the floor. My tail releases her hand; I try to ignore everything in my body throbbing with wild need. "I should call you my torment, not my bliss."

She's red faced, but amusement twinkles in her crystal blue eyes. "I had no idea tails were so sensitive."

"You're going to weaponize this, I just know it," I mutter, opening the glass door to the shower. It's an enormous space, intended to accommodate the most massive of creatures. It's twenty feet high and about fifteen feet wide, featuring multiple showerheads. In one corner, a large chair capable of accommodating fliers waits to be used.

I eye it with more than a few ideas.

With the press of a button, all of the showerheads spray at once. Steam fills the air, along with some fresh, earthy scent coming from an unseen source.

"We're going to make this quick, right?" She's already pulling off her shirt, tossing it across the room. It lands in the sink. Her breasts are held prisoner in a black lace bra.

The whine in her voice makes me chuckle. "Nothing I do with you will be quick. However, I'll be time efficient while cleaning this two-inch cock."

Her eyes flick to the large bulge straining against my zipper. When her pink tongue flicks out to lick her lips, I know without a doubt that if I'm not careful, I'm going to spill into my boxer briefs right now.

"It's very small," she says, tone light. "I'm not sure I'll be able to feel it."

Unbuttoning my shirt, I smirk. "Is that so?"

"Yes," she nods her head with a frown. "I'm not sure this will work out if I can't even feel ..."

Her words trail off as I pull off my shirt, exposing my broad, muscular chest. Working at undoing my belt buckle, I smirk. "What was that?"

"I said," she purrs. "I'd hate to not feel anything, you know? This all seems so perfect, so it would be natural for there to be something wrong."

My belt snaps as I pull it off. She flinches, but grins at the sound. I unbutton my trousers, letting them fall from my hips, landing at my ankles. All I have left are black boxer briefs.

Eyes locked on the outline of my cock, Reverie stares, speechless. I make a spinning motion with a finger. "Come on, *Bilaste*. Your insults are my favorite."

Her eyes flick up to mine. "That's at least three inches."

"Maybe the width" I mutter, shimming off the boxer briefs. My definitely more-than-three-inches cock juts out, swollen with a bead of pre-cum. "Now hurry up. I can't wait for you to not feel this."

Her mouth opens; closes. Unable to wait any longer, I get on my knees, unbuckling her belt. Scanning her face, I search for any indication of discomfort. She seems more shocked than anything.

"Tell me, baby," I say in a low, gruff voice. "Have you ever had a Gargoyle cock before?"

"No."

"Good. Let me set the standard."

Coming back to herself, she tilts her head, smiling. "Does that mean I can compare it to someone else later?"

The vision of her letting anyone else touch her ever again fills me with so much feral rage, I have to take a deep, steadying breath.

When I can finally speak without roaring, I say, "If another man ever touches you again, it will be the last thing he ever does."

She says nothing, because I'm fairly certain I've proved how serious I am. Yanking her trousers down, underwear included, I kiss her soft belly. Reaching behind her, I flick open the bra, freeing her delicious breasts. I'm greedy as I cover a nipple with my mouth, dragging my tongue against its peak.

Reverie's knees buckle, but I hold her steady with my hands on her hips. One of her hands cups the back of my head as the other snakes over my shoulder. Knowing exactly what she's about to do, I growl and release her breast. Unwilling to cum the second she touches my wings, I abruptly stand.

Mindful of my wings, I step into the shower. "Now get your sweet ass in here."

41

Reverie

After an overall taxing day, it's blissful stepping into the steaming shower. Any other time, I'd be soaking myself until my skin's wrinkled, but Luca is naked in front of me.

The goddesses carved him from stone, I swear. There isn't an inch of him that doesn't ripple with strength. And his cock ... I might melt into a puddle from overheating with lust. He'd probably just lick me up with his talented tongue. My body sings with anticipation.

Luca directs me to stand under the spray of water. I groan, closing my eyes, relishing the heat. The tension and emotional destruction of the day melt down the drain.

My eyes flutter open when his body presses against mine. The water soaks his hair as he looks down, water sluicing down his body. We're close enough for his hardness to press into my belly, but I ignore it, too wrapped up in his expression. Eyes filled with reverence soften as his hands cup my cheeks.

"You're so fucking beautiful."

A shiver of pleasure skitters along my spine. "I have no idea how to handle your compliments," I admit.

Luca's expression turns serious as his brows pull together. "Just accept it as patronage of my goddess."

"Well," I say slowly, licking water off my lips. "Your goddess would like you to hurry up, please. I require immediate sexual patronage."

Luca's chest rumbles with a chuckle. Reaching for a bottle of soap, he croons, "Such a demanding deity."

We're quiet as he kneels at my feet, lathering his hands. It's bliss as he applies pressure while they run across my body, massaging at the same time. I moan when he rubs his thumbs along my thighs at the sore muscles. Leaning against his shoulders, I savor his worship.

Luca alternates between watching my face and focusing on his task. When he stands to wash my hair, I luxuriate in the scalp massage.

Finally, it's my turn. He kneels again, with an adoring gaze as I take my time washing him. There's a lot to wash, but it's an opportunity to learn his body. Like the way he hisses at me like an angry chimeragon when I touch the base of his tail.

"Not. Yet." he growls. I pat his ass in acknowledgment, now knowing cleaning his tail is also out of the question. He does that himself, gritting his teeth the entire time.

Task completed, we stare wordlessly at each other. There are no more barriers. No more reasons to delay. His fists clench and unclench; his chest heaves with restraint. I desperately want to shatter it.

His eyes track my hand as I bring it to the underside of his cock — which offers far more girth than long, thankfully — and run a nail under the soft flesh. It jumps as his hips jolt. When he doesn't stop me, I do it again. I worry my lip with teeth, unsure of what to do next.

I want to do it all.

"I don't know where to start," I admit.

His eyes slide to the chair. Pointing, he says, "You said you'd bounce on my small cock. I'd like a demonstration." Without waiting for a response, he sits in the chair; looks at his thick, throbbing cock with expectation. "So. Bounce."

Shy all of a sudden, I take my time walking to the man waiting with a hungry — no, *ravenous* — gleam in his moonlight eyes.

Before I can hop onto this glittering ride, he puts a hand against my chest. "First things first; we both know your tight pussy needs a little warming up."

My words come out hoarse. "It's only a couple of inches. What's the big deal?"

"My fingers ache for your glittering wetness again. Would you deny them?"

His fingers dig into my ass cheeks as he jerks me forward. "Hold on to my shoulders, beautiful."

Obeying, I lean forward, digging my nails into the muscle. It places my breasts right in his face. Instead of taking advantage, he focuses on raising me effortlessly. I stop breathing as he straddles me over his thighs. When he spreads his legs, mine have no choice but to do the same. To my mortification, I see a drop of glitter land on the tile, swirling into the water.

My eyes drag back to his, waiting for judgment. His expression is pure devotion. "I cannot wait to be covered in glitter."

He adjusts me so I'm nestled against his hot cock. The faint ridges wrapping around the girth feel divine against my clit as I hungrily rub myself against him.

"Slow, *Bilaste*," he groans, gripping my hips to slow them down.

"I don't want to be slow," I whimper.

"I know, baby, but let me try to last past thirty seconds. I'm not a virgin, but I swear my cock has forgotten everything it's learned."

Oh.

There's no time to ask questions because when he slides me across his length, pleasure electrifies every one of my nerve-endings. My clit grazes the silky smooth skin of his cock, and I whimper, dropping my head.

"You're the most exquisite woman I've ever met, Reverie," he says, whispering the words in my ear. "For the rest of our lives, I'm going to make sure you never forget."

His hands guide me to move faster; I'm helpless to stop him. I'm desperate to have him inside me; the angst of it all builds my orgasm.

I moan, resting our foreheads together. "Please, Luca."

"Please, what?"

"Please get inside me."

A chuckle rumbles in the thick column of his neck. "Oh, we've barely scratched the surface of what I'm going to do to you."

My hips lash against his, picking up speed. I hold on to his shoulders, squeezing. He hisses. Using one arm to direct my pace, he slides the other hand between us. Pausing in guiding my thrusts, he brings a finger to my entrance.

"Is this what you want?" he breathes, eyes frantically scanning my face. I nod, unable to speak. With his other hand pushing me forward, his finger slips into my body. It's not remotely close to being enough.

Instincts move my hips until his arm is there to push me forward as I roll them back, greedy for his finger. The angle still allows me to rub my clit against the heel of his hand, the friction delicious.

"Eyes on me."

Our eyes lock. Water clings to his face, droplets teasing his eyelashes. His breath is rasping; the wonderment in his eyes is reminiscent of the other night. If he looks at me like this every time, I may get nothing done. We pause again so he can add another finger. It's so much and not enough.

"Eyes on me while you cum, Reverie. I want to see your rainbows."

I bite down on my lip, whimpering as the orgasm builds. When I close my eyes, he snaps, *"Open your fucking eyes, Reverie."*

They bolt open, and he smirks. "That's my girl. Now cum on my fingers, gorgeous."

Staring deep into his eyes, nothing matters except this ... whatever *this* is between us. The Fates, perhaps. Maybe sheer dumb luck. Whatever it is, it has me in a chokehold.

"That's it," he coaxes. "Show me your glow, baby."

As if obeying the command, glitter pours from my skin. He groans, eyes fluttering as he resists closing them. Heat scalds my skin as the pleasure builds. My hips are furious now, chasing the orgasm.

It barrels over my senses, electrifying my spine. I scream, arching my back as he keeps my hips moving.

He hums with satisfaction. "That's it. Keep going."

I sob, closing my eyes, unable to keep them open as the sensation of sheer divinity courses through me. This must be how the Heavens feel. There's no other way. When my muscles stop tensing, they turn languid. He slows my hips until I'm still, panting like I've run a race. He's doing the same, appearing bewildered. We're both covered in pastel rainbow glitter. Some of it's my sweat; some is my cum.

"Stunning." He licks his finger clean, humming.

42

Luca

Everything is glittering. It still clings to my body from the bar. Now, it coats my fingers and the base of my cock. I'm desperate for the whole thing to be slick with sparkles. I want to be surrounded by glitter for the rest of my life.

I'm afraid she's not fully prepped, but I can't wait any longer. I need her.

"Do you think you're ready?" I ask, voice hoarse. Her eyes are wide as she nods. I don't think she's sure either.

"We'll take it slow. Tell me if it's too much. We can wait until later if needed."

"Luca," she says, panting. "If I wait any longer, I might actually die."

Giving her a soft smile, "Remember that in a minute."

Lifting her by the backs of her thighs, I watch her guide my tip to her entrance. I hiss through my teeth, gritting them at the first sensation of her wet silk. When the head of my cock meets resistance, I almost pass out. Moving her methodically, I'm able to enter her, inch by tantalizing inch.

"Luca," she quietly sobs, shaking.

"I know. Me too."

I close my eyes, trying to memorize the moment, while desperately trying to distract myself from the tight velvet encasing my cock. Her muscles squeeze; I inhale sharply.

"Baby." My voice is full of pain. "You need to relax. I don't want to hurt you."

Her body softens, allowing me to sink in a little deeper. "That's it. A little more. Be good for me and stay relaxed."

Reverie's head falls against my shoulder, her legs quivering as I help her take the remaining length. When I'm fully seated, we sit there for a minute, breathless. It's like nothing in my life has ever mattered until now, being inside the most wonderful person I've ever met. She's let me into her body; it's a privilege I take seriously.

When her breath slows and my heart isn't about to burst, I ask, "Are you ready, *Bilaste*?"

She lifts her torso and, for a moment, I'm alarmed at the tears in her eyes. Bringing my hands to her cheeks, I search her face for clues. "Am I hurting you? What's wrong?"

"Nothing," she says quietly. "For the first time, nothing at all."

"Oh," I groan, bringing our foreheads together. "I'm right there with you." Running my hands along her neck and arms, I ask, "Do you want to try moving?"

She nods. I bring each of her hands to my shoulders. "Let's see how you ride this two-inch cock, baby."

She hiccups out a laugh through her tears and moves forward tentatively. Stars burst in my eyes. I let out a feral, embarrassing moan. It emboldens her; she repeats the motion. When I make the sound again, not caring if I sound like an inexperienced adolescent, she picks up the pace.

Instantly, the orgasm roars through my senses; I grab her hips roughly. "Wait. *Wait.*"

Imagining horrific things, trying with every ounce of willpower to make the orgasm stay away for a little longer, I force her to stay in place.

She giggles. A beautiful sound. "I might be able to help."

My eyes snap open. "How can you help me not die from your delicious body?"

"I can sing you into not cumming."

My head snaps back in shock. "You can what now?"

She nods. "Watch."

Before I can truly register what she's about to do, she opens her mouth and sings the most beautiful sounds. As she begins to move, my soul is captivated by her silent command to *sit back and enjoy.*

Enjoy.

Wait.

Enjoy.

Wait.

Enjoy.

Her glorious body moves over mine expertly. Now that I don't have to worry about cumming, I can fully appreciate every inch of her supple curves. Her thick thighs flexing over mine. Her soft tummy bouncing in time with her full breasts. The quiet, whimpers escaping in tandem with her song.

Wait.

Enjoy.

My arms wrap around her body, hugging her close. Her glitter acts as a lubricant, increasing sensations tenfold. Her breasts pressing against my pecs for the first time truly makes me feel reborn. How have I gone through my whole life without this?

Finally, the song changes.

With me.

With me.

Reverie screams, the sound echoing against the glass shower walls. Her pussy walls squeeze my cock like a lifeline as she transports me to another dimension. My orgasm rips through me, shuddering my body viciously. My roar is rough, made of battling stones. A sound I've never made. I barely recognize this body I inhabit as my cock throbs, releasing my pleasure into her.

When our souls come back to our bodies, we're sweaty, flushed messes. I've never seen so much glitter in my life.

She stares at me, stunning, her breasts shaking as she pants. "That was ..."

"Life altering?" I offer, struggling to breathe.

She squints, assessing the bathroom. Steam makes it impossible to see anything clearly. Glitter sparkles in the bright lights, a shimmer heaven for the two of us.

"I've made a mess," she says, grimacing. She raises her hand to suck it all back in.

"Don't," I say, lowering her hand. "I want to set a world record for the most glittery shower of all time."

"You want to go again?" She sounds shocked.

I'm a little offended, especially since my cock is already hardening.

"*Bilaste*. Don't insult me. I need to see something first."

Her brows furrow. "What?"

Gently, so gently, I slide her back until only the tip of my cock remains inside her body. It is completely coated with iridescent white glitter. With a sigh of male satisfaction, I reseat myself. She gasps, then laughs.

I grin. "Making sure my cock is covered in glitter." As I brush a wet curl from her forehead, I say, "Can you put rainbows in my mouth?"

Reverie lifts her hand, and a rainbow grows from her palm. With a teasing lilt, she purrs, "Open wide."

I open my mouth, excited to be the pot of gold at the end of the rainbow.

43

Reverie

We're both exhausted and satiated by the time round two's over. It's been the most emotional day of my life. It's crazy to think that only this morning, Luca was sleeping on the floor — I was *such* a dunghole for that one — and he still held so much secret pain.

Toweling me off, Luca asks, "Will you wear those cute pajamas again? I never had the opportunity to truly enjoy them."

I tuck the towel around my chest, handing him one. "You were never supposed to see them, you know."

Wrapping the towel around his waist, Luca snorts. "I think there are a lot of things I'm not supposed to do that I've done. What's one more?"

"Incorrigible," I tease, leaving the bathroom to find said pajamas. I squeal and giggle as he swats my ass.

We dress and take turns braiding each other's hair. He sits patiently, unaware of the mischief I've engaged in.

Holding up the mirror, I beam. "See your new look!"

Luca eyes his reflection, tilting his head and raising an eyebrow. "Did you braid pigtails into my hair?"

"Yes!" I clap and jump on the balls of my feet.

"This is going to dry and look insane when I take them out tomorrow."

Placing the brush on the dresser, I scoff. "You'll just wash them out at the thermal pools." Luca's silent long enough for me to turn around and eye him with suspicion. "You *are* going to the thermal pools with me, right?"

"If that's what you want," he says slowly.

"It is," I confirm, then look at the bed. "Do you want to sleep on the stone floor again? Or would you like to sleep with me? I'm a bed hog, just as a warning."

Luca twitches his wings. "These will take up far more space than you will."

Removing some pillows, I ask, "How *do* you sleep?"

"With my eyes closed." I toss a pillow at him. He catches it, grinning. "On my back. Not much of a choice."

I frown, realizing the dilemma. "But if you sleep on your back ... how will I sleep next to you?"

Luca comes to the other side of the bed, helping me pull back the comforter. "Carefully, on a blanket."

My jaw drops. "You want me to sleep on your wings?"

Luca huffs out a laugh. "I *could* sleep on the floor again, although I might fight you on that tonight. My right wing is still sore from the stone."

When he sees my crestfallen expression, he points a finger at me. "Knock it off. We're moving on. Promise to never make me sleep on the floor again, and I swear I'll only mention it occasionally when the need arises."

"When the need arises?" I ask flatly.

"Yeah, like if I'm losing an argument, and need something to turn the tides. I can say, 'Sure, I didn't do the dishes, but remember that one time you made me sleep on the floor?'"

"You're never going to win an argument," I retort, smiling as I crawl onto the mattress.

"We'll see." He winks, motioning for me to wait. "Let me get in first. Grab that blanket at the foot of the bed."

While he gets situated, I grab the soft blanket. Luca lays in the center of the ridiculously wide bed, allowing his magnificent wingspan to spread.

He pats the wing on his left. "Climb on."

Crawling toward him with a grin, I say, "Round three?"

He huffs out a laugh. "*Bilaste,* I need sleep. I've barely slept in three days."

Again, guilt has me frowning. "I'm so—"

"Get over here." He leans forward and snatches me from where I kneel in front of a sparkling wing, spreading the blanket.. Placing me on the blanket, he pulls the comforter over us and tucks me into his side.

Giving my forehead a loud, smacking kiss, he declares, "If you apologize again for the last twenty-four hours, I reserve the right to do something that will shut you up."

Running a hand over his chest, I purr, "Like ... what?"

He sighs. "That wasn't meant to be a challenge. Go to sleep, Rainbow Menace."

The exhaustion covers me like a weighted blanket, leaving no energy for snark. Relaxing my head against his chest, I close my eyes. His arm wraps around me, pressing me closer. His tail slowly wraps around my ankle, but in a quiet, comforting way.

"I love you, Luca."

A happy rumble vibrates against my cheek. "I love you, Reverie."

We fall asleep like that, leaving me feeling more at peace than ever before.

***

After sleeping like a rock, I wake feeling refreshed and ... content.

Luca's sleeping soundly next to me, his chest rising at a steady pace. Still curled into his ribs, head on a pillow, I run my hand over the smattering of chest hair, reveling in the touch of his soft skin.

Quietly adjusting, I wince. It's sore between my legs. I can't tell Luca; knowing him, he'll refuse to fuck me for days. It's my fault for letting loose without a care, but I have zero regrets.

We still have one more day here to do whatever we want. Originally, Yureka and I were going to visit the thermal pools. Maybe Luca will want to do that too, although Gargoyles tend to avoid bodies of water. I was teasing him last night. They can't swim; their wings literally won't let them. But if it's shallow enough, maybe he'll want to go.

My fingers trail to his stomach, loving how it isn't flat. Muscular stomachs are pretty, but uncomfortable for cuddling. His is the perfect amount of strength and softness. I follow the trail from his belly button to the hem of his cotton pajama bottoms. As I tease the elastic hem, his stomach tightens.

"You haven't had enough?" His voice is rough with sleep, a delicious grumble against my ear.

Sliding my hand underneath, I search for my new favorite part of him. He's already hard, his cock jumping as I wrap my hands around its girth.

"I don't think I'll ever have enough."

"I couldn't agree more," he rumbles, shifting to face me. His wing draws under his body, bringing me closer. I stretch out my legs and sling one over his hips, working his length. His breathing goes from languid to rapid as one of his hands finds my ass. With a firm push, he closes the gap between our bodies.

His free wing folds over us, creating a private cocoon of heat, breath, and sweet nothings while his hands explore my body.

While I work him with slow strokes, I gasp as his tail caresses from my calf to my thigh. I've never engaged in tail play, outside of biting it yesterday. It nearly brought him down, so what will it be like for him to slide it inside me?

The thought has my heart galloping and my hips writhing. I moan as it slides higher, until its smooth, round head prods my entrance. *"Luca."*

"Is this okay?" he croaks out, sounding strained.

I tilt my hips to give it better access. "Fuck yes."

It has less girth than his cock, so it's only a little sore as it presses in and out at a delicious, slow pace. It's barely in, but I'm soaked already.

"Fuck, Reverie," he growls. "This is transcendent. How are you so fucking perfect?"

I whimper as his tail sinks into me. I increase the pace with my hand. Our hips undulate in time as we match the pace of our movements.

His tail stretches me, offering enough friction to build my orgasm. I press my clit against my moving wrist, aching for release.

Luca's finger crooks under my chin, lifting my mouth to his. I savor the kiss to a painful degree. Do I really get this for the rest of my life if I want it? Is it too soon to actually think of forever? Are we rushing into this?

He pauses during the kiss to give me a frown. "Stop thinking so much, *Bilaste.*"

I giggle, resuming my pace around his cock. "Sorry. I was wondering ..." I hesitate, not sure if it's smart to bring up. What if it scares him?

"Yes?" As he says the word quietly, his tail pumps into me slowly, forcing a shuddering groan from me.

It takes a second of extreme focus until I'm able to say between thrusts, "I was ... just thinking that ... *oh goddess* ... that we could do ... oh, *Luca,* keep going ... that we could do this ..."

My voice breaks as the orgasm incinerates my words, thoughts, and body. I can't focus on touching him, so enraptured by the pleasure throbbing through me. His tail continues to work me, ringing out every wave. When I shudder from the sensitivity, his tail slows, then gradually pulls out of me.

Before I can fully realign with this reality, Luca has me flipped on my back, spreading my thighs as his hips settle between my legs. He's careful to not let his weight rest on me at all. Bracketing my face with his forearms, he peers at me with amusement. Against my belly, his cock throbs.

"Are you trying to say ..." He trails kisses down my throat. "That we could do this every day?"

I nod silently, still recovering. Luca guides himself to my entrance. I wince. His brows shoot up.

"Are you sore?"

I grimace. "A little."

He pulls away, but I grab his shoulders. "No, please. I want this. It's okay."

Luca frowns. "I will not hurt you with my body, *Bilaste.*"

Smiling, I say, "Some of the best pleasure has a little pain in it, baby."

He searches my face for any deception. When he finds none, he hesitates as he resettles. "Okay. But you have to tell me if it's too much. We'll take it slow. Understood?"

I giggle, pressing a quick kiss on his cheek. "Yes, Sir."

Happiness flares when his expression darks. "Don't say 'Sir'. I said that we're going slow; that word makes me want more than slow."

Biting my lip, smiling like a maniac, I say, "Understood."

Watching my every tiny reaction, Luca takes his time entering my body, pausing every single time I look even slightly uncomfortable. By the time he's fully seated, we're both panting like marathon runners.

"You ready?" His voice is deliciously intimate.

When I nod, Luca sets a tortuous pace, drawing out every thrust. He kisses away my whimpers, holding my face in his hands. He makes love to me like it's the last time, savoring each flutter of my eyelids and movement of my hips.

"You are the light of my life," he murmurs, pressing his forehead against mine. He hasn't taken his eyes off me, even as he brings a hand behind my knee, hitching my leg higher so he can go deeper. "I'm going to make love to you every day you let me. On the days you don't want to, I'm going to love your mind."

Emotion swells in tandem with my orgasm. This is the most intense moment of my life, letting Luca fill me with more love than I thought possible.

"Luca." I mewl his name, increasing the veneration in his expression.

"Good. There you go. Memorize it."

His strokes barely increase in pace, driving me wild. He applies a little more pressure with his pelvis, giving my clit the friction it's craving. It's enough to fling me off the edge. His name is on my lips as my back arches.

"You're so incredible," he whispers, keeping the same sinuous movement as his fingers dig into my hips. As I come down from the intensity of pleasure, he finds his own, jerking his hips forward to fully bury himself to the hilt. With the most delectable groan in my ear, he empties himself into me.

When we've both recovered from the acute satisfaction, Luca gives me the softest, sweetest kiss. "I love you, Reverie Songlight."

Melting at the words, I say, "I love you, too, Luca Destau."

When our bodies finally separate, we both groan with regret. He lies on his stomach, watching me. For a few minutes, the only sound in the room is our rapid breaths easing to a manageable level. When my stomach growls, he grins.

Kissing shoulder, he says, "I'm thinking room service is necessary. Thoughts?"

"Goddess, yes," I groan, pulling a sheet around my deliciously sore body. "If you're inspired to make some of that cheap hotel coffee, too, I won't stop you."

"Good thing you inspire me, *Bilaste,*" he says, sliding out of bed. Glittering dick swinging, he pads over to the coffeepot. Once he activates the brew setting, Luca calls for room service, ordering me two apple strudel muffins, plus a copious amount of eggs for himself.

While we wait for breakfast, he twirls a finger, motioning for me to flip over. "Time for a morning massage."

Frowning, I hesitate as I shift onto my stomach. "Morning massage?"

"Yes." The bed dips as he crawls onto the mattress and swings a leg over my hips until he's straddling me. "A perk of tolerating my grating personality."

Tilting my head to the side on the pillow, I smile. "It is a bit of a struggle at times."

Luca playfully slaps my ass. "I'll eat your muffins."

Wiggling my ass, I taunt him with, "You can eat my muffin any time."

He groans, bringing deft fingers to my shoulders. "Don't make me be that stereotypical man where massages turn into sex."

I hum with pleasure as he kneads my sore shoulders. Carrying around two cameras for nine hours takes a toll. Releasing a happy sigh, I close my eyes. If this indicates mornings with Luca, I'll fistfight any woman who tries to eye him with interest.

"So what do you want to do with our day?" he asks, working his thumbs into the tension lining my spine.

"Thermal pools." The words are muffled in the pillow.

His hands pause before he says, "Okay, we can do that."

"I also have reservations for dinner tonight at the Starlight Room."

"Sounds delicious."

I crane my neck to look at him. "Will that count as our first official dinner date?"

Luca grins. "I think it will, yes."

The thought brings a smile to my face. "Sex before the first date. How backwards of us."

"Please stop twisting your neck; you're ruining my work," he scolds playfully. "And yes, I suspect we will always do things in unexpected ways."

Readjusting my head, I say, "Well, we should do some normal things, like meeting each other's parents, friends, etcetera."

"You truly want to meet my mother?" he asks softly.

"Of course!" I exclaim. "Why wouldn't I?"

Strong thumbs make circles on my lower back as he says, "She's showing permanent signs of Fletchling's, Reverie." He pauses, then adds quietly, "I'm afraid it will scare you."

Attempting to shrug, I say, "If you're okay with it, I am, too."

We're quiet for a few minutes while I revel in the best massage of my life. I could have this *every* day? Unfathomable.

But my thoughts wander back to his mom. What it must've been like to find out.

Clearing my throat, I ask, "So the day after we met, you found out about it?"

Luca's fingers dig into a knot inside my shoulder as he says, "Unfortunately, yes. My mother discovered a stone patch on her shoulder. It was small, no bigger than a marble, but it was an immediate cause for concern. The day after we met, she went to the doctor and received the diagnosis."

With my eyes still closed, I say, "That must have been devastating."

He hums in agreement. Voice low, he says, "There's not a strong enough word for it. Within five minutes, both of our lives, our futures, changed."

"How did she deal with it?"

"She accepted it immediately. My mother is made of grace, so she jumped right into planning for her death. It's impressive how much she's both resigned and resilient."

Turning my head to see his face, I ask, "How did *you* deal with it?"

His expression shifts from grim to sad, with a frown deepening the lines on his face. "Honestly? I don't think I have, other than avoiding any discussions with anyone. Kahlo knows; so does my boxing coach. And now ... you."

An ache blooms in my chest. "So you've been essentially dealing with it alone? Do you not have any family to support you?"

Luca pauses in the massage, staring at the bed as he contemplates my words. "Aside from Kahlo, there's his mom — my aunt — but we aren't close. No siblings. My father is gone; as are my grandparents on both sides. So, no — no family."

It all sounds so incredibly lonely. How he persists, knowing his fate, is a testament to his strength.

"Well, you have me," I whisper.

His silver eyes find mine, filled with grief. "I love you, and I'm too selfish to let you go. But Reverie, this is a lot. Have you ever seen a Gargoyle going through the stages of Fletchling's?"

"No," I admit. "But I learned about it when I was younger."

"It progresses rapidly once the first signs appear. Two to three years, at most. I don't want to be a burden."

I wriggle, signaling I want to turn over. Luca hesitates, but swings off my hips to sit on his heels.

Shifting to sit in front of him, I give his hand a squeeze. "Luca, you aren't a burden. I understand the valid concern, but it doesn't make you any less worthy of love. Do you understand?"

He nods, but still appears unconvinced. Adding sternness to my tone, I say, "Luca, do you understand?"

His voice is hoarse as he says, "Yes."

Suddenly, I realize we are still both naked, but it's appropriate for the raw intimacy of the moment. My eyes trail across the soft skin wrapped around his strength like a lavender gift.

Will he waste away?

Will these muscles wither?

What will it be like to take care of him?

It's too soon to think about. Brushing the worries away, I force a brave smile. "Well, we have time, right? I mean, your mom could hate me. And then you leave me."

A ferocity tightens his expression as he says, "*Never.* She's going to love you."

Doubt still nestles in my thoughts, so I shrug. "Only one way to find out."

There's a knock at the door. Luca jumps up, and trots toward the door.

"Luca?" I call out.

He pauses. "Yes?"

"I'm one hundred percent positive that whoever is at the door will not like seeing every inch of you right now."

Confusion shifts to amusement. "Oh. Right."

Grabbing one of the complimentary robes, he wraps the white terry-cloth robe around his body. It's too small, looks ridiculous, but it's somehow very Luca.

While he opens the door to accept the room service, I nestle into the pillows, inhaling a deep, steadying breath. So much has changed in the last twenty-four hours, but even with all the revelations, it feels *right.* Like we've been on this inevitable path toward one another forever.

Flashing me a grin, he walks toward the small table in the corner and places the full tray of food in the center.

Grabbing the other robe, he holds it out. "Want a muffin?"

44

Luca

When lunchtime arrives, Reverie convinces me to leave the hotel room. She's keen to try the thermal pools. The thought of being in a hot tub of water makes my wings twitch, but I can't deny her. Whatever she wants, I'll make sure she has it. Even if I drown.

Stopping at one of the smaller cafes, we ate a quick lunch before heading to the spa. The whole time, she happily holds my hand, looking at me like I hung the moons. Her smile is radiant, and she's light on her toes with every step. Pride puffs out my chest. When I met her, she was so internally curled in on herself, suspicious of everything life offered.

Now, she's luminescent. She doesn't appear to have noticed that her glitter veins are brighter. Her eyes have an inner glow to them, as if the sun itself resides in her soul.

I've never seen anything so beautiful in my life.

By the time we reach the spa, she's practically hopping like a youngling. Hiding my apprehension, I smile every time she does, even when I'm panicking about being in a thermal pool.

The spa's made of interconnected pools fed by hot springs within the mountains. Each pool, about a dozen of them, is a bright shade of blue, almost as bright as Reverie's eyes. Large, iridescent crystals jut from the rocks, all different sizes. Moss covers every inch of the ground, with glowing flowerbeds lining the pathways.

It's quiet, with a harp playing somewhere. Bioluminescent butterflies flit around the guests, landing on fingers and noses.

With shining eyes, Reverie grins. "Yureka is going to be furious that she missed out on this."

I nod. "That means we have to enjoy it as thoroughly as possible."

Our reserved pool isn't ready yet, so an attendant guides us to a communal pool while we wait. There are people already there; a few Sprites, a pair of Elves, and ... a female Glyridite?

I see the exact moment Reverie notices the Glyridite. The woman is wearing a bikini, showing her glitter veins proudly. The pattern is different from Reverie's, like interconnected fingerprints.

The species is rare; apparently, there's a low fertility rate in males. The level of bigotry from others doesn't help, so they tend to keep to themselves. How many Glyridites has Reverie met? I don't get the impression her father celebrates his heritage, either.

Her eyes find mine, brows deep with uncertainty. I encourage her with a motion of my hand. She peels off her robe, revealing a black, modest bathing suit. I need to buy my girl some bikinis.

The Glyridite immediately takes notice; her pretty face lights up, splitting into a huge grin. "Oh, hi! A fellow Glyr!"

Tentative, Reverie sits next to the Glyridite in the pool, leaving a couple of feet between them. I sit next to her on the edge of the pool, soaking my claws in the hot water. I *really* don't want to get in. Unless Reverie insists, I won't.

"Hi, my name is Shimeri!" The Glyridite holds out a glowing glitter hand.

Reverie stares at the hand, seeming to marvel at the contrasts. Taking the hand, she says, "Reverie."

"Oh, that's such a pretty name," Shimeri says, still smiling as she looks at me. "And who are you?"

"Luca."

She eyes my body with a hum of appreciation. "I've never seen a glittered Gargoyle before." Her neon green eyes glance at Reverie's brand. "And part siren? How wonderful!"

Reverie's head snaps back like Shimeri slapped her. My tail lashes nervously. This could go really well or ... really badly.

The others in the pool have stopped talking, watching the interaction. I glance at each of them, contemplating a subtle threat, then decide against it. If Reverie notices, it could harm this interaction before it begins.

Reverie worries her lips, choosing her words with intention. "You ... think it's ... wonderful?"

Shimeri frowns. "Of course. They're your powers. Why wouldn't they be wonderful?"

"Where are you from?" I ask, knowing it can't be Gondora.

The Glyridite lights up. "Slous. Do you know it?"

I nod. "The Land of Many Waters."

Shimeri nods. "Yes, exactly. Lived there my whole life. Where are *you* from?"

"Gondora," Reverie says warily. "Have you been?"

With a tinkling laugh, Shimeri shakes her head. "How can you stand it there? I hear the culture there not only hates our species but also," She holds up five fingers, ticking off each one. "Sirens, goblins, pixies, bogs, and even werewolves. I heard those are completely banned."

All of it's true. She's forgetting dryads aren't allowed to have leadership positions, and it's incredibly Mermaid inaccessible.

"No, thank you!" Shimeri says with a giggle. "I hear it's stunning. Maybe one day I'll visit. If they ever change their tune toward glitter." She raises her hand, allowing a thick rainbow to spring from her palm. "I'd rather play with my rainbows all day whenever I want, rather than have people staring."

With that last part, she sends our audience a nasty look. They quickly resume their conversation.

I like her.

Reverie still appears unconvinced. "People aren't afraid to touch you?"

"Of *course* they are," Shimeri says with a chuckle, trailing the rainbow over the surface of the water. "But I don't want to be touching strangers anyway."

"And the glitter?" Reverie says, perplexed. "You don't hide it?"

Shimeri tilts her head, smooth brow wrinkling. "Of course not. Why do you ask?"

Chin dropping, Reverie gives me a silent plea. I have no idea how to help her with this one. People are afraid of me; I prefer it that way until I decide to show I'm not a threat. I don't feel the need to make sure *everyone's* comfortable around me.

Sputtering, Reverie says, "I-I don't know. I ..." She runs a finger through the glowing blue water, and mutters, "I was raised to hide it."

Shimeri glares at me like I'm the one who raised her to hate herself. I put my hands up. "Don't look at me." I motion to the glitter on my body. "I fucking love it."

Still eyeing me with suspicion, she asks Reverie, "Do you expect to hate yourself forever?"

A lone tear trails down Reverie's cheek. This isn't exactly how I envisioned the thermal pools to go. Half of me wants to scoop her up and berate Shimeri for making her feel this way. The more sensible part of me instinctually knows this moment might be pivotal.

"I ... I think so?" Reverie admits quietly. "My father is a Glyridite, but he's rarely taught me anything about the culture. My mother is a siren, and, well, you can imagine how that goes."

Shimeri nods. "We have some sirens in Slous. They actually do some live action role play, where they pretend to be the sirens of old. People pay money to be tricked into doing things. Hilarious things. There's an entire show revolving around it."

"A show?" Reverie chokes out.

With a laugh, Shimeri pulls out her phone from a bag behind her. She scrolls until she finds what she's searching for. Leaning closer to Reverie, she holds it up. "See? People love it. I've seen all eight seasons at least twice. I love it when this one guy, Rhono, is convinced to give up his entire life savings for charity."

Reverie's silent as she watches, the flickering screen lighting up her face. I watch her micro-expressions carefully, searching for a clue. All I see is her processing cognitive dissonance.

Inspiration sparks in her eyes. "I want to visit Slous."

Shimeri laughs, putting her phone away. "Well, let's exchange numbers so you—," she looks at me, "*—both* of you, can come visit."

Tension leeches from my muscles as they chatter about Slous. Personally, it sounds nightmarish to go somewhere with "many waters," but for Reverie, I'll do anything if it makes her happy.

The conversation goes on a little longer, but we're soon interrupted by another attendant, offering to bring us to our private grotto with a thermal pool. Reverie exchanges information with Shimeri before we're escorted to a small alcove.

Candles are lit everywhere, with soft moss covering the floor and hanging from the ceiling. A small waterfall feeds the pool, steam rising from the dark blue water. On the hooks, by the now-closed door, are robes and fresh charcoal gray towels.

This intimate thermal pool is designed specifically for fliers, with the interior edges significantly deeper, with a half-circle of carved stone fashioned as a sitting bench. Still makes me anxious, but the way Reverie's expression lights up, I'm determined to hide my discomfort.

"If you need anything, please ring this bell," the attendant says, handing me a bell before leaving us in privacy.

We strip, tossing our clothes onto the floor. As soon as I'm situated in the thermal pool — with a moderate amount of nervousness — Reverie joins, quick to straddle me. It's been less than twenty-four hours since we finally gave into this magic drawing us together, and I'm sad that all of it wasn't spent inside her.

She presses against me, wrapping arms around my neck, letting out a sigh. As Reverie's head comes to my shoulder, I wrap my arms around her delicious body. The water is almost too warm; just enough to relax away the tension. The way Reverie relaxes against my chest, I can tell she's experiencing the effects, as well.

"How are you?" I murmur; this environment requires soft voices.

She lets out another happy sigh and snuggles closer. "Like this is surreal. I'm sad that I've been fighting this. So much time wasted."

"Technically, we fucked up a whole year of potential."

"*Ugh,* don't remind me." Her head snuggles into my neck. She plants a kiss on my collarbone. "I'm sorry I was so mean to you." She sniffles. "I wish you had told me sooner."

My heart aches at the misery in her voice. "Oh, *Bilaste.* Why are you crying?"

"Do you need me to list all the obvious reasons? Namely, finding out you're going to become stone one day?"

I wince, staring at a candle's flame. That's the way I feel right now: like a candle being burned down to the inevitable end of the wick.

I have about twenty years until my body betrays me. Twenty-five years at most until I become a burden, then a memory, while everyone moves on with decades left to go.

Painful emotions clog my throat. If we lasted that long, Reverie would be forced to deal with that. Would she regret it? A useless husband, unable to provide or protect?

"If you need to go, I would understand," I say quietly. Bringing a hand to her hair, I run my fingers through the strands. A comfort to both of us. "I wouldn't blame you. In fact, I wish I'd told you sooner. I feel like I tricked you." I press my head against her forehead. "Will you forgive me?"

Reverie sniffs. "There's nothing to forgive because I'm not mad anymore. I was only angry that you lied and refused to tell me. But I also understand why you didn't tell me. I hid being a siren from you because I couldn't bear the thought of you viewing me differently. It's not that much dissimilar — you just found out sooner."

The lingering deep fear of being rejected eases, allowing me to take a deep, uninhibited breath for the first time in days. "Can we agree to never lie again? No matter how hard the truth is?"

"I swear it."

Reverie holds up a pinky, and I lock it with mine. We shake once and share a giggle. She leans back to look me in the eye. "I have an idea."

I bring my tail to trail up her leg as I ask, "What's that?"

"You said you're financially struggling because of your mom, right?"

I shift, grimacing. Another excellent example of not being able to provide. "Uh, yeah, but I'll figure it out; you don't need to worry."

She runs nails through my hair, sending shivers through my body. It must be a spell she's casting. "Are you trying to sway me into saying yes to something, *Bilaste?*"

She giggles, kissing the tip of my nose. "No, just trying to return the pleasurable favor."

When her fingers rub the tips of my ears, I let out a groan as I close my eyes.

It's so amazing, I almost miss what she says next. "What if we joined forces?"

Surely I misheard her. My eyes fly open to see her watching my reaction intently. "Join ... forces?"

Reverie nods, rubbing my earlobes. "We've been competing, but if we join our companies together, we gain higher profits. Imagine how much more we'll be in demand; the two best photographers in one company?"

The idea's intriguing. I wouldn't have to sacrifice my ethics to help my mother. Plus, I'd get to work with her all the time? A dream.

She hisses as my tail snakes around her lower back. My hands sweep along her sides, grazing her breasts, and finding her cheeks. Unshed tears make her bright blue eyes resemble waves in a tropical sea.

Running my hands along her neck and her arms, I whisper, "*Bilaste,* that's incredibly thoughtful. I'm interested in discussing it more."

Reverie rolls her hips forward, grinning. "Kahlo is going to be so mad."

I let out a deep chuckle. My tail slowly wraps around her torso. Her back arches, offering her breasts. Spreading my fingers below her shoulder blades, I raise her a little higher. Dipping my head to take a nipple into my mouth, I say, "He'll be fine."

Her fingers are immediately in my hair, pressing my face closer. When I lightly nip her nipple with a fang, she sucks in a sharp breath, then releases a throaty moan. *"Luca."*

My tail finishes its journey, wrapping around her neck. Switching breasts, I squeeze her throat lightly; her hips scoot closer until her pussy settles right on top of my thickening cock. Her breath's raspy as my hands roughly snatch her ass closer until our bodies are flush.

I claim her with a searing kiss, keeping pressure on her airways, and move her over the length of my hardness. Her entrance is *right there*, but I want to tease her until we're both wild with need.

Water splashes as the pace increases. Our foreheads press together, mingling our jagged breaths. Reverie breaks from the kiss to trail her tongue along my jaw and throat. Tightening my tail, I force her to straighten. Eyes flaring with surprise, she's helpless as I stand, my tail releasing her temporarily.

Grabbing her sumptuous hips, I turn her until she's kneeling on the rocks, leaning against the edge of the thermal pool. Water laps at her pussy lips like an ocean against the shore as I press between her shoulder blades, forcing her to bare everything for my viewing pleasure.

She hisses in pain. I pause. "What's wrong?"

"Ugh, my knees," she says, grimacing.

After a quick assessment, I grin. "Easy to fix."

My tail snakes around her body again, this time around her abdomen. Reverie gasps as it lifts her from the water. Her sweet ass raises. I groan at the sight. "Lean against the edge. I'll do the rest," I promise, already focused on her swollen lips.

She looks over her shoulder, double creasing her brow. "Can you hold me like this?"

I raise an eyebrow. "*Bilaste,* I can do all sorts of things with this tail. This barely scrapes the surface of what it will do to you. But first, let me reacquaint you with what it's like to be fucked like a Gargoyle."

45

Reverie

If today's experiences are a preview of tail play, ideas are an endless stream in my debauched mind. I'm weightless with his tail supporting my body. A finger slides along my growing wetness; my moan is guttural. Resting my head against my forearms, I whimper as it sinks a little deeper.

"Oh, *Bilaste.* You're glittering so good for me already."

Luca is the only man who has made me proud of my glitter, especially during sex. It's like his own soul craves it. The finger disappears with a sucking sound.

Luca hums. "You taste incredible."

Sweet goddesses, this man will be my undoing. My back arches when the finger returns, instinctually trying to offer more than he's currently taking. It sinks a little deeper, playing with my entrance in slow circles.

I whimper, biting my fingers, trying to hold back the echoing sound. The grotto is cozy, but made of merciless stone. Every sound will travel. Judging by Luca's dark chuckle, he's thinking the same thing.

"Best of luck, *Bilaste,*" he rumbles, sinking the finger in deeper. "Because this is the warm-up."

Of this, there's no doubt. He works the finger deeper while his other hand slides up my spine. Goosebumps pebble my skin, and my heart rate increases. When the hand rakes along my scalp to tug my hair back, I can't help but release a sharp gasp.

A groan rumbles in his chest. "Goddess, Reverie. When you make sounds like that, I can't decide whether to fuck your mouth or eat your moans."

The finger plunges. I grit my teeth, digging nails into the stone. He has me bowed backward, so my hands barely support my weight. It's all him, holding me in place for his use. I'm displayed for easier access; the smooth head of his cock brushes the inside of my thigh.

"Please," I rasp out.

His hand eases its grip on my hair, allowing me to put more weight onto my hands. The finger working my pussy pulls out halfway; a second finger joins.

"Please what?"

I have no fucking clue; begging is the only way I know how to communicate right now. Those fingers thrust at a tortuous pace. Luca grabs one of my breasts roughly, pinching the nipple.

"Please ..." Luca increases the pace of his fingers, bringing the hand on my breast to cup my jaw, lifting me again. "... what?"

My ragged breaths make it hard to speak. His hard cock rubs *right there* perfectly on my clit in gentle swipes, driving me out of my fucking mind. The words are nearly sobs as I sputter out, "P-please give me more."

"I can feel how much you want this," he purrs, moving his fingers and cock in tandem. "You're so wet for me. But not wet enough for how I'm going to fuck you."

Luca leans forward and whispers in my ear, "I want you to cum so hard, your clenching cunt almost snaps off my fingers."

His voice is full of masculine sin. A strangled whimper breezes past my parted lips. "Y-yes, please."

This man will make me beg for the moons and stars, and he'd do everything in his power to pluck them from the sky. The rapture of his cock against my clit has me mindless with lust, sparking the inferno of an impending orgasm.

The hand cupping my jaw wraps around my mouth, and Luca's fingers pick up the pace. The barely there sensation of his cock teasing my clit is my undoing, a scream ripping from me, filling his palm. He lets out an awed groan.

"So good, *Bilaste.* Look at how you come undone for me."

My body shakes violently as the orgasm works its way through my body, pulsating my muscles. Stars fill my vision; for a moment, no sounds exist.

When I'm finally able to suck in another breath, Luca purrs, "That's my girl. You did so well."

Releasing my face, Luca slides out his fingers. My arms, unable to hold my weight right now, buckle to rest my forehead against my hands. My hot breath slaps against the cool stone as Luca shifts behind me.

There's a sucking, then a popping sound, as he slips his fingers out of his mouth. "I want to taste you every day, baby." The scalding tip of his cock presses against my entrance. "Right before I do this every time you let me."

A scream lodges in my throat as he works himself into me at the most agonizingly slow pace, filling and stretching inch by salacious inch. Rough hands spread my ass cheeks.

He lets out a keening groan. *"Fuck."*

The tail lifts me a little higher. I'm helpless as he pumps into me. Slow at first, but soon, it's a punishing pace that sloshes water everywhere. I hear his wings snap open. Fingers dig into my flesh as my ass bounces against his hips.

My teeth dig into my hands, a desperate attempt to hide my screams. It's a poor gag against the sounds, because there's *no damn way* people in the other grottos can't hear the uninhibited way we're fucking. He brings two fingers to circle my clit, vanquishing my sanity.

Already, another orgasm builds. It's a heady realization that I can have this every day if I so choose. That Luca will be here, craving me the same way. My days will be full of every expression of love available. That thought pushes me over the edge.

The orgasm slams into me like an avalanche. Behind me, Luca grunts and slams to the hilt, cock throbbing. I exhale a shuddering breath, feeling satiated.

Luca runs worshipful hands over my body with heaving breaths. "I love the way you take me, *Bilaste.*"

My hand aches as my teeth part, releasing the ruined flesh. There's definitely going to be a bruise there. "I love the way *you* take *me.*"

He chuckles, lowering me so I can attempt to balance on my own two feet. Easier said than done. Luca's firm, protective hand holds my belly when my knees buckle.

"Careful," he murmurs, turning me to face him. Tilting my head with a finger, Luca presses a reverent kiss to my lips, mingling our ragged breaths. "You're so fucking perfect."

I nuzzle his nose. "You aren't too shabby yourself."

His chuckle is a hug to my heart. "Do you think they heard us?"

I blow air out through my lips dismissively. "*Pfft*, so what if they did?"

"That's the spirit," he says, smiling. "Here; have a seat." Luca helps me ease back into the water, then sits next to me. Wrapping an arm around my shoulders, he tugs me tight to his side. Placing a kiss on my forehead, he brushes away a wet strand of hair from my cheek.

I let out a happy sigh, more at peace than I ever have in my entire life. "I love you, Luca."

"I love you, too, *Bilaste.*"

Watching the small waterfall gurgle water, I ask, "So what do we do next?"

Luca snorts. "If you think this was our last round for the day, you'd be sorely mistaken."

"Sorely being the optimal word," I joke.

He stills. "Is it too much?"

"I'll tell you when it is," I assure him.

We spent the rest of our time enjoying each other's company, talking about nothing in particular. It's incredible, spending time with him like this. Intimate, quiet, and comfortable.

It's in this moment, where everything appears to align as intended, that I realize one very important thing: If I only receive a week with Luca, it's all worth it. Twenty years? Sounds like a blessing above all blessings.

I want to spend the rest of his days making sure he knows that my love doesn't come with terms and conditions.

46

Luca

"Okay, rapid fire question and answer," Reverie says, sipping her femire.

We're sitting in the Starlight Room, the hotel's exclusive restaurant, lit only by bioluminescent plants. The small but mighty light sources cast an ethereal glow around the space. Small waterfalls cascade over the rocky walls, deepening the intimate ambiance. Tiny pin-points of light prick the black ceiling, reminding me of Cilyestia Pools.

Unfortunately, Reverie is not in a dress made of glitter, but wears a silver satin dress revealing enough to show off her glittering veins and brand. She looks fantastic. Her growing confidence expands the pride swelling within my rib cage.

The waiter has already pulled the empty plates, and we're waiting for our slices of blueberry cheesecake.

We spent most of the dinner trying to learn obscure facts about one another. Apparently, this new game is the solution to learning the most, the fastest.

Taking a sip of my whiskey, I say, "Any limits?"

"None."

I sit back, appraising her. "And we have to be fully honest?"

"Fully," she agrees.

It doesn't sound *too* bad. Scary, sure. But intriguing enough. "Okay."

"Age of first kiss."

I laugh. "We're starting at the beginning, huh?"

Reverie grins, taking another sip of her drink. "Keep up, Destau."

"Eight. Her name was Imelie. Behind a slide. You?"

"Is that going to be your question?"

I frown. "So I can't ask it back without it counting?"

"Nope." Her delicious lips pop the P.

"Then, no. My question is, did you hate growing up as an only child?"

"Absolutely," she says fiercely. "I wish there'd been someone else to loosen some of their damn expectations."

"My parents were never like that." I say pensively. "That must have been stressful."

"Still is," she says with a grimace. "Favorite sports team?"

"The Lucifers."

"You enjoy clawball?"

"I enjoy a good beer, junk food, and screaming at teams of men pommeling one another over the ownership of a randomly appointed object."

"But you're not gay?" she quips, pretending to sound surprised.

I dip fingers into my ice water and flick them at her. She giggles, wiping a droplet from her cheek.

Drying my fingers off, I ask, "Top place you've always wanted to visit?"

"Oasha. I heard the desert landscape is stunning."

"Maybe we can book a wedding or something there," I say, contemplating how to make that happen for her.

"Favorite time of day?"

"Morning. I apparently love a good cup of hazelnut coffee nowadays."

Reverie grins, lighting up the space with her joy. "I love hazelnuts."

Returning the smile with one of my own, I say, "I know."

Watching her for a moment, I take in the softness of her expression; at the inner light that electrifies her gaze. If I could, I'd peel back that pretty head of hair and nestle right into her mind. See the world as she does.

But her viewpoint on reality, for better or worse, is hard won. I may not know everything about her, but I know life has dealt her some low blows. I want to know all of them; I want Reverie to feel seen.

"Biggest heartbreak?"

The smile falls, but not by much. Instead, her mouth quirks, and she looks up at the corner of her left eye, contemplating the answer. Voice quieter as she says, "Morlin. He was the one I told you about weeks ago. He dated me for months, and I thought he loved me." Reverie scoffs. "As much as a twenty-one-year-old man can love a seventeen-year-old girl."

My instinct to protect flares. "Seventeen?"

"Yep," she says with a grim expression. "He apparently always wanted to sleep with a Glyridite, and I was the stupidest one he could find."

"You were seventeen," I say with a gentle tone. "It's not your fault."

Reverie's body language tenses up, shoulders rising and arms crossing. "Anyway, that's my answer. That's my biggest hurt, especially after what he said about me."

So much glitter oozed out. My stomach rolls with disgust. That's what she told me that day we were rock climbing. My fingers twitch, wishing for a specific skull to crush.

"What's *your* worst relationship?" she says, making it sound like a challenge.

I give her a sad smile. "Dated a woman named Rylyian for four years in my early twenties. We lived together for most of it. She was controlling and neurotic,"

"What happened?"

"She wanted kids, and I didn't."

Reverie frowns. "You don't want kids?"

"I was twenty-two. It felt too young for such a big responsibility."

"Did she get married right after you broke up?"

"Yep. Popped out three younglings within the following four years."

"Goddess," Reverie says, shaking her head. "I can't imagine having four kids at my age right now."

I laugh. "Me neither." Assessing her reaction, I ask, "Do you want kids?"

She shrugs as her hand floats to her visible siren brand. "I worry, you know? My children, and their children, and *their* children will be branded. A never-ending cycle unless the laws change."

I nod. "I understand deeply about generational trauma."

Reverie sighs, then frowns. "Who's turn is it now?"

"Mine. Technically. I did ask you if you wanted kids."

Reverie grins. "I'll let you have one freebie. Only because I like you."

"Well, thank you, Miss Nonya; Your generosity is noted."

A voice interrupts the conversation. "Two blueberry cheesecakes." The waiter places the plates in front of us. "Enjoy."

I eye the blue slice and lift my spoon. "If you had to eat one dessert forever, what would it be?"

Reverie scoops a bite and holds eye contact as she tantalizes me with a slow swoop of her tongue against the spoon. With a raised eyebrow, she says, "Can it be something else other than food?"

Immediately, I'm shifting in my seat. Goddesses save me, but I'm hard as fucking stone right now. After taking a sip of water to soothe my sudden dry mouth, I say, "Uh, sure. What, you want something like rocks or marbles?"

Reverie takes another teasing bite, dragging her tongue along the groove of the spoon before shoving it into her mouth.

Goddesses fucking goddesses.

"Maybe a certain someone?"

Digging my nails into my pants, I'm vibrating with restraint. "You're playing a dangerous game, *Bilaste.* You're already sore enough. Are you so determined to not sit for days?"

Surely, she doesn't think I haven't noticed her tiny winces every time she shifts in the seat. I'm both pleased and worried, but she doesn't appear bothered, so I've focused on feeling pleased.

"You asked," she says defensively, flicking her tongue out to lick up a stray piece of cream. There's the tiniest sound of it smearing against her tongue. I dig a fang into my lips to prevent a moan escaping.

Speaking of cream, I'm about to ruin these fucking pants.

After exhaling with extreme care, I say, "*Bilaste.* Are you forfeiting the game in favor of sexy food play? Because I swear, I will have these desserts taken to-go, and I will haul you to the hotel room where I will lather you with multiple types of fucking cream before you can say, 'blueberry.' Would you like that?"

Reverie straightens, eyes widening. They dart around; she leans forward. With a dramatic whisper, she says, "How fast can we get it to-go?"

I signal to the waiter, trying not to come off too impatient, when I only want to roar for him to hurry the Hells up. "If he's not here in sixty seconds, I'm grabbing it with my bare hands."

"Yummy," she purrs with a shimmy of her shoulders.

Gritting my teeth, I shake my head in disbelief. "You're actually going to put me in an earlier grave than necessary."

Reverie pretends to wipe away non-existent food, dragging her thumb along her bottom lip. I want to dig my fangs into it. With too-wide eyes, she pouts. "But I'll make it worth your while."

I sweep my gaze over her with deep appreciation. "I know you will."

"Yes, sir?" the waiter says, appearing out of thin air. Benefits of phantoms.

I motion to our barely touched slices. "I need these boxed up, please. My partner is sick, and we need to get her back to the room immediately."

The waiter gives Reverie a worried expression; she's glaring at me.

"Yes, sir, of course," the waiter rushes out. "I'll be right back." He disappears, leaving Reverie to curl her nose in disgust.

"Now he's going to think I've soiled myself or something."

I let out a dismissive grunt. "It would show in that flimsy thing you call a dress."

"It's not flimsy; it's satin."

"It's going to be on the floor in three minutes," I say smoothly. "One last question."

Her eyebrows perk up. "What is it?"

"What's your favorite sex position?"

"I would normally say from behind, but your tail offers intriguing possibilities."

I laugh. "I'm excited to find out what you have in mind."

"Here you go, sir," the phantom waiter says, handing over two paper boxes.

"Thank you."

I pack up our slices, trying to maintain my focus and not spill them. It's difficult to not weigh the merits of swiping away all of these plates to splay her across the table.

The Rainbow Menace is now leaning on her elbows, offering a deeper view into her cleavage.

I'm mentally tallying the spankings for each offense.

Standing with the boxes held in one hand, I hold out the other one. "Come, *Bilaste.* Let's make dessert more hands-on."

"Hopefully more than *on* hands," she quips, gracefully coming to stand at my side, braiding her fingers through mine.

Looking at the light of my life, I grin wide enough to flash my fangs. They immediately catch her attention, and she swallows hard. She *should* be nervous.

"Let go, sparkles," I say, trying to aggravate her. To bring her down to this mix of irritation and desire that I'm stewing in.

"Don't you *dare,*" she seethes, sounding more serious than she has in minutes.

"Glimmer?"

"That's my cousin, so no. And even if I didn't have a cousin, it'd still be a no."

"Shimmy?"

"I might murder you."

"Gleamella?"

"That's it; no cheesecake pussy for you," she hisses as we step out of the restaurant.

"No," I whine, smiling. "Don't take away my *cheesecake pussy.*"

"You were warned."

"Barely."

"Consider this a blanket warning, valid in perpetuity or whatever."

I tap her butt as we come to a stop in front of the elevator. "I want to 'in perpetuity' this ass."

Her nose wrinkles in distaste. "Ew."

"What do you mean *'ew'?*"

"I mean, what are you perpetuating in me?"

I shrug, motioning for her to step into the elevator when it opens. "My dick, most likely. Maybe my fingers. Maybe—"

The same family as yesterday stands in the elevator, watching us. Reverie has no clue, because they only saw her rear end. Me, however? Yeah, this is awkward.

Giving them a stiff wave, I shuffle to the side and let them out. The mother gives me the nastiest look, ushering her kids away.

"Well, that was unfortunate," Reverie says, stepping over so I can shove myself into the mobile coffin.

"You have no idea," I say, pressing the button to our floor, cheesecake still in hand.

47

Reverie

As the transport brings us back to Gondora, I view the city differently now. The towering buildings rising from white puffy clouds are more welcoming. Perhaps it's because Shimeri made me realize my powers are beautiful — something Luca has been trying to prove to me — and showed me how to integrate fully into my identity.

When we land on the transport dock, I let Luca take care of my suitcases, earning me a grateful smile. I hadn't realized when I rejected him last time how badly he needed to take care of me. In these last few days, I've learned so much more about him, all of it wonderful.

The memories flutter with happiness inside my belly. I have so many new memories to organize in my mind. There's now a whole mental filing cabinet dedicated to him.

Unfortunately, when we arrive back in Gondora, we have to go our separate ways. While his mother has finally woken up, much to our relief, he wants to wait for our first meeting. Luca's positive she wouldn't want to meet me while in the hospital.

Which leaves me time to get ready for dinner with my parents.

The complicated relationship with my parents leaves no shortage of resentment. The older I get, the more frustrated I've become. Today is the day we clear the air.

Standing in my bedroom, I inspect my outfit. This time around, I'm not only wearing what makes me feel comfortable ... the sweater won't be tagging along.

The longer I stare at my reflection, the angrier I become, because I don't need to be afraid of my powers. Shimeri wasn't. She wasn't also part siren, but even that side of me ... why do I need to hate myself? Because society said so?

I'm over it.

Stripping, I decide to wear a strapless summer dress. The weather outside is balmy, despite the constant breeze sweeping through the city. But the pale rainbow stripes bring out my glittering colors. It's too on-the-nose; my father will hate it.

I can't wait.

Piling my curls on my hair so my brand shows, I apply pink lip gloss and smack my lips together. Picking up my phone, I take a selfie for Luca.

Reverie: Look at what I'm wearing!

Luca: You're stunning, *Bilaste*. I'm glad you're showing the world your beauty.

Reverie: My parents are going to hate it.

Luca: Is that good?

Reverie: Yes. It's time we had a talk about the choices they made while raising me.

Luca: Want me to come over after? My mom is awake, thank the goddesses. She'll be released in two days. She's excited to meet you.

Reverie: Yes, I'll let you know when I'm done. I can't wait to meet her too.

Grabbing my purse, I breeze out of my apartment, excited to have the confrontation that's been a long-time coming. As the Dragxi flies me through the clouds to the suburban settlement on the outskirts of Gondora, I consider what I'll say.

But as I raise my hand to knock on their door, I'm still not sure. It's probably best to play it by ear. My goal is to not let this turn into a shouting match.

We'll see how long that lasts.

My mother opens the door, beaming. Her ashy blonde tendrils fall loosely over her shoulders. Even in her sixties, she's stunning.

"Darling, it's so wonderful to see you!" she gushes, gathering me in a warm hug. I squeeze her back tightly. Though we're often at odds, I still love her.

Mom ushers me inside. In a sing-song voice, she calls out, "Sparks, she's here!"

"Is that my girl?" Dad yells from their kitchen. His booming voice makes me grin. As he rounds the corner, wiping his hands with a dish towel, I rush over to him. He gives me a solid hug, and I'm relieved. Despite not seeing eye-to-eye on my choices or clothing, I love my parents.

"Come, dinner is almost ready," he says, releasing the hug and steering me to the dining room. Their home is a cozy one-story, with floor to ceiling west-facing windows. It's an open floor plan minus the bedrooms on the far side of the house.

Everything's built with comfort in mind, with plush sitting areas, dozens of pillows everywhere in case you want to lie down in a random corner. No one ever does, but Mom refuses to believe there won't be a day those piles of pillows won't be needed.

The dining space holds a polished wood table with benches with even more pillows to sit on. Large Monsteras and ferns line the walls, basking in the glow of sunset. Dimmed sconces line the earth-toned walls, with candles lit all down the center of the table adding ambiance.

It's clear where my obsession with cozy vibes came from.

"Sit, sit." Mom ushers me to the same spot I've sat in my entire life. I obey, letting them fuss over me. Dad brings me a glass of water, promising my favorite fruit juice when dinner's plated.

He cooks over the stove, finishing my favorite dish: roasted vegetables and braised quail.

Mom kisses him on the cheek before rushing back to the table, sitting across from me. "So, tell me what you've been up to. It's been weeks since we've seen you!"

After taking a sip of water, I tell them about some of the most recent weddings, lingering on the story of Bella and Azmodeous. Mom's rightfully shocked about Azmodeous' mother. I tell them about the Orc wedding, lingering on the ceremony site details.

As Dad brings dinner over, perfectly plated, he asks, "So has my little girl found anyone special yet?"

Mom's equally intrigued, leaning forward. "Yes, please tell me you've found someone."

Taking a deep, steadying breath, I say, "Yes. I've met someone."

Two sets of eyebrows raise, and matching smiles split their faces. Mom even claps. Dad forks out our portions as he asks, "So, tell me about him. Or her. Tell me about them."

"Well," I start, gauging their reaction. "His name is Luca, and he's a Gargoyle."

"Oh!" Mom claps her hands together. "We love a big, strong man!"

Dad casts her an indecipherable look. "Is he in the industry, too?"

I nod, cutting into my quail. "He's a photographer too. We're actually technically competitors." I frown. "Although that's probably not true anymore. I think."

"Amazing," Mom says, expression turning wistful. I can already tell she's going to fan-girl over him.

Dad cuts right to the chase, as usual. "How does he feel about being with someone who is mixed?"

My fork screeches against the plate. Staring at the quail, I contemplate my words. Sometimes, the internalized bigotry starts inside the home.

Refocusing on slicing the quail apart, I say evenly, "He doesn't care."

Dad hums in a way I know he doesn't believe me. Fine. I guess we're doing this already. Placing my utensils down, I school my features. "Say what you want to say so I can go back to dinner."

Mom's eyes bounce between the two of us, trying to decide when to jump in. Dad, with his dark blue eyes, looks pained. "I know you've been hoping for someone, but we all know how cruel the world is to those who are mixed."

"How cruel *some* of the world is," I correct. "And after having a conversation with a Glyridite in the Orc mountains, I'm coming to realize that bigots don't exist everywhere." Grabbing my fruit juice, I mutter, "Even if they're in my home."

Dad's eyes flash with warning, but Mom speaks up. "What is that supposed to mean, Popsicle? We aren't bigots."

I scoff, sitting back in my chair. "You both raised me to hide who I am. To be ashamed."

Mom's face warms with anger. "That's not fair. Sirens are branded from the moment they're born. I tried my best to prepare you for what the world would do."

"That's valid," I say carefully. "And I appreciate everything you've taught me about the outside world and its arbitrary laws. But you also taught me to be ashamed of it."

My eyes cut to Dad. "Luca brought me to Cilyestia Pools last week. He didn't have to ask; he knew I would love it. You've never taken me."

"He stepped foot on hallowed ground?" Dad's back goes ramrod straight. "This Luca presumes too much."

"He presumes enough," I say hotly. "It's *you* who have presumed too much. You assumed the world would be cruel, and instead of helping me embrace my power, you gave me clothes to cover my body, and never let me love it."

My voice raises with each word, so I take a breath. "This past month, I've been forced to look at my upbringing in a new way. Maybe Gondora isn't for me; I've learned people like me are welcome in other places."

"You'd leave?" Mom says, stricken.

I shrug. "I don't know. Frankly, it's a new thought for me, too. But you—" I point at Dad, "—made me feel like my glitter was a cage. So whenever bigots mocked me or fetishized me, I felt like I deserved it. That it was a required experience as a Glyridite."

Mom is almost in tears as I say to her, "You did that as well. Sirens are so much more than sexuality, but you never helped me believe that."

Her brown eyes shine with tears. Dad's pale face reddens as his fists clench. A muscle feathers in his jaw; I know he's trying hard to speak without yelling. I gained my disposition more from him; fiery and resentful of the world.

I don't want to be the latter anymore.

"Popsicle," Mom pleads. "Please forgive me. I tried my best, truly."

"I know you did," I say, softening. "You both did. But you need to understand how much the fear-based upbringing stunted me until now."

"What's changed?" Mom asks, voice quavering.

An easy smile teases my lips. "Luca. Since the start, he's loved my glitter. He loves it when I sing."

I don't care if you're covered in glitter or sing me to my death. My heart and soul are entirely yours to do whatever you want with.

The memory of his words lends courage. Directly at Dad, I say, "I need us to move forward differently. You're no longer allowed to refer to me as mixed. You're no longer going to tell me to wear certain clothing."

His eyes flicker over my outfit; he purses his lips. "Even when you flaunt every vein for the world to see?"

That's when it hits me; this is about more than glitter. I look at Mom, truly look at her, and realize she's wearing a lot of layers. Sifting through the Mom filing cabinet in my mind, I realize that she's always worn layers. Even in the heat.

“Oh my goddess,” I say, laughing. “Dad, are you *sexist?*”

Mom brings her hands to her face, watching him with wide eyes. How did I not see it before? My father is many things, including patient and loving. But because of the way they encouraged me to view my powers, it never dawned on me there was more to it.

Dad seems more confused than angry. “No, I’m not. Why would you think that?”

I motion to my dress. “So you wouldn’t care if Mom wore this dress?”

It’s fascinating watching him process my question. Conflict flickers; he looks at my mother. At her clothes.

Now he’s bewildered, wrinkles deepening between his brows. “Maybe?”

“Okay ...” I bite back a laugh. “Well. Maybe that’s enough revelations for the evening.” I look between them. “This sounds like a discussion for you both to have in private.”

Without another word, we resume eating, but in the corner of my eye, I watch Mom roll up her sleeves.

I smile.

48

Luca

The moment Reverie says I can come over, I snatch up Reggie and leap off my platform. Coasting through the air traffic, I grin at passersby. It's been an entire afternoon since I've seen her — one afternoon too long.

Reggie flies next to me, easily keeping up. His forked tongue flies out from the side of his mouth, moving his legs as if they help him move forward. Silly chimeragon.

My fist hovers to knock on her door when it flings open, revealing the love of my life beaming from ear to ear. She's wearing a sheer white tank top, revealing her nipples. Shorts hug her curvy hips, revealing those strong thighs I love.

"Hi!" she squeals, leaping forward for a hug. Gathering her in my arms, I breathe in her raspberry scent. Carrying her into the house, with Reggie hot on my heels, she giggles into my chest, smooshed against my shirt. "Ineedtobrefplez."

Chuckling, I release her, setting her on the ground, and closing the door behind me.

Reverie grins. "How's your mom?"

"Mom is good. She's excited to meet you."

Excitement isn't a strong enough word — Mom's thrilled at the prospect of my finally bringing a woman around. Something I haven't done in years.

"Will I get to meet her soon?" she asks, eyes shining with hope.

I nod. "She said we can come in a couple of days."

"Can't wait," she says, kneeling in front of Reggie to scratch his ears.

Looking around Reverie's apartment, I realize I've walked right into a heaven. Glitter is everywhere. On everything. Every shade in existence is in here, on the cozy piles of pillows, lightbulbs, and yes, even the sink.

There's a picture of her with two adults on the wall. The woman features a siren's brand, and the other is a male Glyridite. I walk closer to inspect the image. It's in a park, and Reverie is about fourteen years old.

"Are these your parents?"

Reverie comes to stand beside me. "Yep." She lets out a bitter laugh. "Dinner with them was interesting, to say the least. I told my dad he isn't allowed to dictate what I wear anymore. Turns out he's also a little sexist, although I don't think he knew it. Even Mom was surprised at the realization."

I wrinkle my nose. "He controls what you both wear?"

She rolls her eyes. "Yes, but I won't let him shame me anymore. I'm tired of their outdated views on how my future should look."

I kiss her on the forehead. "That's my girl. Tell the patriarchy to fuck off."

Walking into the kitchen, I open cabinets, inspecting their contents.

"What are you doing?" Reverie sounds apprehensive, as if I'm going to judge her for missing certain spices — which I might, because why doesn't she have any kinds of pepper?

"Do you not have any pepper?"

She closes the cabinet I'm inspecting. "You want to know about pepper?"

I face her, smiling. "Are you not good at cooking?"

Flustered, Reverie crosses her arms. "I mean, I won't win any awards, but no one has died yet."

Unable to resist teasing her, I say, "The optimal word here is 'yet.'"

A sound I haven't heard in at least a few days vibrates in her throat as she growls in frustration. "Did you come here to make fun of my spice rack and my cooking skills?"

"Of course not," I say smoothly. "I also need to check to see if you clean your toilet."

Reverie scoops up Reggie, who immediately nestles into her embrace. *Traitor.* She gives me a prim look. "You can leave now. We think you've already overstayed your welcome."

Tilting my head, I give her a smug grin. "Reggie won't stay." I make a kissy sound. "Come 'ere Reg. We're not wanted here."

The Beast of Betrayal gives me a look that says, *Are you kidding?*

Reverie crows with victory. "Okay! Goodbye! Nice knowing you!" She pauses. "I guess I'll have to go find myself another partner who doesn't care about my peppers." Then, *"Sir."*

I take a menacing step forward, my claws clicking on her glittering white tiled floor. "Say that again."

She widens her eyes innocently. "What? *Sir?*"

I glare at Reggie. Baring my teeth, I bark, "Down."

Reggie doesn't hesitate, kicking out of her arms and scampering away to a pile of pillows. He promptly begins to nap. I give Reverie a glare that wipes the smirk off her beautiful face.

"What's wrong?" I croon. Taking a large step forward, I flush our bodies together, dipping my chin as I take in the fear on her face. It's not only fear, though; her eyes sparkle with excitement.

In a low rumble, I say, "Reverie, never forget that I'm one of the most powerful creatures to fly or walk on this continent. My softness is hard-earned, and freely given. But not my first instinct."

Threading my fingers through her long, soft hair, I yank her head back. My cock twitches at her little inhalation. "What was that you said? Some of the best pleasures come with pain?"

She's unable to nod; instead, I hear her gulp. Music to my ears. Releasing her hair, I pick her up with my tail. Reverie screeches, semi-panicked, as it easily lifts her around the waist. That damn smile shifts into something downright devious.

Wrapping her fingers around my tail like it's my cock, she strokes. The growling groan coming from my throat is a sound I've never made before in my life.

"Where. Is. Your. Bed?" I ask through gritted teeth.

Still stroking, she points to a door across the room. Stomping across the apartment, I barge into the room and toss her onto the glittering bed. She curls into a fit of giggles until she sees me still glaring at her.

"That wasn't nice." I look around the room until I spot what I'm searching for. A wide, full-length mirror leans against her wall. It's far from the bed, so I place it right across from the bedframe.

"What are you doing?" she demands, sitting on her heels.

"Poke the Gargoyle, get a pointy end in return, Reverie," I say conversationally. Grinning, I fist the collar of my T-shirt and rip it in half. Rolling it into a ball, I throw it at her face. It plops into her lap.

Reverie jerks back, scuttling to her pillows, watching me with wide, excited eyes.

"*Luca*. What are you *doing?* I was ***kidding!***"

"Yes, well, I'm *not,*" I say impassively, snapping my belt out of the loops, making her lick her lips. I point at her clothes. "Take those off. Now."

"No."

"I recommend you do."

"Make me." She gives me a stubborn glare, but the corners of her mouth twitch as she fights a giggle.

"Okay." I round the edge of the bed. She tries to leap away; my tail lashes out, grabbing her ankle. Yanking her backward, I cackle as she shrieks, grabbing every pillow possible for purchase. Grabbing her arm, I flip her over, keeping her in place with my tail.

Her wide blue eyes glow the color of tropical waters. Her breasts jiggle as she pants. Bending over, I curl my fingers into the top of her shirt. Her pulse pounds against her sternum.

"You said 'Sir'," I remind her, my tone full of salacious promise. "Do you remember what I said would happen if you did that?"

Her throat bobs as she swallows. "Um, something about it making you not want to go slow?"

"Correct." With a tug, I split her shirt in half. It's flimsy, ripping apart like paper. Reverie inhales sharply, bringing her arms to cover her breasts. I carefully coax them to her sides. "Are you still sore?"

Dazed, she nods. "I took some medication though. It's okay now."

I'll still have to pay close attention. Slipping out of my trousers, I let them fall to my ankles. Her eyes home in on my cock, still held at bay by my boxer briefs. I motion to her shorts.

"If you like those, I recommend you protect them."

She shimmies her hips and tosses the shorts at my face. I catch them one handed. With a feral grin, I raise them and inhale. It smells like her arousal; the scent tightens my balls. Reverie blushes from the tip of her nose to her breasts.

Tossing them over my shoulder, I survey her delicious body, with only a thin piece of satin covering the one spot I'm desperate to sink into. Her glitter veins are like a road map, guiding my eyes to endless destinations.

With a casual tone, I begin collecting pillows as I say, "So you like to be a brat?" She shakes her head, which makes me chuckle. "I thought we agreed not to lie to one another anymore."

Reverie stays silent, watching me build a tower of pillows. A blush pinkens her cheeks as she watches my every move, chest heaving.

I continue, "Well, we both know you're going to give me a taste of all twelve Hells every single day, so I figure it's a good idea to establish expectations of what said sass will cost you."

"I'm not going to obey you because you command me," she snipes.

When the tower of pillows is tall enough, I playfully pat her knee. "I don't expect you to obey me, just like you can't expect me to let you be sassy without consequences."

She squeezes her legs together. I give her a crooked grin. "If I didn't know any better, I'd say you're nervous."

"Am not," she says defensively. "I'm just wondering if we are going to fuck in a pillow fort."

I throw back my head with a laugh. "The idea is intriguing; you certainly have enough pillows."

My tail releases her ankle. I crook a finger, motioning for her to sit up. To my delight, she obeys without protest. I think she's more curious than anything else.

I easily flip her over onto her stomach. She makes an *oof* sound, watching me over her shoulder. I grab the edges of her underwear and slide them down. Giving me the best view in the whole fucking universe.

I take a moment to admire her sweet ass. Bringing a hand to one plump cheek, I rub it firmly, loving the way it jiggles. Giving it a playful smack, I grunt with appreciation when she squeals, lifting it higher.

"Perfect. You're a natural," I tease.

Her brows furrow as she tries to puzzle together my words. "A natural at what?"

Before she can react, I clamp my hands around her waist. She shrieks as I deposit her directly onto the pillows. I've arranged the pillows so that the highest point is directly under her hips. She's also facing the mirror, so she has nowhere else to look at but me taking her from behind.

Reverie tries to sit up, but I stop her with a hand. "No, *Bilaste*. Remember, I'm setting expectations."

She laughs, wiggling her ass. I groan as her pussy glistens with glitter. Climbing onto the bed on my knees, I move each of her thighs wider, until she's obscenely bared to me. I gaze at her reflection. She's resting her chin on both hands, grinning wildly.

"Do you like what you see?" She taunts.

Ignoring her question, I run a finger along her swollen slit. Her eyes flutter as she lets out a moan. Her ass deliciously tilts further, showing her eagerness.

My cock is desperate for release, but I will not waste this opportunity to teach her a lesson. Pressing my finger into her entrance, I groan at how easily it slides in. Her body is eager for much more.

When I confirm that my finger fully slides in without resistance, I add a second.

There's a little resistance; easily remedied.

As I move them in and out, I glance at her reflection. Her eyes are closed.

"Reverie, open your eyes."

She opens them, dazed. With my free hand, I roughly smack her ass. Her eyes brighten with awareness, fully paying attention now. Increasing the pace of my fingers, I bring my thumb to her clit to give her the friction I know she needs.

"See, when you call me 'Sir,' it does something to me, Reverie. I can't quite explain it, but I know it makes me want to fuck you so hard, you forget your name." When her head drops with a moan, I spank her again. Her head pops up; I shake my head.

"No, you're going to look in that mirror the whole time. I want you to memorize everything I'm going to do to you. All of it. Every sensation. Every sound. Every pump of my cock. And you're going to be a good girl by cumming on this tiny cock, never forgetting what happens when you tease me."

"Y-yes," she moans. When her eyes close, I spank her again. Her pussy muscles tighten.

"Oh, you like that?" I croon, doing it again. She throws her ass back. To reward her, I added a third finger. Her body greedily accepts it. "Now cum for me, baby, because I won't be inside you until you cum, and I *really* want to be inside you."

I increase the pace, never breaking our eye contact. The only sounds are our heaving breaths and my fingers inside her wet core. Her glitter veins grow brighter until she's glowing from the inside out. Her body tightens until she rocks her head back, crying out in a sob of pleasure.

"That's it. Your pleasure belongs to me," I mutter, entirely focused on my body inside hers. When I look up, her eyes are closed, mid-orgasm.

I spank her *hard,* and her whole body seizes as her orgasm intensifies. Her eyes open, but she's so lost in sensations, she's not focused on me. She's a beautiful, obedient creature.

Grinning wide enough for my cheeks to hurt, I pull out my fingers. She's barely recovered, stupefied and panting. Brandishing a claw, I cut off my boxer briefs at each side of my thigh, letting the torn fabric fall to the mattress as I press my cock to her entrance.

"Watch me," I say in a guttural voice. I glanced at the reflection, pleased to see her listening. Pushing my hips forward, the head of my cock sinks into her pliant wetness.

"Fuuuck," I groan, my entire body shuddering. I work myself inside with tiny thrusts, willing her body to fully accept me. Grabbing her hips, I tilt them a little higher, reveling in the white glitter coating my shaft.

"Luca," she says, breathless. "Stop taking it slow and fuck me."

My smile is vicious with glee. "Gladly, *Bilaste.*"

I slam into her to the hilt. Reverie screams. Glitter pours out of her whole body in colorful waves. Her hair brightens until it's illuminating the room. Digging my fingers into her generous hips, I voraciously rock our bodies together, not letting her spend any effort while I fuck the absolute Hells out of her.

My heart gallops as sweat pours down my spine.

"Look at me," she whimpers. I've been so engrossed in watching where our bodies join, I completely forgot to watch her face. I'm thrilled to see her grinning wildly. Her fingers dig into the sheets as she holds on for dear life.

My instincts roar; I increase the pace. She's helpless in my hands, letting me wring satisfaction out of her. The Gargoyle in me demands to *claim.* To *please.* With a vicious snarl, my wings flare open, knocking over picture frames. In the reflection, I resemble an unhinged beast ruining an ethereal creature. It shoots a thrill through my body, knowing she loves this as much as I do. Our dichotomy is what makes us work.

Her body tightens, signalling she's close to cumming again. To shove her over the edge, I have my tail go between her legs, pressing into her clit. She sobs, dropping her head into the mattress. I don't make her look at me; she'll remember what it feels like to be claimed by sensation alone.

In a room full of glitter, with her soaking my cock in sparkles, I bring us both over the edge.

49

Reverie

Today, I'm meeting Luca's mother, and "nervous" isn't a strong enough word for how I feel. What if she doesn't like me? What if I don't like her? What if she's one of those mothers, like that Vampyre mother, who's obsessed with her son in a creepy way?

Luca assures me this isn't the case, but since he's an only child, and a male, I'm reluctant to believe him.

She lives on the outskirts of downtown in a condo skyhigh overlooking Infinity Falls, a sky park where waterfalls mist into the air. Luca explained it costs a lot to let her live there, but it makes her happy. Since she doesn't have much longer ... he doesn't care that it depletes his savings to make it happen.

My heart both melted and broke when he told me that.

Nestled in his arms as we fly through Gondora, I lean against his chest, reveling in his steady heartbeat. I probably should've taken a Dragxi because my hair is going to be a mess, but I also love flying with Luca.

Finally, we land on the condo's launch pad. Luca helps steady me on my feet. He chuckles, playfully tugging on a knot of hair. "You should've braided it."

I stick out my tongue, working the tangle with my fingers. "Duly noted, dunghole."

Chuckling, he ruffles my hair, despite my sounds of protest. Laughing, I toss my hair into an extremely messy bun. Either his mother will like me or she won't; if she's the type to hate someone because their hair is a mess, that's her problem, not mine.

When we reach her door, Luca pulls a key out of his pocket and opens the door. It swings open with a creak.

"Mother, I'm here!" he calls out with a soft voice.

We step into a small apartment that's darkly lit with the curtains closed. It smells clean, but is devoid of life. I give him an uncertain look, but his eyes are busy scanning the space for his mother.

"In here," a forlorn voice calls from a short hallway.

"Stay here for a moment," he murmurs, kissing my forehead. I watch him disappear down the hallway, crossing my arms over my chest as I study the space. It feels like a cave, but not in a cozy way. Magazines pile on surfaces, as well as other bits of clutter. The sink is empty, and everything's organized. It's just ... I don't know how to explain it. Like someone has decided what's most important, and aesthetics isn't one of them

I'm willing to bet the apartment is clean because of Luca.

"So you're the one who has my son enamored," a voice croaks.

My head jerks toward the voice, taken aback by Luca entering the room, holding a female Gargoyle in his arms. She's reduced. I've never seen a single female Gargoyle who didn't stand tall and proud. This woman is ... smaller than me. Pale purple wings hang from her back. Bits of her skin are pocked with permanent chunks of stone.

Luca gives me an unreadable expression as he walks over to a lounge chair by a curtained window. I trail behind them, unsure what to say.

When I find my words, it sounds lame, even to my ears. "Um, yes. That's ... me."

His mother watches me with silver eyes, bright and observant. While Luca grabs a blanket to lie on her lap, I stand in the middle of the room.

The woman motions to the couch across from her. Three of her fingers don't move.

"Please sit."

I obey, worrying my lip, my fingers twitching with the need to fiddle with something. I sit and watch Luca open the curtains. His mother breaks her gaze on me to watch her son work through a routine. The way her eyes track his every move as she frowns, I can tell that she not only loves him, she's worried for him.

"Um, it's nice to meet you," I offer, unsure of what else to say.

The woman turns her focus back to me, her eyes coasting over my colors and brand. There's not a flicker of a reaction; I don't know if that's a good thing.

"Your name is Reverie?" she asks, watching Luca come sit next to me.

"Yes, ma'am."

Luca puts a hand on my knee; her gaze homes in on the movement.

With the curtain open, sunshine streaming through, I can see the stone striations marbling her body, not unlike my glitter veins. Where mine holds power, hers holds death. The realization is painful. This will be Luca in twenty years or so. He gives me a knowing look.

This is about his showing me what's in store for him. One day, he won't be able to fly or walk. One day ... He won't wake up.

I swallow the thick emotions choking me. "I just realized your son never told me your name."

She gives him a sharp look. "I assure you, I raised my boy better than that."

Luca sighs like he's burdened beyond belief. "Mother, you have. I figure she can call you Old Crone."

I jerk back at the joke, appalled, but to my relief, she cracks a smile. "Incorrigible."

They both look at me when I bark out a laugh. Chagrined, I say, "I call him incorrigible."

He flashes me a grin, bumping me with his shoulder playfully.

"I'm glad to know the woman in his life sees him for who he is. My name is Soleil," she says kindly, smiling with her eyes. "My son has spoken highly of you for a long time now. I'd thought he was delusional and that his brain was turning to stone."

He told her about me a long time ago? That fact does a little something to my soul, knitting up another tear created by others. To be fair, I thought about him every single day since the first time we met. "Soleil, you've raised a good son. I want you to know that."

Soleil huffs out a laugh that sobers almost immediately. To my dismay, her mouth quivers as silver lines her eyelids. Her voice cracks as she says, "Yes, I have."

She reaches for him. Without hesitation, he kneels at her side, grabbing one of her shaky hands. Soleil places the other hand on his cheek, brushing away his hair as only a mother can.

I can't help it; I cry. The way she watches him, like he hung the moons and stars, hurts. Soon, she'll be gone, leaving behind Luca with the knowledge of what his future holds.

Her eyes trail to mine, softening when she sees the emotions clear on my face. He looks at me, devastation pinching his features. I let out a laughing sob. "I'm sorry, I didn't expect all three of us to be crying within the first five minutes."

Soleil chuckles, patting his hand. "Go sit by your love, Luca."

Luca lifts the hand still in his and brushes a light kiss against the top. He sits back next to me, wrapping an arm around my shoulders while our tears dry.

Clearing her throat, Soleil huffs out a heavy breath. "Okay, enough soppiness. Tell me all the ways my son has made you angry so I can properly chastise him."

So, I do. It's a morning of laughter, complemented with tea made by Luca. As she and I talk, he cleans the space. She tells me stories of him as a youngling, and I adore the way her face shines with delight as she regales me with stories of Luca's father, Fane. When she brings up his death, the delight extinguishes.

"A little bit of me died with him," she says sadly. She gets misty-eyed as she peers out the window where the sun's setting. Raising a hand to her mouth, her lips quiver as she says, "At least I'll be able to see him soon."

Luca's in her bedroom, changing the sheets. Unsure of the right thing to do, I listen to my heart. Standing, I fall to my knees at her side, like Luca. Soleil's attention snaps to me; her expression softens to one of love. I cover her icy fingers with my hands. "I'll take care of him when you're gone. I swear it."

Soleil glances toward the bedroom to check he's still in there. To me, she says, "I fear for him, Reverie. He's rightfully proud and so strong. I worry about what this will do to him." Despair sags her features. "*I* did this to him. I won't be around to take care of my little boy when he starts to deteriorate."

I can't help it; I let out a sob, crying freely. "I'll do that for you, Soleil. You can join Fane knowing that your son is loved until his last breath."

Her silver eyes, Luca's eyes, search my face for the truth. I bare everything, letting her see the love I have for him and the ways I'll fiercely care for him as he does for me.

Finally, she gives me a curt nod. "Thank you." She clears her throat, then inhales a shaky breath. "Now, my dear, I tire of crying and sentimental things. It's an exhausting thing, dying."

Giving her a watery smile, I sit up, furiously wiping away tears as Luca walks into the room. He freezes, his eyes bouncing between the two of us. His wings twitch as if there's something here he can fight, even though there isn't.

Appalled, he growls, "What in the Hells did I miss?"

Soleil straightens, casting him a glare. "You aren't too old for tail lashings, Lucasta Tremblae Destau. Watch your mouth."

Fighting a grin, Luca ducks his head. "Yes ma'am. I apologize."

We spend the rest of the evening chattering about weddings while Luca cooks her lunch — giving me a smug smirk as he pulls out pepper from the cabinet, might I add. By the time we leave, my heart is full, yet heavy. Giving Soleil a final kiss on the cheek, I wait as Luca carries her to the freshly remade bed, tucking her in. An attendant will be arriving within the hour so Luca and I can head to brunch without worry.

When he steps out of the bedroom, quietly closing the door behind him, he gives me a long look. It's as if he expects me to break character and bolt. I have to admit; a part of me wants to run from this inevitable heartbreak.

But as he steps closer, those silver eyes filled with so much vulnerability, there's only one thing I can do.

I wrap my arms around his chest, breathing in his scent of petrichor. "I love you, Luca. I'm not going anywhere." Hoping to alleviate his doubt, I smile. "When it's time, you can become a beautiful glittery gnome in my garden."

The joke lands; Luca laughs as his big arms envelop me, holding me tightly. My heart fills with warm confidence. Twenty years filled with his hugs and love will be enough for me.

He will always be enough for me.

50

Luca

After the emotional visitation with Mom, I sweep Reverie into my arms and take off for The Brunching Basilisk, her favorite brunch spot. We're meeting with Kahlo and Malona. Yureka is coming with her best friend, Tobias. I'm excited to show Reverie off to the world officially.

Upon her suggestion, I landed on a platform a little ways away from the restaurant, allowing us to stroll through the shopping market. With her small hand in mine, I escort her through the crowd, watching her face brighten when she sees a dress she likes, or when a busker catches her attention with a performance.

I'll never tire of watching her experience the world. I'm fairly certain she has no idea that when she's truly excited, glitter swirls in her irises. In the bright sunshine, her pale skin glistens. I see the way people stare at her and, more than once, I see envy. Some are disgusted, but I suspect it's a disguise for envy. When their disdainful eyes trail to me, I curl my lip, revealing a fang. No one is going to ruin my girl's day. I will spend the rest of my life protecting her from bigotry, if she'll let me.

All of them avert their gazes, as they should.

Finally, we arrive at The Brunching Basilisk, where our friends are already waiting. Four pairs of eyes home in on Reverie's fingers intertwined with mine, and pride puffs my chest as Kahlo gives a low whistle. The Slogoth slime has left his system, allowing him to stand tall next to Malona, one arm slung around her slender shoulders.

"Does this mean you both owe me a 'thank you'?" he says smugly, striding forward to pull me into a rough hug, forcing me to release her hand.

"Good to see you don't have socks taped to your wings," I say dryly, smacking his back a little harder than necessary.

He chuckles, stepping back next to Malona. She stares at me with those doe-wide eyes that sparkle with amusement. Giving me a wink, she hugs her best friend. While the three women hug and squeal, I hold out my hand to Tobias.

He's an Orc, with pale blue skin, two fangs jutting from full lips, and a body more soft than muscular. Both pointed ears are covered in colorful piercings, with a lip ring centered on his bottom lip. His blue and black outfit billows around his large form. With a firm, commanding handshake, he grins. "The name's Tobias, but you can call me Toby."

"Lucasta, Luca for short," I say, approving of his grip. A strong handshake equals a strong man. I take note of his coal black hair that has blue streaks throughout, matching the shades of blue eyeshadow framing his bright blue eyes. He certainly follows a theme, embracing his physical attributes.

"I've heard so much about you," he purrs with a lusty appraisal.

I may or may not flex a little as I smirk. "All good things, I hope."

Toby glances at Yureka. With a little resentment, he replies, "Unfortunately, I wasn't informed of *how* handsome you were."

Yureka makes a face. "I wasn't about to talk to you about my friend's crush's plump ass."

"Oh, so you think my ass is plump?" I tease.

Yureka's cheeks darken as her eyes dart to Reverie. "I mean, Reverie knows this. It's not a secret. When we first met, I told her about—"

"Yureka, please stop talking," Reverie says, laughing at the nervous rambling. Giving me a salacious once over, she says, "No one can deny what a hunk of delectable flesh this man is."

I frown. "This is getting to be a little more odd than expected."

Kahlo clears his throat. "I need coffee. Can you stop ogling my cousin so we can get seated?"

"Yes, let's," I grumble, reaching for Reverie's hand again. Gracing me with a dazzling smile, she intertwines our fingers. I lean down, kissing her forehead, inhaling her scent. She can talk about me all she wants; I'll never tire of the fact that she's mine.

The hostess walks us back to our round table. She hands out the menus as we all sit. "Your attendant will be here shortly and share today's specials. Enjoy."

Reverie sits to the right of me, with Yureka on my left. Next to her are Tobias, Kahlo, and Malona. All of us grab menus, reading over the different dishes. It has typical brunch fare, but Reverie said she always orders the Fanged Frittata. It doesn't actually have fangs in it, apparently, but it doesn't sound appetizing, regardless.

"I think I'll get the Slithering Strudel," Kahlo declares.

Toby scoffs. "Everyone knows the best dish here is the Forked French Toast. They drizzle it in a venom reduction syrup that makes you mildly hallucinate."

Yureka makes a sound of protest. "I'm not carrying you home, Toby."

"Maybe I'll get that instead," Reverie says, giving me a sly look. "I wouldn't mind a little hallucinogenic."

"I have some gibbonroot, if you want," Kahlo offers.

Malona smacks him on the arm. "I can't believe you brought that nonsense to brunch."

Kahlo has the good sense to look contrite. With a voice softer than I've ever heard, he says, "Sorry, love, habit."

Reverie and I exchange a glance at the nickname. At that exact moment, our female waiter slithers to our table. Basilisks are half-snake, half-fae, with longer necks and arms. This one wears a rather revealing bandeau top, with a name tag that reads, "Scaleana."

Her dark skin glistens with red scales that reach from the maroon ophidian bottom half. From the crown of her head to the tip of her tail is about ten feet long, making her a more petite example of her species.

Batting her golden, reptilian eyes, Scaleana reveals wickedly long fangs. "Good afternoon. My name isss Ssscaleana. I'll be ssserving you today." She glances around the table. "Can I interessst you in a round of mimosssasss?"

"Oh, goddess yes," Malona moans, beaming. "Three carafes, please."

Kahlo gives his partner a look of pride, which she ignores.

Scaleana nods. "Of coursse. Anything elssse?"

"Waters?" Reverie asks.

The waitress nods and slithers off. Yureka leans into Tobias. "I've never seen a Basilisk in person before. They're so beautiful."

Eager to cause mischief, I lean on my elbows to look at Kahlo. "Didn't you date a Basilisk last year?"

My cousin gives me a glare full of daggers, then glances at Malona. She peers at him, curious. "Uh, yeah. But it was a fling. Nothing serious, I swear."

Malona lets out a melodic chuckle. "Sweetie, I don't care who you've dated before. As long as you're happy being with me now."

Relief sags Kahlo's muscles. He nods eagerly. "Absolutely."

Reverie and I exchange another look, similar to the one we first shared at brunch when these two met. Kahlo has been a notorious playboy his whole life, so watching him anxiously searching her face for a lie warms my heart with amusement. I'm glad for him.

Then Kahlo turns his focus to Reverie. "How was the Orc wedding, by the way?"

Reverie huffs out a laugh, side-eyeing me. "Not too many hiccups."

"Did you get to use the thermal pools?" Yureka asks with a slight tone of envy in the words.

My cock pulses at the memory as Reverie says, "Oh, yes, they're lovely. We got a private grotto. I'm hoping to book another wedding there soon. It's a unique space."

"My wings wouldn't stop twitching," I add.

Kahlo nods in sympathy. “Sad I couldn’t go, but it sounds like you both had fun.”

“Three carafesss of mimosssasss,” Scaleana announces, placing two on the table, and reaching for the third held by the tip of her tail. “Isss everyone ready to order?”

Kahlo immediately begins pouring the drinks while everyone gives their orders. I’m eager for the Slootberry waffles — they’re my second favorite fruit.

Resting an arm on the back of Reverie’s chair, I tell Kahlo, “Just so you know, I’m the new official second shooter for Edges of Glitter.”

Reverie elbows me in the ribs. “We never made anything official.”

Twirling a strand of rainbow hair around a finger, I say, “Mere formality.”

“You can’t be serious,” Kahlo says, aghast. “Don’t you have your own company to run?”

“Actually, we figured it’d be easier to join our companies together,” Reverie says, taking a sip of her mimosa.

My cousin shoots Malona a glare. “Did you know?”

The Cherub laughs. “No, but it makes sense.”

Kahlo takes an angry sip of his drink. “The two of you working together? There won’t be any business left for the rest of us. You know that, right?”

“That’s the plan,” Reverie says brightly.

Toby frowns. “Wait, what’s going on?”

“It’s quite simple,” Malona says, leaning on an elbow while holding her mimosa. “Kahlo tried to impress a girl and was slimed by a Slogoth and needed a replacement photographer for Reverie. He asked Luca, his cousin, who just so happened to be the same guy that ghosted Reverie over a year ago, and then they spent the last month having all sorts of problems working together. But somehow, now they’re doing the Pegasus pump and apparently joining forces.”

Giving Reverie wide, innocent eyes, she asks, “Is that about right?”

Meanwhile, Reverie's choking on the sip of mimosa in her mouth. Yureka lets out a delighted cackle. Kahlo groans. Tobias looks more confused.

Patting a hand between Reverie's shoulders while she coughs, I say, "Did you seriously just say 'Pegasus pump'?"

Malona shrugs, sipping her mimosa without a care in the world.

Reverie takes a sip of water. "Luca should at least be flattered that you likened his dick to a Pegasus."

I pretend to preen, plucking a piece of invisible lint from my shoulder. "I am flattered. Thank you, Malona."

"Maybe a miniature Pegasus," Kahlo mutters, clearly still miffed about losing his job.

Everyone laughs, even though he wasn't aiming to be funny. Malona kisses his cheek, and his sour expression shifts into a smile.

"So ... you ghosted her?" Toby says.

Reverie nods emphatically. "Oh, yeah! But I've forgiven him on account of the Pegasus pump."

"Please stop saying that," Kahlo pleads. "I don't want to envision my cousin—"

"I don't neigh when I cum, if that's what you're wondering about," I say, grinning ear to ear.

He groans, covering his ears while humming. I laugh, sipping from my glass. I love my cousin, but I enjoy annoying him more.

"Luca?"

My chuckle's interrupted by a female voice. Everyone at the table looks over to see a short Fire Sprite smiling at me, with a tall golden-skinned woman next to her.

Standing, I hold out a hand. "Kyrielle, it's nice to see you." I motion to everyone at the table, giving their names. "Everyone, this is Kyrielle. She teaches self-defense at the battle gym."

The Fire Sprite, with light orange hair and fiery eyes, beams. Motioning to the woman, she says, "This is my best friend, Orliana."

I shake her friend's hand. "Enjoying brunch, too?"

Kyrielle smiles. "We're on our way out, but we love coming here. Best waffles in the city."

"Couldn't agree more," I say, my stomach growling in agreement. "Well, enjoy the rest of your day. See you at the gym?"

Kyrielle flexes a set of impressive biceps. "One day, I'll kick your ass."

"Looking forward to it," I say, genuine with the words. She's an excellent fighter.

They wave goodbye and leave as Scaleana arrives with all of our food. As the plates are passed out, Reverie kisses my cheek.

"I love you," she says softly into my ear. Goosebumps skitter along my skin from her warm breath.

Turning my head, I duck my head to capture her lips with mine. She tastes of hazelnut coffee. Behind me, there are gagging sounds. Not wanting to make Kahlo throw up, I break the kiss far sooner than preferred.

I'm staring into those turquoise eyes as I hear my cousin mutter, "Fucking Slogoth ruined my life."

I grin. "Funny, because it changed mine for the better."

Grabbing my fork, I cut into my Slootberry waffles, listening to my growing family chatter. My heart expands six times its size with happiness.

51

Luca

The crowd roars as twelve chimeragons race on the makeshift racecourse. Reggie is number nine, and his smoky mane flies in the wind as his stumpy legs gallop in the air. He's tied with a gold chimeragon named Chuck.

"Come on, Reggie!" Reverie screams, eyes alight with stress. Next to her, Sparks claps furiously, hollering the same. They're both standing, with Laurel still sitting on the bench. She leans back, sharing a smile with me.

"People take this seriously, don't they?" Mom whispers, shifting in her wheelchair.

Just as I'm about to respond, someone screams from behind us, "Bumble, Mommy has a raw fish ready for you! Win, baby, win!"

Mom and I share a chuckle. So far, this chimeragon festival has been interesting. There are races, like this one, and other activities. A costume contest; a hothound eating contest; the biggest roar competition. The latter is often more hilarious than impressive. Hard for a fifty-five pound animal to sound intimidating.

My shadowy chimeragon races to the front of the group, forked tongue waving like a banner in the wind. A blood red chimeragon nips at his tail, eliciting a few boos.

Reggie chirps when the blue ribbon of the finish line slams into his serpentine eyes. A festival judge places a ribbon around his mane with a congratulatory pat on the head.

I whistle; he bounds over, almost careening into a few heads. Holding my arms open, he barrels into my chest, licking my chin frantically.

"You did so well, buddy," I say, scratching his furry ear. Attaching the leash to his collar, I hold on to the handle while he floats in the air like a balloon. Reverie reaches up to stroke his flank.

"What a good boy," she coos. He mewls with pleasure, bopping her on the head with a flick of his unruly tail.

Handing her the leash, I grab the handles for Mom's wheelchair. "I think it's time for some celebratory fried chocolate chip cookies. What do you think?"

"Yes, please," Mom says, eyes sparkling with excitement. Not just because she asked for Reverie to cover her in glitter — much to Sparks' dismay. This is most likely one of the last times she'll experience the world around her, and I know how much she loves chocolate chip cookies.

She won't say it, but I suspect she also knows the final episode is hurtling at an unforgivable speed. In the last three months, her pocked skin is worse, and the stoning episodes are more frequent.

Thinking about it makes me want to crack in half with violent sobs, so I shove away the thought.

There are murmurs of agreement from everyone, cementing the decision for snacks. Weaving through the crowd, I guide everyone to the nearest food stall. Sparks offers to pay before I can insist, so while he orders everyone a cookie, I bring an arm around Reverie's shoulders. She snuggles into my side, and I kiss the top of her head.

Today is the first time I've spent real time with Sparks and Laurel; it's been interesting. When Mom and I showed up resembling purple disco balls, his face turned an alarming shade of white. Reverie warned us ahead of time, stating her sleeveless shirt and short skirt would disturb him. But the way he reacted, you would've thought we'd shown up naked.

I'm proud of her rejection of his controlling ways. When people stop to stare at two glittered Gargoyles, she merely lifts her chin, daring someone to comment. It's been incredible to watch her grow into a newfound level of confidence.

We've been inseparable these last three months, spending every single day together. It's been nothing short of *bilaste.*

Laurel holds out a hand. "Can I hold Reggie?"

Reverie hands over the leash. "Just keep him away from the other chimeragons. He's going to gloat over his win."

Her mother laughs. "Does he not know that modesty is a desirable trait?"

"Probably not," I say, chuckling. "But why would the fastest chimeragon in Gondora want to be modest?"

Reggie meows in agreement, landing on my shoulder, teetering on the tips of his four paws. He falls off when he whirls around toward the sound of a roaring chimeragon, slapping my cheek with that damn tail. All around us, chimeragons of all colors bob around like overzealous balloons. It's an overstimulating experience for him; he'll sleep *really* well tonight.

"Five freshly fried cookies," Sparks announces, handing one to Mom first, then his wife, then Reverie. Finally, I receive the last cookie, which I promptly split in half. Holding it up in the air, Reggie's slobber wets my fingertips as he gobbles up his victory dessert.

We're silent as all of us munch on the crispy dough and chocolate morsels. My mother closes her eyes, savoring her cookie with a happy hum. Another memory burned into my brain.

When I look at Reverie, she grins with a smear of chocolate on the bottom of her lip. Without thinking, I wipe it away with my thumb and lick it off with a quick swipe of my tongue. Behind her, I see Laurel's eyes widen. The woman is more pious than a virgin acolyte.

Giving her an apologetic smile, because I don't want her to hate me, I ask everyone, "What else should we do?"

Sparks grabs Laurel's hand. "We need to head out, unfortunately." He smiles at my mother. "It was great to meet you finally."

Mom beams. "Likewise. You both raised a wonderful daughter."

Laurel smiles softly, resting her temple against Sparks' shoulder. "We did, didn't we?"

"Okay, enough of the compliments," Reverie grumbles, taking back Reggie's leash. Exchanging hugs with her parents, she says, "We'll see you at the farmer's market next week?"

"For hazelnut coffees and fresh bread?" Sparks quips. "You bet. See you soon, Popsicle."

Reverie rolls her eyes at the nickname but gives him an affable smile. "Text me later."

While they walk away, I look at Mom. "So, what do you want to do?"

Reggie lands in her lap and promptly curls into a ball for a power nap. She pets him affectionately. "Can we go visit Infinity Falls?"

"I've always wanted to go see it up close," Reverie says, immediately enthusiastic.

The thrill of knowing what will make both of them happy splits my face into a grin. The longer this day can last, the better. Pushing Mom forward, I announce, "It's settled. Infinity Falls, here we come."

After dropping off the rented wheelchair at the entrance, we summon a Dragxi — normally unheard of for fliers, but I can't carry all three of them, sadly — and stop at Mom's house to drop off Reggie before heading to the entrance of the falls.

It's busy today, especially with the limited access to the cloudavators. Renting another wheelchair for Mom, I help get her situated, and the three of us join the slow-moving line.

"Do you think they'll care if I shoot off some rainbows?" Reverie asks, tone anxious.

I give Reverie a raised eyebrow. "Do you think anyone will have the gall to say something if so?"

She laughs under her breath. "Fair enough. I enjoy having a purple guard hound at my disposal."

"I enjoy being a guard hound." I kiss her cheek.

Mom harrumphs. "You better show off your rainbows. It's illegal to disappoint the elderly."

Reverie gazes at my mother with a level of adoration I could never have dreamed of from a partner. Grabbing one of her hands, Reverie says, "Well, when you put it that way, I'll release extras."

While Mom asks her questions about her Glyridite powers, I enjoy the quiet exchange, trying to solidify it as a core memory. Unfortunately, not being blessed with a photographic memory like Reverie means my average brain will eventually shove aside memories for new ones.

Luckily, in my backpack is my camera.

Soon enough, it's our turn. Rolling Mom onto the cloudavator, I step aside to make sure Reverie has enough space. Magyck will protect her from plummeting to her death, but I don't want her to be nervous at all.

"I haven't done this in ages," Mom says with uninhibited glee. A rush of happiness brings a broad grin to my face, knowing how important this is to her. Reverie rubs my arm, then kisses my shoulder. She also knows how important this is to me.

Bringing an arm around her shoulders, I tuck her into my side, and place a hand on my mother's shoulder. Reverie wraps her arms around my waist with a happy sigh. Having both of them here feels incredibly right and deeply significant.

The metal platform hosting the line of ticket holders disappears as we rise into chilly mist. It clings to our skin and clothes. I check the blanket on my mother's lap, tucking it in a little tighter around her hips.

She smacks my hand away. "Stop fussing. I can take care of my own blanket."

I straighten, huffing out a sound of frustration. When she doesn't let me do the smaller things, it makes me feel more helpless. "I'm trying to be a good son. No need to be rude."

Reverie's arms hug tighter in quiet comfort. I caress my thumb along her now-wet arm.

My mother's irritation softens. "Apologies, my light." She brings a hand to mine. "Thank you for caring."

Swallowing the lump in my throat, I nod. Before I can say anything, the cloudavator lifts us into blinding sunshine. I blink rapidly, taking in the scene. While we can see the falls from Mom's apartment, it's an otherworldly experience, rising above pillowy clouds to be baptized in bright warmth.

And the roar of rushing water.

Infinity Pools comprises dozens of floating mountains, each catching mist that pools and surged off the edges, only to feed the mist all over again. The never-ending cycle keeps the area balmy. Thanks to the sunshine refracting off the fraying edges of the waterfalls, rainbows surround us.

My mother lets out a wistful sigh, running her fingers through the mist swirling at our feet. It's been over a year since she last flew of her own volition. A prison sentence for any flier. Even when I offer to fly her whenever she wants, it's not the same kind of freedom. She doesn't complain, but I know it must bother her.

How could it not?

A long bit of cloud rises from the edge of the cloudavator with a perpendicular handle attached to a rudder at the bottom. Pointing at it, I say, "Go ahead. Take us wherever you want to go, *Mamai.*"

She doesn't hesitate, leaning forward to grasp it with both hands. The cloudavator silently floats toward the largest waterfall that is at least fifty feet wide and a hundred feet tall. Colorful birds swoop through the mist, chirping happily. Some have reported wild Pegasi roaming the individual mountains, although I've never seen any.

When we're close enough to the waterfall, my mother points. "Look, Reverie! A rainbow!"

My partner grins, extending a hand. A similar rainbow springs from her palm, brilliant and overwhelming in its size and depth of color. My mother claps with delight, eyes full of wonder.

Reverie kneels next to my mother, grabbing her hand. "Here. Want to hold it?"

Somehow, my mother's eyes widen further, jaw slackening. "I can do that?"

"Of course." The love of my life shifts the end of the rainbow to rest on my mother's wrinkled palm. When my mother moves her hand, the rainbow follows. She lets out the happiest laugh; one I haven't heard since before my father died.

It nearly makes me weep with joy at the sound. Their faces blur as tears fill my eyes while they both play with rainbows. The mist soaks us to the bone, but my soul's so warm, I can't even feel the light chill from a breeze. While they play, I pull out my camera, lifting it to my eye.

I catch the moment they look at one another, elation reflected in each other's expressions. Wide smiles and sparkling eyes. A two-foot wide rainbow sprouting from my mother's hand. The one thing my camera can't capture is their conspiratorial giggles.

I'm printing this image as large as is unreasonable and featuring it in our future living room.

Putting the camera away, I'm content to watch them spend time together. Time is running out for my mother, and I'm content to memorize every little detail.

Sensing my stare, Reverie looks up for a split second. The sun lights up every iridescent inch of her; she resembles a goddess. *My* goddess.

Whatever she sees on my face brightens her further. After gracing me with a soul-shattering smile, she refocuses on my mother.

Yes, I think spending the rest of my life with her sounds like an excellent idea.

52

Reverie

Six Months Later

"What do you think?" I stand back from the finalized collage by our bed. Luca and I have spent the last weekend packing my old apartment and moving me into his.

It makes sense, since we're combining our businesses and he has a built-in office. After a lot of debate, we decided to call it "Glittering Skies Photography," a nod to both of our original company names.

Since we joined forces, business has been booming. Saving money on expenses by living together will help, too.

Luca's chest presses against my back as he wraps his arms around me. "Looks beautiful. I especially like the one of you."

I laugh. "Which one?" The man never stops taking photos of me, so there are a dozen of my favorites taped next to the ones I've taken of him.

Luca's fang nips my earlobe. "All of them."

Smiling, I hug him tighter to me. "That's fair. How much is left to unpack?"

He grunts with unhappiness. "I think there are at least four more boxes of pillows."

His apartment was too austere for my tastes, so I brought every stuffed and soft creature comfort possible. My glittery pillows and blankets cover the surfaces.

Luca may or may not be slightly panicking over my doom piles already. But that's fine, because I cannot believe he irons his sheets as a weekend treat.

Turning to face him, I wrap my arms around his neck. "We'll need lots of them if we ever want to make that pillow fort."

His expression darkens with lust. "I enjoy using pillows with you."

My thighs clench as I nibble on my lip. I know it drives him wild when I do that and, as expected, his focus immediately homes in on the movement. The word that drives him crazy sits at the tip of my tongue, but instead of saying it, I kiss him. He tucks his hands under my ass, hoisting me up so I can wrap my thighs around his waist.

Life with him these last six months has been phenomenal. Every day, I get to wake up next to my best friend, who happily gives me an orgasm or two. We photograph every wedding together, much to Kahlo's chagrin. It's his fault for trying to dance with a Slogoth, as we remind him every time he complains.

Luca breaks the kiss, smiling. "You ready to go?"

I wriggle in his hold, giggling. "I'm so ready. I can't wait to make you a disco ball."

He puts me on the ground, ruffling my hair. "All day, every night, *Bilaste.*"

Today, we're going to Cilyestia Pools so I can see it during the day. The last six months have been so busy with weddings, joining companies, moving, and his mom, that this is the first afternoon we've had to go see it again.

Remembering what it was like last time, I happily skip to the balcony. Luca chuckles, grabbing our picnic supplies.

Reggie hops on his feet, chirping with excitement. As soon as Luca scoops me up, depositing a kiss on my forehead, the chimeragon starts flying.

Luca walks to the edge of the platform. I gaze out at Gondora, loving the view. The glass ceilings of the buildings, the sky traffic, and the mist rolling through. A rainbow of Dragxis dash colors against the gleaming gold buildings.

"You ready?" Luca murmurs, searching my face for any hint of discomfort.

I love this man.

"Onward, lavender steed," I declare, pointing into the vague distance..

Luca likes to show off all the dismounts he's created. Today, he walks to the very edge, balancing on his claws.

"Oh, noooo ..." he says with fake dread. "I think I'm falling ..."

I cackle as gravity yanks us forward. "Oh, noooo ... we're going to die ..."

"Goodbye cruel world," he says mournfully, licking the tip of my nose before his wings snap together.

"Hold tight," he whispers.

We're in free fall, buildings rushing by. I shriek with delight, pleased to see Reggie keeping up. He coos with pleasure, giving me a grin, his forked tongue waving in the wind.

Luca's wings crack with a boom as they take up the sky, lifting us again. Now we are shooting upward, with him pressing me into his chest. I'm smiling so hard my face hurts. I love flying with him.

Soon, we're out of Gondora, flying past floating islands and pillars of clouds. The sun is high, bringing out the colors of everything, including my veins.

We fly slowly so Reggie can keep pace — he's faster hurtling toward the ground than actually going long distances — and when he's tired, I cuddle him in my arms. Luca wraps his tail around us both for safekeeping.

I know we're close when my skin hums, eager for the magyck of the falls. Looking into the distance, I see the tallest fall rising into the fluffy white clouds. Already, rainbows glisten. The pools are like a twinkling gem in the sky, a beacon for my blood.

The moment we land, I'm out of Luca's arms, placing Reggie on the ground. Laughing, I spread my arms wide to release a rainbow that rips from my chest, streaking upward like a wall of color. It's the biggest rainbow I've ever made, and I love it.

There's a click, and I whirl around, still leaking rainbows, to see Luca taking a photo with his phone.

I throw a ball of glitter at him, and it explodes in his face, the shimmer splattering on his face like paint. He blinks at me, then grins.

"Disco ball time?" He asks, tone hopeful.

I point to the green moss at my feet. "This goddess requires supplication."

Within two seconds, he's kneeling in front of me with a grin so genuine, it makes my heart ache. Placing my hands on his cheeks, I bring my lips to his mouth. On an exhale, I breathe colors and sparkles into him. When I've commanded enough, I straighten to see my handiwork. It spread across his formidable form, the glitter catching the sun rays.

In a haughty tone, I say, "You may rise, my most loyal subject."

Luca stands. Like a little boy, he flaps his wings to see if it comes off. None of it does.

"Do you doubt my ability?" I say in my best condescending voice.

Smiling, he shakes his head vehemently. "Of course not, my goddess. Simply awed by your supremacy."

We hold the stare until we break into a fit of giggles. At our feet, Reggie hops and chirps. Luca slings an arm around my shoulders and we walk over to the pools. In the daytime, more colors of glitter are visible than they were at night. The falls are rainbows upon rainbows. It's like dozens of Glyridites have released every inch of their power, coating anything with a surface. When I see a Lunite flit by, I point it out with a squeal.

The orbs of light hibernate in the sun, but I send them some glitter, regardless. When I'd asked, Dad wasn't sure if they were souls, so I'd rather play it safe.

The bright green moss stops abruptly at the pool's edge. Leaning over, I can see the glittering boulders at the bottom, dozens of feet down. They're distorted by more rainbows, but still visible.

I'm tempted to jump in, but Luca steers me away. "Keep your shirt on; let's have lunch. I'm starving."

I laugh, wrapping an arm around his waist. Finding a shaded spot, we unpack the picnic supplies on a blanket. As I plate the food, Luca pours our femire into shatter-proof cups. Taking a sip, I watch him concentrate on making sure everything is arranged according to his idea of perfection. When he almost drops a plate, I frown.

"Are you alright?"

For a split second, I see nervousness in those silver eyes before it's wiped away by an amiable smile. "Of course. I keep thinking about that night when you stripped in front of me. I damn near came in my trousers."

I laughed. "In hindsight, it was a crazy thing to do."

His lopsided grin warms me from the inside. "I'm glad you did."

We eat in silence, observing the small animals that call the pools home. Reggie rolls around in some glittery tall grass, popping his head up with glitter all over his mane, making us laugh.

When lunch is done, Luca packs and I pull out a camera. We wanted to have some photos from here to print at home. Setting up the tripod, I position it in front of the pools, making sure the settings will capture the most color possible.

I wave my sexy Gargoyle over. "Come on! Hurry! I want to go skinny dipping!"

Luca chuckles, taking his sweet time. His tail flicks anxiously, betraying his emotions. What in the Hells is going on with him? I eye it with suspicion.

He mocks my expression with narrowed eyes. "What?"

"Your tail." I point at it. "What is wrong with you?"

He stares at his tail like he's never seen it before. "No idea what his problem is. I'm fine."

I roll my eyes. "Come on. Let's get this over so I can go cannonball into the water and you stand on the sidelines as a fake lifeguard."

He throws his head back, laughing loudly. "If anything, you'd have to be my lifeguard."

"Please don't get in the water. I'm not sure I could lug your hulking body over the edge of the pool."

"I am not hulking!" he says with fake outrage, coming to stand next to me. "I'm just ..." He trails off, failing to come up with a retort.

"Hulking?" I offer.

He narrows his eyes. "I'm going to give you a good hulking. Right after these photos."

My core clenches at the promise. "Okay, no funny faces."

I rush over to the camera and set the fifteen second timer. Squealing, I rush back to him, hugging his side. We do this a few times, and each time, Luca makes a face. By the sixth attempt, I'm actually irritated with him.

"Lucasta, can you please stop? You're making this more difficult than it needs to be," I say crossly.

He raises his hands in supplication. "Alright, I'll behave."

Rolling my eyes, I set the timer and rush over.

"Let's do a spin," he suggests, grabbing my hand. I grin, and let him spin me repeatedly. The world spins by in melted colors; I let out a gleeful cackle.

The camera clicks. Luca catches me, planting a kiss on my forehead. "One more and we can be done," he promises.

Huffing in frustration, I reset the timer. I rush back, and Luca spins me again. When the spinning stops, I expect to see Luca over me, but he's kneeling on one knee, grinning. In his large hands is a small blue ring box, holding an asscher cut yellow diamond, with triangles of white diamond at the sides.

I bring my hands to my face as the camera clicks.

"Reverie Vayla Songlight, you have been the light of my life since the moment I saw you. Even when we were at our most broken, I knew there wouldn't be a day where I wouldn't try to make you happy."

His face blurs behind glittery tears as it hits me exactly what's happening here. He's proposing.

Luca wants to marry me.

I laugh out a sob, bending over, trying not to have an actual breakdown.

Luca continues, his voice wavering. "You've accepted me, flaws and all. A goddess beyond reason." He swallows hard, grabbing my right hand and separating the middle finger. Pulling out the ring, he asks, "Reverie, will you make me the luckiest man in existence, and be my wife?"

The fact that he's nervous is adorable. I nod furiously, still unable to speak. I watch him slide the ring on; of course, the fit is perfect. Knowing him, he probably measured it while I slept. I bring it closer, admiring the way the diamonds sparkle in the sun.

"Do you like it?" he asks, sounding anxious. I look at my soon-to-be-husband and with my biggest, brightest smile, I enthusiastically nod.

"Oh, Luca, I will absolutely be your wife." Throwing my arms around him, I squeeze his neck tightly. He returns the embrace, holding me while I cry.

When we separate, he's grinning like a fool, flashing his fangs. "Does this mean I get to make love to my fiancée now?"

Fiancée. A word I've used almost daily for years, but never directed at myself. After so long being alone, my life is full of unbelievable love. This man has helped me step into my own, gaining the confidence I've searched for my whole life. With him, I'm safe being myself. Decades of his love would be a gift from the goddesses.

I answer Luca's question by taking my clothes off.

53

Luca

One Year Later

Fidgeting nervously with my yellow tie, I inhale a shaky breath, trying to steady my pulse. My heart has been racing all morning, from the moment I woke up with Reverie in my arms to the moment I put on my white suit. Deep breaths are doing nothing for my nerves.

Kahlo glances up from the couch. He stands, looking worried. "You good?"

He's wearing a khaki suit with an orange tie. Since he's the only groomsman, the only other person in the room is Reverie's father, Sparks. He's wearing a typical blue suit, but with a yellow tie covered in glitter.

They're both watching me with concern.

Letting out a nervous chuckle, I say, "I've never been on this side of things. It's more terrifying than I thought it'd be."

Kahlo comes to stand next to me with a grin. Clapping me on the shoulder with a rough shake, he says, "I never thought there'd be someone dumb enough to do this with you."

I growl, narrowing my eyes. "Did you call my wife dumb? Because I will snap your tail in half if you are."

Kahlo steps back, hands up. "Just a joke. Please don't break my tail. Malona really likes it, if you know what I mean."

I know exactly what he means, but instead of saying that, I snipe, "No, I don't know what you mean. Please don't tell me about your sex life with Reverie's best friend."

"So you *do* know it can be used during sex?" he teases, taking another step back. I flick out my wing, smacking him in the face. He chuckles, rubbing his cheek. "Someone's become a groomzilla."

I turn back to my reflection, smoothing a flyaway hair. "Not a groomzilla, dunghole. I want things to be perfect for her."

"Knowing my daughter, you simply need to be there," Sparks says, trying to be helpful.

But he doesn't understand. Sparks hasn't seen his daughter panic over the color of napkins and which band to choose. As much as I try to tell her that it's not about the caterer making sure the vendor meals are delicious — I know our friends will appreciate it — she won't listen. I've been working overtime to help with everything possible.

I hope it's enough.

The suite's door opens and our wedding planner, Euresta, peeks her head around the door. "How's everything coming along?"

Turning from the mirror, I declare. "Well, we're dressed. That's half the battle."

Euresta steps into the room, an envelope in her hand. "The other half is keeping your composure when you see her because Luca ..." Euresta gives me a meaningful look. "She's probably the prettiest bride I've ever seen."

"I highly doubt 'probably' needs to exist in that sentence at all," I retort.

She laughs. "Okay, you're right. I never thought glitter could be so ..." She trails off, her face darkening with a blush.

"Stunning?" I offer. In the last year, it's been incredibly frustrating to see the way people treat Reverie, or rather, her powers. She's stepped into her strength with grace, but when people act surprised that glitter is beautiful, I want to smack them upside the head with my claws out.

Euresta recovers quickly. "Yes." She holds out the envelope to me. It's covered in white glitter, not unlike Reverie's ...

I snatched it from Euresta's hand. She recoils with surprise, but I ignore her, lifting the envelope to my nose. Relieved it doesn't smell like my favorite spot in the world, I give Euresta a sheepish smile. "Sorry, just a little excited."

She gives me a look that tells me she doesn't believe me one bit. "Yes, well, I'll be back in five minutes to get you situated for the First Look."

Eager to discover what my wife has written, I practically rip apart the envelope and pull out the letter. The message springs tears to my eyes.

Lucasta,

Two years ago, you rose through the clouds, bringing wings and cheesy sex jokes. I never told you this, but I almost called you the next day. I stared at your number so many times, but I stubbornly thought that if you didn't reach out, neither would I.

I regret robbing us of that year, as I know you do, too. But we're making up for lost time, and that's the best we can do for one another.

Today, you officially become my forever. No matter what the future holds, you're my forever. When your body fades and your spirit rises, I'll sit next to your stone statue every morning. We'll keep having our morning coffee, and every night, I'll tell you how my day was.

Because no matter what, I can't imagine a life without you. You are everything I'm not, and so much more. Your kindness is your ultimate strength, and I'm so honored to be the one who witnesses it daily.

So, starting from now until whenever it's over, I'll love you the way you have me: no terms or conditions.

I love you.

Reverie

P.S., I know the white glitter made you panic. I hear wives should keep their husbands on their toes — Sir.

Carefully placing the letter back into the envelope, I close my eyes as I hold it to my heart. I don't deserve her, but I'll spend every day trying.

Handing the envelope to Kahlo, I say, "Please put this somewhere safe. I've never been so serious in my life; *do not fucking lose this.*"

Kahlo nods, solemn, as he takes it from me. "I will."

At least he can be serious ... sometimes.

Euresta knocks on the door again. "Okay, Luca, are you ready?"

Inhaling a shaky breath, I look at Sparks. His throat works repeatedly. "You take care of my little girl, okay? She's never been so ..." He trails off. A flicker of shame makes him break eye contact. His throat bobs as he whispers, "You're exactly what she needed."

I walk up to him and, much to his dismay, I wrap Sparks in a big hug. He stiffens, then wraps his arms around me, returning the gesture. I clap him on the back. "She's my deity, Sparks. I literally worship the ground she walks on. You can rest easy knowing this."

Grinding his jaw, shoving down his emotions, Sparks can only nod. He's never been good at showing emotions, so I know this is the best he can offer.

"Luca," Euresta says impatiently.

With a final grin to Kahlo, I follow Euresta out of the suite to the First Look spot. Our wedding photographer is already there, one of our colleagues, Nura. I hear the shutter snap repeatedly; it's a struggle to ignore. I itch to take my own photos, because there's no one else I trust enough to capture the beauty of Reverie. It rarely happens, but I currently envy her photographic memory.

"Okay, stand here," Euresta says, directing me to face the ceremony site. We're getting married at the same location as the wedding where we first reconnected. The sun will set as the ceremony begins, so right now, golden sunset light streams through the dappled gumdrop trees.

The arbor is covered in garlands and yellow poppies, as I always imagined. However, the one thing I never imagined was the glitter.

I wanted Reverie to start her life with me being entirely herself. She fought against it at first, but it was the one thing I refused to budge on. Which is why everything is covered in glitter. The moss; the logs; the hanging vines. Sparks added his own touch by commanding translucent glitter to float in the air, adding a mystical quality to the entire scene.

When the sun sets, everything will glow like Cilyestia Pools. That's when she'll walk down the aisle to me.

Nura walks in front of me. She snaps a photo of my expression with a smile. "Nervous?"

"You have no idea," I mutter. She laughs and lifts the camera, signalling Reverie is approaching.

My galloping heart might snap my ribs. It's difficult to steady my breath and trembling hands. I hope I don't lose my shit, but I know I will. Because it's her.

There's a tap on my shoulder. I close my eyes for a beat, willing myself to keep it together. When I turn, I'm awestruck for a moment.

Because my wife is a goddess. Her beautiful turquoise eyes shimmer with tears as she smiles warmly. One of my favorites. Her shimmering hair's styled into an elegant twisted braid, showing off every color.

She wears no makeup; instead, she's used glitter to add enhancements to her features. Sheer glitter highlights her cheekbones, and gold glitter rims her eyelids.

But her dress ... it takes my breath away.

It's nothing but slow-moving glitter, constantly shifting pastel colors like a piece of glass swinging in the sunshine, capturing rainbows. The train trails behind her, lightly floating above the moss. The sweetheart neckline shows off her brand and veins, both of which glow.

All I can do is carefully kneel in front of the goddess in front of me.

"Bilaste," I breathe. Bringing my hands to her arms, I caress her soft skin. "You're ..." I shake my head. "There are no words for what you are."

"You're so *handsome,*" she says, laughing through a sob. She kneels with me. I make a sound of protest, but she presses her fingers to my lips. "It's not like I can make the dress dirty," she jokes.

I still don't want her kneeling; that's my task. But she's always made sure we're equals, so it's not surprising for her to join me on the moss. She touches my suit absentmindedly, adjusting the tie.

I'm still speechless. How am I so lucky? Around us are the clicks of cameras, but I can barely pay attention to our small audience when she presses her lips to mine. My wretched cock stirs, but I don't blame it. She looks delectable.

Breaking the kiss, she gives me a devilish, knowing smirk. "Did you read my letter?"

I bring my mouth to the shell of her ear. "After the ceremony, you better be prepared to spread those pretty thighs, *Bilaste.*"

"Looking forward to it," she murmurs with another brilliant smile.

I lift the gold diamond necklace around her pretty throat. "I see you received my gift."

She peers down her nose at it, then grins. "Baby, I love it. Thank you."

Nura walks up, patiently waiting for acknowledgement. Bringing a hand to my wife's cheek, I whisper, "It could never compare to your beauty, *Bilaste.*"

Her eyelids flutter closed, undoubtedly memorizing this moment. Her eyes open, and they're full of delicate tears. When one falls, I kiss it away, happy for the glitter on my lips.

"Now let's go get married."

54

Reverie

It's painful to separate from Luca, but Euresta insists on giving me a moment to reset myself while the guests arrive. Luca wants to greet everyone, even though our wedding is small enough to allow time later for greetings. Frankly, if he were here, I'm not sure I could resist dragging him to a room.

He's truly so handsome in his suit. It was blindsiding to know he had already been planning our wedding at that brunch so long ago. Knowing that at the time would've made me run for the clouds, but now, it fills me with so much joy, it's painful to contain.

Drying my eyes, I sit next to Yureka and Malona. They're both wearing yellow satin dresses with white ribbons around their waists. Malona is ringing her hands, casting me worried frowns.

Laughing, I ask, "What has you in such a tizzy, Mal?"

Looking pained, she says, "I need to tell you something, but I don't want you to think I'm trying to steal your big day."

Chuckling, I give her a look of disbelief. "How could you steal my *wedding* day?"

She huffs. "Okay, true, but ..." Instead of saying anything else, she raises her right hand and shifts the silver hand on her middle finger to reveal a huge sapphire. "Kahlo proposed last night."

Shrieking with joy, I snatch her hand, examining the emerald cut sapphire. "This is stunning, Malona!" Feeling nothing but happiness for my friend, I say, "Congratulations. I don't see it, but I'm glad he makes you happy."

She laughs. "He has a side you don't get to see. I promise he's sweet and dedicated." Dreamily, she says, "And that *tail.*"

I cackle. "Those Gargoyle tails are the stuff of legends."

Next to us, Yureka pouts. "I want a Gargoyle."

I nudged her with an elbow. "Luca's friend, Alair, is attending. He's not too bad looking." Not as handsome as my husband, but that's okay. "I can introduce you two?"

Yureka perks up. "Yes, please!"

"Ladies, it's time!" Euresta says, sweeping into the room with the type of energy only a wedding planner can exude.

The butterflies, quiet until now, make a painful racket against my rib cage. I can't believe I'm getting married. Almost two years ago, I sat at the bar with Prestley, feeling sorry for myself. Thinking no one would ever want to be with me.

Luca is more than I could've dared to dream for.

Malona brushes a kiss against my cheek. "See you at the end of the aisle."

Yureka kisses the other cheek. Both of them know what in the Hells I've been through to have this moment.

When they leave, I'm left in the room all alone. The whole bridal suite is in disarray, not unlike most bridal suites. I examine each item, memorizing every detail. Luca is envious of my ability when it comes to these kinds of moments, and I wish there were a way to share the gift with him. Alas, I'm the memory keeper; I always will be.

When it's time, Euresta comes to escort me to the partition hiding me from the guests and Luca. My hands flutter, desperate to fidget with something, but my glitter offers no purchase. The bodysuit underneath is there for people who want to hug me, but that's it.

"You're stunning, Reverie. Here are your flowers," Euresta says, keeping one eye on the aisle as my friends walk down to the arbor as she hands me a bouquet of yellow poppies; I clutch it for dear life. My heart sets a painful pace. The anticipation heats my skin.

Why do I feel like this? I just saw him.

Yet, as the partition slides away and I see him there, waiting for me, I understand now why First Looks never take away from this moment. All eyes are on me as the quartet plays my favorite song. Euresta places a hand on my back, giving a gentle nudge forward.

On shaking legs, I walk to the slow beat, smiling at my friends and family.

Each step forward is one step away from who I was. I was so angry and alone.

With Luca, I'm not lonely anymore. Everyone deserves to be loved this way. Not everyone is this lucky, but as I walk barefoot on the moss, I send a prayer to the twelve goddesses that everyone has a chance.

Tears trail Luca's cheeks as he grins so wide, his fangs are front and center. All around us is shimmering glitter, courtesy of Dad. Later, Mom will sing a song intended to lift spirits. Wearing a beautiful strapless dress, might I add.

As I pass the end of the aisle, I glance at the memorial set up for Fane and Soleil. She died three months ago; but she's here in spirit. Although she's buried with the love of her life, we honor both of his parents with a candle, photos of them, and a single yellow poppy.

Luca holds out a steady hand, helping me up the stairs.

"Hi, you," he whispers, his silver eyes swirling with moonlight.

Giving him my biggest, brightest smile, I whisper, "Hi."

***

The ceremony is quick; we weren't eager to do a ridiculously long ceremony. There was a handfasting, an exchange of vows, Mom's singing, and it was time for the first kiss.

Luca cups my face, delivering a reverent kiss. Our guests cheer, but instead of letting me go, Luca wraps his wings around us for privacy. Everything fades until we're the only ones here.

Breaking away from the kiss, he watches me with soft eyes. "Hello, wife."

"Hello, husband."

Bringing his hands to cup my neck, he nuzzles my nose with his. "If I recall, I promised to spread your pretty thighs."

"Yes, Sir, you did."

Eyes flashing, he grits out, "You have one minute to find a room. I don't care where we are; I'm filling you with my cock."

"Even in front of my dad?"

Luca growls. "Do not test me, *Bilaste.*"

Sweeping his wings back, revealing us to the world, I thrust the bouquet into the air with a crow of victory. Everyone stands and claps, but I'm focused on tugging my husband forward. The dung-hole actually resists. I shoot him a scathing glare. He raises his eyebrow in challenge.

"Move faster, and I'll kneel."

The words light a fire under his tail, and he sweeps me into his arms. I squeal, wrapping my arms around his neck. Peering over his shoulder as he stalks down the aisle, I throw my bouquet to Malona. She catches it, beaming from ear to ear.

Euresta steps in front of Luca, about to say something, but jumps back when he snarls. He's in full Gargoyle mode and I love it. I give her an apologetic smile, and understanding dawns.

She grins back to our guests. "Okay, everybody, photos will start in about ... thirty minutes. Please let me show you where the drinks are."

I hate to break the news to her that thirty minutes may not be enough time.

The doors close behind us. Luca prowls to the bridal suite, using his tail to open the door and slam it shut. Looking at me, he snarls, "You have it coming, you know."

Laughing, I pretend to shake with fear. "Oh, no ... I'm so scared of the big, angry Gargoyle."

Depositing me onto my feet, he lifts a finger. A black claw shoots out. Before I can tell him to stop, he's reaching through my glitter and slicing my bodysuit straight down the middle.

I smirk, shucking off the ruined material. "I brought three."

"Good," he says, pushing my shoulders so I kneel. "Now show me how my wife sucks cock."

He's radiating lust, his entire being shaking. Pleased to see him reduced to his baser instincts, I unbuckle his belt, then his trousers. Tugging them past his hips, I rub my mouth over his boxer briefs where his swollen cock twitches.

"Fuck," he grits through his teeth. I curl my fingers at the hem, lowering it. As each delicious bit of his skin appears, I plant a kiss. By the time I reveal his cock, he's panting with wobbling legs.

Bringing the boxer briefs to his knees, I give his tip a tentative lick. His face twists with fury. "Reverie. You're testing me. Is this truly your first act as my wife?"

Grinning, I slide my tongue along his shaft until I reach his dark purple head, sliding it into my mouth.

"Mhmm," I hum. He sucks air through his teeth as his head falls back. Bringing my hands to work his girth, I work him the way I know he likes. He brings a hand to the back of my head, threading his fingers through my hair, most likely ruining it. His thumb caresses my scalp as I wet his entire length with glitter.

Just as my jaw begins to ache and my knees are begging for relief, he says, "My turn."

55

Luca

This woman will be the death of me. Not my heart turning to stone, but the way she teases me, knowing it drives me insane.

Exactly where I want to be.

Her mouth makes a popping sound as she releases the head of my cock, licking the pre-cum. She's so goddess-damned pretty, watching me with round eyes and a mischievous smirk.

"I'm glad you're pleased with yourself," I growl, tugging off my jacket and unbuttoning my shirt. I want to be fully naked for what comes next. There's nothing I'm craving more than the sensation of her body against mine.

I study the room, seeking furniture that we can destroy. There's a piano, but that's out of the question. I eye the table covered in random piles of stuff. I motion for her to stand. As soon as she's on her feet, I scoop her up, wrapping her legs around my waist.

She doesn't waste any time, immediately kissing me at a fevered pitch. She's still "wearing" her glitter dress, but I don't care.

Walking over to the table, I use my tail to sweep it all away. Something shatters — probably a lamp — but neither of us breaks the kiss to find out what it is. She stays wrapped around me as I hold her with one hand and use the other to touch every inch of her luscious body. She feels like heaven, all soft heat. Her fingers find their way to the base of my wings, stroking them.

My cock thumps painfully, but I ignore it as I bring my tail to her soaking entrance. She moans into my mouth, shoving her hips back eagerly. It's not as good as my cock inside of her, but it's a close second. Playing with her heat, rubbing the glittery seam, I wait until she's mewling with need before sliding it into her welcoming body.

Pumping my tail in and out of her, I lay her back, keeping her legs wide and her knees tucked to her chest. It offers the most obscenely gorgeous view of my tail working her into a needy mess. Her eyes are closed as she whimpers with each thrust. I bring a thumb to her clit, making circles in the way she likes it.

When her legs drop, I bark, "Grab your knees."

Reverie obeys, clutching her bent knees with white knuckles, like they're an anchor to this reality. Too bad they won't help her.

I pause, focused on my tail pushing deep inside of her. The way her muscles squeeze sparks stars in my vision.

Steadily fucking her with my tail, I work her clit until she's a sweaty, sobbing mess. Glitter leaks from her body in undulating waves, coating everything. My favorite, though, is the white glitter coating my tail.

When her body tightens with a violent shudder, I remove my tail. She opens her eyes, confused. "What's—"

Her words cut off as my tail comes to her open mouth and slides inside. Watching her lick the glitter off the tip makes me groan. She's going to destroy my sanity. As she sucks the head of my tail greedily, engaging both of her hands, I line up the tip of my length to her entrance. Her body has adjusted to mine by now, so when I ease into her, I'm easily welcomed with her tight heat.

Taking her from both ends tests my endurance, especially once I begin moving. When there's no expression of discomfort, I increase the speed until her breasts are bouncing and she's moaning around my tail.

"You're such a fucking good girl," I snarl, grabbing the back of her thighs and spreading her wider. I want to see every inch of her flesh bared to me. I'm rutting up to the hilt, no better than a wild beast. My tail muffles her cries as it pumps in and out of her pretty lips. Filling her in more ways than one, feral satisfaction burns through my veins.

She's fucking mine.

This is *my* wife.

All of her attitude and smiles are *mine.*

The sound of us joining is obscene. The table's barely able to hold her up, but I don't slow. I drape her calves over my shoulders as I claim her deeper, mindless as she screams around my tail.

When her body shudders violently and her thighs don't stop shaking, I know she's close. Bringing my thumb to her clit again, I send us both over the edge, joining her ecstasy with a grateful heart.

As my pretty wife comes down from her orgasm, I rub a hand up her soft sternum. She hums, giving my tail one last lick before I remove it. Still inside her, I lean forward and brush a kiss against her lips.

"Well, Mrs. Nonya, shall we go celebrate our wedding?"

Reverie Destau gives me the greatest smile of them all. "I can't wait."

As I redress and she resets her outfit, I can't help but think I'm the luckiest man alive.

Epilogue

Thirty-Three Years Later

Today's sunrise is gorgeous. It's all pinks, oranges, and the softest shade of purple. Like Luca's skin. The thought makes me smile.

Grabbing my coffee, I whistle for our chimiragon, Silfer. He bounds down the hallway, his white wings flapping. Grinning, I open the door to our backyard. Songbirds chirp happily as a breeze shifts through my hair.

Sitting in my favorite chair, I wrap one of Luca's quilts around me. He's made so many quilts, a hobby he picked up about five years ago. This one is made in our wedding colors, with shades of yellow and orange.

While Silfer plays in the tall grass, I gaze over the cliff edge, sipping my coffee. It's our favorite flavor, hazelnut, made with cinnamon and nutmeg.

To my left, I see our garden full of lush bushes and raised flower beds. Some are yellow poppies, but also Luca's favorite, plumerias. The colors warm my stony heart, and I hum as I look to my right.

Luca's stone form kneels, his head raised to the Heavens, in the way he used to look at me. In his last moments, I stood above him as he willingly turned to stone for the last time, so he's frozen the way he wanted: gazing at me with nothing but love, covered in purple glitter.

I brush my fingers over his frozen wing, missing the way he used to shudder when I touched them.

It's been six months since he left. Every morning, I have coffee with him, just like I promised. It's honestly the only way I can get out of bed sometimes, knowing he's waiting for me. I was with him in his last moments; I'll spend the rest of mine with him.

Later, our adopted son, Cazmere, will come to have dinner with his new bride, Serel. Luca refused to pass on his genes to his children, so we happily adopted a baby Gargoyle and raised him as our own.

Silfer chirps as he flies toward a foolish bird, almost catching it by the tail. I quietly chuckle; I wake up for him too. Without him and Cas, I'm not sure I could resist taking one last leap with Luca.

I promised him twenty years would be enough, and we got so many more than that before the symptoms kicked in. He refused to put me through the struggles of caretaking, so he let it consume him here in the garden. I held his face as he turned to stone, with absolute reverence in his eyes and my name on his lips.

As I sip my coffee, I sift through our memories together, like I do every single morning. Sometimes, I talk with Luca as if he'll eventually speak back, reminding him of the best times.

Luca carrying me over his shoulder as he brought me into this house for the first time, promptly worshipping me on the counter.

The blissful smile on his face when he held Caz for the first time.

The joy of watching our son grow into a handsome, intelligent, kind man.

Every "I love you" and every whispered word of adoration in my ear.

Our first and only fight as a married couple, about where to position him in the garden of all things. I wanted him near the poppies, but he insisted it would be easier next to this chair, the one he always sat in. So I could be as close as possible to him.

The last time he said *Bilaste.*
Do I regret it? No.
Was this pain worth it? Yes.
I'd do it again in a heartbeat.
Because love stories belong to people like us.

Bonus Content

Want more of the characters you love? Scan or click this QR code for bonus content.

Acknowledgements

On September 18th, 2025, the Universe sent me a divine download in the form of an incredible story. I finished the first 78,000 words in six days. What you've just read is 75% of the first draft. I don't say this to brag — I say it with the recognition that Luca and Reverie came to me as a gift, and I'm so grateful.

So, naturally, I'm thanking the Universe first and foremost for this gift. Even if I only have thirty-three years left on this earth, I know the Skies of Avalon will remain one of the best things I've ever created.

Of course, I must also thank my husband, who kept me grounded, fed, and cared for while I dug into the deepest recesses of my soul for this series. When I finished Glittering Skies, I wept for two days, overwhelmed by what had just happened. Josh, thank you for holding me, keeping me fed with nuggets, and always enabling my ADHD whims.

This story would also not be here without the rabid love of my friends Bex, Emily, Nikki, and Sarah. Y'all are my Hype Hoes and I love you.

My beta readers are also integral to the success of this book. Big thank you to Caitlin and Claud for giving vital feedback that strengthened this story!

My writer's group, Happily Ever Authors, has been a foundational aspect of this journey as well, including my critique Cohort. It's a blessing from all twelve goddesses to have found a group of authors who are the biggest cheerleaders in the industry. Late night sprints, critiques, and celebrations. Or sometimes staring at my exhausted face in bewilderment when I write 20,000 words in a day. Y'all have been so incredibly supportive, and I'M SO GRATEFUL.

To all five of my readers (lol) who took a risk on an indie book, thank you. I wrote this book for you. If you're aching for more Luca and Reverie, make sure to check out Heimlock, the third book in the Skies of Avalon series. I've included some scenes as a tiny apology for the epilogue.

About Jenna Avery

The origin story of Jenna Avery is complex, weird, and requires numerous alcoholic beverages to regale. The current story? She's an elder millennial with a penchant for evolving and growing. This is a polite way of saying her ADHD makes her choose a new hobby every three months. By the time you read this, who knows what she'll be into. Just ask. Otherwise, she lives with her horde of kids and pets, a golden retriever husband, and a rotating residency of soon-to-be-dead plants.

www.ingramcontent.com/pod-product-compliance
Lightning Source LLC
LaVergne TN
LVHW100509110826
845146LV00002B/572

* 9 7 9 8 9 8 7 1 8 9 0 3 0 *